The Nipple of the Queen

C.D. HOPKINS

iUniverse LLC
Bloomington

THE NIPPLE OF THE QUEEN

iUniverse books may be ordered through booksellers or by contacting:

iUniverse LLC
1663 Liberty Drive
Bloomington, IN 47403
www.iuniverse.com
1-800-Authors (1-800-288-4677)

ISBN: 978-1-4917-2112-4 (sc)
ISBN: 978-1-4917-2113-1 (e)

Printed in the United States of America.

iUniverse rev. date: 03/26/2014

Contents

Acknowledgments

For their invaluable contributions of time and expertise, my deepest thanks to Barbara Leith, superb writer, reader, and editor; Donna Reed, generous and dedicated proofreader and computer wizard; and Martin Reed, who, with Donna, brought my computer back from the dead.

Being Occupied

"You ruined my life," my husband said, as we were separating. On the spot, I began to wonder. Up till then I had thought that if anyone's life was ruined, it was mine, and I thought I knew who ruined it, and it wasn't me. "You ruin everything," he said. There I was about to draw the line, but he was saying, "You can have the house. I never liked it, it was like living in a museum." So all I said was, "Thank you." End of the marriage. Twenty years.

After a while, I fell in love with another man, oh, not really in love. He was one of those New Men who have to tell you how they feel. He said things like, "I feel close to you" and "I own anger," but the last thing he said was: "With you, Ruthie, I've discovered what it is to be my very worst self. I couldn't have done it alone. I'm almost grateful." Again I was surprised. All I could think was, "Why me? If he needed all that help, why couldn't he have gone somewhere else for it?" It never occurred to me to say, "You haven't done me much good either, Buster." Instead I wept a bit (it seemed to be expected) and said I thought it would be nice if just once someone, it didn't matter who—children, husband, lovers, friends—would decide that knowing me had been good for them. But he only laughed, not very nicely, and stumbled off into the afternoon. I was living on an island then, and I remember yelling after him, anticlimactically: "I hope you miss the ferry and have to stay in that crummy hotel!"

At the time, I didn't take his departure too much to heart. I sat down in my sunny living room and looked out at the distant water, thinking something like, "Well, *it's* always going to be there." I don't know whether I meant the view or the water. But after a while, as my anger faded, I began to realize that I was alone again, which before had never much bothered me. And I found myself thinking, "What if it's all true? What if I do bring out the worst in people and ruin their lives? What if it's true that I ruin everything?" I hadn't had such an attack of dread in years, not since my children grew up and went wrong, doing drugs and worse, and cried at me: "Why did we have to live on an island? You never taught us anything about the world." Then, as now, I was amazed by my destructive potential. Perhaps the time had come to give the matter some thought.

So, okay, I thought, say I did all these things. How was I going to stop? "If you don't know, maybe you don't want to stop," I heard myself suggesting. But, even as an experiment, who could maintain this line of reasoning? Consider the way it was coming out: "If you don't know how to stop doing what you don't think you're doing, what that means is: you wish you were doing it." This was maybe the first time I realized a complex thought could be stupid.

I could see the ferry now, small—my friend, I hoped, on it. "You're a dope," I said, to both of us, and my dread subsided. But now I was sad, oh, sad. Mis-accused, I thought, like Circe, legendary for turning men into animals. Some myth! A man washes up on your shore; you rescue him, feed him. Love casts its spell, and what happens? He changes. Not for the better. Who's responsible? You. Or so he says: you wanted a barnyard, not a companion. Not true, you say. He only grunts. You don't want to see him too clearly; it's hard on your feelings. What can you do but make him want to escape? Else, you'll have him for life—in no form you can want him. That's relief, when he sneaks away into the night, goes stumbling off into the afternoon. Disappointment comes earlier, when he changes.

But maybe they don't change, I thought, sitting in my sunny room, the ferry now vanished. Maybe they were always the way you finally see them. Such alternatives: terrible powers—defective judgment. Here I foundered: no reason you can't have both. Recovered: or neither. And foundered again, transferring my gaze to the mirror. (Better to have gone on staring at the water.) How long had I looked like that—I mean slightly shriveled, like one of those peaches that sit too long in the bowl on my kitchen table? Doleful, I wondered, "Didn't I used to be more cheerful?" I didn't want to put blame where it didn't belong, but oh, how I wanted to put it somewhere. (A moment's regret here for not having accused my departed friend.)

So I thought: "Hey, whose 'worst' are you supposed to be bringing out? Theirs. At forty-five, a man's going to turn into something new?" But I was passing the mirror now, on my way to the kitchen, and all I could think was: Or a woman either? No, disregarding for the sake of argument the effects of time, I had to say nothing took it out of you like human relations.

"Maybe you should give yourself a little rest," I thought, making myself a cup of tea, "stay out of the world a while." Where I lived, it should've been easy. I meant to give it a try, but life stepped in, and the next thing I knew, I'd fallen in love again.

All I saw, on that Friday morning when he came to fix my roof, was a strong, dark-haired man, smiling up from my bottom step. He wore a blue shirt, unbuttoned halfway down his chest, the sleeves rolled up. His face and arms were brown from working long hours in the sun, from clambering around, I supposed, on the high peaks. I took one look and forgot to care whether my roof got fixed that day or ever.

I can remember the sound of the day as we stood looking at each other—a few birds, the bees buzzing in the rhododendron. I can hear myself asking:

"Would you like some coffee before you start on my roof?"

"Sure," he said, and came into my house.

I waited for him to say, "This is an old one, isn't it?" but he wasn't looking at my house, he was looking at me, and the look in his eye was one I had come to recognize. I knew better, but I could feel my own eyes begin to twinkle.

"Would you like a muffin?" I asked.

"I always like a muffin."

We both laughed, I hate to think why.

I sat him down at my kitchen table, and we sized each other up across the peaches and the muffins. Yes, he was a handsome man. Blue eyes to match his shirt, a good head of hair—wavy, no gray. I'd already formed a pretty good idea of the rest of him. As for me, I could feel myself plumping up, unshriveling. Even the peaches in the bowl looked better. It was plain to both of us what was going to happen, but we had all day; we took our time. I didn't even mind when he said, as they all do, "You live way out here by yourself?" No, I didn't care what he said. We had a long conversation.

I was a foolish woman, wasn't I? We were a mile from the nearest neighbor. But what did I care? I wasn't afraid. I didn't mind knowing nothing about him. All I regret is the end of that ignorance.

Well, he was a man of much sweetness. Even his breath was sweet. It had a faint scent like a newly mown lawn, or chamomile. His skin, too, seemed to emanate this grassiness and it was very smooth and fine, with none of those pale clammy places on the lower belly or the inner thigh. I'd fallen in love by the end of the day.

Evening came before I knew it. Saturday went by. On Sunday I began to wake up, woke up first and saw him sleeping. I sat looking at him. Had he changed a little already? Wasn't he a little larger, his features, relaxed in sleep, a little less fine? As I watched, I saw there was something stray about him.

By and by, he woke up too; he looked dazed—like a big three-year-old, frightened. When he recognized me, he seemed glad to see me.

"No more of that just now," I said. He said:

"I'm hungry."

I was a little while understanding that he meant for food.

We ate breakfast. He said, "I think I love you, Ruthie. What about it, shall we go get my clothes?"

"Clothes?" I said.

"Yes, they're at my brother's."

"At your brother's?"

"It's where I've been living."

"But why?"

"I always do, between wives."

"Between wives!" I said. "Have you been between many?"

"Only three."

I thought, What have we got here—a Bluebeard?

"Come on, Ruthie, let's get a move on."

"What's this hurry?"

"We've got to make the ferry. I've got to get my brother's truck back." But now I was the one who was dazed, and I sat there. "Come on, I want to borrow my brother's car."

"Why do you have to borrow your brother's car?" I asked. "Don't you have a car of your own?"

"The engine seized last month. I had to junk it."

"Oh," I said, reassured, I suppose, because the demise was so recent.

"How about it, Ruthie? Are we getting my clothes?"

I took a long look at him. Then I said, "We can get some of them."

That seemed to satisfy him. We set off for the ferry. The ladders on the truck rattled, as we bumped along my dirt road.

He shared a tiny room with his nephew: white crib in the corner, a rollaway cot, yellow dresser (decals of white ducks across the drawer fronts). His few belongings were in cartons under the crib.

"But why do you stay *here*?" I asked. He didn't answer, just draped some shirts over my arm.

He told his brother, "Every man needs a vacation." His brother seemed glad enough to let him go. Maybe he hoped he'd be gone for a lifetime. He lent my roofer an old white Oldsmobile. We had to shout over the muffler's rumbling.

Now, I thought I would also like a vacation. I stopped answering the phone. I woke up happy, and happily every morning I'd whip up an omelet or a batch of muffins. We'd walk down to the beach; he'd take my hand. We'd wander along the cold sand, go wading. We sun-bathed and shade-napped, ate lobsters and clams. I never thought of my roof. The weather continued fine.

But at the end of ten days, the skies clouded over; the next day it rained, and the following day also. My roof began to leak, and when he heard the water pinging into the bucket, my roofer jumped up, and how he glared at me!

"I can't spend my whole life lying around. I have to earn a living." Even his hair looked angry.

"So who's stopping you?" I said, and before he could answer: "You could start with my roof."

"Are you crazy? I can't fix your roof in the rain."

"Then," I said, "how can you fix anyone else's?"

"That's not the point. We've been lying around for a week."

"Almost two," I said. He roared:

"Don't correct me!"

I knew to be quiet. There was nothing else to do anyway. He wanted to leave now; otherwise, his whole life might be wasted. Never mind that I might have a life of my own not to waste.

So I waited, and he calmed down and said, more kindly:

"You see, Ruthie, if you had an occupation of your own, you wouldn't be so content to just lie around."

I suppose I could have laughed. Instead I surprised myself by crying. I was crying (need I say?) from disappointment. Why did he have to be so dumb, I mean make such dumb assumptions, and just when I'd gotten used to him and would miss him when he left? I was almost afraid to look at him, for fear of seeing how he might have changed in the last few minutes.

"Now, Ruthie," he said, coming back from the exit he was making, taking me in his arms, "I have to leave now . . ."

"Good-bye," I snuffled.

". . . but I'll be back. I just have to go make some money."

I was unable to answer. My own worst self got in there and got my tongue. I was feeling comforted, and I liked it there, nestling in his arms. I didn't see why I had to give all that up just yet.

"But," he said, firmly, taking me now by the shoulders, "we can't lie around like this all day anymore. It uses up all my energy."

But you have more than most, I thought. Aloud I sniffed.

"Here," he said, handing me a filthy handkerchief from his pocket. "I'm going now." And kissed me on the cheek.

I went over to the window and watched him get into his brother's car, the old Oldsmobile, gathered back the curtain and watched, standing to the side so he couldn't see me, like one of those sea captains' wives in the old movies. The music swells, and you know he isn't coming back. I felt it—all that emotion, so pure and spurious. I stood at the window until I could no longer hear his car.

And now it was time to tend to my own business, which was antiques. I was a "picker." Twice a month or so I'd go in my van to far places and bring home quilts and cupboards to sell to dealers. I didn't deal with the public myself, although at one time there was a sign on my lawn that said, "Ruthie's Rarities." A friend made the sign and put it up. When he was no longer a friend, he took it down again. I would've taken it down myself. I was just getting around to it.

So now I went, to Maine and Canada. I had to make a living too, late in life though I'd realized. What had I been thinking all those previous years—that the future was mine, that it was all before me? "Do I have a future?" I asked myself, the day my husband said good-bye. But soon enough, "What future?" became the question, and shortly thereafter I was into antiques.

For the house I'd been given was not empty. It was full of furniture, mostly eighteenth century. No sooner was I living alone than these chairs and tables began to pester me, looming at me in the night, tripping me in the morning. And not just the furniture but all my collections—the red-ware, sponge-ware, the baskets hanging from the beams—were doing their own collecting, I mean of dust. "Now, what do I need all this for?" I began to wonder. There was so much of everything, because all the time I was doing the things a woman does to raise a family, I was also out, in the barns and cellars of people I didn't even know, finding forgotten cupboards, old bottles, broken chairs. I was in my own cellar, refinishing, restoring. I had to have furniture around to work on, the way some women have to have a baby to raise. I'd live with it a while and then, like as not, sell it. I never thought, though, of ruining a pleasant hobby for the sake of a career.

But with my furniture turning into such a nuisance, the thought occurred and every day got stronger, until one morning I said good-bye even to things I'd thought were mine for a lifetime. I called some dealers I knew; soon my house was as bare as if Shakers lived there. In the Shaker spirit, I saw no reason not to turn a profit, and that was the beginning of my antique business, which flourished, owing to hard work and a certain shrewdness.

Where was all this shrewdness when it came to men? Not entirely absent. Driving around Canada and Maine, I had time to think. It would be just as well, I thought, to pack up my roofer's clothes and send them to him, maybe with a note about how much I had enjoyed knowing him. And yet, I thought, driving along those empty roads, the radio my companion, when had I ever enjoyed my few flings at rational living? What rewards lay there for a restless spirit? Thus, no sooner had I decided to send my roofer his clothes than I sent him a postcard, saying when I'd be home. And no sooner was I home (a day earlier than I'd expected) than he telephoned, and over he came on the next ferry.

All that was very well—another honeymoon. Then my troubles began.

"So," he said, "do you do things like this very often—just take off on a trip, without telling anyone?"

You could hardly expect that I had told him everything on a postcard. I had explaining to do.

"Let's see this stuff." And no, a barnful of old furniture did not delight him. "You went clear to Canada, you paid money, for this junk?"

"It's not junk."

"Looks like junk."

"Look again when I get it cleaned up."

"Cleaned up isn't going to help. This stuff is broken."

"Yes, it's broken. I'm going to fix it."

He said, with a lip-curl, "You?"

"Me."

"Oh, Mrs. Fix-it! She's so smart, why doesn't she get up there and fix her own roof?"

I knew better, but I said, "I don't like heights."

His face got red; he pointed his finger. "You think you could!"

"Oh, calm down," I said, painting varnish remover on the nearest chair.

"Huh," he said, turning away, "I guess I can see when I'm not wanted."

"Be fair," I cried, running after him; he was heading for his car. "I won't do this now, but I'm going to have to do it sometime. I've got dealers coming next week."

"So, no more lying around now, only when it suits her. What am I supposed to be doing while you play furniture-repair?"

Well, I was getting snappish. "You could fix my roof."

He looked sulky. "I haven't got my ladders."

"Then why don't you go home and get them?"

"I'll go home, all right."

He was gone for a week.

When he came back, he wanted to learn about antiques. He wanted to go on my trips with me.

"What for?"

"I want to be with you."

"But what about your roofs?"

"They won't run away."

I'll give it a try, I thought. We went.

We went together, every two weeks from June through September. He was a help. I no longer had to hire neighbor boys to unload; I could bring back more furniture, tied to the roof. I was no longer lonely. But I paid a price. I paid literally, because he was helping, and in other ways; his company was not entirely pleasant.

"You'll take the next left," he'd say, for he soon knew my routes.

"What's this?"

"Baker Street."

"No, why are you *telling* me?"

"Because I want you to *turn*. Blinker lights on."

He wanted to drive. His driving scared me. We'd go hurtling down the middle of the road, the double horn blast at full toot. He identified with trucks. Ran red lights. What were stop signs? Sometimes I thought he even watched for my shudder.

"There's no reason to be nervous. I'm in complete control."

"That's what makes me nervous."

"Look, don't tell me how to drive."

Once I asked him, "Did your engine really seize or did you have an accident?" He didn't answer. He gave me such a look.

We would argue, yet the nights were tender; and sometimes we stopped in the afternoon, at a lake, made love in the woods, checked early into a motel. We were leisurely; my business suffered. There were times when I wished that I were alone.

Between trips, for a few days he'd go back to the mainland. I welcomed his absences, though I missed him. It began to seem to me that the only time I did my own work was when he was gone. When he was there, what was I doing? Cooking meals, not fixing furniture, cleaning up after him, doing laundry. What was he doing? Oiling my gutters, replacing my downspouts, re-shingling my entire roof. For none of this would he let me pay, but I did not like this kind of bargain.

"It'd be nice," he'd say, from his lofty ladder, "if you'd bring me a cup of tea. And then, Ruthie, you could run to the hardware. I'm going to need some more of these nails."

"Listen," I told him, at last, "this makes me uncomfortable. You're giving up too much." And so, I felt, was I.

He rose to new heights. "Since when has giving got to be on an equal basis?"

"But you're giving up your life. You're living mine." And I was living his, I thought; I felt I owed him.

"Ruthie, is that a sensible remark? We're making a life together."

"That's the problem, all right."

He laughed. He gave me a squeeze. Oh, with all his misguidedness, the man had warmth.

"If it'll make you feel any better, I've got a pile of shirts that need buttons, and I ripped my jacket when I was fixing the porch."

But I'd thought I was through with all this tending. Gazing out at him as I sat sewing, I thought: "Do I want to be the woman he wants if I have to be the woman he wants me to be?"

We were now into October. He was spending less and less time on the mainland. Maybe there were no roofs to work on; maybe his brother didn't need him. Came the day when he didn't want to go back.

"I want a home, Ruthie. I want a stable home life."

"There's no stability here," I said.

"Stop walking around, come here and sit down. I want to do some serious thinking."

"Fine, you do it," I said. "I've done enough for a lifetime."

"Now, look, Ruthie, I'm not kidding."

And neither was I. "Let's not talk about it."

"Ruthie, I love you. I want to live here."

I could feel myself filling up like a bottle, with dismay. "I can't give you a home," I said.

"Why not? You're living in a six-room house."

"Space," I said, "isn't the only consideration."

"Of course it isn't. We love each other."

"Do we?"

I was at a stage in my life where it seemed to me that I had never loved anyone—not father, nor mother, nor husband, nor any child. I mean I was at that stage on that particular day, but it was recurrent. The next day I might love the world. Who could trust such feelings?

"I don't know if you'd want to take a chance on me," he said, and reached for my hand, "but I've got nothing against getting married."

I have not had so many proposals in my life, and this one brought the tears to my eyes.

"One marriage is enough."

"I don't regret my three."

"But I regret my one."

He was hurt. "You said you loved me." In fact, I had said that, several times. "How can you love me and not want live with me?"

But it was the only way, I knew, to keep such love alive. And that's selfish, I thought, not wanting to explain. Selfish. I began to slide toward my doom.

The weather turned cold: November. We made the last trip north until spring. Together we filled my barn and cellar with furniture for me to work on during the winter. He put up my storm windows, brought in my hoses. "What," he asked, not facetiously, "would you do without me?" The same as I did before, I thought, recollecting the previous winter, how bleak, how long, it had been. And how I'd been lonely and had the flu. "I'm getting too dependent," I told myself, as well as him.

"Let me take care of you," he said.

I grew sad when, even for a few days, he went back to the mainland. And I was not the only one. You would've thought he was going on a ten-year journey.

"Why do I have to leave? Why can't I stay here?"

Yes, why can't he? I began to wonder.

He had a peculiar gift: he made me happy. He had a loving touch. I think I could have found him in a dark room, among other people, by his sweet breath and the way he touched me. Sometimes he would stroke me as if I were a dog or a cat, his hand automatically, almost absent-mindedly, finding familiar places— the forehead, the cheek, the jaw; the ribcage, the hip, the flank. It was a hand that knew me in a way I didn't know myself, I mean sensually in a soothing way. I would feel myself go soft, ripe, like a hard cheese that has been set in a warm place. I am afraid that this happiness is what I loved him for.

Naturally, I couldn't leave well enough alone but had to ask whether he knew what he was doing, had to tell him how the stroking made me feel.

"You're just in a soft emotional state," he said, gruff, offended. "What good does that do if you don't want to live with me?"

He went home after Thanksgiving, came back upset. "I have to clear out, Ruthie. My brother's mother-in-law's coming. Now, Ruthie, what am I going to do? Do I have to go to a rooming house? Am I going to live with you? What's it going to be, what's the story?"

He held me by the shoulders. I was tired of struggling. Why did I have to be the one with the judgment? I said:

"Let's get the rest of your things."

He had more than I thought. "What's this—a coat collection?" He laughed. I laughed too, because he was laughing. He took me down into the cellar. "What's this?"

"My furniture." In the gloom it didn't look like much—a double bed, a metal desk.

We spent the weekend packing things into cartons. He kept finding more and more to pack. Why did we have to bring it all now?

"My brother needs the room."

I supposed we could put it in the barn.

"Why should my stuff be in the barn?"

"But where will we put it?"

"We'll find a place."

I had thought to use my van for the move. We rented a truck. The metal desk was very large. That was not a double bed; it was king-size. In his brother's cellar were more cartons. They had on them the dust of months, maybe years. I could see they had spent time in the cellar—not just his brother's? I began to have misgivings. This looked like a move for life.

"Listen," I said, "let's leave this for later."

"We've got the truck *now*."

"We can get it again."

"Why wait?"

"What if we don't work out?"

"Ruthie," he said, dignified, "you agreed we'd live together."

"I agreed to live with *you*, not all this."

"What nonsense," he said. "Grab the end of the mattress."

We could barely work the desk through my doorway; it had grown larger in transit. The lamps had quadrupled. There was a sofa I'd never seen before.

"Where did all this come from?"

He didn't answer. "We'll put my chair by the fireplace. You can sell the settle."

"But I like the settle."

"Stone age," I heard him mutter.

I ran upstairs and sat on my bed, staring out at the choppy sea. I felt tricked, in some not so indefinable way. He followed me up. "Ruthie, what's the matter?"

"I don't like what's happening."

"What's happening? I'm trying to get moved in. And you're not being much help, Ruthie, to be truthful. You're not making room for me."

I said, between laughing and crying: "But you're so much larger than I thought."

"Ruthie, you're talking like a child."

It was true. I even sounded like one. I said:

"I have to go for a walk."

"Now?"

But I was off and running. "What have I done?" I thought. "I've made a mistake." I ran down to the beach. There was a cold wind blowing.

I walked up and down the beach. Maybe my mistake would be good for me. Maybe I would learn from it, the way you were supposed to do with mistakes. What would I learn? Oh, to be less rigid and more accommodating, more flexible, less controlling. It was the beach where we had gone when we first fell in love.

"So," he said, when I got home, "did you have a nice walk?"

The settle was gone—and my couch that was made from a hired man's bed. His desk had replaced a blanket chest. There was hardly anything left of me in the room.

I could see then that he was enormous. How he loomed above me! I said:

"I want you to move out."

But my voice must have grown very small, because he didn't hear me.

Every day he seemed to grow larger. He put up his king-size bed. There was no room for me in it. He filled the bed. He was a giant. He made giant noises too, in his sleep. When he snored, the whole house shook, and sometimes I could not tell his inner rumblings from the blizzard outside. I would wait until he slept, then creep to the guest room. In the morning, if I did not get back to his bed before he awoke, he was angry. "Well," he'd say, "did you get enough sleep? Were ten hours enough or do you need a couple of hours more?" I would not answer. He couldn't hear me anyway.

Sometimes, when he was downstairs or outside, I would look around and try to see, really see, what was there. I would say, "That is the change from his pockets, there on my chest of drawers. That is his comb. That is his electric razor, permanently plugged in." I thought if I could tell myself what was his and what was mine, I might be able to remember what was me. But I'd get distracted. I'd think, "My jewelry box used to sit there. Where did it go? When did it disappear?" I would hunt for my belongings. Some I found. They were in cartons under the guest bed.

As the winter wore on, his clothes began to get larger. I suppose they had to. I tried not to notice. I became very busy. One of the things I did was hunt for my own clothes. Sometimes I had to change the object of my search several times; some days the only thing I could find was my bathrobe. I realized that I was becoming more flexible, but there were days when I could not get up. One night I left my bedroom slippers in the bathroom. By the next morning, a pair of his shoes had taken their space in the closet. The shoes I wore that day lost their place also, and the rest ran and hid under the shelf in back. His shoes covered the shelf like an army and then they began to advance across the closet floor.

Every day there were more cartons under the guest bed. I did not look in them. I knew that someday everything I owned would be in cartons. Where would I be? Would I have disappeared? I dreamt that I saw his foot in the guestroom doorway. His big toe filled the doorway from threshold to lintel.

From this I understood that I was getting smaller.

I lost track of time, but all that went by was December. It was the winter we had over six feet of snow, even on the island. For a week after New Year's, we were snowbound The electricity failed, and the heat. The house was warm from the wood he had chopped; we had groceries that he'd fetched from town on a sled.

"Where would you be now, if it weren't for me?"

"Oh, I don't know," I said, bitterly. "How am I supposed to know? I don't know where I am now, never mind where I'd be."

"Ruthie," he said, "what are you saying?" and I knew he'd never asked the original question.

Maybe, I'd think, I'm making it all up. For, sometimes, wasn't he a perfectly normal size, the size that he was when he first moved in? And didn't he have the same blue eyes and the same skin, only a little paler? And there were my slippers in their rightful place and only a few cartons under the guest bed, with "Canning Jars" written on them. But no sooner had I decided that the problem was me than he'd say, "Ruthie, let's get rid of these plants. I could use a lamp on that table." I'd know there was no sense in dallying, and the next thing I knew, the cartons would be multiplying.

Blizzard after blizzard, the worst one in February. When it stopped and we had dug out, I walked to town, to the market. He wanted to come along. I said I had to go by myself. We argued. I went, dragging the sled behind me, and every step I took even though it was hard work, made me feel lighter, which is how I knew I was going in the right direction.

I went to the bakery. There was a long line, a crowd. We took numbered tickets from one of those machines. I got my number and went to sit on an empty shelf to wait. It was going to be a long wait, but I didn't mind. No, I didn't mind. When an old man ahead of me decided to leave and tried to give me his ticket, I burst into tears. His number was fifteen, mine thirty-two. I don't suppose he knew what to make of my crying, but I knew. I went home and said:

"I want you to move out."

"Move out!" he cried (meaning that my real voice had returned). "What do you mean, 'move out'? Are you crazy?"

"Almost, but not quite," I told him.

"I can't believe what I'm hearing."

"I'm sorry, but it's true."

"Ruthie," he said, kindly, "have you noticed the snow?"

"It'll be spring soon. You can have until then. But then you've got to be ready to go."

"Go where?"

"I don't know."

"I can't believe this," he said, to himself, and to me, "I never dreamed you could act like this."

"Nor did I."

"Now, look, Ruthie," he said, in that kindly way, putting out his arms to draw me to him. But all I could see was how he had changed, what he had turned into, and I leapt away.

"No more talk," I said. "Just action."

"How can you live with yourself?"

"Better than with you."

"How can you treat me like this?"

But I could not tell him.

We packed everything up again, in the cartons. There seemed to be fewer and fewer things to pack. The clothes did not seem so large. I began to be fond of them again. I thought how I had just packed these same clothes, a few months ago. I thought about what I was losing. He looked forlorn. He looked like himself. He looked at me and asked, "Why?" How could I do this? Tears fell down on the coat I was folding. Were they real tears or not? Were they mine?

He went back to his brother's. The mother-in-law was gone now, had perhaps never been there. His brother was not too happy to see him, his brother's wife even less so. That made four of us, unhappy. He kissed me good-bye. "You'll know where I am." And went into his brother's house, a man with nothing.

I suppose you think I was all right, once I got home. I wasn't. There was a hole in my life. He'd made all that room for himself, and now it was empty. For two weeks my clothes remained huddled together. It was up to me, I then realized, to move them. I had to coax my shoes out of their hiding place; my jewelry box found its own way back to my bureau. By the end of the month, my house looked the way it used to. But it did not feel the same. It had a memory, like villages that have survived an occupation.

History

511, CLOVIS DIES.

Kathleen reads this silently; she has to twist in her seat to see the words. The timeline is stenciled high on the wall. Fluorescent light makes the blue letters gleam.

485, MEROVINGIAN FRANKS UNDER CLOVIS.

Yes!" Mr. Mahajan says, looking up from his desk, his eye caught by the movement of Kathleen's hair, which is wild and curly and red, the same deep burnt red as the filaments of saffron that Sushila uses to tint the rice gold. The hair looks crinkly, like the saffron; it looks—but this is foolishness—expensive. "Yes," he says, less certainly, forgetting what he intended to say.

401, VISIGOTHS INVADE ITALY.

He stares at the textbook on his desk, open to pages 58, 59, the accounts of one R. Roberts appearing on the left; R. Roberts owns a cleaning establishment. Perhaps—his eyes shift to page 59, to the accounts of N. Lamb, internist. Dr. Lamb's figures are more complex, the capital and income statements more of a challenge. But American girls dislike a challenge. They quit coming to class when the work becomes difficult. In four weeks, twenty-six students have vanished—dropped out, he fears, though they all may be ill. Each Tuesday evening there have been fewer, until tonight there are only these four girls. It may be bad luck to take attendance; he's not sure the office requires it. There's no one in the office at night except a girl to answer the phone.

Sighing, he decides on R. Roberts. No, he will do Dr. Lamb.
It's impossible to make bookkeeping simple; the most he can do is
try to make it clear. Of course, he should have decided beforehand
which exercise to put on the board, but Anil was fussing all
through supper; the child has caught Sushila's cold. Soon, no
doubt, he will catch it himself; the landlord keeps the apartment
too cool, barely 60 degrees in Anil's room, according to the
thermometer hung on the crib. The electric heater has helped at
night, but Anil might burn himself during the day.

286, DIOCLETIAN.

She likes these weird names: Diocletian, Pepin. There's Pepin
the Younger and Pepin the Short. And Clovis—she likes that
name, too, hates her own name: Kath*leen*, Kath*leen*. "Kathleen,
Kathleen," Mrs. Feldman calls up the stairs, and Kathleen wants
to quit on the spot, wants to go home and go back to bed, but of
course she can't do that. "Kathleen, now, today, Kathleen, you'll
remember about the dining room window sill?" Every single
Friday it's the same thing, and it's just useless to try to explain.
"But, Mrs. Feldman . . . ," she says sometimes. Mrs. Feldman says,
"I'm late, Kathleen," or "Not now," or "Don't argue with me," as if
you could argue with Mrs. Feldman. It's not fair—you can't dust
the windowsill unless you move the artillery fern, and if you move
the artillery fern, you have to put it back where it belongs. Only,
if you so much as look at the fern, it's dropping these things like
little brown seeds, so there's no way, ever, to prove that you dusted
unless you put the fern somewhere else. And she tried that—left
the fern on the dining table, in the center, under the chandelier,
but the following Friday Mrs. Feldman said, "Kathleen, I can't have
that fern on the dining table." Kathleen would not have that fern
in the house, but it was a present from the Feldmans' daughter,
Rachel, pictures of whom Kathleen must dust; eighteen of them
hang in the upstairs hall, and downstairs there are twelve pictures
of grandchildren. What you do about pictures to prove you dusted:
you always leave some of them hanging crooked. Then Mrs.
Feldman says, "Really, Kathleen! Try not to leave the pictures every
which way." Mrs. Feldman is on Kathleen's hate list, just below a

basset named Albert. Mr. Feldman is nice, though; he has a nice face. He's what you call a cantor in the Jewish church. He's home a lot, because he's retired, but he always keeps out from underfoot. Most of the time, he goes to the cellar, and she can hear him practicing his singing down there.

Tracy—she likes the name Tracy. Tracy Gordon sits in front of her. They can sit any place they want, but she and Tracy usually sit together, go outside at the break for a smoke. Tracy's knitting a muffler—fuzzy, soft yarn, a lovely dark green. Bob might like a muffler like that, if only Kathleen knew how to knit. She glances at the clock. Ten of seven. In twenty minutes she could have learned.

She glares at Mr. Mahajan, willing him to start teaching something, but his pale brown face hovers close to the book; he wears thick, heavy glasses, like binoculars. When he moves his head slowly from side to side, a camera is what he reminds her of, the kind they have on *Nature* or something, where they're panning around the floor of the ocean. They're showing you white worms nine feet long, underwater volcanoes making steam.

"Yes!" Mr. Mahajan says, pushing his chair back. "Let us look at Dr. Lamb." He stands at the blackboard. "Where is my chalk?" He had it, he knows, when he wrote *Chapter 4*. Then what did he do? Sat down at his desk. He goes to the desk and looks under the textbook; the chalk is nowhere in sight. Sushila says he is absentminded. For days he has neglected to call the landlord, not forgotten exactly—he often remembers, but not when he is anywhere near a phone. And he is entirely within his rights: when the landlord supplies the heat, the temperature at night must be 64. It is the law, Mary Mirsky says. Mary Mirsky found a mistake in his work, a stupid mistake, a copying error. She said, "What's wrong with you, Ramesh? You haven't seemed your usual self." What is his usual self? He checks and rechecks his work. He is known for his accuracy, not for his speed. He must not make mistakes.

180, ROMANS DEFEATED IN SCOTLAND

It's all defeats and invasions. Last week she learned the parts of a castle from the poster that's tacked up next to the blackboard. So now she knows about crenellations, and she knows this new word, "keep," but she doesn't know a whole lot about bookkeeping, only what she's learned from the book. *Stop*, it says. *Before you go on, do Exercise 4.1.* She does, not looking at the solution, which is printed right below. *Now check your work*, the book instructs, and she's usually got it right. But the teacher just copies from the book. He should make up some exercises himself. Plus, they're doing only one chapter a week, and there are eighteen chapters in the book. Four more classes, she paid fifty bucks. She's paying the teacher to look for chalk.

He runs his fingers along the chalk tray, his fingernails filling with powder and dust. No chalk. They should leave him more than one piece. The first evening, they left him none; he had to send a girl to the class next door. Borrowing—he is always having to borrow; he had to borrow to buy his car. And the car is always breaking down; he still has not had the defroster fixed. Some morning soon, there will be frost. Next month, there could be snow. Sushila says, "You work for a pittance. When are you going to ask for a raise?" And "When are they going to promote you? You should be head accountant." But Mary Mirsky is head accountant at the firm of Mirsky & Green. She will stay home, Sushila thinks, once she is pregnant, and then the job will be his. But Sushila is the one who is pregnant—and Anil not yet a year and three months. Anil's room is too small for two cribs, but how can they afford to move?

"Where is my chalk?" he cries, in Hindi, his voice sounding high and wild. The unhelpful girls stare back, giving no sign that they have heard. He must calm down, calm down and think. At the beginning of the evening, he had the chalk.

Kathleen knows the chalk's in his pocket. That is where he usually puts it: his pants pocket, in with his handkerchief; in his handkerchief pocket are pens and pencils. But she's not going to tell him, because she hates him; he's wasting so much of her time.

He reaches in for his handkerchief, to wipe the dirt from his fingertips, feels the chalk, but it's too late; he has already pulled out the handkerchief. And the chalk has leaped onto the floor, where it breaks into three pieces, none longer than a centimeter. He picks them all up—let the foolish girls giggle—and writes *31 December* on the board. The chalk scrapes, and the girls cry out, but he writes on, ignoring them: *Accounts Payable, Accounts Receivable (A/R)*. He is whispering the amounts as he writes: *Miscellaneous Expense, Rent Expense, Rent Expense, Supplies Expense.*

"As of December 31," he turns to face them, relieved to find his voice under control, "the accounts of R. Roberts are as follows . . ." He reads the entire list out loud.

"He hasn't got a full deck," Tracy says, as they stand outside at the break. The end of her cigarette glows in the dark; when she takes a drag, her face looks mean. She has short blond hair, practically punk, left longer on top but not spiked. "I thought he was going to break down and cry."

Once when Kathleen was still in high school, the chemistry teacher did break down. He was drawing a blast furnace on the blackboard; then he muttered, "Who gives a shit?" Next thing they knew, he walked out of the room, and they got this substitute. Didn't know squat. It could happen again, she supposes. Mr. Mahajan wrote *Rent Expense* twice.

But Tracy is off on another tack. "I'm trying to keep my husband's books, right? It's not like I'm taking this class just for fun."

So who is? Kathleen thinks, and she's mad at Tracy, more like miffed, because Tracy thinks she's special or something; she's always saying "my husband." You don't see Tracy out cleaning houses, vacuuming dog hair off the sofas and wiping up where the dog has just pissed on the floor you washed an hour before. She gets to stay home with her little kid; her husband paid for the class.

"Payroll's Chapter 10," Tracy says, "and we aren't even going to get that far." But all Kathleen says is "Yeah"; she's biting her tongue not to say, "I could care." Rosario and Melinda come out just then, and Tracy says, "We should report him."

"Who?" says Melinda.

"Mr. Mahajan."

"Report him for what?" Rosario asks.

"Well, Jesus—for total incompetence."

Kathleen blows her smoke straight up. "He might be an okay accountant."

"Don't be an asshole," Tracy says, but Kathleen doesn't like that, either, calling her an asshole; she's feeling real prickly. She doesn't like the way Tracy laughs. "If we had to have an incompetent teacher, why did they have to give the job to a foreigner?"

Does that make sense? Kathleen thinks. She throws her cigarette onto the lawn. "I'm going to hit the ladies' room." She saunters off toward the building.

The rest room's clear down at the other end of the hall, like about the length of a football field, just before the exit to the parking lot; she might as well get in her car and drive home. Except her textbook is still lying on her desk—nine dollars she paid for that book, an hour and a half of taking shit. She doesn't dare go to the ladies' room. She'd walk out the door and never come back, plus she'd never read the book on her own. She stops at the drinking fountain instead.

"Next week," Mr. Mahajan says, "I think we must have a test."

If he could take back the words, he would. Four pairs of eyes have gone narrow and fierce. But surely it is usual to test the students. Ah, but what use will it be? When he said, "What goes into the income statement?" they could not even say, "Income from fees." They needed only to refer to the book, but even that was asking too much. "Income from fees," he had to prompt, "yes?" Bored vacant eyes, two pairs blue, one pair brown, the hazel eyes of the redhead so sullen. Why did she look at him with such scorn when he said, "You have all read Chapter 4?" Their silence, their doltish lack of response must entitle him to his little joke. He doubts they have even read Chapter 1, and what can he do if they will not read?

"A test on the first four chapters," he says.

He wishes he could forbid the blond girl to knit; the click of her needles always distracts him, but she is a very tough-looking girl. She has a tough name, the name of a boy. He remembers because the first evening, she was listed twice on his roll, as "Gordon Tracy" and "Tracy Gordon," so that now he is uncertain which it is. That first evening, he asked, "There are two?" and then felt a fool, but he had to make sure. There were no men in the class, and surely the office had made a mistake, but American girls sometimes have men's names; there is a woman named Sydney at work.

"I hope you study hard," he says. "I know the work is becoming more difficult but, with application, you will be able to master it, and someday, perhaps, you will work as bookkeepers."

The girls are collecting their books. Tracy or Gordon rolls up the green scarf, thrusting her knitting needles through like spears. She says to the Hispanic girl, "We'll see," in a voice that sounds to him ominous. It is the only thing any of the girls have said, and suddenly he is afraid, afraid that none of them will come back. He has frightened them off with talk of a test.

"Wait, please. Let me take attendance. Who is here? You are . . . ?" Rosario, Kathleen, Tracy, Melinda. "Thank you," he says. "Good night."

But not one girl says "Good night" as she leaves. On the hard floor their sneakers squeak as they walk.

Tears come to his eyes. He is so tired. He was up and down all last night with Anil, for Sushila insisted she felt too weak, although he is sure she has only a cold. Mornings, she claims she has nausea and cannot get up to fix the tea, and so it is he who must feed Anil; there are jars in the cupboard of pureed food—applesauce and vegetables—that Anil used to like, but no longer, it seems. The child pushed the spoon away and said, "No!" his body sagging in the high chair, and would not sit up but kept sliding down, evading the spoon, turning his head. Alien flesh, made of food from a jar. At that age, he himself ate real food. He remembers—but he might have been older—remembers being fed by his sister. They are sitting in sunlight on the floor, and Pinky is feeding him tahiri, popping the rice and peas into his mouth with her fingers; he wants to do it himself. She is laughing, "What a big boy!" and he reaches for the peas with both hands, the yellow-green peas; he likes them best, wants to pick them out of the rice. But she says, "No, no, only this hand," and holds his hand down. "Only this one."

He blinks back the tears. He won't think of home, of his mother and father, long dead, or of Pinky, with whom he lived until coming here; she would still take him in if he asked. But he won't ask, because of Sushila. Pinky is right: Sushila is spoiled. It comes from being an only child, and it is true she is still very young, but for over two years he has made allowances. When he first brought her here, she did nothing but cry, and he thought she had married him for his green card. Now she wears pants and has learned how to drive and demands to have a car of her own. When he says he wishes her not to wear pants, she says, "Then how am I to keep warm?"

No, life is not as he had hoped.

Tonight he made a fool of himself.

In the ladies' room, Kathleen sprays Wild Musk on her wrists. She gave Bob Wild Musk for Men, not that he uses it. He always smells like the dope he smokes—his clothes, his hair, even his blankets. She can't smoke dope; her mom would smell it, and then she'd say, "All right, lady, move out." And she wants to move out, only she can't. She'd like to move in with Bob. It was a mistake to tell him, though, because that's when things began to go wrong. Anyway, she thinks that's when. She asks what's the matter; all he says is "Nothing." But something is—she knows that much. It could be he's met someone else.

She backs on tiptoe into the stall, but the mirror still only shows to her waist. She can't see if her sweater looks grungy down there where it hangs past the knees of her jeans. White—she knew it would be a problem. She climbs up onto the toilet seat. If someone came in, they'd think she was weird. The sweater doesn't look all that bad from a distance. "What're you doing, Kath?" she says. It's not like she plans to go in—she's just going to see if Bob's light is on, going to drive by, she won't even stop. She could creep up to the window and look.

She climbs down. That's sinking too low. If he's got another girlfriend, she'll know soon enough. She looks at the heart she drew last week on the towel dispenser: *Bob + Kath*. Since then, someone has written *Life sucks*, and someone else printed ARE YOU SURE? but you can't tell if the arrow they drew points to *Life sucks* or to her heart. It's better to know if he's cheating on her; it's always better to know. It's like what she copied from over the blackboard: "There is only one good, knowledge, and only one evil, ignorance."

A famous philosopher said that.

Socrates.

Ramesh Mahajan lies awake in the dark, listening to the breathing of his wife. She was asleep when he got home, pretending, perhaps, to be asleep. But now, he thinks, she truly is, and he moves closer, trying to get warm. Her long, thick braid lies between them; he sighs and rolls over on his back. The heater in Anil's room creaks off and on; he turned it down when he came home. Anil had crept out from under his blankets; he sleeps in a garment that resembles a snowsuit. He must have been too warm, Ramesh thought, but children may simply crawl in their sleep. By now the child may be too cold. Perhaps the heat should have been left where it was. But a man should not have to think of such matters. He swings his legs over the side of the bed—Sushila does not stir—shivers, as he steps off the rug, and encounters the icy floor of the hall.

His son lies under slatted shadows thrown by the bars of the crib onto the white blanket, onto the cool cheek. Ram slips a finger into the neck of the snowsuit: warm but not too warm. Below, on the lawn: the shadow of the fence, the grass between pickets faintly aglitter and the tops of the parked cars as well, it seems, but without his glasses he cannot be sure.

He had meant to call the landlord. Oh, why is there no one else to keep watch?

In Delhi, it would be daylight now.

Mr. Feldman sings in the basement, his voice floating up each carpeted stair. It's the loneliest singing Kathleen ever heard; it's making her feel worse and worse.

With her sneaker she nudges the mess on the carpet—dirt and vermiculite, pieces of fern. The clay pot isn't broken, but it did crack. Today is an evil day. She knew it was evil the minute she got here; nothing's been right ever since Tuesday. An awful mistake to go over to Bob's, and she never should have knocked on his door. "Oh, it's you, Kath." She can still see his face; he thought she was going to be someone else. "I'd ask you in for a beer, but I've got this heavy-duty test . . ." And meanwhile, he's sort of closing the door as if he thinks she might barge in, and he's doing this sort of shuffle like when is she going to leave? She's so stunned she can't think of a thing to say, and she can hear Bruce inside, real loud.

So she just said, "Forget it."

He never loved her. The least he could've done was tell her. She's going to be stuck at home her whole life, and the only thing she's ever going to do is clean houses.

"I have a friend," Mrs. Feldman began this morning, before Kathleen even got her jacket hung up. "She's a spotless housekeeper, but now it's too much—her husband's just had an operation. I was going to give her your phone number, but I thought I should ask you first."

So what could Kathleen say but "All right"? She didn't even ask if it was an apartment or a house. Never mind that she was thinking of phasing down. She's never going to be a bookkeeper anyhow. Just more and more houses. Mrs. Feldman's friends. Of course, that was before she dropped the fern.

She told herself to be extra-careful, like when she was dusting the chandelier, because if anything could go wrong, it would, though she's never broken anything before. She kept waiting to unhook a crystal and have it come zooming down, nicking the table, the finish of which you can see yourself in; it's got about fifty layers of Pledge. But that didn't happen, and when she got around to the windowsill, it was like her mind must have gone somewhere else. She picked up the fern and her wrists went all weak, and now look what she's gone and done.

She didn't need that. She says, "Fucking shit," and she raises her foot and stamps on the pot, which is when Mr. Feldman comes up out of the cellar, and Kathleen can't help it, she bursts into tears. Because he's seen her. At least he's heard her. Because she's going to get fired.

She drops to her knees and claws at the dirt, trying to scoop it onto the dust rag. The pieces of broken pot are sharp, and she's glad. Maybe her fingers will get cut.

"Is there a tragedy?" Mr. Feldman says. But all she can do is nod. He comes over. "Sweetheart, you'll cut yourself." His hand cups her elbow. "Get up, please."

"I'll buy you another one," Kathleen bawls, but Mr. Feldman says, "No, no. Please." And he murmurs something under his breath in that language Mrs. Feldman talks to him in. "The plant had lived long enough. It was not a very good plant." He goes and gets her a paper towel. "Come, no more crying." So Kathleen stops. "You go on home. I'll clean this up." But that is too nice. She starts crying again and points to the clock and tries to explain: she hasn't worked her three hours yet. "Not to worry." He pats her shoulder, and then he's leading her toward the door and picking up the money Mrs. Feldman leaves for her under the crystal candy jar. "Don't give it another thought."

He gets her windbreaker out of the closet, tucks the money into the pocket. "You go home and have a nice nap." He opens the door. "We'll see you next week."

So Kathleen walks in a daze to the car. She'll get them some other kind of plant, a Boston fern or a creeping Charlie, or something like a cactus that doesn't drop leaves.

She goes home and has lunch, though it's only eleven, and then gets into bed and sleeps and sleeps. When the little kids come home from school, she takes them to McDonald's for milkshakes. The next day, she studies her bookkeeping. Her mother says she's impressed. Her mother makes everybody quiet down when they're screaming, and she closes the door to the TV room. Also, she answers the phone in case it should be "that wretched Bob." But Bob never calls, though a boy named Jake does.

"I always liked that one," her mother says.

In the closet of Ramesh Mahajan's bedroom is the tissue paper-wrapped picture of Pinky's holy man that Pinky gave Ramesh when he left home. On Saturday, he unwraps the picture, a photograph of the baba's face: Stern, intelligent eyes, gaunt cheeks, wisps of white hair to the collarbone. In Pinky's house there is a shrine with the same photograph and candles and incense. At night, she leaves offerings of food in brass bowls; in the morning, the food is always gone. Rats eat the food, Ramesh fears, but he would never let Pinky suspect.

He gazes into the baba's eyes, which ask, "What right do you have to pray?"

"Baba . . . ," Ramesh begins, but agrees: he has no right at all. He has been negligent, remiss. No wonder things have gone wrong. He sets the picture on Anil's bureau and lights incense and two votive candles, bought last winter when the electricity failed; he had thought it was disconnected. The holy man tells Pinky what to do when she asks. "Baba . . . ," Ramesh begins again. And hardly has he uttered the word when the answer comes: Call the landlord.

He does, and the landlord answers—Ramesh doesn't get the answering machine. He says, "It's only 60 degrees in my son's room. Last year it was always at least 68. When will you be able to fix the heat?" And the landlord says, "I'll come take a look," which is much better, much more encouraging a response than Ramesh used to get from the old landlord when the faucets leaked or the sink stopped up, although they never used to have trouble with the heat.

By late afternoon, the apartment is warm, and Sushila is sitting in the living room, watching television, while Anil staggers from doorway to sofa and then back to his father's knee in the kitchen, where Ramesh sits, making up the examination for Tuesday. He makes the questions as simple as possible: multiple choice and blanks to fill in, so that surely all of the girls will pass. But he has a more difficult section as well, about journal entries and financial statements, not too difficult, since the test will be open-book; they can model their answers on the examples in the text. Monday, he'll copy the test at work—thirty copies, just in case.

Sushila comes to the kitchen and says, "It's time for me to feed Anil." She looks very pale and beautiful, even though she is wearing pants. "Would you lift him into the high chair?" she asks, and Ramesh and Anil play a game, Ramesh roaring like a tiger and Anil running as best he can. Which is not at all; he crawls on the floor, with Ramesh laughing and crawling after him.

But on Tuesday there is another access of doubt. What will he do if the girls don't show up? For how long will he need to come to the class room in the event that a pupil might come back? And will they continue to pay him for teaching if he is merely sitting and waiting?

But it's insulting, Kathleen thinks. She studied so hard, and look at this test. "'Assets = Liabilities + Capital' is called (a) journalizing, (b) a transaction, (c) the accounting equation." You'd have to be a retard not to pass. You'd have to be a retard to make up the test. Unbelievable. Tracy is right: Mr. Mahajan deserves to be fired. She knows so much more than he's tested her on. She could probably work as a trainee right now. The last part is harder, but not much. She's never coming back to this class.

And neither are Tracy and Rosario. They exchange phone numbers out in the hall. Melinda didn't come tonight. "She had the right idea," Tracy says. They are all going to go on by themselves; they can go a lot faster without Mr. Mahajan. If one of them gets stuck, she can call the other two up. But there's no reason why they might get stuck, except sometimes the book isn't all that clear, like once in a while it leaves out a step, but you can usually figure it out.

Tracy says, "Let's go have a drink. I don't have to rush home tonight."

So the three of them head for the parking lot. As they pass the rest room, Kathleen says, "Wait up." She scrabbles in her purse for her pen and, crossing out *Kath* in the heart, writes *Pepin*.

～

All three girls have gotten one hundred. He was wrong to despair; they have learned, after all. He's pleased—with them, with himself; their scores speak well for him as a pedagogue. There is only one thing that perplexes him: the red-haired girl, Kathleen, has written something at the bottom of her test, and he doesn't quite understand what it means. "There is only one good, knowledge," it says, "and only one evil, ignorance." At first, he took it as a kind of tribute, but now he isn't so sure. It is one of those sayings of the sort Mary Mirsky collects—she saves adages from Chinese fortune cookies. On her desk is a sign that says: PERFECT MAY BE THE ENEMY OF GOOD, BUT TRY TO BE PERFECT IN YOUR WORK.

And he does try, he has always tried, but sometimes mistakes will happen. There are worse things than mistakes; almost always they can be rectified. While he proctored the exam, he was reading the timeline and saw that someone had made a mistake. It nearly caused him to laugh out loud, for *Gaul* has been misspelled *Gual*. It looks so queer. How long has it been there, and why did no one ever change it? Students must have stenciled the timeline. Probably no one ever noticed. And so there it is: MEROVINGIAN FRANKS UNDER CLOVIS TAKE CONTROL OF GUAL. Clovis—he doesn't know who that was. But there are worse evils, surely, than ignorance.

The Nipple of the Queen

It was a good day for greens—"blues," Eddie called them, but this was just to tease her. The stones were green, the same briny green as the waves that tumbled them up onto the sand and dragged them back, washed them in again, casting them into heaps with other stones: black, orange, gray, maroon, high on the beach where the sharp grass began, or stranding them singly, lone rocks lying wet and green near a nugget of red jasper or an egg of Maine granite— the beach spangled, the stones glistening, the tide ebbing in trickles around them.

They were serpentine, or so the man who used to run the rock store had told her years ago, almost twenty years ago, when, spreading a handful of gold and brown and green stones on the top of his glass display case, Ada pointed to the greens and said, "This is jasper, right?" It took the wind right out of her, hearing, "No, that's serpentine." It was deflating, like falling out of a swing when you were a child or having some adult say to you, "Pride goeth before a fall." She had always been afraid of that sin, the sin of pride.

Being wrong—but she had not been wrong, only mistaken, only misguidedly confident—somehow it had made her not want to ask what the other stones were: the polished browns whose black veins formed patterns like rivers and tributaries, the fine-textured golds with their grain like burled wood. Unusual stones, but none of them in her rock books, and now it was too late to ask; the store was closed and the man no longer there—retired or dead. The kind of thing that made you feel old.

"Well, you *are* old, sweetie," Eddie said, laughing at her when she said she was beginning to feel old (but she must tell him something to explain why she was so impatient these days, why she was snapping at him). And immediately, she wanted to contradict him: "No, I'm not!" Belligerent as a child. She was feeling more and more like a child; she was thinking more and more about childhood, and that was what old people did. She was seventy-two; that was old.

It was this gypped feeling that made her feel like a child. The impatience, too, a strange impatience that kept rising like an urge, like a tickling, as if she just wanted to get on with it, whatever it was, as if she had spent her whole life delaying.

It came over her at the worst times—when she was walking across a parking lot with Eddie, or when they were down here at the beach and it was one of his bad days and he had to walk so slowly. She should be glad he could walk at all, and she *was* glad, but it was like walking with her own grandfather and she a girl of six or so. That was what it reminded her of: his grip on her arm, so loving and yet so stern.

She had felt that same impatience back in June, when the house was overrun with grandchildren, everybody there at once: the three boys and their wives, all those little hellions running around making so much racket that even Eddie said, "I think I'm getting—what do they call it these days?—peopled out." She should have put her foot down and said no when the boys first suggested it. She should've told them Eddie wouldn't be up to it. And it was tactless, their coming from the ends of the earth, Texas and California and even France, as if they all thought this birthday would be Eddie's last, when even the doctor couldn't predict. But it was good of them, too.

Gypped. She had never felt like that as a child and never once until just lately. That was what made her snap at Eddie, snap at that poor little devil Claude, who knew no better than to dump out all her jars of rocks, the sorted ones. What a mound they made on the closet floor, all the greens and blacks and her few golds, years and years of sorting by color, by size. Her small rocks, so hard to come by on this beach; none of them was larger than a navy bean. But what was he doing in her closet, and how could she help being angry?

She didn't want to snap at Eddie. She wanted to question him, and that was like a child, too: Why had they done this and not that? Why had they come here always in August when they could have spent the entire summer, and why had they never considered renting a place, or even buying? They always stayed in the motel. And then went back to Connecticut, where the weather was hot and muggy and she wished her life away, longing for fall. They could have stayed here, where the cool breeze blew straight off the Bay of Fundy and you could still get a twenty-five-cent cup of coffee at the little place in town where they always ate lunch. Other summers they could have stayed here. Not now.

She hadn't thought they would come, hadn't even dared hope. But Eddie said, "I feel much better, and we're going. I have to see what's on the beach."

His red jasper. He picked up nothing but red jasper, and all red jasper was his. Oh, she could keep the maroon kind, but not the bright reds, rosy, carnelian, the Chinese reds, Venetian. And the stones with the scarlet flecks so dense, so close together, that you could hardly see the dark matrix, those were his, too; they looked crazed, as if baked. She had hated to see the kids playing with them, the huge brandy snifter he kept them in tipped over on the rug. "Can I have this one, Grandpa? Can I have this one?" Of course he said yes. Then there were red stones in the lawn and underneath the sofa cushions; she was still finding them in July. What did children care about red jasper?

The rocks—each one different, each dry stone with its minuscule seaprint of salt rime, whorls that disappeared in the collecting bag, to reappear, patternless, a dusty film that needed to be wiped off when she oiled the stone's surface, bringing out the color; she used Nivea. Already she had gone through the jar, a small jar, that she had brought with her.

"Room smells like a funeral parlor."

She noticed he hadn't said that this year. He had always thought she should get a tumbling machine, but that made stones look artificial, like plastic.

"You ought to do like me," he would tell her, rubbing a red stone up across the bridge of his nose, down, following the contour of the nostrils, his glasses lifting, unhitching themselves. It was a wonder they never broke; he would grab at them but not always catch them. They would land on the stones he had emptied onto the towel, to keep the sand off the bedspread. The hollow clicking of plastic against stone was so familiar that she didn't even need to turn her head to see the white towel, the red stones, the escaped glasses that looked both roguish and abandoned. In the light from the table lamp, his hair was blond gossamer, and that unsettled her, because in his youth his hair had been very dark and then, later, white but always thick; and not until chemotherapy gave him the angelic baldness did he begin to look to her like a stranger, for which, heaven help her, she could not quite forgive him. But he still had something, a radiance. Waitresses smiled at him, extra-warm, checkers in the market, too, and women strolling along down here with their own husbands—campers those people usually were, with RVs parked in the woods beyond, though for the most part, as today, the beach was empty.

"Blue," he called back to her, and she said, "Where?" then, "I see it," as if she didn't see several, all of them too large but still too beautiful to leave. You could think of yourself as being on a kind of rescue mission: saving the stones from being pulverized into sand. Of course that was foolish, and someday she might bring back the ones she hadn't needed or could bear to part with, though how could she bear to come to this beach again? She would go to the beach in California that Ed Jr.'s wife had told her about, where you could find moonstones (they were probably agates, not moonstones, but no matter). "How big are they?" she could hear herself interrupting, because Judith was already telling her about another beach, close by the first one, maybe an hour's drive, where you could find jade and the sand was black. A strange question—she could see Judith thought so—though perhaps no more strange than hiding the wooden bowls full of special stones in the cupboards under the window seats; but there must be no more scenes, no more dreadful scenes. Poor little Claude. She must have terrified him: "No! Those are Grandma's!" His mother rushing in, fierce and stricken: "What has Claude done?" But nothing, nothing, a child of three. Judith, mystified, echoing, "How big?" as she plucked a stone from this or that bowl, fingered it. Judith in the window seat, the bowls beside her. So perhaps it had not been a mistake, succumbing to temptation, showing Judith the stones. "Come visit," Judith said. "Come next summer." But what did that mean, whom was she inviting? Surely she must know that Eddie was not up to much travel. It had taken them three days to drive up here instead of one.

At least, Ada thought, bending down, picking up the green stones, wiping the sand off on her sweat pants, at least she had not said anything ghastly, anything incriminating; she had not said, "Why, I'd love to come."

But she would love to, for somewhere she would have to find the small white stones for the pharaoh's gown, the small golds for the arms, for the legs, more blacks for the hair—like stiff strings of beads. She had enough greens for the gown of the queen. She must look at more pictures; perhaps both breasts were bare. But perhaps only one—she wasn't sure. Frescoes in tombs: all the heads in profile. But the torsos front, then the legs from the side. Six legs crisscrossing, showing through the skirts. Herons in the foreground, long-legged ibises.

Pay attention, she told herself, giving her head a shake if to dislodge water. Eddie was thirty, forty feet ahead of her almost to the fish weir, and that was as far as they ever walked. He wasn't wearing his cap, and he should be; his blue windbreaker billowed behind him.

"Put on your cap," she yelled, but she was downwind, and he didn't turn around. Beyond him, the cliff rose high and dark, the beach curving into its base and spruce trees furring its top; they were foreshortened in a way she would have got wrong, her perspective was so rusty.

Ahead of her, in the dingy sand, lay a piece of red jasper that Eddie had missed, not a small one, either, and that wasn't like him, though when he had walked here, the water might have covered it; his footprints were no longer at the water's edge but upbeach; the tide ebbed so fast—an inch a minute, she thought it was; it must be about to turn. There was a point where the outgoing tide met the tide coming in, and what was that called? She bad never known; perhaps there was not a word. She squatted down.

Yesterday he had missed a stone much larger than this one, and she'd thought it was because the tide was coming in, wetting stones that he had only seen dry. But red jasper didn't need to be wet for you to see it, and therefore how much more horrible for her to have teased him about it, holding it on her upturned palm as they sat across from each other at the table in the little restaurant. "Look what I found. I'll give it to you if you're real good." And his tired smile, forgiving and even wry. "Well, I'm too far gone to be anything but good, so give it here." She would simply slip this stone into his collecting bag when he wasn't looking.

But other rocks she could show him at lunch—the ones he called his "aerial photographs," rocks marked as though by islands or continents; and she saw one now, a flat green oval, mapped blue like sea meeting shore, like the coast of Maine itself. Once you were hunkered down, you saw all sorts of treasures that eluded you when you were standing up. She wanted to look in the piles of stones up near the beach grass, dig down; the smaller stones were all underneath, though why was that? It was like the sermon on TV that she'd been listening to before Eddie said, "Will you turn that thing off?" about the three men who grew potatoes and two of them sorted their potatoes, but the third man just threw them into his truck, and the potatoes sorted themselves as they were driven to market. It was a sermon about different ways of sorting, she knew that much, and she didn't care about that, about what the point was; she'd never intended to listen to a sermon. Only, the big potatoes ended up on top—that was what was interesting; she would've thought they'd end up on the bottom, being heavier. It was the same with the rocks. Eddie would know why that was; she kept forgetting to ask him. She would ask him at lunch.

The stone was drying in her hand, and she licked it to bring back the color, her tongue tasting salt. He would cock his head, squinting, holding the stone up close and then at arm's length, deciding what the story would be. "Ah yes, I remember taking this one. We were over in Sumatra, or was it Brazil?" Always places the two of them had never been.

"Ada," she heard him calling as she pocketed the stone, slipping it in with the jasper, because why mix it up with her own stones and then have to search for it—she might not remember, might be tempted to keep it for herself. Even with her sweater on, she was chilly; the wind was picking up. Why didn't he have enough sense to wear his cap?

She pushed herself up, the breeze cold on her shins; with the toes of her sneakers she nudged her pant legs down, first one, then the other.

"You coming or what?"

She mimed: Put on your cap. But he cupped his hand to his ear, so she yelled the words.

He shook his head, laughing—not hearing, she guessed, not understanding. She shrugged. The water between him and the fish weir was aglitter with sunlight, and she squinted, thinking she saw something out in the blueness that was deeper than the sky's—something dark and round, stationary; it could not be a buoy.

"A seal!" she said, pointing.

If he would only turn around, he could see it much better than she could. But he motioned her to come on, so she did, plodding toward him; her feet were cold. Yesterday she had tried to get him to look at a barge that was slowly passing in front of the island, Grand Manan Island; every summer they talked about going to Grand Manan. And he had not looked at the barge either—oh, maddening man! But still, she must talk to him gently, she must not snap at him. She had snapped at him only this morning.

He was walking on now, not waiting for her, and she squatted down again, seeing a green, seeing a brown; it was a good day for browns, too, though none of them would ever find their way into the mosaic; they were all too large. The small waves plapped in close to her feet, curling over on themselves, sending in a listless foam. It was lucky the tides had been right this week, low in the morning, so she and Eddie could get down here when the whole beach was exposed instead of having to wait until afternoon, the way they did last week; he was always too tired in the afternoon. She'd thought he was going to be too tired this morning. But this had been a good week, and she'd had no call to snap at him, seeing him so slow to get moving, still sitting on the edge of his bed when she came out of the shower and he was supposed to be dressing, seeing him slumped there like a doleful boy; he looked so old, and somehow that was all right for her but not for him. His arms were so thin and flabby, and when he was young you could not even dent the muscles, pushing on them with your forefinger.

"Why can't you wear those T-shirts I bought you?"

Was there ever anything more irrelevant? It should have been a joke, it had always been a joke, but it didn't sound like a joke when she said it. He had always worn those sleeveless undershirts with the V necks, "old men's undershirts," she used to call them, as if she could get him to change; he was changing before her eyes. But a joke, a joke between them, so to say, so that he could say, "Ah, I see you've gone and bought yourself some new dust rags." Then to snap at him, for no reason, as if she wouldn't have been glad to give up her life if it could have saved his, like Queen Alcestis and her husband, King Admetus, except that they were both then saved by Apollo.

Maybe, instead of Egyptians, she should do Greeks.

But no, the hair, she could see the hair, and sometimes she found herself idly sketching the figures, planning; the queen would be the central figure. The stones could be glued on a backing of masonite, a large square of it, or else Plexiglas.

A wave foamed in up around her feet, rising over the toes of her sneakers, and she said out loud, "Damnation." Now Eddie would want to go back to the motel so that she could change her shoes, and she did want to look in the piles, where, long ago, they had seen a man with a walking cast sitting in the stones that were warm on top, cold underneath; his crutch lay there next to him. The very picture, she told Eddie, of true determination, or else pure greed. They had spoken to him, and he'd said, "I'm getting these for my daughter." No doubt he was telling the truth, and she shouldn't have laughed, saying, "That's a lame one if I ever heard one," because then Eddie was exasperated. "Do you have to say everything that comes into your mind?" As if she did. Only, if everyone took as many stones from the beach as she did, someday there would be no more, because there could not be an infinite supply, and where did they come from, anyway?

Another wave washed in. She thought: I should move. But it was too much trouble to move. A tiny fragment of red jasper eddied in the foam, and she rocked forward, making a dam of her hand, the slurry of icy grit numbing her fingers so they opened, the water rushing through and the fragment as well, she was afraid, because now it was nowhere to be seen; there were just bubbles quickly collapsing on the sand's surface as if they had been sucked dry from underneath. She dug down, wedging the sand aside with the heel of her hand; it was like digging for a vanished crab. But then there it was, and not where she was digging but simply lying on the surface, an almost perfect red circle; it must have been under a bubble. She had found the nipple of the queen!

"Ada!"

Over the waves she could hear the stones in his canvas collecting bag clinking together as the bag swung against his leg. He had given up and come back for her, and she wished he hadn't.

She stood up, dancing back stiffly before another wave could get her. "Now, don't go scolding me." He had put his cap on; at least he had put his cap on. "Look, there's a seal," she said, pointing with the arm he'd been about to take. And there was the seal; it had appeared as soon as she had spoken, as if by magic, and submerged as she pointed, so it was gone when he turned around to look.

"Well, there was one."

He frowned. "How do you know it was a seal?"

"I saw it before. It was watching us."

"My dear," he said, humoring her; he had always humored her. He had always asked, "How do you know?" and she had always hated it.

"I saw the whiskers," she said, though she had not seen the whiskers. "Well, I did," she said, shoving her hand into her sweater pocket, poking the queen's nipple down into the fuzzy seam. She wanted to look in the piles; she was too tired to look in the piles. "Are you too tired to look in the piles?" she said.

"No," he said. But he was too tired—she could see it, see that he was more tired than she was. "I'm fine," he said, linking his arm with hers.

He steered her up the incline to the heaps of stones, pod-shaped and flat, their ends tapered by tides that would not be that high again until winter. He was a man, she thought, who would not have begrudged her the whole beast. And she felt herself melt, as she always had, and heard herself concede:

"It could have been an otter."

Dreams

Just before noon on Saturday, Emma's ex-mother-in-law phoned from Arizona. Emma had not heard from her since the divorce.

"I dreamed about you last night. I had to tell you. I dreamt you were all together—you and Bill and the children, but you were the strongest," her mother-in-law said.

At first Emma took this to mean that in the dream she had been the strongest, just as, perhaps, she had been in real life. But what her mother-in-law meant was that she had seen Emma more clearly than the others. It could come to the same thing, Emma thought.

"I saw you lying in bed," her mother-in-law said. "You looked calm and very happy."

"That was certainly a dream," said Emma.

"Your arm was at your side, and in it—guess what?"

"What?" Emma said.

"A baby!"

Both laughed. "That could only happen in a dream," Emma said.

"I know, I know," said her mother-in-law. She sounded exhilarated. "It was a newborn baby, but it didn't look newborn."

"You mean," said Emma, "it didn't look real?"

"It looked real, but it was like a baby in one of those Old Masters' paintings." Emma tried to imagine what her mother-in-law was seeing. "Who's the artist that painted all those cherubs?"

"I don't know," said Emma. Her own real babies had not looked like cherubs.

"Anyway, it was a beautiful baby. Now, why do you suppose I had a dream like that?"

"I don't know," Emma said.

Her mother-in-law was not the first person to have such a dream about her. Only a few weeks ago, Emma's closest friend had dreamed that Emma had a baby. "You were so pleased about it," her friend said. "I couldn't understand why you were so pleased."

"It made me happy," Emma's mother-in-law said. You were all together, and you were all happy."

"Dreams," Emma said.

"Yes, aren't they funny?"

"Yes," Emma said. She didn't know why her friend should have had such a dream about her. In other people's dreams, children made her happy.

"I've got something to tell you," Emma's mother-in-law went on. "I got a postcard from that son of yours. It was from New York City. What's Jeff doing in New York?"

"I don't know," Emma said. "I didn't know he was in New York."

"Is he through with school?"

"Maybe so," Emma said.

"But is the semester over?"

"I don't know."

"But don't you hear from him?"

"No," Emma said.

"Your son and mine!" said her mother-in-law. "How do you suppose they managed to turn out so much alike?"

Emma had her theories, but she said, "I guess it's only natural."

"Here, I'll read you the postcard. 'Today I took my first ride on the Staten Island ferry.'"

"We took him when he was little, but I guess he doesn't remember."

"Then he says: 'My life is full of stress.' What do you make of that?"

"I suppose," said Emma, "he expected something different."

"Well, we all did," said her mother-in-law.

Emma thought about that. Maybe there were people who expected what they got. Maybe there were people who got what they expected.

"We do the best we can," her mother-in-law said, "and after that, it's up to them."

Emma thought about that, too. Just last week she had met her daughter for lunch. "You brought us up all wrong," Ginny told her, over salad.

"I suppose I did," Emma had agreed.

She did not say, "I did the best I could." Her feeling had always been that she should have done better. She saw the two of them sitting there: chewing, ruminant.

"You shouldn't have been such a mother."

I shouldn't have been a mother, Emma had almost said; there was a time when she didn't yet know that.

"You shouldn't have always had to run things."

"I ran things?" Emma said, remembering differently.

"You should've made us do things."

"How?" Emma asked.

"You should've made us want to."

"How?" Emma asked, again.

"You shouldn't have had to be such a mother."

No, I shouldn't have had to be, Emma thought. "They forced us into it," she said, into the phone.

"What?" her mother-in-law said.

"I was just talking to the cat."

"Oh," said her mother-in-law. "I thought it died."

"It did."

"You got another one?"

"A kitten."

"Well," said her mother-in-law, "it's company for you."

As a matter of fact, Emma did not now own a cat. After the old cat died, she did not want any more animals. At one time, she had had a great many: ducks and geese, the cat, a goat kid. She imagined that she had so many animals because the children liked them, but the animals were Emma's, nobody else's. Several years went by before Emma realized. By then the children had grown up, and so had the kid. It had turned into a cantankerous nanny goat, formidable but rather foolish. The grown children teased it and made it chase them. Emma remembered how it had followed her around as a kid. She wondered if the goat would have turned out differently if it had had a kid of its own.

"Probably worse," she said.

"How do you mean 'worse'?" asked her mother-in-law. "What's worse than what?"

"I was thinking about the goat," Emma said, "and all the animals."

"Oh, the goat," said her mother-in-law. "I never could understand why you kept that creature. It had the worst disposition."

"Maybe," Emma said, "it had reason."

"You were so attached to it. Sometimes I used to think you liked animals better than children."

"They were easier," Emma said. She was watching twelve-year-old Jeff throw stones at the goat. She had watched for a long time before she stopped him.

"They were a lot of work," her mother-in-law said.

"They were all a lot of work," said Emma. She had given away all the animals except the cat.

"I know Bill got awfully tired of them."

"Bill got tired of everything."

"How *is* Bill? Do you hear anything?"

"A little, now and then," Emma said, "from Ginny."

"What do you hear?"

"Oh, mostly about his girl friends."

"But doesn't he call you?"

"No," Emma said.

"He doesn't?"

"No, why would he?"

Her mother-in-law seemed to think. "Maybe he wouldn't. But I don't see why he can't call me." Emma said nothing. She heard her mother-in-law sigh. "I don't like not knowing what's going on." There are times in your life when you'd rather not know, Emma thought, but you can't pick and choose them. "Emma, I miss your letters."

"I just don't write letters any more," Emma said.

"I know, I know. I don't either. But I want letters anyway. Isn't that crazy?"

"No," Emma said.

"Anyway, it was Papa who was the great letter-writer."

Emma said, "I remember."

"He used to come home and say, 'Any news from the children?' I saved your letters. They're a record." But not of what went on, thought Emma. "Do you know, sometimes I'm glad he didn't live to see you split up?"

Emma said, "Well, it was hard on everybody."

"I know it happens all the time, but I never thought it would happen to you two."

"Neither did I," said Emma.

"But Emma, I never have understood it."

I believe, Emma thought, it was because of the goat. First the animals went, then the people. They had all found homes of their own.

"It was time," she said.

"I suppose that's it," her mother-in-law said. "Middle-age—it's a hard time. In my dream you were a young woman."

Emma was silent. She was thinking about her middle-aged dreams. Once she dreamed that she was full of eggs, large eggs, like the eggs of Muscovy ducks. She had to move very carefully, but not for fear of breaking them. She knew the shells of the eggs were tough, like the shells of duck eggs. She dreamed of eggs, never of babies; also she dreamed of giving birth.

"Well, I had to tell you," her mother-in-law said, and waited, but Emma did not answer. "When you find out what Jeff's up to, let me know. And if you hear from that son of mine, tell him to call me."

I won't be hearing from either one of them, Emma thought— but relented and said:

"I'll ask Ginny."

And a Woman to Hate

When I was between the ages of three and eleven, my Uncle Brett was my favorite person in the whole world. For sure I loved him more than I did my dad, who, once, when he had Corey and me over for the weekend, said, "So how's your uncle, that pious sap?" Maybe I didn't love Uncle Brett more than I loved my mother, but he was easier to be with. He never got mad at us. Mom got mad at me and Corey every single day. It didn't seem to matter whether we did anything we weren't supposed to or not. Just the fact that we were us seemed to annoy her, and I knew it had something to do with the way she felt about my dad, who had gotten married again and now had a baby girl named Jennifer.

"Wouldn't we *all* like to have a baby named Jennifer!" we heard her say to Aunt Jodene, whose stomach was getting bigger and bigger every week. Corey and I knew what that meant, though nobody had told us.

"Not really," our aunt replied. "I mean, I wouldn't name her Jennifer. I might name her Charlotte, except I just heard that was the most popular name for a girl in England. There're probably too many Charlottes already."

"The son of a bitch!" Mom said.

"Damn it, Sandy, can't you try . . . ?"

"I'm trying, I'm trying!" Mom pretended she was wailing. "But I'm never going to find anybody, not at this rate."

Somewhere around this time, when she was pretty discouraged about just about everything, she asked who the hell was going to want to marry a woman with two boys like us, two peas out of the same pod. We would drive anybody nuts. Then she said, "Oh, God, I didn't mean that," and grabbed us and hugged us, but it was something neither Corey nor I forgot, though I don't think we would have remembered it at all if she hadn't turned it into such a big deal, so we had to pay attention and get our feelings hurt. But then it was like we were never going to get over her saying a mean thing like that, and she was never going to get over saying it.

"Just forget it," Uncle Brett told us, and his finger made an invisible "X" on my forehead, "and let her forget about it. If that's the worst thing anybody ever says to you—hey, it's nothing. Besides, your mother's under a lot of stress. Come on back this afternoon and watch the Red Sox."

People usually thought Uncle Brett was our grandfather, but he was our grandmother's youngest brother, our mother's uncle. Mom liked to tell us how, when she was four years old, he used to come wake her up before the sun rose, to take her fishing. He'd throw pebbles at the window screen and tell her to come on, and off they'd go to Revere Beach or Hull, Mom with just a jacket on over her pajamas.

"It seems incredible now, him taking me out there in the dark, but I loved it, I just loved being with him. I'd be all wrapped up in a blanket, sitting in the fog. The sand was cold—was it ever cold! But pretty soon the fog out over the water started to turn pink and then it thinned out, and the sun came up and burned it off. When I started kindergarten, I used to fall sound asleep during rest period."

I thought it was weird for Uncle Brett to take a girl fishing, especially since she said she'd "never caught a damn thing," and Corey asked how come he never took us fishing. Uncle Brett said it was because fishing wasn't what it used to be. But then another time he said the main thing was, his fishing days were over. "You get sick and tired of something, you don't want to do it anymore."

He got sick and tired of fishing, my mother said, at about the same time as Aunt Jewel divorced him. I didn't remember much about Aunt Jewel; I was probably about six when she left. She was tall, she didn't like kids, and she always wore an apron. "He never should've married her," Mom said, after Aunt Jewel had been gone a while and we were sure she wasn't coming back. And we heard her say to Aunt Jodene, "Why couldn't Jewel have left thirty years ago, so he could've had a life with someone nice?"

But Jodene just snorted. "Brett wouldn't have given someone nice the time of day."

Mom didn't answer for a while. Then she said, "No, I think a really together woman could've turned him around."

Emboldened by what I'd heard, I later asked if Aunt Jewel had been a witch.

"Why would you think that?" Mom said. "Of course she wasn't a witch. She was just a real me-firster. It's lucky they didn't have children."

Aunt Jewel was a Catholic, and Uncle Brett had converted. The only Catholic kids we knew had lots of brothers and sisters, so I asked why Uncle Brett and Aunt Jewel never had any children.

All Mom said was, "Guess it just wasn't in the cards." But then she thought about it some more and said, "Actually, he probably should've been a priest. Trouble is, he was already married when he found his calling."

This sounded right to me. I could see him wearing one of those black robes, like the priests. I could see how he'd look, with his silvery hair. Sometimes, when Mom came to get us early in the morning, we drove home past the Catholic church, and once in a while we'd see the red-haired priest, standing out in front with the dark church doorway opening behind him. He would be standing in the sunlight, with his face lifted up, and he had the same holy look that Uncle Brett had when he was praying. His cassock billowed around his legs. Rainbows drifted toward him from the fountain.

On the wall behind Uncle Brett's bed, there was a cross hanging from a nail, and dangling from the cross was his rosary.

Sometimes I got up on the bed and unhooked the rosary. I liked to hold it between my hands until the black beads got warm. I didn't want to have to say "Hail Marys" and "Our Fathers." I just wanted to hold the rosary. But Uncle Brett said it wasn't something to play with. He told us about the Blessed Virgin, whose framed picture hung on the wall opposite his bed. "I worship her," he said, and his eyes were as solemn as the Blessed Virgin's. "She is the holiest woman that ever was. In the beginning, there was Eve and then there was the Virgin Mary . . ." He stopped and sat there, frowning. "Now, you take your Aunt Jodene—I don't know if anybody's ever got around to telling you boys, but someone ought to tell you it isn't right to have a baby when you aren't married. Still, it's better she should have it. She's not a bad person, Jodene. She's just got an unruly spirit. I was like that when I was young." And he sighed. "We were all children once."

Sometimes, when we stayed over, Sunday morning he'd take us to early mass. I didn't know what to think of it—all those people kneeling and praying. We didn't do any of that at home, and Mom never made us go to Sunday School or anything. When Corey and I slept over and the three of us knelt to say our prayers out loud before getting into bed, I knew that "God bless Mom and Corey and Aunt Jodene and Uncle Brett" was the order Uncle Brett wanted me to ask the Lord's blessings in. At home, though, if I remembered to say a prayer, I asked Him to bless Uncle Brett first, every other night, so both he and Mom would both get blessed first the same number of times.

"I guess it's all right that he's taking you to mass," Mom said. "I don't know what you're going to get out of it, but it probably won't hurt you. They wouldn't let him take me, when I was little. I never thought I missed anything. Just don't bring home any crucifixes." I said she ought to be going to church too. She said, "No, that's not something you can tell another person to do. I don't have any business in church. I'm not a believer." Another time, she said, "I think of it as a kind of ritual—you know, to get you calmed down and focused and thinking about something else besides your own troubles. So you can be grateful to be alive even if you haven't got a perfect life. Some people go to church. I play solitaire." She played three games every morning, while she drank her first cup of coffee.

Even at seven or eight I didn't think it could be the same thing. I remembered waking up in the night, hearing whispering. There was a full moon, and in its light Uncle Brett's face looked like marble, like the face of the statue of St. Francis of Assisi. He was kneeling with his hands clasped under his chin; the rosary with its crucifix was looped over his little fingers.

". . . and bless my nieces Sandra and Jodene and my great grand-nephews Tommy and Corey, and bless Jewel," he said, after naming everybody else in the family, which took him a while, because he'd had two brothers and two sisters and they'd all had children and grandchildren and even great-grandchildren, and he asked for them to have a blessing whether they were alive, like my aunt and another uncle, or dead. Uncle Brett, being the youngest, was "only" sixty-five.

It was when he was around sixty that Aunt Jewel had moved out and said she wanted a divorce.

"What're we going to do about him?" Mom asked Aunt Jodene. "I never saw anybody so devastated. Isn't that strange? I mean, here he's been miserable for thirty years, and finally he's rid of her, and he's just bereft."

Aunt Jodene said, "But you know converts always take it to heart more than people born into a religion." Aunt Jewel could demand a divorce, but that was something Uncle Brett just couldn't imagine.

He couldn't imagine it even though it had happened.

"I keep thinking she's going to come back," he used to tell us. We'd be sitting on the daybed, waiting for the Celtics to come on. One of those times, he said, "I keep wondering how a woman could hate me so much." He gave our shoulders a squeeze; Corey and I both said, "Ow!" "Would you believe, these last few years, she wouldn't even sleep in the same room? And she wouldn't eat with me anymore—we were cooking separate suppers. I don't understand what happened to her." He thought for a minute.

"When women get to a certain age, they go off their rocker. Some of them."

I didn't like it when Uncle Brett talked about Aunt Jewel. It scared me, because it was like he was mad and sad at the same time. And I didn't see why he was so sad about the divorce. Everybody in the family said Jewel was a Holy Terror.

"The poor guy," Mom said to Aunt Jodene, "he was just so pussy-whipped he doesn't know what to do with his freedom. The women are going to mob him, they're going to be jumping out of the trees . . . ."

I looked at Corey, ready to snicker. He didn't know what Mom was talking about either. We heard a lot in those days that we didn't understand. But that didn't stop us from listening.

"He's the nicest, most loving man I've ever known," Mom went on. "Nobody, but nobody, ever measured up to him."

"Certainly not Daddy," Jodene said. And the two of them laughed. Then Jodene said, "But he was a nice drunk, Daddy was. Remember how he'd give us dollar bills?"

"Once Brett gave a man a hundred dollars," Mom said, "a complete stranger who came into the store, somebody down on his luck and he needed to get to New York . . ."

"Chicago," Jodene said.

"It was New York," Mom said, and I looked at Corey. "He told me New York, I got it straight from the horse's mouth."

"Well, he told me Chicago," Jodene said. "And it was a hundred and fifty. Of course, he never saw it again, but then he didn't expect to."

"We were standing on the beach right opposite the Arcade when he told me," Mom said. "You weren't even there. You were only three years old. He never took you fishing."

I heard a coffee cup being set on its saucer. "He never took you to tap-dancing lessons," Jodene said.

"That's because I wouldn't take tap dancing," my mother said, and they both began to laugh, and Jodene said, "It was two hundred dollars to the guy who was trying to get to Denver."

Then they both quit laughing, and my mother said, "Poor Brett."

I didn't see what was poor about Uncle Brett if he could give away money, but I knew that wasn't what they meant. I was sorry I'd listened. Sometimes, I wished we'd known Uncle Brett in the days when he would've taken us fishing instead of to church.

From time to time, there were men who called up, wanting to speak to "Sandra," or "Sandy," and Mom made us rehearse saying, "Just a moment, please" instead of "Who?" or "Okay" or just shouting, "Mom!" Having been a babysitter herself, she didn't trust babysitters, so she only went out on Saturday night if she could line up Uncle Brett, which she mostly could.

Uncle Brett always made a big to-do about how glamorous Mom looked. "You look radiant," was the thing he told her most often. And she would lean back, holding his hands as if they were doing some kind of dance, then go into a big hug followed by a big, noisy kiss. She'd ruffle his hair and swing away again, one hand letting go and then the other. Uncle Brett just stood there, looking pleased, his hair all mussed.

"You're so cute," she'd say.

"You're pretty cute yourself." He'd smooth his hair. It was embarrassing.

After she left, he kept standing there in the middle of the living room for a long time, smiling. Then he said, "Well, boys, how 'bout we make us some popcorn?" Once in a while he said, "You know that mother of yours? She's a pretty hot ticket."

Uncle Brett had a bed that he said was queen-size. It was the bed he used to sleep in with Aunt Jewel before she wouldn't sleep in the same room with him anymore. I don't think Corey and I stayed overnight until after Aunt Jewel moved out, because if we had, we would've had to sleep on the daybed in the family room, where we watched the Celtics, and I don't remember ever doing that, plus when Aunt Jewel quit sleeping in Uncle Brett's bedroom, she would've had to sleep on the daybed herself.

Sometimes, before she moved out, Uncle Brett would sleep over at our house. We'd wake up and find him on the sofa in the living room.

"Your Uncle Brett's going to be visiting us for a while," Mom would tell us.

But he never stayed more than two or three days. He'd have breakfast with us and dinner. His toilet kit sat on the back of the toilet tank, and I don't know how old I was before I realized that it was not called a toilet kit because of where it was. Ordinarily a box of Kleenex sat there, but it would be moved over to the built-in cupboard where the towels were kept. In the toilet kit were Uncle Brett's razor and his aftershave lotion and some stuff to clean his teeth, which were false, anyway the upper ones, though we never saw him without his teeth, never once. But we saw his teeth in the bathroom sink.

Mom was in a better mood when he stayed with us. She whistled while she cooked dinner, and she wore her red satin bathrobe in the morning.

"It's nice to have a man in the house," she always said, smiling.

"One more day, then I'm going to have to go back to Xantippe and face the music."

"Brett . . . ," my mother said, sometimes, but he would hold up his hand.

"Don't even suggest it."

We were sorry to see him go. He brought home batteries from the Radio Shack he managed. When we were probably too young, he brought us a Walkman, but Corey dropped it down the stairs and wrecked it. I didn't see how he could have done that. He just stood there and dropped it, and it bounced halfway down the stairs and then it wouldn't work. I went for him, I was going to kill him. But Uncle Brett picked me up and carried me into the living room.

"Now, you've got to remember he's three years younger than you." He held me close on his lap, so he had to lean back to see into my eyes. "He hasn't got to the age of reason."

"I don't care," I howled. "I hate him."

Uncle Brett rested his chin on top of my head. "I know." He sighed, and I could feel his warm breath. "You two remind me of your mother and Jodene." He kept his chin there. "You, especially—you remind me of your mother."

I thought he meant because Corey looked like my dad, with brown eyes and reddish brown hair. Me, I had hazel eyes like my mom and lighter hair like her too, except she did something to hers to make it come out blond. Dad's new baby, Jennifer, had dark brown eyes and red hair like her mother, and neither Corey nor I could believe she was our sister. Dad said she was, but we didn't see all that much of her. We were supposed to go to our dad's every other weekend, but somehow that never worked out the way it was supposed to. Dad would have to cancel out at the last minute, and then my mother would call Uncle Brett, crying on the telephone.

"He's done it again, the son of a bitch, he's left me high and dry, and we already have the limo . . . Brett, could you . . . ?"

He let us stay up late, watching wrestling. Corey would fall asleep, and Uncle Brett would have to carry him to the bedroom, though I didn't see why we couldn't just leave him there on the sofa. It was crowded, the three of us sleeping in that bed, even if it was supposed to be big enough for a queen. I'd end up rolled over too close to Uncle Brett or else too close to Corey, all tangled up together.

"That Corey—he climbs you like you were a tree," Uncle Brett would say. He called Corey "The Climber" and me "The Kid That Throws All the Covers Off." But I had to. Sometimes it just got too hot. Uncle Brett made Corey sleep on the outside so he'd climb me instead of him, but then there I was, wedged in between the two of them, with Uncle Brett's arm and Corey's leg pinning me down so I could hardly breathe. And it wasn't just the heat. Uncle Brett talked in his sleep. I was mostly too sleepy to remember what he said, but I know once he said, "You turd," because I went home and asked what that was. He also snored, and so did Corey. I'd just have to get out of the room. I'd climb out the foot of the bed and go get the afghan out of the linen closet in the hall so I wouldn't freeze to death after I'd cooled down.

The afghan had been knitted by one of Uncle Brett's girlfriends, the one Mom couldn't stand because she was just like Jewel.

"Yeah, she's a pushy broad, all right," Uncle Brett laughed. "But she sure as heck plays a mean game of golf."

"Brett, you damn fool, don't you dare marry her."

"Don't worry, hon." He winked. "You're my best girl."

But we could tell that Mom really meant it. "Listen to me—she'd make you miserable!"

He just chuckled. "But there's something about those women who can do that."

Of another girlfriend, Mom said, "That woman's a gold-digger."

"Then she's in for a disappointment. Nothing left to dig."

"You're such a pussycat," my mother said, and in my mind I must have connected it with being pussy-whipped.

"I suppose it was just easier for him to give Jewel what she wanted," Mom said later to Aunt Jodene. "I mean, look at the poor guy—no house, that car . . ."

All Uncle Brett would ever say was, "Well, you know Jewel wasn't rational."

He was living in a different apartment by then, a one-bedroom place overlooking a tiny park. In the distance you could see a bit of the Atlantic Ocean if it wasn't too foggy. In the same building lived his newest girlfriend. Mom liked her better than some of the others, though we never met most of them. She told Aunt Jodene she didn't care how many girlfriends he had, so long as going out with them didn't keep him from babysitting.

"Amen to that," Aunt Jodene said.

Mom invited Uncle Brett and his newest girlfriend over for an apple pie she had baked. Aunt Jodene was there with her new baby, Tamsin.

"What kind of a name is that—Tamsin?" Jan was dumb enough to ask. "Isn't that the name of a plum?"

"That's damson," Uncle Brett said, and even I could see that Jan had just cooked her goose.

"I guess she cooked her goose," Jodene said, after they'd left, and my mother said, "I'd say so."

The way the golfer had cooked *her* goose was: she'd said Uncle Brett spent too much of the weekend babysitting. Saturday nights she wanted to go out to dinner or to a movie.

"I had to tell her, 'See ya later,'" said Uncle Brett. "I'm a contrarian." His eyes looked big behind the glasses he'd taken to wearing. "Nobody, but nobody, tells me what to do."

"Aunt Jewel used to," I piped up before I realized I was being as stupid as Jan had been.

"Tommy, you're excused," my mother said.

"You said so," I cried, "you told Aunt Jodene. You said Uncle Brett was pussy-whipped—me and Corey heard you!"

I just didn't want to end up with all the blame, but I'd cooked my goose; I knew that right away. I didn't yet realize that I'd cooked Mom's too.

After that, though, Uncle Brett wasn't as friendly as he used to be. He was always nice and polite, but things weren't the same. He didn't ask us over very often, and Mom had to find a high school girl to sit with us. I thought eleven was old enough to stay home alone, but Mom said no. There were nights when she didn't come home, and Ginger slept in her bed.

"We hurt his feelings," Mom said. "It was my fault. I never should've said that, but you shouldn't have repeated it. It's an insult. I can't explain what it means, but it's bad. Uncle Brett's a darling man, but he's very . . . fragile."

He was babysitting Tamsin now, so Jodene could go out. On the few Saturday nights when Corey and I went over, there was Tamsin in her smelly diapers.

"Now, Tom," Uncle Brett said—he had started calling me Tom instead of Tommy, "isn't it time you learned how to change a diaper?"

I said no, it wasn't, and it wasn't anything I was going to need to know, because I was never going to have any smelly babies when I grew up.

"Oh," he said, "every man needs children."

"You never had any."

His forehead wrinkled. "No, but I'd have liked to."

He went ahead and changed the diaper, washing Tamsin off with a Handiwipe and sprinkling her with pink powder. They were those Huggy diapers, like you saw on TV.

"There's my little darlin'," he said, holding her ankles together in one hand and jiggying her legs till she quit crying and laughed. "Just look at those dimples!"

I felt like I hated him. And I hated Tamsin. I could see Corey wasn't too happy either. He was sitting at the kitchen table, with his face propped in his hands, looking at nothing, though there was going to be a fight on Cable pretty soon.

We watched the fight, Uncle Brett holding Tamsin on his lap the whole time because if he put her to bed, she would just cry. I thought of all the times we used to sit on that sofa, the three of us, with Uncle Brett in the middle, the bowl of popcorn on his lap. He used to have one arm around each of our shoulders, as if he were our dad. But now he was all Tamsin's; he'd just forgotten all about us.

"He doesn't like us anymore," I told Mom.

"Oh, baby," she said, and I almost didn't mind, "Uncle Brett still loves you."

"No, he doesn't."

"He does, but you're growing up now—you know?" She reached out and drew me over to her. "The thing is, he likes *little* children. We all went through it. You two had a long run." But it wasn't fair—him not liking us anymore just because we grew up. "Oh, God," she said, and she hugged me close, "don't I remember—I had to watch him fall in love with Jodene." She tipped my chin up and made me look into her eyes. "And now, honey, it's Tamsin's turn."

"I hate Tamsin."

"I know, I know." She kept looking at me. Then she let me go and looked out the window. "He's always happiest when he has a baby to love." She added something, so softly I didn't know what she'd said, or maybe I couldn't hear it because it didn't make any sense. It sounded like something about a woman to hate. She looked at me again, but she wasn't thinking about me. She had a funny, crooked smile.

"Poor Jewel," she said.

Rescue

"See that streak of dark water? That's where he's feeding—just about halfway between those two boats."

Beh-oats, Liz repeated in her head. Tew beh-oats. Had to be the same man she'd heard Sunday—Downeast plaintive or else Canadian.

"You'll see his back, you'll see him surface four, five times. Then he'll dive and you won't see him for a while."

She came on up the path, toward the group of whale watchers. They stood well back from the edge of the cliff.

"You watch real close, you might see a fin."

The late, low sun was blinding; she brought her hand up to shade her eyes. Somewhere, out there between those two boats . . . One of these days, she'd bring the binoculars.

Sunday, watching the tourists sitting on the outcrop opposite the island, she had thought how well-equipped they seemed—with cameras, binoculars, so many visible signs of being ready for anything, although there had been that one moment, no more than an instant, when they looked to her like a tribe of something—monkeys, baboons; it was the way they perched there on the rocks.

". . . right where those gulls are," the pleasant tenor voice had said, floating to her through the wind from somewhere below, behind the rocks; perhaps there was a ledge.

She had found the gulls, or were they just whitecaps? Gulls, because then the two decorous puffs, like mist, already drifting across the water, and the two dark slivers, barely surfacing, then submerged, the drift of spray vanishing. A pair of finbacks, the voice had said; they could have been shadows cast by the streaky clouds. "You'll see a humpback's tail, you won't see a finback's." A man with binoculars had claimed to see a fin.

"You'll see a humpback's tail . . . ," said the man in the yellow T-shirt; Liz was close enough now to see his lips move, see how several of the women glanced his way.

She was pleased with herself—a little wave of pride, as if she had identified a bird.

"He's there every time I go over to the island," she tells Molly, who couldn't care less and doesn't want to listen. Why should she? Her baby's down for his morning nap; this time is precious. Stolen. Liz can remember what that was like—it's only been a quarter-century. She'd like to tell Molly she has all her sympathy, but the fact is, Molly has only some of it.

When she pulled into the driveway, Molly was down on her hands and knees, weeding around the three-foot tall poppies her garden is full of, deep pink double poppies, annuals that self-seed, becoming weeds themselves. Molly's head was almost hidden by the sage-colored, tattery leaves she must have thought camouflaged the rest of her.

"I see you," Liz said, softly; she rolled down the car window and called, "Can I get you anything in town?" Reassuring them both by not getting out of the car. Molly backed out of the foliage like some reluctant woodland creature. "I'm going to run in the market, maybe hit the hardware . . . ."

Molly got to her feet. "Gee, Liz, that's nice of you." Two polite steps across the unmown lawn. "But there's nothing I need right now, not that I can think of." Something fawnlike about her: the long legs, the delicate brown of her hair. "Thanks anyway, though." Another two steps, one to the side, one backward.

Not an offer to thank anybody for. Liz is pretty sure Molly knows that. Two months alone, and it's as if the whole world has X-ray vision, her every nerve and cell exposed, except nobody is looking. Liz knows that too; she's at her own mercy. "I think I'd better come up and save you from yourself," a friend down in Boston suggested a few weeks ago. And he did come, but it was too late already. She didn't want to be saved.

Now, how did she allow herself to get out of the car, invade the lawn, Molly's territory, examining the poppies—their doubleness, their tripleness? And how did she manage to start talking about this man over on the island who's always there, no matter when she goes over, telling people about the whales that are feeding and mating out in the icy bay? She wasn't invited. Two summers ago, when she first rented the cottage across the meadow for a week, she and Molly never even met, but the next summer, when Liz rented for a whole month, they had coffee together several times, and even this June, glad to see each other again, they'd exchanged visits, Liz being invited in to see the room Molly had fixed up for the baby she was about to have. Now it's August, and Liz is lonely enough to pack up and go home, but the couple she sublet her apartment to in Cambridge won't be moving out till just before Labor Day. Exile— that's what it feels like: exile. She can't go home again, at least not yet. A mistake to commit herself to stay here for so long, expecting to get so much done that she couldn't do at home: reading, writing, sorting out her head. Two more weeks; then she'll go stay with friends. Only, which friends? She'd thought she might stay with George.

"At first I thought this guy was a tour guide," Liz explains, and Molly's pale brown eyes gaze past her, hopelessly. "There was a tour bus down in the parking area—you know, where you park for the lighthouse."

"I don't remember," Molly says. "I haven't been over there in years."

The lighthouse on the island is only twelve miles away, and you can drive to it over a bridge. Molly has lived in this little Maine town her entire short life, a case of cultivating her own garden, Liz decides. The island is in Canada, a foreign country.

"Then I thought he was someone hired by the Canadian government . . ." The fan that cools the VW's engine comes on; to reassure Molly, she left the motor running. "But now . . ." Molly's attention has contracted to a pinpoint, about the diameter of her pupils.

She's tired, she wants to get back to her weeding. Liz knows she should let her off the hook. Instead, she gets reckless, was already reckless, reckless and perverse.

"I think he's there all day, every day," she says. There, like the lighthouse, even on days when she herself is not, when she is mowing her own vast lawn (part of the rental agreement). "Granted," Liz continues, "I came to this conclusion on the basis of only two sightings . . ." She's about to explain that, the first time, she didn't actually see the man, merely overheard him, but that is when sympathy finally wins and she almost cries, "Oh, Molly, forgive me, I'm not really like this. I'll be myself again as soon as I get back to Boston." For Molly is gazing in despair at the muddy toes of her sneakers." What do you suppose would make a man want to do that?" Liz finishes, and Molly comes to life again after only a very short silence, which nevertheless is not a decent interval.

"Oh," she says, "I found that clipping for you. I finally got around to clearing off the dining table, and that's where it was."

And she bounds off across the lawn on tan young legs and disappears into her house. Liz goes back to the car and switches the ignition off, to ensure that Molly will come back out.

It's a long wait. Maybe the baby woke up or Molly got a phone call. Liz wanders around the yard, examining the piles of weeds and the flowering plants: the poppies, hollyhocks. In early July there were lupines, swaths of purple, of white, of pink growing wild here and on the island. There were irises in Molly's garden, deeper violet than the lupines, with a bright yellow beard that reminded Liz of a caterpillar, the way it cleaved fuzzily to the petal, nosing toward the blossom's heart. Molly thrust a bouquet of those irises into Liz's arms. But that was July. And then Timmy was born.

Molly has been in the house for so long that all Liz's courage has drained away, leaving her prey to gravity, as if she might sink down upon the lawn, sink down to her knees. She should go away, mind her own business, or else offer something genuine—baby-sitting, the use of her car. Cut Molly's lawn? Not when Nick could do it.

Empty gestures, anyway, since not from the heart.

Week before last, when they met at the mail boxes that are twinned together at the roadside on one pole—careless, not thinking, altogether on impulse, Liz said the fatal words: "Come have coffee."

Dismay struck Molly's face like an instant frost.

"I mean, when you have time . . . ."

Molly's features had thawed as swiftly as they'd frozen, but Liz doesn't forget. She isn't to be bought with a smile.

"I just don't have any time," Molly apologized, but Liz couldn't forgive her for that, either. "I never knew a baby was going to take up so much time."

Liz could have persisted, said to bring Timmy along, but she wasn't that cruel, nor so kind as to make the only offer that would count. As she strode back down the driveway with the one letter she'd received from the larger world, she had remembered her own mother—in her late middle-age, ten years older than Liz was now—saying, "Come visit me, dear, when you're not too busy," her voice quavery, lonely. Liz remembered her own outrage. "For God's sake, don't put it like that. I *want* to see you!" But from then on, not wanting to in quite the same way and never quite forgiving her: the sweet milk curdled.

"Here," Molly says, behind Liz, suddenly, and the poppy cupped in Liz's hand breaks off. Of course.

"Look what I did!" Liz cries. "I'm so sorry!"

Molly's flourishing the article, neatly trimmed around the edges. Maybe she was in the house for so long because she was trying to find the scissors.

"You can float it in a bowl," Molly says. "Here, listen to this."

It's the article she told Liz about at the beginning of the summer, a short account of how some people, heedless of the sign warning in both English and French about strong currents and swiftly rising tides, had tried to wade back across the sand bar from the lighthouse and been swept off their feet, out into the bay, "'from which it was their good fortune to be rescued by a passing pleasure boat,'" says Molly, and Liz wonders why she is reading this to her, then knows: it is so Liz will take in that phrase, take it to town on her tongue: "a passing pleasure" and "a passing pleasure . . . boat." She can hear it already, how it will come at odd moments, like a line of poetry, Coleridge or someone, not even anybody she would read, except to teach: how it will drift through her mind when no better words will come, be one of those phrases she says aloud when she is alone too much, like *Defense de fumer* from the Paris Metro.

Molly hands her the clipping. "Let me pick you some of those. They won't last very long, but I've got so many . . ." Her hand-pruners materialize from beneath a pile of weeds and she goes around the garden, snipping poppies and more poppies, forgetting, Liz guesses, that Liz was on her way to town.

The hawk tucked in its fierce brown-striped head as it banked—a marsh hawk, Liz thought it was, a small hawk; she would look it up in the Audubon guide. She trusted photos more than drawings. She always brought the bird guide with her, even though she wasn't the kind of bird-watcher who sought out new sightings. There were ospreys and eagles. In Florida, in the Keys, she had seen ospreys nesting atop the concrete utility poles, but here she had yet to see a nest. Remote birds, keeping to themselves.

The hawk dived, leveled out, skimmed across the meadow, barely clearing the spears of fireweed—pale, this year, not the strong hot-pink they had been last year and the year before. Yesterday she had tracked a great blue heron that flew up over the alders from the pond to roost in a dead tree on Molly and Nick's land. Ungainly birds, lumbering into the air with such a flapping, the long, awkward legs still dangling, not yet retracted. She had almost hit the one that erupted from the marsh as she drove into town with George. A month ago already. The long legs had barely cleared the hood of the car.

The hawk was spiraling up now over Molly's house, circling her front yard. Molly was out weeding again. Every spare moment. She and Nick had planted apple trees.

She was not weeding. She was simply kneeling there, her face red and bloated from weeping.

"*La plage est exposée seulement a la marée basse . . .*"

The sign is red, as a warning sign should be. The warning in French takes eleven more words than the terse English version and not just because of all the articles and reflexive verbs, either. ". . . *vous pouriez vous retrouver coincé . . .*" It is more complicated to be stranded in French, somehow less passive, more personal— something really happening to you, a hint of being cornered. All summer Liz has been meaning to climb down the red metal ladder attached to the cliff and go across to the second island, maybe even to the third with its lighthouse straight off a postcard, white with red trim, the same red as the ladder zigzagging its way up the opposite cliff. If she wanted to, she could do it today. The lower rungs are still free of the swirling green water; the narrow connecting beach is still getting wider.

He's here again, the whale expert, sitting on the knoll above, on grass as bright as moss after rain; it looks as soft. The listeners are grouped below him like disciples.

There seems something not quite relaxed about him, though he sits forward in apparent ease, with grace, his arms loosely hugging his shins (blue jeans, green T-shirt today). But it is conscious ease and grace, a posture; his face is too impassive.

She could be wrong. She may just imagine it. She caught him out of the corner of her eye as she went past. He has sandy hair, is of medium build, a man in the youth of his middle age, his face sun-weathered like a fisherman's.

"*Vous circulez à vôtre risque,*" the sign ends. It begins: "*Hazard Extrême.*"

"They winter off the coast of South America," he's saying, just as he did the last time. Her toe stubs against something on the path, a tree root growing across. Hurts more than she would've thought. "They follow the Gulf Stream . . ." Swimming all that way singly or in pods? She stands before the sign. A long journey for a lone whale, thousands of miles.

On Sunday, a young man sitting below her on the outcrop said he was in the navy, on a submarine. He'd heard whales on the sonar, their bleeps and whistling. Their singing. There were tapes of whales, but she would never buy a tape—it wouldn't be the same as hearing them in person, though if she ever mentioned it to George, next thing she knew he'd be getting her one. He's a good man, and she ought to be nicer to him. She doesn't want to be nice to anybody.

"I've been in the navy for seventeen years," the young man had gone on, and she remembers the odd, sudden pang—like pity. He was not as young as she'd thought, though his profile was youthful. Everybody is beginning to look young to her. Just this summer. Something draining out of her—judgment, stature. Something replacing it—feeling limited, unsure, mortal, like losing a language, not knowing it any longer, which is different from never knowing, different from before you learned. Isolation is dissolving all her attributes, and it hasn't been worth it; she has nothing to show for it; she is not even sure that she has endured.

"*Se retrouver*"—to find oneself again, to find each other again, to find one's way. She had liked that and then, in sudden irritation, thought: Why one word and not another?

"He was right down there 'bout noontime," the whale expert says.

That would have been at high tide. Almost low tide now. A man and a woman are climbing down the ladder, the last few rungs, coming across. The man stops to skip a few stones, the woman waits. Then they proceed across the isthmus, are lost to sight. Their voices rise from below. The ladder rattles.

"There!" she hears, from behind her, and turns around to see where he's pointing. "There he is!"

The tourists, as a group, raise their binoculars.

~

When her husband gave her the binoculars, that last Christmas, he made a big point of what good binoculars they were. Zeiss. He didn't tell her she was still going to be paying for them at Easter, after he'd left. They were supposed to help her watch birds. Supposed to distract her from watching him, was more like it, though he'd over-estimated her attention, over-estimated her persistence in following moving objects.

Looking out at the bay from the cottage's upstairs window, trying to see some waterfowl, she always gets first the alders below the window, then the town across the cove (hill of white houses where she knows not a soul, though the produce man in the market calls her "dear"). Today she saw a woman in her back yard hanging out laundry (sheets, towels, jeans that looked like men's). She could even see the clothespins in her quick hands, their pinch and spread, like opening beaks. But as for the ducks, or whatever they were (cormorants—maybe loons?), they were too small. They bobbed, they eddied. She kept losing them as soon as she found them, heard them better than she could see them, their wings beating the water as they bathed: cards slowly shuffled.

She had not taken George over to the island. She had taken him down to the beach, her beach, a cobble beach. There was a way of walking on a cobble beach, and he didn't have the knack of it. You had to walk lightly, swiftly, a fluid distribution of weight— heel, toe—as if you walked not on the stones but on the pockets of air between them.

He had stumbled and fallen, rolling like a bear.

"Sugar!" He would utter no obscenity. Of course it made her swear more than she normally would. She knelt beside him, asking if he was hurt, but it was an act considered, and the delay was not lost on him. "My ankle—I think it's sprained."

She helped him get to his feet, saying, "Lean on my shoulder." She never meant so heavily. He always seemed to take her more than literally, and she knew she never meant to give as much as she offered, so there was always this discrepancy. Anyway, he was a huge man.

"I need a stick," he had said, and on his face, as he looked around, up and down the beach, as if conjuring a stick for her to fetch him, was that same expression of distaste, even disdain, that she had seen the evening before, when at dusk he arrived. The sun had been setting, the clouds purple and magenta, the darker clouds mimicking the shapes of the islands, their edges lit a coppery cerise. She had led him inside, for him to see, from every window, a different portion of the sky. And had surprised on his face that look: nose wrinkling, nostrils vellicating.

"It smells damp in here," he said. "Is there water in the basement?" Later on, he said, "For this *cabin*, you sublet your apartment till *when?*"

There was no stick, only the skeleton of a spruce tree, someone's Christmas tree, the branches stubbed off, protruding like spokes. It was half-buried in the stones, festooned with dry kelp. She could imagine him using it as a cane, stumping along, and a nasty little snicker caught in her throat. She stooped suddenly to pick up a rosy scallop shell for her collection, and he lost his balance, nearly went down again, crying, "Damn you! Why did you do that?" As if he didn't know. "If you're going to do it again, next time warn me!" She should have warned him not to come up here. Well, she had; he came anyway.

In the car, driving him to the medical center, his hand rested on her thigh, so that when the heron erupted from the marsh, for an instant it was as if the heaviness of his hand were in the air, in the long, heavy legs that folded themselves up only at the last minute as they cleared the hood.

When she leans into the raspberries that grow along the road where everybody parks when the cul-de-sac is full, the binoculars swing forward into the canes, as if there were a magnet hidden in the thorns. The berries are filmed with dust; they taste of earth and then, when you get past that flavor, tartly sweet. A woman walking up the road with her husband stops.

"What are you picking? My husband said blueberries, but I said, no, blueberries up here grow down low." The husband is walking on, a stately retreat.

"Raspberries," Liz says, not smiling because her teeth might be red or have seeds stuck between them. "Try one." She squeezes between the cars' bumpers, offering the berry on her palm as on a plate.

The hand is red-stained, even slightly muddy. She has on old jeans, as usual, a T-shirt a neighbor in Cambridge gave her that says "M.I.T." Her hair is growing out salt and pepper brown, though there isn't a distinct line where the dye ends. Why dye? This lady looks very crisp, not to mention clean, like somebody who goes to the hairdresser every week, if not more often; hair is not naturally that shade of red this late in life, if ever.

So—a female of another species altogether. Still, shouldn't she be able to control that recoil, that involuntary step backward as Liz emerges from between the cars? The way she picks up the berry: as if her fingers were tweezers.

"Thank you." She hurries up the road, calling, "Jerry, wait! I've got something for you."

"A berry for Jerry," Liz hears herself muse. She's supposed to be a poet.

Today he has no disciples. He stands a little back from the cliff's edge, his arms folded. Stands, looking out across the water as if he already saw something—Nova Scotia? It's his stillness. People stop. They don't know what he's looking at. Paying no attention to them, he begins.

"Look over there to the right of that rock, there, with the cormorant on it, you'll see three whales."

Everybody looks, Liz included.

Someone asks, "How do you know where they'll be?" He replies, preposterously, "I hear 'em." She doesn't want him to be a charlatan. "I hear them when they spout."

That makes her feel better instantly, just as when the young sailor, the one who'd heard the whales from his submarine, said,

"This is the wife." She was glad he had a wife. He had swiveled around so his back was to the drop-off, and she'd wished his wife would tell him not to sit like that, but the wife, invisible behind the rocks, said nothing; she must have been sitting down there with the whale expert. It would be a long way to fall—thirty, forty feet. "She drove up to meet me in Halifax," the sailor had continued. "Four months ago, she met me in Bethesda." Every time he had a week or so in port, she would come to meet him if she could. "So it isn't true, what you hear about sailors—how they've got a girl in every port." And the wife's laughter rose, joining his. "He's got the same girl," she said. "Keeps me busy traveling around, I can tell you."

"Sort of like a whoosh," the whale expert says. "Different sounds for different kinds of whales." The blow-holes are different shapes, he says, as if that explains the different sounds.

Liz has seen enough of him by now to know that he always uses the same words, the same phrases. He is not a guide, so what is he? Does he come here for the same reason she does? He must have a home but evidently doesn't want to be in it. She would like to ask him: Is this a penance?

The three whales are finbacks. Again. "If you look real close, you'll see the fin." Liz gets the binoculars focused, sees a fin—quite far back on the body, near the tail, which you don't see. These are big whales, the biggest—sixty, seventy feet, though they look miniature, the size of porpoises, the bay is so vast. There are boats out there again too, boats full of whale watchers. Pleasure boats. The whales seem to have no fear of them but surface at will, a smooth, rolling glide, the dive implicit as they break through the water, spouting. Those plumes that appear so delicate must be as powerful as geysers, gallons of water raining back into the ocean. Liz is waiting for one of the whales to come up under a boat, waiting for something to happen.

Gone, George had infested her dreams for a month, weighing upon her conscience, like Molly's weeping. Not an isolated occurrence, that splotchy face, but what was to be done about it? Liz wanted to watch marsh hawks, not know these things.

She must offer to baby-sit. Years, decades since she'd held a baby. Like riding a bike, she told herself; you didn't forget. Molly and Nick must get out—go to dinner, go to Calais or Milbridge and see a movie.

She must offer. They might not take her up on it.

Looking through the binoculars makes her feel off-balance, and she can't help wishing she had someone to place a hand on her arm, to steady her. She had to go sit down on the grass after a child bumped into her, ran into her, chased by his sister, the mother calling, "Christopher and Hilary, stop that running." But no apology. "You're going to fall over the cliff," the mother yelled at them, and Liz said, not all that quietly, "Good," though she was also admiring their recklessness, their energy, their high color, their cheeks reddened by wind and running. Their coloration seems almost too brilliant, too rich—their glossy dark hair, olive complexions—unnatural, almost, like the colors of flowers that grow here along the coast, ordinary flowers—phlox, petunias, Molly's poppies, her irises. It's the salt in the air that makes the flowers glow like that, Molly told her, back in June, before she turned into Molly's nemesis.

She avoids Molly, making it a point not to go out to the mail box if she sees Molly working in her front yard. Forwarded bills. Magazines that, without her requesting a change in address, have nevertheless gone ahead and made the change, no forwarding necessary. The occasional postcard—that's all Liz gets anyhow, nothing interesting, though sometimes the postcards are interesting: infrequently there is one from her daughter who did a medical rotation in Florence, of all places; the postcards arrive two months after they were mailed. And yesterday there was a note from George, saying the ankle was just about as good as new and he hoped she was being careful, if she was still walking on that treacherous beach, because if she should fall and break a leg down there, it might be days before anyone found her. He added that this concern was strictly for her welfare and cautioned her against any misinterpretation as wish-fulfillment, which would be so like her.

He concluded with the hope that she'd gotten somebody in to have a look at the cellar, to see if she had a lake down there.

This can't go on.

She sits bolt-upright in the rocker, feet planted on the hooked rug that Molly made, back when she had time to do things like that, crafts and hobbies. Nick and Molly have been gone for at least five minutes, and Liz is still afraid to move. The baby lies across her thighs, where Molly placed him. What a strangely inert weight—so warm; the heavy little head the size of a grapefruit; either his neck is sweating or it's her own hand. She has never sat in this rocking chair before, doesn't trust it. If she lost her center of gravity, she might rock backwards and Timmy roll out of her lap, up and over her chest and shoulders, yes, if her feet lost contact for so much as a second.

"Christ!" she says, wishing it were over already. The baby stiffens at the sound of her voice. But he's a lively body now, not that dead weight, and her hand automatically finds a more natural way to support the head. She begins to relax, hoping Molly hadn't seen the panic (though would she have cared? So eager to be gone, the two of them, going to meet friends for dinner). In the refrigerator is a bottle half-full of breast milk for Timmy. Queer looking bottle, not glass. Soft plastic.

She bends forward and in a burst of courage hoists Timmy up against her shoulder. The burp position, her mother's generation called it, but already, in her own, you set the baby on your lap, your hand against the midriff, and rubbed the back. She hasn't forgotten.

"Don't spit up," she tells Timmy, not ready for that yet. Not yet. "Wait till I've calmed down a little more and had my dinner, okay?"

The peanut butter sandwich in her purse has one bite taken out of it. She got back from the island late.

Things she knows by now: he has a red pickup truck with a canopy; he drives faster than the speed limit, stirring up great clouds of dust. She lost him just as they reached the village, he speeding on, probably turning off somewhere, she creeping along at the sedate fifty kilometers prescribed by the signs.

The oblivious dog that had been there earlier, sleeping in the road when she drove past, was still there, in the shade cast by a rowan tree. Some day someone would run over him, thinking he was already dead. Both times, he raised his head to look, then laid his chin on his paws again. If she lived here, she would have to have a dog, though even a dog, even someone of your own, a mate, a husband, a family might not be enough. What a coward she has turned out to be.

She rocks back, resting her head against Timmy's, wondering whether, if she put him back in his crib, he would start crying again.

"Two females and a male," the whale expert announces, and a stout woman near where Liz is sitting laughs and says loudly, "Wouldn't you know!" She wears brown-tinted glasses and a red bandana, tied under her chin the way hardly anybody does anymore.

"Those kids," she goes on. "They got my dog all excited, running around like that. Max!" she bellows. "I mean, hell, I've raised my kids and I don't want to have to put up with someone else's, right?"

"Right," Liz murmurs, looking around for the dog, which comes scrabbling down from the outcrop. An old dog, brown and white water spaniel. His wet nose is cold against her ankle.

"Max, sit!"

He settles briefly on the toe of Liz's sneaker, thumping his tail against the grass. Five, six thumps. Liz pats his neck; he gets up and wanders off.

The woman seems not to notice. "It's not that I've got anything against kids per se, but I believe in discipline. Mine always minded. Didn't yours?"

"Oh, always."

"Right. I'd tell them, 'Cut that out.' They did or they got what-for."

Liz watches Max sniff at the tree-root that grows across the path, then trot back and over to the sign, against one of whose posts he relieves himself.

"When I hear all this on TV about not spanking," the woman goes on, "and you get it in the magazines too, I have just one comment: What a bunch of b.s."

Liz tips her head back, massages the back of her neck, where it still aches, as if she's been wearing a yoke, though she took off the binoculars at least half an hour ago. She doesn't have to say anything. This woman wants to talk; she has that eagerness as if she hasn't spoken to anybody except maybe Max for the last month, and Liz figures she owes her, owes somebody, owes the world; maybe it all evens out. She lets the woman tell her where she's from (St. Andrews), asks if she's on vacation (she is), questions that keep her from asking Liz anything, not that she would. Finally Liz asks if this is the first time she's been here to watch the whales. She says yes, so Liz tells her about the lone whale that was here, last time, and the woman says, "Well they need a dating service don't they?" Liz, on her best behavior, laughs.

Then she's had enough. She offers the binoculars. "Would you like to try these?"

"They're no use to me. I'm blind in one eye."

Liz blurts, "I think I always close one eye anyway."

"Where'd my dog go?" the woman says, suddenly. "Where's Max?"

"Maybe with the children . . ." Liz begins, but she's gone, heading down the path to the parking area, though Liz is sure Max never went past them.

She watches the whale expert. His blue T-shirt flutters in the wind, his sandy hair blows straight back. She's never going to know what his story is, why he comes here, where he goes.

It's a while before she hears the dog barking, faintly: bursts of sound that gust with the wind. She doesn't even know where it's coming from until someone she can't see calls, "There's a dog down there!" The groups of whale watchers look toward the lighthouse, one motion, like a school of fish turning, and then they're running over, beyond the sign, beyond where the red ladder goes down.

Liz ambles over to the edge of the crowd and asks someone what kind of dog is down there. "Is it a spaniel?" It is. "Is he hurt?" Doesn't seem to be. The trouble is, the tide's coming in.

People are whistling and calling, "Here, boy!" Liz edges in, so she can see what's going on.

It's Max, all right. He's running back and forth in the middle of the beach between the islands, now an island itself. Just the crown is still dry; the rest is awash with water that looks shallow but laps together, the strong currents crossing each other and angling out in a visible riptide.

"That's Max," Liz says. "How'd he get down there? Doesn't look like he fell."

"You'd better go get him before he gets swept out," a man says.

"Me!" Liz yelps.

The dog's real owner pushes in beside Liz, panting and puffing, crying, "Oh, my God!" She goes down on her hands and knees, calling Max, who whines and wags his tail, barking. "He's going to drown," she wails. Liz tells her, "Nonsense!" A whole cliff-full of people isn't going to let a dog drown. "But he hates water," the woman says. "He's a water spaniel, but he can't stand water."

"Well," Liz says, "he must've climbed down there somehow . . ."

"Over there," someone says. "Over by the ladder."

They go over to look. First there's a path, then the ladder, built out from the cliff, clearing boulders the last ice age must have sliced away, sharp rocks covered with kelp to the high-water mark, halfway up the cliff. The lowest are under water already; seaweed undulates on the surface.

"If you can get him over here," a man tells the dog's owner, "then he can climb up the rest of the way."

"Oh, no, he's an old dog. He can't climb."

"He might've gotten down that way," Liz tells the man, "but he'd never make it up. His legs are too short."

"Oh," cries the owner, "he can't even swim. He almost drowned once in a lake." Liz hears the tinge of hysteria as she shouts, "Doesn't anybody have a boat?"

People look uncomfortable. They don't have a boat. They don't want to go down there and get Max. Liz doesn't see the whale expert, wonders where he went.

"Someone," she says, "will have to climb down."

"I can't climb," the owner says.

No one else seems willing either. Liz thinks: Am I really going to have to do this—climb down those rungs, get my feet soaked, get swept out to sea with a forty-pound dog? She turns to the owner and says, "Where's his leash? Give me his leash. You've got a leash?"

"It's in the car."

"Well, go get it."

The owner whispers, "All right," and hurries down the path, tripping on the tree root, catching herself. God knows how far away she had to park, somewhere down the road behind Liz.

"You're going to go down after him?" a woman asks, in amazement.

"I was hoping some man would volunteer."

And a man has volunteered, for here comes the whale expert, up from the parking lot with a coil of rope. Max's owner trots along behind him as he heads for the dirt path, starts down the ladder. A cheer goes up, and there's a little light clapping, about what you'd hear at a tennis match.

He's down the ladder in no time at all, climbing across rocks, slipping on seaweed. From the set of his shoulders as he strode through the crowd, Liz knows he didn't want to do this.

Now the crowd swarms over to the cliff's other side and stands there, waiting for him to reappear. The sand bar has shrunk to maybe three feet wide, six feet long. You can see the water rising on the opposite cliff; it must be a couple of feet deep at the foot.

"Max, darling, go with the man." Max sits down on his sand bar and howls.

People laugh. The whale expert is wading through water that's halfway up his shins, but his jeans are wet above the knees. As he approaches Max, the dog gets up and starts forward, tail wagging; then he veers. He's down at the water's edge, lapping up seawater.

A child says, "He's drinking the ocean."

The whale expert collars Max and ties on the rope, gives him a pat, tries to get him to come on. But Max isn't leaving dry land. The collar is pulling off over his head. People groan. The man backtracks, pushes down the collar, grabs the dog around the middle. Max squirms free; he runs into the water, the rope playing out. "Damn fool," Liz says. He is swimming in the shallow water, but you see the current. The whale expert plays him like a fish, reeling him in, dragging him forward. Then he's close enough; the man splashes in and grabs the dog.

More cheering. Liz wishes she could see the expression on the whale expert's face. But she left the binoculars up on the grass. Now he's carrying the dog through the frigid water. Liz loses sight of him as he reaches the cliff.

"I thought he was going to drown," says the owner. She dabs a tissue up under her glasses.

People are laughing now—the relief—and they start to chat, to talk to one another. They are telling each other what they had thought was going to happen. Liz has seen this phenomenon before; she's remembering the first time, when she was a child. A couple of cars collided out in front of the house, nothing major, nobody hurt. It happened at dinner time; the whole street came out, and people didn't go back in when the cars drove off. They stood around on the sidewalk and the lawn for another quarter of an hour, telling each other what they'd feared had happened. They told it again and again, even though nobody was listening to anybody else. Even Liz's mother. She kept saying excitedly, "I'd just finished making the carrot salad. I was just about to put it on the table," until Liz's father, behind the two of them, his voice low and deadly, said, "If anybody cares . . . ," and that stopped her mother short, shut her up; for that moment Liz despised her as a babbling fool. But then her mother said, "Well, all right for you, bub," and Liz marveled at her, at her resilience. Her father's voice hadn't quelled her; it had only insinuated itself into Liz's ear, vicious as a weasel, and gone in and killed her loyalty for one long instant.

She moves off to find the binoculars. They're still there; Liz almost wishes they'd been stolen. From the knoll, she watches the frantic reunion, the dog who was saved in spite of himself. It's so easy for a dog, Liz thinks, as people clap the hero on the back.

He walks on, immune to acclaim. His clothes are soaked and muddy, his arms are scratched. Going home to change—at last he has a reason. He lopes by, water sloshing in his sneakers.

A glance. The first time he's ever looked at her, and she doesn't even feel seen. Her heart lifts anyway; she finds that miraculous. A shamefaced look, his eyes averted instantly.

Still, it included her, if only as a witness.

Clams

"This one's sticking his neck out," Melissa said. "I think he's going to go for the cornmeal."

She was sitting at the end of the dining room table, intent on the clams, steamers, which had been packed in ice in the refrigerator for two days before she remembered them. Amazingly, they were all still alive. Harry's daughter, Rose, had brought them up from the Cape for his birthday, but Melissa had somehow forgotten to cook them, for which she was apologetic though not, he thought, contrite. She had not forgotten his birthday; he was seventy-eight.

This morning he had watched her touch each clam on the end of its protruding neck or on the strip of pale flesh that showed between the edges of its shell, and all of them, cold as they were, had moved: shrunk back, or closed their shells even tighter, some of them more sluggish than others. Into the metal bowl they went, into salted water meant to simulate seawater. He doubted she had any idea how much salt to put in. "Seawater" was not listed in her cookbooks' indexes; he had looked. Nor would she know how much cornmeal the clams could be expected to eat. But they were all going to die anyway, so what did it matter?

"One of them's moving down below, maybe on the bottom layer. It's making some of the top ones move. Did I ever tell you about the clams I saw in Spain?"

"About twenty times," Harry decided not to say, because then they would've gotten into an argument over whether she had told him about the Spanish clams every year they had been together or told him several times in one year but not in others, and he didn't want to talk about it. He was trying to listen to the PGA tournament. From where he sat, with his back to the living room, he could see the TV screen's reflection in the window pane opposite.

"It was on the Costa del Sol," Melissa began. "They were hot pink, really a beautiful color. They were the same color as dogs' penises."

Phil Mickelson was about to make his shot. Melissa professed to like Phil Mickelson. If she turned her head, she could watch, but she would rather watch clams.

"I don't know if dogs all have the same color penises," she went on, as she always did, "but when I was little my grandma had a dog, I can't remember what kind of dog, I can't even remember its name, but I remember its penis, because it was this really intense pink, and the dog used to sit there in the middle of the rug and lick it. I think I wasn't supposed to notice that."

Mickelson's drive went straight where it was supposed to. There was a lot of clapping. One of Phil's good days. But you never knew—tomorrow he might be all over the course, hitting balls into the bunkers, into the pond. Harry had no patience with such inconsistency.

"A lot of the clams I'm talking about had their necks stuck out, like snails, maybe because they were dying or maybe because they were so fresh. They were still moving, though, over the ice, but I can't remember how they moved, maybe I'm thinking of snails. But I remember the color. I remember they didn't look to me like food, because of the color."

Maybe he should trade places with Melissa, though in order to see the TV screen, he would have to turn his chair, since it was next to impossible for him to turn his head. Too much arthritis in the neck. Melissa did not have arthritis in her neck; she had it in her hands and in her knees.

"Aren't you going to ask me if it turned me on?"

"Why would I do that?" he said, before he knew he was going to.

"Doesn't it ever occur to you that you never ask me anything?"

"Why would I have to?"

She grinned at him triumphantly. "See? You do too hear me."

Privately, he thought Melissa talked so much—too much—because she was going deaf. It didn't seem to bother her anymore that most of the time the harpsichord was out of tune when she played it. She was listening, she said, to the inner music. But she could have done that without actually playing, could have slid the stops off and played on a totally silent keyboard, and then he wouldn't have had to listen to an out-of-tune harpsichord, an instrument he disliked even when it was in tune. But, she said, she needed to feel the pluck of the plectra on the strings, though recently she had seen a program on PBS about the plasticity of the brain. Musicians' brains lit up whether they were reading the score in their minds or actually playing. In that case, Harry said, why couldn't she just pretend to play, on some other surface such as the table, as she'd told him she had to do the summer she studied with a famous harpsichordist in Amsterdam and had no access to a practice instrument. "I just told you why," Melissa said, so he gave up and spent a lot of time in the cellar, from which distance the harpsichord sounded more like a piano.

Slowly, he was tidying up the cellar, not that it was his disorder, but someone had to organize things. Melissa had lived in this house for forty-four years, and though she claimed to have cleared out the cellar thirty years ago or so, it was apparent to Harry that she had never actually thrown anything out. He was not telling Melissa what he was getting rid of. He simply put this and that into a dark green trash bag and dragged it out for the Friday morning pick up. Thus had the cellar been delivered of who knew how many ancient cans of black olives, corn, bottles of mixed red and yellow pickled peppers, boxes of pudding mix that the mice were getting into, old packages of black beans and lentils that were now hard as stones. That was just in the make-shift pantry he had created in order to get this surplus out of the kitchen. He had also managed to get rid of a badly broken rocker that was probably some kind of antique. The twin wooden lions' heads that had once adorned it were displayed on the coffee table in the living room, but the chair itself hadn't been usable since some time in the sixties, when Melissa and family had moved east from California. They hired a private trucker whom they found through a newspaper ad. Only when the truck was in the yard did her then-husband see that it had no rear doors, nothing but a canvas curtain that laced shut none too securely. As the truck jolted its way up the dirt road that functioned as a driveway, the rocker had bounced out and broken into eight pieces: the two arms with their lions' paws lying, separate, in the dust; the back had somehow landed intact except that both lions' heads fell off; the two rockers detached from the legs, but the seat and legs landed and stayed as-is. Anybody else would have thrown the pieces out, but Melissa said, "No, I bought it for eight dollars in Culver City."

"Why did you hire such a truck?" Harry once asked her. "You must've known you were asking for trouble."

Melissa thought about it. Then she said, "It was because of the driver. He said he hoped we weren't too fininicky."

"Finicky," Harry corrected.

"He said 'fininicky'. And he did stop and stuff all the pieces of the chair back in."

Out of the corner of his eye, even though he was looking past her, Harry could see that Melissa was stirring the water in the clam bowl with her forefinger. He knew what she was doing: trying to simulate ocean currents. She did not have Alzheimer's; she was just peculiar. No doubt she had always been peculiar, at least by Eastern United States standards. She had lived in Topanga Canyon, home of the Manson gang. Potters and artists also lived there, not necessarily hippies, some of them perfectly normal people. Once, when she and Harry were visiting her nephew in L.A., they had driven up to where Melissa had once lived. Except they couldn't find it. Everything looked different. Gone was the potter's studio that used to be up the road. She was uncertain where the entrance to the dirt driveway was that led for half a mile to the cabin. They had driven seven miles to this hot, dusty place, a thousand feet in altitude from the Coast Highway, and for what?

"I think it might have been in here somewhere," Melissa said, but there was a chain barring their driving in. "We could walk in." But they were in their late sixties then. They were wearing sandals, not walking shoes or sneakers. "We used to have to park up here when it rained. The road turned to mud. We slid off it once. We'd gotten rained in, but we tried to drive out anyway. We were trying to take the kids to school. Just as we came over the peak down there, there was a curve, but the car kept going straight. I remember hanging in mid-air a long time. Then the car plunged down into the brush. It must've landed on the brush, but Michael kept going—it was like landing on a mattress. We drove straight over a well we didn't even know was there. The cover collapsed, but we kept going, we drove right up onto the road, as if it were just nothing." She was full of stories. "That was the best driving I've ever seen. Another time . . ."

"Please," Harry said.

"I was going to tell you about the snake in the road."

She had already told him about the snake and also about the bottle of home brew that had ended up in the middle of that same road. If roads could talk, this one would have a story. It wasn't really a road, but it wasn't like a driveway either. No one remembered how the bottle had gotten there, but once it was, no one dared pick it up. It lay baking in the hot sunlight, day after day, gathering explosive power. Day after day, Melissa and Michael drove around it. Finally Michael went out one night to retrieve it. He took a bottle opener with him and a flashlight but lost his glasses somewhere in the dark.

"Oh, that home brew," Melissa said. "It always had to be capped at night—usually about one o'clock. That's when it always seemed to be ready." She smiled, as if she enjoyed the memory. "I used to like to watch the potatoes and the raisins roiling around in this five-gallon water bottle we kept on the kitchen table. It was like watching fish in an aquarium."

"Why didn't you just get an aquarium?"

She looked at him as if he were a Martian. "I don't like fish!"

But she would stand and watch a pot of oatmeal cooking. It reminded her, she said, of lava. She had never seen lava in real life.

Tiger's ball had landed in the rough. Not one of his better days. He'd been off his game ever since coming back from his months-long withdrawal. Melissa said serve him right, but Harry didn't like to watch this happening to his hero. He didn't like watching Tiger fail. He was angry with Tiger anyway, though if Tiger had been playing brilliantly he would have forgiven him anything.

"I wonder if I could be killing them with too-fresh water," Melissa said. "One of them just raised his snout. There's a grit of cornmeal floating right where he could eat it, but he's not eating it . . ."

"He," Harry said. "*He?*"

"It's true," Melissa acknowledged, "I don't think of any of them as female. How do clams reproduce, now that we're on the subject?"

"How should I know?"

The TV announcer was saying something about Ernie Els.

The only thing Melissa would know about Ernie Els was that his last name was sometimes in crossword puzzles. She did not care about Tiger Woods or Phil Mickelson, though of all the sports Harry watched, she claimed golf was the least offensive. Then came baseball, then basketball. Football was the worst—the noise, the clamor! She wouldn't have minded watching tennis or ice skating. Once, she told Harry, she promised her uncle she would go to a football game in which her college team was playing. And she did go, and it was total torture. She had sat for hours and hours in the bleachers, standing up when everyone else did, her mouth wide open as if sound were coming out. "Rahs," another crossword puzzle word. She was stirring the clams again.

"Maybe," she said, "I should've put them in a shallower container, like that pyrex bowl I use for lasagna. Maybe they shouldn't be all on top of each other . . . Maybe you can't really call it a bowl . . . ."

"Jesus God!" Harry cried.

"Watch," she said, tapping the clam's snout to make it recede, adding, "They're not going to eat the cornmeal."

"I don't care." They could be full of sand. He didn't care. "For God's sake, will you please just cook them?"

The butter she melted for him to dip the clams in must have been rancid. She wouldn't know; she didn't use butter. But it was rancid. It made the clams taste bitter. He spat the first one out.

"You're trying to kill me. They're spoiled."

"That's impossible. They were all alive."

"Then it must be the corn meal."

She tried a clam. "They're delicious."

"Then it must be the butter."

"Then eat them without the butter."

"*You* eat them." He didn't eat clams without melted butter.

"No, they're *your* clams. I'll go buy some butter."

But the clams would be cold by the time she got back. She had ruined his clams. He felt entitled to sulk. She would eat them herself, no doubt.

She didn't eat them. They weren't hers she said. She put them in the refrigerator, and there they stayed. Garbage day came, and out the clams went, along with the cellar trash bags for the week. What were they going to tell his daughter?

"We just won't say anything," Harry said.

"Not even thank you? But Rose will want to know if you enjoyed them."

"She's too busy," Harry said. "She doesn't care."

But what would they say if Rose asked, "Were they good?" Only Melissa could answer that truthfully.

"Tell her you can't remember," Harry advised.

"No," Melissa said. "That's what *you* can tell her."

But Rose never asked about the clams. Perhaps she was too busy, as Harry said.

~

Harry brought a book home for Melissa from the Senior Center, where he went for a line-dancing class every Tuesday. The book, a novel, was lying on a table among other books, so he figured they must be up for being borrowed. He said he'd browsed through it and thought she would like it, though in fact all he had done was scan the back cover. The book was called *The Elegance of the Hedgehog.*

Melissa said it could have been written by Dostoevsky. Here was a character fit to be the mate of Dostoevsky's Underground Man, though certainly this intellectual concierge had a better disposition. Harry didn't care what the book was about, so he couldn't manage to pay attention.

When Melissa gave him the book to return, it seemed to him she was trying to give him the wrong book. He had no recollection of the title but remembered that the book's cover was bright blue. This book's cover was navy.

"It is too the same book, and it isn't navy."

The cover was a dark, dullish blue, so, all right, maybe it wasn't navy. There was probably a name for this color, but, if so, he didn't know what it was.

"It's not the same book."

"You said you browsed it."

"I never would've brought this book home," he insisted.

"Why? You said you thought I'd like it. Why did you think that?"

"I didn't." He felt caught-out, as if in a lie, but it wasn't a lie. He couldn't remember. All he knew was: this wasn't the book. "It's the wrong book, and I'm not taking it back."

He was angry, and he didn't know why. Usually Melissa would back down. But she wasn't backing down this time, which meant she must be sure she was right. And she wasn't right. She was dead-wrong.

"Is this how it begins?" she asked.

"What?"

"Dementia."

He waited a long time before he answered. He was waiting for some doubt to start wending its way through Melissa's brain. But none must have, because she conceded nothing. What he finally said was:

"Yours or mine?"

They ended up in the same nursing home, at first together, but then the attendants said they squabbled too much, and Harry had even tried to hit Melissa. He missed. In his younger days he wouldn't have missed. In his younger days, he wouldn't have *tried* to hit her. He would either have hit her or not. He wouldn't have hit her. Maybe he should have hit her while he still was capable. It was the yelling—it disturbed the other patients. All the terrible arguments they'd never had. Throwing out her lentils, Melissa cried, her black beans. When had she ever thrown out anything of Harry's without asking?

"I never had anything to throw out," he yelled back. "I came to you empty-handed."

But, she said, his hand was always out. That was when he tried to hit her. His hand had never been out; he had always pulled his weight. He did the laundry, he unloaded the dishwasher. He had lived with her for thirty years, and never had they had such arguments. She was going blind, and in her mind's eye, saw things she had never seen before.

"You were having an affair with that bimbo in your line-dancing!"

"So, what if I was? But I wasn't."

"You were! You started showering every week!"

"You showered every day, and you weren't having an affair."

"How would you know?" Melissa shouted. "You don't know anything about me."

They were eighty-five and eighty-eight by now. Melissa's hair, such as there was of it, was white; her scalp was pink. Harry, just about bald, had liver spots on his head. They couldn't hear each other. That was why they shouted. No, they shouted because they hated each other, the way only old people can do—because they had lived together too long and were both infirm. It seemed to Harry unfair that Melissa couldn't walk on her own—not unfair to her, unfair to him that she had to be pushed around in a wheelchair. He himself used a cane but only when he was outdoors, therefore only in spring or fall; winter was too dangerous, summer was too hot. Sometimes he went out, alone, with his cane, and sat on a bench a few feet from the birdbath. There was a pair of cardinals that came to drink, though not to bathe. Hummingbirds too came to some kind of vine that had trumpet-like flowers; it might be a trumpet vine. The flowers were so large that the birds almost disappeared, as if they had flown into an alternate world. He already was in an alternate world, one that had been waiting for him all his life. Melissa was in it and yet not in it. She couldn't go with him; he was utterly alone. So they hated each other—they were almost like siblings—and the nursing home people separated them, putting Harry in a room with another old man.

They didn't even have to see each other, though they did see each other sometimes at meals. But then Melissa began taking her meals in her room. And then she took to her bed and would not get up, though the attendants got her up anyway and pushed her to the TV room, where she could be with other people, though she could neither hear nor see them or the TV.

Sometimes Harry, in the night, when he couldn't sleep, would limp down the hall to the doorway of Melissa's room. He would stand there, out of sight of the attendants, but not going in. She was in the far bed, next to the window, and in the moonlight he could see how thin she had gotten, her face sculpted in a way it hadn't been for years: the bone structure, which had slowly disappeared, was re-emerging like peaks from melting snow. She looked less and less like herself as he knew her, and had a blank expression in the daytime. But now, though she could neither see nor hear, she looked serene, as if she were dreaming calm dreams.

They thought it would be better if Harry didn't visit her, but Harry wanted to push her up and down the hall in her wheelchair. How could it do any harm, he asked. How would she even know it was him?

In Perilous Times

"Where did you get those pretty long curls?" the lady sitting next to Tove said, but Tove stared at the bus seat in front of her; it was scratched all over with words she couldn't read. "I have a doll at home with curls like yours, except hers are blond," the lady went on.

There was a haze, like noise, between the lady and Tove, like when it was too hot out on the playground and the sun was too bright and the air got wavy; the transformer you must never go near would be buzzing, and the buzz was too close, like the lady's voice.

"She has real hair. You can brush it and comb it."

She was an old, old lady like Auntie, and her voice was soft, like Auntie's voice. But Auntie was thin, and this lady was fat; she took up so much of the seat that Tove was squeezed almost up against the window.

She wasn't supposed to be back here. She was supposed to be up where the other children were. It was Michael's fault—first he'd grabbed her nickel, then he gave her a wrist-burn over her charm bracelet. Now the skin was red and it hurt, and the little silver book-charm had made a cut. Not a bad cut, she hadn't cried, but what if he had broken the book? If he ever did that, she'd tell on him. Daddy and Auntie and Mrs. Grant. The silver book was her only charm and she had to wear it all the time, except not when she was home because at home they knew who she was. It opened up and there was her name, written with something sharp like a needle. The next page told her street: 236-16th. Santa Monica was the town, and the state was California. The last page had the day she was born: February 16, 1938. Auntie had to unfasten the bracelet—Tove couldn't do it herself—and Michael had better not try or she'd tell his father and he'd get strapped.

But she couldn't tell about the nickel because, if she did, Michael would get her. He'd jump off the bus first, when it was their stop, and stand on the curb and not let her out. She'd have to ride to the end of the line; at the end of the line they put you off. But the worst thing would be if she tried to jump out and the bus doors snapped closed on her foot. She'd get dragged all the way down Carlyle, and no one would know till the bus stopped again.

So she had to stand on the sidewalk and watch while all the other children got on. Michael got on, but she hadn't dared, and then she was the only one. "What're you waiting for?" the bus driver said, and he made the door flap so she was afraid. "Come on. I haven't got all day." But she didn't have her nickel, so she couldn't ride the bus. "What's the matter with her?" he said, but no one was going to tell on Michael. Then Mary McCassey came down the aisle, and Tove heard her say, "Michael took her nickel." The bus driver snorted, "Oh, for Pete's sake," and he said to get on, so Tove did. But she had to sit with the grown-ups in back, and the lady got on at the very next stop.

"She's a very old dolly," the soft voice said. "I've had her since I was a little girl. I probably wasn't much older than you, and that's over seventy years ago."

The lady smelled sweet, but it wasn't nice. It made Tove feel like she couldn't breathe. It was like when Auntie said leave the window open, and then the smell of the jasmine came in. And so did the darkness and so did the fog. It would all come in and fill up the room, wisping in through the holes in the screen. And out in the ocean the foghorn was going, and Tove was too afraid to sleep. She would try not to fall asleep, so she wouldn't smother in the night, but then she heard the mourning doves cooing, and that was how she knew it was morning. Their wings squeaked when they flew to the ground to eat the loquats that dropped off the tree.

Tove would lie there, afraid to move, then run down the dark hall to Auntie's room.

Auntie's nose whistled when she was asleep. The lady was making that sound in her chest. When she bent down to look into Tove's face, Tove could feel the breath on her cheek. It puffed on her cheek the way Auntie's breath did when she got to the part in *The Three Little Pigs* where she'd take Tove's hand and blow on the back: "I'll huff and I'll puff and I'll blow your house down."

This lady had no right to breathe on her. Mama couldn't breathe on her. The people where Mama was all had T.B., and maybe this lady had T.B. too. Auntie said, "Now, don't get too close," so Tove always stood near the door. Then Mama blew kisses from where she sat, and Auntie reached out and caught the kiss, saying, "Where, oh, where is it going to land?" Mama always had to think. "On Tove's forehead" or "On Tove's nose" or "Right on Tove's chin." Wherever she said, Auntie would pat, but Tove would be trying not to breathe. Mama's chest didn't make a noise like that, so it could be the lady had something worse.

"Would you like to know my dolly's name?"

Michael had said that Mama would die.

Tove turned her head away. Now the sun was in her eyes, and the window was so dusty outside and inside that she couldn't find a place to see out.

"Maybe you'd like to try and guess."

A fly buzzed against the glass.

Where were they now? Not the drug store yet, because at the drug store the bus always stopped. Then it turned and went up the hill, and that was when she knew where they were. It was Mary's street, Twenty-Sixth. It was the street the tank had gone down. Michael said the tank came down his street, but there weren't any tread marks on Seventeenth. The tread marks went right past Mary's house; Tove had seen them herself. And Daddy saw them but Auntie didn't. Mary and her mother had seen the tank. "It was one of ours," Mary said, and Daddy threw back his head and laughed. "Whose else would it be?" He patted her cheek; then he frowned at the two rows of cracks in the street. "If they've got so much time on their hands, they'd better get down here and patch this up."

But the street still had holes, it still wasn't fixed, because the soldiers were busy marching and shooting. They marched down the street where they had their tents under the palm trees on top of the palisades. That place used to be a park, Auntie said. There used to be grass, but now it was dirt. A shame, she said. Daddy said, "Oh, Lot." The soldiers were keeping Santa Monica safe. Down in the cliff there were hidden big guns that could sink a ship thirty miles out to sea. A Japanese sub could never get close, but the soldiers had to make sure the guns worked. Sometimes she could hear the booming that felt like breakers after a storm. There were other guns too, called anti-aircraft, down near Douglas, where Daddy worked.

"Someone is shy," the lady said, and Tove felt a pat on her knee. It made her jump, like when she heard guns. The bus was slowing down.

The doors thumped back, and a breeze came in. That meant people were getting off. But she couldn't see whether it was the drug store stop; she was on the wrong side of the bus.

"I've got an idea," the lady said. "What if I tried to guess your name?"

Stupid lady. She'd never guess. Only one other person was ever named Tove: Mama's friend, her bosom friend, Tove Number One. But that Tove had gone away, back to Denmark, a different country, a long time ago, so long ago that Tove couldn't remember her at all. "We begged her and begged her to stay," Auntie said, "but she had a mother in Denmark, you see." You could have mothers in different places. A friend of Michael's had two mothers. You could have a godmother, and that was what Tove Number One was. She'd be her mother if Mama was dead and if Daddy and Auntie got killed in the war. But Tove Number One might already be dead, because she had never written a letter, "and she'd know," Auntie said, "what a letter would mean to all of us but especially your mother." If Tove Number One was dead, there was only one Tove in the whole world.

A special name, Mrs. Grant told the class, but that was after she said, "Who is Tove?" The way she said "Tove" made it sound like "stove." "Am I pronouncing that right?" she said. "Is it Tuv?" But Tove could not say a word; there were too many children sitting on the rug. "Will Tuv or Tove please raise her hand?" Too many children. Mrs. Grant waited. Michael was whispering, "Tuv or Tove," and then he was pointing. "It's To-va," he said. "She's Number Two Tove, Number Two." The children laughed. Mrs. Grant said, "Class!" An unusual name, quite beautiful. "Can you tell us about your name?" she asked. But Tove was wishing she'd never told Michael. She was wishing her name was Peggy. Then, later, she wished her name were Mary.

But if it was Mary, the lady might guess.

"I'll have to put my thinking cap on."

That was the same thing Mama said.

The bus started up and began its turn, and Tove thought she was going to be squashed. Big fat lap, big fat knees.

"Oh, my goodness! Excuse me, dear."

The lady reached up and straightened her hat; she smoothed her black skirt over her legs. Her cheeks were bright pink. That was rouge. She must have forgotten to rub any off. Sometimes Auntie would forget too; sometimes she forgot to put any on. Then Tove said, "Put your pink cheeks on," because she didn't like the way Auntie looked.

"Wouldn't it be a funny thing if you and my dolly had the same name?"

Tove sneaked her hand to her wrist and covered up the little silver book.

"Shirley—I'm going to guess Shirley, but that isn't my dolly's name. I'll bet you were named after Shirley Temple. You're going to tell me if I guess right, aren't you?"

The lady must think she was very dumb. You weren't supposed to tell strangers your name. You weren't even supposed to talk to them. If a stranger followed you in a car, you ran away as fast as you could. You ran up to the nearest house, but you didn't go in. You said, "Call the Police." A little girl Auntie knew got in a car, and they found her the next day under the pier. Another little girl went into a house, "and look," Auntie said, "what happened to her." Her poor little body was cut up in pieces, her arms and her legs, just not her head, and the pieces got tied in a gunny sack, and the gunny sack got thrown on the lawn. "And when her daddy went out to bring in the paper, what," Auntie said, "do you think he found?" Tove could say it along with Auntie. "He thought," they both said, "it was just a dead dog. Then he looked inside and saw the head." When Auntie said that, she made her eyes big; they got dark, like witches' eyes. Tove would make her eyes scary too. Then she'd say, "Tell it again."

"Well," the lady said, "I guess it's not Shirley. I wonder if it might be Sharon."

They were at the place now where the tread marks began. The pavement had come up out of the street, and that made the bus bump along. It bumped up the street just like a tank.

"My soul," the lady said, and she leaned all over Tove again. At the top of the hill the bus turned down Carlyle. Yesterday Tove could get off right here. Because yesterday she was sitting with Mary. She got to go play at Mary's house. They played store with Mrs. McCassey's cans of pineapple and something Mary called fruit cocktail. But now Tove couldn't see Mary. She heard her call, "Bye," then Mary was gone. When the bus started up, it made smoke that stung.

"Oh, these fumes," the lady coughed; the sound of her cough made Tove feel sick. "I shouldn't be around these fumes. I used to drive, but now I'm too old."

Just like Auntie. She was too old, Daddy said. When they went to see Mama, she said, "Let me drive." But Daddy said, "You know I can't, so don't ask." It was a long ride to someplace hot. Auntie got mad, and her voice got loud. "I was driving before you were born." She would look out the window and not talk after that. Then Daddy said, "Don't be unreasonable, Lot. You don't want Tove to see you sulk." Auntie said, "I get to do something I want. If I want to sulk, I'm going to sulk." But Tove didn't get to sulk.

They were going down the shady part of Carlyle, where the pine trees grew along the sidewalk. Two more stops, and she could get off. The lady was rummaging in her purse.

"Would you care for a mint?"

Tove's heart gave a thump. A mint was some kind of candy, she thought. Giving you candy was what kidnappers did. Then they told your father, "Pay this money." And Daddy couldn't pay the money. Tove knew; she had asked Auntie. "Your poor father?" Auntie said. "He can hardly make ends meet as it is." The kidnappers would kill you anyway. That was what happened to the Lindbergh baby. They would even kill a baby.

"It's rude not to answer," the lady said. "If you don't want a mint, you should say, 'No, thank you.' I'm sure your mother must have told you."

Shut up, Tove said but not out loud. The prickles were starting high in her nose. She mustn't be rude, but this lady was rude, to try to make her talk to a stranger. Tove hung her head so far down that her curls came together under her chin.

"Such pretty hair," the lady said. "You ought to have pretty manners too. I'm sure you must have a pretty name. Do you think I should try to guess one more time?"

But it wasn't like when Auntie guessed: "What can this be that has such cold feet? Is it a little dog, is it a moose?" She knew before she said, "Why, it's a girl!" She didn't have to feel Tove's face; she was just pretending it was too dark. "I think . . . I think it's someone I know. Let me see—I think it's *Tove!*"

"Cheryl," the lady said, and Tove burst into tears. She didn't care if the children heard. No one would hear; the bus rumbled too much. No one would hear even if she screamed.

"Oh, my heavens." A hand touched her hand. "Have I hurt your feelings, is that what I did? I'm a stupid old woman. I should've known. Now, don't cry. Here's a handkerchief, dear."

The handkerchief smelled just like the lady. It made Tove's nose run worse. The bus was stopping, and where were they? How many times had they stopped? Carlyle was pine trees and then it was date palms; it was pine trees as far as Seventeenth. That was her stop. It was Michael's stop too, but she couldn't see Michael or anyone else. There were still pine trees, it wasn't too late, but how was she ever going to get out?

It was too much like when there was the air raid and they sat in the dark hall and heard the guns. There was too much noise and it was too loud, and the lady just kept talking and talking. Auntie said, "Are we going to get bombed? Oh, we're going to get bombed," and her voice was scared. Tove knew they were going to be bombed, and she didn't have her bracelet on. Daddy said, "Lot, get ahold of yourself. Look at how brave Tove is." But nobody could see in the dark, and she didn't know how to be brave.

She tried to squirm out of Daddy's arms, to run get her bracelet from Auntie's room, but Daddy held tight, not letting go. His chin was prickly against her cheek. She yelled, "Let me go," but his arms were so tight that she couldn't breathe. She started to cry. "Stop that," he said. "Stop that right now." And he gave her a shake. But she couldn't stop.

Then Auntie's arms came and got her. "There, there. What's the matter?"

"My bracelet," Tove shrieked. The big guns kept booming; the whole house shook. What was she talking about? Daddy asked. Her bracelet for when they were bombed, Tove wailed. So someone would know that was her arm.

"What have you been telling the child?" Daddy said. "Have you lost your mind? Don't you have any sense?"

Then Auntie cried, but Tove stopped. She didn't care if they did get bombed.

"Blow your nose," the lady said. She stroked Tove's hair back from her face. "Good heavens, what a commotion!"

And then she had Tove by the wrist. "Why, what's this? It's a little book. What a cunning charm—and it opens up. 'Tove,'" she said, and it sounded like "stove." "But that can't be your real name, can it? It must be a nickname. And look where you live. You're very close. I'm just here on Twentieth."

She dropped Tove's arm. "I'll write a note. I want to find out where to get that charm. I want to get one for my little grandniece." But she couldn't seem to find a pencil in her purse.

She snapped her purse shut. "I'm going to have to get off. Hop up and pull the cord, there's a dear."

Tove stood up and pulled the cord. She didn't sit down; she kept standing up. Michael was all by himself up in front. He was still sitting down. He was still on the bus.

"Thank you, darling. I'm Mrs. Johnson. And now I'll tell you my dolly's name." She took hold of the back of the seat. "It's Dorothy. Some day we'll have you to tea."

The bus made a sound like a poo when it stopped. Mrs. Johnson pulled herself up.

"Good-bye for now."

"Good-bye," Tove said.

Mrs. Johnson went up the aisle, and Tove let the handkerchief drop. It dropped onto the toe of her shoe, and she kicked it forward under the seat.

Nineteenth, Eighteenth. There were the palm trees. Michael was reaching up for the cord. Tove, quick, gave the cord a yank and ran to get dibs on the pole. She'd make Michael give her nickel back, or she wouldn't tell him about the mint. He was so dumb he would talk to strangers, and next time he'd be the one that was kidnapped.

A kidnapper! He was right behind her.

The bus stopped, the doors flapped back. She flew down the steps, and nothing could catch her.

Come With Me, Marlene

Yesterday I phoned about a sales position at a shell store. It was not a full-time position; they needed someone for Saturdays. Shells, Unlimited was the name of the place. I could see why it was not called The Shell Shop. Even as I dialed, I was thinking what a challenge it would be to say, "I sell shells," if somebody asked.

I liked the voice that answered my call, a man's voice; the way he said, "Shells, Unlimited," I thought he sounded kind. I pay attention to voices—I am attuned; this man's singing voice would be baritone. "You understand," he said, when I had told him my name, "this isn't just a job for the holidays, Marlene." He sounded solicitous, rather as if he were explaining to a child. And then anxious: "This is a permanent position."

Because of my voice, people tend to think I am very young. From years of teaching music in the public schools, I have lost my middle range. Eight classes a day, nine on Fridays, years spent shouting down the tone-deaf and the talkers—and what I have left is my upper register. I can speak lower, but then I croak like a drinker, and sometimes I am mistaken for a man.

"The woman you'd be replacing was with us for eleven years."

In the high little voice I was using yesterday, I said, "Yes, I understand."

"Do you have small children?" was what he said next, working his way around to what he couldn't ask. In my croak I assured him that I did not, and now I could hear him wondering: How old, how old?

"Have you any retail experience?" This, after a pause.

"Limited," I said, but he didn't laugh.

I faulted him for that. I had already been imagining the shop: the cases that would be entirely of glass, the smaller shells in clear plastic trays (pearly or speckled, like so many buttons); then the shelves on the walls where the larger, more resplendent shells would be displayed—the chambered nautilus, perhaps the frilly clam, the green snail—and would there be fossils?

"Could you be a little more specific?"

"I've worked in a department store."

I was praying that I would not have to admit that my experience consisted of half a day or that I had acquired it forty-one years ago when I was sixteen and in another state. I did not suppose it would help things, either, if I had to say it was a Christmas job.

"I see," he said, though of course he did not. They had put me in yard goods the very first day, showed me how to measure the material against the yard stick at the table edge, make the neat scissor cut that started the tear. One swift rip—and voila! "Dear," they said, "you go help that lady. Go on."

The lady had in her arms a bolt of cotton, the kind they used to make housedresses out of: royal blue background, white flowers— big ones. Flimsy stuff and not the least suitable, because she was as fat as I was—not hugely, grotesquely fat but still, as people liked to put it, "a bit on the heavy side." I was thinking how awful she would look in that print, but maybe she was buying it for someone else.

I unreeled it. The bolt went thump, thump down the table, and the customers and the sales ladies turned to watch. Mr. Livoli— he was watching me too, lounging over there by the wall where the fabrics were shelved, a slight man but so beautiful: brown eyes, brown hair; he was assistant store manager, and he wasn't very old. He was watching me, and his lips were smiling. All around there was silence and good will. In the background they were playing "Oh, Come All Ye Faithful."

I measured the four yards; I made the little cut. Then, as I held the material up, I lost all faith. I hesitated so long that Mr. Livoli said, "Ready, set, go!" The customers and the sales ladies laughed.

I yanked hard with both my hands and heard a harsh rip, then a groan. It was a communal sound, like a song. For here was this ruined piece of goods, not ripped across but with a long, puckery rent that had turned and followed the warp. No one said, "Why, it could've happened to anyone." No one said, "Never mind, never mind." Mr. Livoli said, "Come with me, Marlene."

"Marlene?" the man in the shell store was saying, and I think he was asking me how to spell my last name or wanting to know how far away I lived or whether I was at present working during the week. I suppose I must have answered something, but I was seeing myself being led over to the counter where the undergarments were—corsets and panties and bras and those pink knit undershirts that older women wore, heaps of things that had been pawed through and disarranged. I was hearing Mr. Livoli say, "See if you can get this mess straightened out." He said nothing about how that material must have had a fatal flaw. He said: Put this here, put this there, and when you're through, make sure there are five or six of everything in all sizes, you can restock from here, and he showed me where: there were shelves under the counter behind sliding doors. Then he picked up a bra and stuck his fist in the cup. "Pooch them out so there aren't any dents. Like acorns," he said, just before I went deaf.

I was kneeling on the floor, staring at boxes. My eyes were full of tears, so I couldn't see sizes. The customers were reaching around me and over me and tripping over my feet. A lady said, "Where are the nightgowns?" but I pretended not to hear. They were playing "Away in a Manger" by now, and that is what the choir sang when I was an angel in the Christmas pageant at age six. I wore a white robe and a silver bead halo and knelt in straw. In the manger, playing the part of the baby Jesus was my Shirley Temple doll, swaddled up to her hard composition face in gauze. And my father was a king, one of the Wise Men; in his purple robe he preceded the other kings down the aisle, the three. of them singing, "We Three Kings of Orient Are" to the accompaniment of the organ. He had the first solo, but what with "Away in a Manger" and the customers tripping over me, I could not remember how the words went or hear my father's tenor.

"Isn't there anyone who can help me?" the lady who wanted nightgowns cried so loudly it was as if she had uttered my own thoughts, and Mr. Livoli came over and said, "What's going on here, Marlene?" Because I was crying, I could not take my head out of the cupboard. The Dean of Women thought a Christmas job would be good for me—and for no other reasons than that I was failing Physiology and had no friends and was overweight. But I would rather have been in school, where in French class someone had written on the blackboard in English: "Marlene is a pig."

Mr. Livoli took me by the arm; it was not an unkind grip but firm. He made me stand up and said, "Come with me." I felt the customers' eyes as he led me away and up the stairs: a great crying girl and this small, dapper man. He took me into his office and said, "Sit down," while he himself perched on the corner of his desk and folded his arms. I sat there, blowing my nose, my eyes fixed on his shoes, the latchets of which I would have done up had they been undone; the leather was highly polished especially at the toes and, like his suit, brown. "Now, what am I going to do with you?" he said. I had only one answer in spite of having been asked that question so many times: "I don't know." There was only one thing I was good at: I could sing; my mother had sung in the choir, and all my aunts and uncles had fine voices except the ones who came into the family by marriage. "You think you could iron some curtains?" he said, and I nodded.

He took me to a small room where there was a tall, narrow window whose big panes were so grimy I could hardly see the rooftop of the building across the alley. He switched on the light— one bulb dangling from the ceiling—and pointed to the ironing board and then to a stack of boxes. "Calm down," he said, and vanished from the doorway.

I went over and closed the door. Now I could no longer hear the Christmas carols, and everything was quiet. I began to feel at peace and at home. The curtains were lime-green dotted Swiss and pale yellow organdy. As I ironed, I was humming to myself and then singing along with my father the way I had done, although nobody had told me to, at the Christmas pageant: "Born a king on Bethlehem's plain/ Gold I bring to crown him again." When I was an angel, I had not only the silver halo made of beads but also white curved wings made of organdy stretched over a wire frame. I was not yet fat, my mother sang in the choir, and my father was a king.

But at twelve-thirty, Mr. Livoli opened the door and beckoned. Lunch time, he said. Go to lunch; up the street I would find a Walgreen's, and after lunch we would try me in Notions. So I went to lunch; I even remembered to turn off the iron. But after lunch I went home on the bus, and I never went back, though who knows?—if he had said I could keep on ironing curtains or if he had sought me out, come and stood beside me at the lunch counter and said, "Come with me," I think I would have left my coke and my hamburger and gone.

"So you have quite an education," the man in the shell store was saying; I must have been telling him about my teaching credential. It is a trick of mine that I can say one thing and be thinking something else; it has stood me in good stead; it has been my salvation, though I still cannot hear two different melodies at once, not precisely at once; they are always just off. "Do you happen to have a background in science?"

That question annoyed me, because how much scientific background did you need to sell shells one day a week? I have a very fine book on shells that I got at a remainder table somewhere, which is how I know about the green snail and the frilly clam. I could not think, though, of any way to work this information in without seeming to boast or perhaps even to lie, so I said, "I have a general background." What I would have liked to tell him was, "My background is rich and varied." I would have liked to say that I looked on exotic shells as emissaries from distant lands and that it would be a pleasure to work among them. In short, I would have liked to say something to impress him, but I was already remembering where I had first encountered that phrase "rich and varied"; it was in General Science, where they placed me after I failed Physiology. What was being described was the oral flora in the saliva of the rat. The complete sentence went: "The oral flora is rich and varied," and I can remember thinking: But this is poetry. It was probably short-sighted of me not to get that reference in there somehow, hinting as it did of a scientific background. On the other hand, why should I be so eager to please? While I was thinking these things, I remembered something else: how, from the destructive distillation of ants, you could make formaldehyde, which is what morticians inject into dead bodies, and of course it has other uses; but I could not remember what the destructive distillation of ants was, if indeed I ever knew. I went from there to marveling at the mind's retrieval system and to wondering what caused you to recall the things you did—the phrases and fragments that appeared out of nowhere and came together as if they must form a pattern. I was thinking that perhaps the problem was a matter of scale. For example, if you were looking through a giant kaleidoscope, you might not be able to tell that all the pieces were pointing toward the center; all you would see was the space that they pointed to; it would be vast, like the sky. When, at my father's funeral, the minister said, "Our Father, who art in heaven," I thought he should have said "Our fathers" but did not correct him.

I knew that my conversation with the shell man was not going as well as when we started, but that is what always happens. When I first began to teach, the children loved music, they loved to sing, they were quiet when I said, "Put your hand here, on your diaphragm." They did not giggle and poke each other, they were not hyperactive; I never had to shout to make myself heard or stand at the piano and play crashing chords. All I had to do was say, "Children," or start to sing. I did not yet find it difficult to teach Christmas carols.

"Maybe you'd better tell me a little more about yourself," I thought I heard him say, the man on the phone; but I was thinking how nerve-racking it would be to have to deal with the children who were free to roam around on Saturdays. They would come into the store to browse and steal shells. And then, again, I might be called upon to sell things I did not believe in, such as earrings made out of starfish or sand dollars. And what about the crafts-persons who wanted to buy shells for unworthy purposes: decorating the tops of balsa wood boxes or gluing them onto rocks to make paperweights? I remembered how tired I used to get, standing up all day, especially the last few years, whereas now I could lie down any time I liked and had thrown out my Supp-Hose. If I went to work at the shell store, I would have to be there every single Saturday and would never be able to go to Europe or Australia, which is where some of the best shells come from.

So I said, "I haven't worked for two years, and I'm looking for some structure to my life."

There was silence on the line, but it was too late—I couldn't take it back. I wanted to protest: But you only asked for a little more, and look—I've given you everything. It would have been useless; people don't want more than they bargained for.

"Probably the best thing," he said, "would be if you came in."

I knew from this that his store must be a terrible place to work. He proceeded to give me the address and directions, but I merely pretended to write them down. The time is past when I will go with anybody who wants me or pretends to want me or is just curious to have a look at me. I look forward to only one more permanent position. This made me wonder whether the woman I was to replace had died.

"What happened," I said, in my worst croak, "to your last woman?"

"Oh," he said, "She got a full-time job."

He sounded, in his innocence, so puzzled that I murmured, "That's too bad." Because I could see how, after eleven years, you might start to count on a person and consider that he or she would be with you forever, "from the beginning of the world to the end of time," which is how it was worded on a legal form I was once asked to sign, absolving the company of all responsibility, as if you could ever be absolved. I was sorry for him because he did have a nice voice, the sadness of a baritone.

Somehow, without meaning to, I had managed to disconnect, or else the phone company had cut us off. I thought I would not call back but instead look at my shell book, in which there were some beautiful pictures: a large iridescent spoon made from the shell of the green snail, a chalice made from the chambered nautilus. Then there was the swan mussel, hinged in the shape of angels' wings, and the spiky murex, gathered long ago for the purple dye that made cloth worth its weight in gold. I wished there were fossils, for they bring tidings of distant times, giving voice to the mute and the extinct.

When my father came down the aisle in his crown and his purple robe, he was carrying a casket of loose gold beads. His eyes were cast down; he was wearing a fake beard. I sang, "Gold I bring . . ," and the shepherd boy kneeling beside me said, "Ssh," but I sang, "King forever, ceasing never . . ." My father started up the steps to the manger, treading softly on the red carpet. It was impossible to tell whether he was smiling, but I thought he was. As he knelt in the straw, the whole choir sang, "Star of wonder, Star of light," and he gave me a fierce and dreadful look and toppled forward so that his face smacked down on the face of the Shirley-Jesus doll. He was trying to tell me something—that I should not have sung, that I was in a pageant and supposed to be still. The gold beads from the casket spilled everywhere—onto the carpet and into the straw, and some of them rolled down the steps, making no sound at all.

Nothing to Laugh At

"So, what are we here for today?" Dr. Flanner said to me, who was perched on his examining table like a fat bird, an old crow; actually I was sitting there like a normal person, with my legs dangling over the edge. But it riled me—the way he talked, the way his nurse talked, medical technician, whatever she was. At age sixty I do not need to be told to put the johnny gown on so the strings tie in back. Also, I am too old to be called "dear."

I thought of saying, "I don't know what *you're* here for." He was sixty-five, sixty-six, ought to be home with his nice wife, cultivating dahlias or some such. I know he does grow dahlias, as well as roses, asters, snapdragons, zinnias, hollyhocks. Every year I drive past his house—it's not much out of my way. His snowdrops always seem to come up before other people's; he has I don't know how many varieties of narcissi; his tulips are beyond compare. Last summer he had the biggest sunflowers I ever saw, and once I saw him and his wife planting bulbs along the stone wall. It was about six o'clock in the morning on a weekday. So this was how he spent his time before going to the hospital or the office, where he was going to have to deal with sick people and people who thought they were sick. It pleased me somehow—I mean that he had a real life. I knew something about him he didn't know I knew, and that part pleased me almost as much. I could figure out, too, what he was going to have to do next: scrub his hands and his fingernails to get them as clean as they always were when I saw him—immaculate.

On the other hand, there was so much I didn't know. I heard myself saying, "I don't know why anyone's in any particular place at any given time." Underneath the office, workmen were making a terrible racket with electric drills, and they were hammering. "Why do they have to do that now?" I continued, by way of illustration, but he said, "They're converting Dr. Thorpe's office into an oral surgery." People are always answering questions I haven't asked.

He went over and sat down on the stool in front of his little metal desk, a desk that attaches to the wall; I always wanted one of those. He patted the chair beside the desk (it had my skirt and my blouse draped across the back) and said, "Come on over here, Marlene," so I slid down. "Are you depressed again?" he asked, opening the Manila folder that contained my chart.

I don't know what he meant "again." I have probably been depressed my whole life. His bifocals were sliding down his nose.

"You ought to have your temples tightened," I said. He blinked at me. I tapped the earpieces of my own glasses.

"Ah," he said.

I flinched, because "Ah" was what he was going to tell me to say when he looked down my throat. I hate that; I don't suppose anybody likes it. It has always seemed to me too bad that we have to have all these orifices that lead to dark and peculiar places, tunnels and caverns; I don't see why we could not have been solid bodies like statues. "All right, give me another six inches, all right," a workman was shouting right underneath where I was sitting. How could Dr. Flanner pay attention to my medical history with all that going on? I had certainly done myself no favor; it is hard enough to get people's attention without competition like that.

"Let's see—you were here eight months ago," Dr. Flanner said. "Everything checked out fine—your cardiogram, your mammogram, all the blood work. You were feeling depressed then. You said you couldn't make yourself care about the earthquake in Mexico or the volcano in Columbia."

He had written that down? I was sure I had not said "Columbia." I would never have said "Columbia." I would have gotten it right. If he was going to take down my exact words, why couldn't he at least be accurate? I myself would have written down something more abstract, such as: "Patient not interested in earthquakes and volcanoes" or "Patient lacks interest in foreign affairs." Yet it touched me and gave me heart to think that what I had said was written down somewhere, if only on a medical chart in a Manila folder kept in a metal file cabinet and even if it was not quite right.

"So what's bothering you now?" Dr. Flanner asked, but I was wondering why, among all the things I could have mentioned, I chose to tell him about earthquakes and volcanoes. I could remember very well that what had sent me over here eight months ago was my receiving in the mail a little folder from the phone company that said: "Now you can star in the most exciting new 'talk show' in your area! Phone-A-Friend Service."

The way this service worked was explained inside the folder. You could dial one number if you wanted to talk about ROCK to MOVIES, so I guess that meant Cultural Events, and another number if you wanted to talk about INFLATION to SPORTS, which must mean Current Events, and a third number if you wanted to talk about RETIREMENT to GRANDCHILDREN, so there was a place for personal concerns, after all. You could dial one of those numbers and be connected with up to four persons who might be discussing something even more interesting than what you yourself wanted to talk about; "something better" was the way the phone company put it, which made me think that whoever wrote that brochure either had no knowledge of human nature whatsoever or else a great deal of unfounded faith. For example, they said you didn't have to converse—you could just listen, and I didn't understand how they expected that to work. What if all four persons wanted to listen instead of talk? I knew it was much more likely that not one single person was going to want to listen, and I based that conclusion on personal experience, which was: if you want somebody to listen, you are probably going to have to pay them. The thought of all these people sitting in their homes, dialing Phone-A-Friend, did worse than depress me; I was frightened. As if a seed had been planted in me, I could feel something growing in all my tunnels and caverns: It was temptation. Some day, at some hour when I felt weak and riddled, I was going to pick up the phone and dial one of those numbers. There would be consequences. It would not be like an earthquake or a volcano but more like when they demolish superannuated buildings by collapsing them from inside.

"Marlene?" Dr. Flanner said, so gently that I was sorry I had told him so many lies, but it was for his own protection. "What's been on your mind?"

"Nothing," I said.

He ran his hand over his hair; it was that wiry kind of hair, iron-gray. He had less of it on top, I noticed, and a lot more in his ears. Surely eight months ago he had not had such tufts sprouting there, as if his ears were growing mold. I was reminded of something I had seen in the back of the vegetable drawer a few days ago and had then forgotten about: an apple, maybe, or part of a cucumber or a zucchini. I don't suppose it matters now what it might have been at some point in the past or even what it was on its way to becoming, but I did know what a mistake it had been to come to Dr. Flanner's office on this particular day, when everything was as it was: his ears sprouting like that and the workmen, who had been quiet for a while, hammering again. If I had wanted mold and noise, I could have stayed at home, where the town was digging another trench down the street with a backhoe. First there were the men with the jackhammers and then there was the backhoe, and it wasn't as if they hadn't already done this just a month or so before: dug a trench, laid sewer pipe, pushed all the dirt back in with the bulldozer. Then the trucks dumping asphalt and the steam rollers, and now here they went again, this time laying pipes for natural gas. They would have to fill it all in again and dump more asphalt; the trucks and the steam roller would have to come back, but I no longer trust that there is some plan, obscure to me though clear and logical to someone else. I didn't know how Dr. Flanner could be so confident that the men drilling and hammering underneath us were in fact doing this because of the office next door. And how did he know that this office was actually being converted into an oral surgery? The workmen could be doing almost anything in there—ripping up floors, building new walls or tearing them down. It could be that some morning, after working in his garden, he would arrive at his office to find that the workmen had removed the sink where he expected to scrub his hands and his fingernails. It might be that when I got home, I would find that the town had by accident dynamited my house even though they meant only to blast ledge. For all I knew, I might not get home.

"What are you doing these days?" Dr. Flanner asked.

I said, "Thinking," realizing too late that I would seem to contradict myself; everyone knows how hard it is to think about nothing. I also remembered that he had asked me that question the last time I was here. If he had to ask again, that must mean he had not thought my answer worth writing down, as it may well not have been. I tried to recall what I'd told him. I suppose if I had been making an effort to look on the brighter side, I might have found pleasure in our perfect accord, both of us agreeing that whatever I had said was not worth remembering.

"Don't you go out," he was asking, "you know—see friends, go to the movies?"

"Of course," I said.

Sometimes I would go to the free films down at the library—Charlie Chaplin, W.C. Fields. I went with a neighbor, a pretty good friend, I guess, if you can count as a friend somebody who has no idea what you are thinking. The last time we went, it was winter, December; the street people had come in to get warm. My neighbor waggled her eyebrows and said, "Count your blessings," as if I weren't already trying to do that every day as it was, telling myself, "You have your health, you have your retirement income," which wasn't what it would have been if I had not stopped teaching at age fifty-five, but still . . . From time to time I would also remind myself that I had never yet experienced a fire or an earthquake or a pestilence, had never been on a hijacked plane or ship. But were these really blessings or merely the result of certain precautions? As soon as she said what she did, I began to wish that my neighbor were someone or somewhere else, and I wished that the street people did not exist. The chairs were hard, the screen was small; we had to wait for a long time between reels. While we waited, my neighbor talked, and it was as if she were projecting her thoughts onto my brain, as if she thought I was as blank as the screen. She told me what her granddaughter had said, what her son-in-law thought about tax reform. She said she planned to connect to the sewer if her town ever got around to putting it in. But she never asked me anything, not even: had I connected to the sewer? If the movie hadn't begun again, I would have called a cab and gone home.

And it was the same when we went to the museum, to the Impressionist exhibit they had downtown. I thought: Now I will get to talk to her about the paintings. But she rented one of those lecture-cassettes with the earplugs. It seemed a queer way to view an exhibition—the people filing past the paintings so slowly, their thoughts all turned inward and their vision too; they stood in front of the paintings, listening, I guess, for what they were supposed to see. They had no idea how much noise they made: their feet shuffling across the carpet, lungs breathing in and out, somebody—a woman—saying, "I like his earlier work best. I don't like those big fat nudes." They have to say it out loud or they don't know what they think, have to say it out loud—it doesn't matter who hears.

"Well, all right," Dr. Flanner said. "Hop back up on the table and let's have a look at you."

He checked my reflexes, heel and knee; he listened to my heart with his stethoscope and then my lungs. "Breathe," he said, and I breathed, wondering what he heard. He looked into my ears and eyes, and I wondered what he saw. The workmen were calling back and forth, loud as crows.

"Open up wide."

He had gotten one of the flat sticks from the jar on the shelf—tongue depressers, that was what they were called; even my tongue was supposed to be depressed.

"Good," he said. "Say, 'ha, ha, ha.'"

Losing

Let it be one of her good days, Lynn thinks, as she parks in front of her daughter's apartment building. She takes the tiny silver-wrapped package out of her purse and puts it on the passenger seat.

Let her not be wearing that wig, she prays, let her have on real shoes, not those rubber boots. Let her not bring that coat she found in the thrift store, or was it the trash? She gets out of the car and goes up the steps into the entryway and rings the buzzer.

"Who is it?" Jennifer says instantly, over the intercom.

"Me." But it has started already. "You didn't forget I was coming, did you?"

"I just woke up."

It's noon. "Do you still want to go?"

"I just have to get dressed."

"I'll wait in the car."

"You can come in."

"No, I'll wait in the car."

"I have to wash my hair."

Not one of her good days, clearly. "I'm going to go read my book," Lynn says.

"If you're in a hurry, I could wear my wig."

"I'm not in that much of a hurry," Lynn says. Could bite her tongue. And she had thought she was prepared; she's been preparing all morning. "Happy birthday," she says, but the intercom has gone dead.

Half an hour goes by. She looks at the silver package. Inside is a silver-lidded box and inside that, silver earrings—for pierced ears; Jenny's ears at least used to be pierced. If you don't wear earrings, the holes probably close up. Three months ago, when she went to see Jennifer, was Jennifer wearing earrings or not? Lynn can't remember. When she last saw Jennifer, earrings were not what was on her mind.

The package is so tiny, a person might sit on it. She was going to surprise Jennifer, let her discover it. When Jenny was small, they would hide her birthday presents, the way they hid Easter eggs— behind the couch cushions, under the afghans, tucked into the corners of window sills. What a cruel thing to do, Jennifer said; she would never do that to children of her own. "But you loved it," Lynn protested. She and Ben would say, "Warmer . . . warmer . . ." Jennifer said, "You were mean—both of you." But she had loved it; Lynn is almost sure. Maybe wait and give Jenny her gift during lunch.

Lunch. Where can they go for lunch? She's supposed to have thought about this already. The French place is out. The waiter stared, Jenny said. The food smelled funny; it smelled like shit. Why were they giving her shit for food? she asked the waiter, just before she walked out. Chinese food—she used to like it. Or there's that nice Mexican restaurant. Unless she's wearing her wig. If she's wearing the wig, she can go right back in and take it off: fake blond hair. Why wear a wig when her hair is so pretty? Same fine chestnut hair she had as a baby—if she'd just keep it cut, hell, just brush it. And if she's wearing the coat with all the ink stains? The deli— they're used to her—or else Brigham's.

Lynn lights a cigarette, tosses her book onto the back seat. Forty-five minutes. Who can read? She rolls down the window and hangs her head out, breathing air still dank from this morning's rain. Leaf buds are sprouting on the trees already, spears of daffodils in front of the gray stucco building. Not even a crocus in her own yard as yet. Maybe nothing will come up; each year there's less. Where do they go, what happens to the bulbs? Just rot in the ground or get eaten by animals? Moles or voles or whatever they are, those things with the noses like fire sprinklers. When she was in the delivery room, having Jenny, she kept her eyes on the fire sprinklers in the ceiling.

An hour. What is Jennifer doing? A number on her—that's what. Maybe gone back to sleep. Or could she have fallen down in the shower? Probably just lying on her bed, thinking. Pills? It's usually pills.

She leaps out, runs up the steps, rings the buzzer. No answer. She rings again. Nothing. Against her forehead she can feel the cold metal of the mail slots. What should she do—ring all the buzzers, hope someone will answer? The superintendent—he doesn't live here, works somewhere else during the day. You never can get him, anyhow, Jenny says. When she locks herself out, she has to wait until after six and, even then, sometimes he doesn't come to let her in. She spends the night sitting in the ER's waiting room. So she says. It's probably true.

Lynn rings again.

"Who is it?" Jennifer says, but Lynn can't speak. "I'm going to call the police if you don't leave me alone."

"I'm going home," Lynn says.

"Oh, it's you."

"As well you know."

"How would I know? A lot of men have been ringing my buzzer."

"I've waited an hour," Lynn says, and, she hates herself for it, but her voice has that quaver. "I can't wait any longer."

"An hour! I'm sorry. I didn't know it was an hour. Somebody called up. You should've come in."

"Jennifer, are you anywhere near ready?"

"I just have to get dressed."

It is all too familiar. "I'll give you five minutes." Backtracking. But it's better than yelling, better than going in, and, no, she can't say it: "After what you did Christmas, you think I'm ever going to set foot in your apartment again?" Can't say it, and it's all nonsense, anyway. She was back in that apartment two weeks after Christmas—feeding the cat, throwing out the spoiled food, hunting around in the mess for the clothes Jenny needed. Since then, no. But when next? How soon?

"Make it seven minutes," Jennifer says.

"All right, seven. Not an instant longer."

"I'll be right out."

If only she could believe her. Or if only Jennifer wouldn't come out at all. Get well or else stay in the hospital. Then I could leave, Lynn thinks. And she almost says what she promised herself she wouldn't: "I wanted to give you your birthday present."

But when she goes back to the car, she puts the little package into her purse. Not because Jennifer will sit on it. It's bait, damn it, bait. Yesterday the gift was just earrings. Pretty earrings, the perfect earrings. Filigree drops as delicate as Jenny's ears. Just right for that Pre-Raphaelite dress Jenny got at the Antique Boutique. Purple velvet and silver. She can be so lovely, though where can she go in velvet and silver?

Jennifer comes out. She's wearing a yellow dress with short sleeves. She's wearing the rubber rain boots. No coat. It's too cold for no coat, but they'll be in the car. Something strange with her hair—eight inches of frizz except at the scalp, where it's growing out. The deli, Lynn decides, leaning over to unlock the door.

"How do you like my dress?" Jennifer says, getting in. "I got it for three dollars at the thrift shop."

"It's a pretty color," Lynn says. She gazes at her daughter. The violet eye-shadow is nice, makes Jenny's eyes somehow browner. "Can I give you a kiss?"

"Sure."

"Happy twenty-third."

"Thanks," Jennifer says. "Where are we going to eat?"

"Where do you want?" She wasn't going to do this. But it was Jennifer's idea, after all, to have lunch.

"I don't care," Jennifer says. "I'm not very hungry."

"I'm starving," Lynn says. Probably that *is* what's the matter with her stomach. She should've brought an apple along. Something.

"I ate a lot of potato chips while I was talking to Lorna."

"Great."

"What's that supposed to mean?"

Don't answer that, Lynn tells herself. "Would you rather have Chinese food or Mexican?"

"Suit yourself," Jennifer says. "I said I wasn't hungry."

"Then we'll go to the deli. Maybe you'll want dessert."

"They said I can't come back to the deli for a month."

Don't ask why, just don't ask, Lynn thinks. "Then we'll go to Brigham's," she says, to Jennifer.

"There was this creep of a man who was bothering me, and I didn't see why I had to talk to him."

"It's okay," Lynn says. "You don't have to tell me."

"So I told him to fuck off . . ."

"Which street do I turn on for Brigham's?"

". . . and he starts yelling at me . . ."

"Which street?"

"We could've walked."

"I'm too hungry to walk."

"This guy was a loon. He was yelling his stupid head off. 'Don't you tell me to fuck off, you little bitch . . .'"

"Softer," Lynn says. Who cares which street? She turns left.

". . . so I yelled back, 'You fucking bastard, leave me the fuck alone . . .'"

"Be quiet a minute. I have to think."

"You should've turned down Central," Jennifer says. "Now you have to go up to Foster. There isn't going to be any place to park. We shouldn't have taken the car."

"The deli's got a parking lot," Lynn says. It just comes out.

"I hate that place. It wasn't my fault. I didn't ask that man to hassle me. Men hassle me a lot."

"Do they?" Lynn says. No inflection.

"They're always talking to me on the street. They say, 'How's it goin', baby?'"

"Original," Lynn says. She turns right and cruises past Brigham's. There's no place to park. She turns right again and goes up to Third Street. There's a parking lot around here somewhere, if she could think how to get to it. She needs to turn left, but you can't. She goes straight across.

"Are you lost?" Jennifer asks.

"Not yet," Lynn says, though the question seems to carry heavier implications.

She cuts across some street she doesn't know the name of. It forks to the right. Central must be somewhere to the left.

"Where are you going?" Jennifer says. "You're going the wrong direction."

"Maybe we should eat somewhere else. That Chinese place—it's near here, isn't it?"

"I hate Chinese food," Jennifer says.

"Good," Lynn says. She turns right, into a dead-end street.

"Why're you being so nasty? What's the matter with you? Why are you so fucked up?"

Oh, Lynn thinks, if I ever got started telling you! She turns the car around and heads out. "Listen, you think we're going to be able to get through lunch without squabbling?"

"I feel good today."

"Good," Lynn says, again. She finds the street she wants but has missed the parking lot. She's too far down, and the street is one-way. Maybe they'll spend the afternoon driving around the city.

"What's the matter with *that* place?" Jennifer says. "Why don't you park *there*?"

Lynn backs up. Once you get it into your head that there's no place to park . . .

"Terrific," she says, and scoots in.

"It's our lucky day."

Lucky days. They sure could use one.

Jennifer has a cheeseburger and French fries, so she must be hungry. What does that mean, though? Next to nothing. The potato chips she said she ate—did she? Threw them up, maybe. And the fate of the cheeseburger?

Bulimic, the doctors said. Thirteen, she was then. Not uncommon, they said. Get her some therapy. "How?" Lynn used to ask—how, if the patient won't stay in the therapist's office?

Oh, lunacy! Lynn thinks, remembering the thin thirteen-year-old standing out on the sidewalk. She can see herself, parked out of sight around the corner. Where is the therapist? On his own couch, probably. Reading or sleeping—anyway, earning money.

And later, when the whole family goes—what then? The patient sits with her back to the therapist, forefingers plugging her ears. Very ill, he says. But Islands of Health. It sounds to Lynn like a destination. They'll embark on the search. Some expedition! The father jumps ship, *mal de mere* for the mother. Medications for all. By now, who is the patient?

What can she ask Jennifer, what's a harmless question? Not "How are you?" Not "What've you been doing?" None of her business, better not to know. And yet, how is she?

She looks at her daughter from across the small table. Earrings, she sees earrings—big brass hoops.

"You want to split an order of onion rings?" she asks.

"No, I'm going to have dessert."

"I should've brought you a birthday cake."

No, what's she thinking of? A fruitcake at Christmas. Her special cake with the nuts and the dates. Never mind that Jenny had said, "Hey, make one for me?" You're supposed to know she was naturally going to start a fast on Christmas; you're supposed to be able to predict, second-guess. Making fruitcakes, Lynn thinks—is that her life's mission?

She hears herself groan. Jennifer laughs.

The laughter has a strange, private sound as if something were funnier than it ought to be. At the concert last fall—that same snicker. They should get out of here. Quickly, quickly.

But Jennifer's ordering a chocolate sundae. No funny business—please, Lynn telegraphs, as if Jennifer had promised, as if Jennifer ever promised. This charade of trust. The hospital letting her out for the concert. Then the laughter; the violinist looked funny. Seats in the rear of the hall, at least. A little common sense, not enough. Jennifer was plump then. Now she's thin. Not too thin, not yet. Beautiful and delicate, not fragile.

Like the earrings. Lynn takes the silver package out of her handbag.

"Happy birthday."

"Gee, thanks."

But Jennifer sets the gift down on the table. "Guess what? I've decided to be the first woman president." Announcing her candidacy. This is no private confidence. The old couple at the next table turns and stares. "You aren't saying anything. Aren't you interested?"

"I want to know how you are," Lynn says.

Wants to know: is Jennifer just being provocative? Or is she heading for the hospital again?

Jennifer says, "I'm fine."

"I'm glad."

"Wouldn't you like me to be the first woman president?"

"What can I say?"

"Well, what do you think?"

"I want you to be happy," Lynn almost says, but she knows better. Knows. She says, "Good luck."

A hand with red fingernails and a lot of rings sets down the sundae. Jennifer scowls.

Lynn says, "May I have the check, please?"

Jennifer picks up her spoon, takes one scoop and stops. "Shit, why am I eating this?"

"I guess you must want to."

Jennifer laughs. Her face clears. She picks up the present and unwraps it. "Oh, pretty!"

She can't consciously be mimicking herself at three—holding the filigree drops up to the light, the way she did with the Christmas ornament: silver peach with a blush on one cheek. The curve of the peach, the curve of the nose. Baby nose. The nose is adult now.

"*You're* pretty," Lynn says, and Jennifer looks down, replacing the earrings on their cotton. What a rare thing to see her blush. "You're more than pretty. You're lovely."

It's true—she *is* lovely, anyway she could be. If she'd not do these things to her hair, wear these clothes. She's lovelier, Lynn thinks, than I ever was. It's almost, for a moment, as if they were sisters.

And she says, "Now you're the same age I was when I had you." The ten years, the twenty-three—they're cancelled.

"You suck!" Jennifer says. She gets up so suddenly she knocks over the sundae. The melting ice cream starts to run out toward the earrings.

Lynn cannot move. What has she done? What has Jennifer heard? Not the closeness. The comparing.

"Oh, God, I didn't mean it that way." As if Jenny at twenty-three should have a husband, a baby.

As who should have?

She'd known she'd do something. When doesn't she blow it? Christmas. Ten minutes. Then howling and shoving. "Get out of here, you evil woman." Out in the corridor, followed by fruitcake. Only ten minutes. How Jennifer changes!

Changes, Lynn thinks, as she pleases. For Jennifer hasn't left; she's still standing beside the table. Her eyes are narrowed, but they aren't murky.

"You're not such a bad bitch," she says. "Just stupid."

She's gazing at the earring box in its pool of ice cream. Are you going to take them? Lynn asks her silently. But no, Jennifer is not. She wants the earrings, but even more she wants to refuse them. Lynn watches her taking leave, regretting. She knows, she knows what she is doing. They're yours, Lynn almost says. If you want to leave them, leave them.

"Thanks for lunch," Jennifer says. She turns to go. "I'll walk home," she says, over her shoulder.

And then, just in case Lynn doesn't get the point, she shivers as if she's already out in the cold.

The Magic Chair

"Susan!"

Oh, she knew who that was, calling to her from across the parking lot. She'd seen him in the market, when she was down by the bread. He was over by the meat counter, wearing a gray pullover on this day, of all days, when it was going to be ninety. She'd thought he'd come after her, but she hadn't looked around.

She slammed the hatchback, enclosing her groceries, and turned to smile at him.

"Leonard."

He stood too close to her, as usual. Didn't know he was too close. Newly single.

"You're out early," he said.

"So are you."

"Wanted to beat the crowd. It's going to be a scorcher."

That's right, she thought, let's talk about the weather. She was noticing his hair: it used to be so thick. Just a few long, gray strands now; the fringe above his ears stuck out every which way. Somebody should tell him to get a trim. Somebody should tell him not to wear that sweater. He'd never have gone around like this ten years ago, even five. He was a terrific-looking man when she and Wayne moved in. Those hot-shot Lewises who lived right on the lake—she still couldn't quite think of him as "Leonard." No, he was Barbie Lewis's father, the owner of Rusty, a setter who'd meander a good two miles in his search for treasure. She used to wave as she drove by; he'd be out walking Rusty. She'd glance back in the side mirror, think: Interesting face. Sometimes she stopped the car, if no traffic was behind her. "There's that bad dog. I saw you this morning, Rusty Lewis."

"He eats chicken bones," she'd tell his owner. "Some day it's going to kill him."

"Oh, I know, Susan. I'm sorry. One of the kids let him get out again."

"Tin foil," she'd say. "He eats tin foil too."

Leonard would grin and look sheepish, like Rusty. "Bad dog," he'd say, patting Rusty.

And now Rusty belonged to Eileen Lewis, and Susan hadn't seen him for an age. Leonard must not have walking rights, although he still lived on the lake. He'd rented a cottage—not that far away, just around on the summer-house side. "It's my neighborhood," he had told Susan. "Twenty-five years. Why should I move?" And into his voice crept that tone of resentment she'd hoped never to hear again. Had a belly-full of that with Wayne, and not just Wayne—every man since. Every man with his own hard luck story. Now Leonard. She hadn't expected it. He was such a nice man, always courteous, a sunny man; she'd envied Eileen. On Saturdays, when she drove by their place, admit it—she had kept one eye peeled, because Leonard was usually out mowing the lawn, and without his shirt he was a sight to behold. Where he lived now—she knew the place—all he had was pine needles, not a blade of grass.

"So what've you been up to?" she asked, but he was still too close. The glass under her elbows was hot, when she leaned back.

He seemed to lean forward. "I've been painting my kitchen."

"In this heat?"

"It stays cool inside. I get a nice breeze."

"What color paint?" He was just about standing on her toes.

"Yellow. You think that's all right?"

"Why not?" Susan said.

"Well, I never know about color. Eileen did all that."

"Typical," Susan said, turning so her hip and only one elbow were against the glass. She had to look at Leonard over her shoulder. "I haven't run into Eileen lately."

"Probably too busy with her lawyers." He moved around to face her; his forehead was sweating. At least Wayne had the sense to move out of the neighborhood. Couldn't wait to move on, was more like it. "She's screwing me but good."

No, don't tell me, Susan thought. She turned around and peered in at her groceries. Defrosting in there, the car like an oven. All her Lean-Cuisine lasagna, diet sherbet.

She said, "All that'll be over one of these days."

"I suppose," Leonard said. "What do you think about blue for the bedroom?"

She could see sky reflected in the glass. It was blue; it was distant. "I don't really know," she said. "I just paint everything antique white."

"What's antique white?"

"Oh, you know, Leonard—just off-white, sort of cream." She gave the top of her Rabbit a tap. "Like this."

"You paint all the rooms that color?"

"That way I don't have to think about it."

"I don't think I was ever actually in your house," he said. "I was always in such a hurry when I picked up Barb." Was he hinting or not? She just didn't know.

"Well, it's all antique white."

"Susan," he said, and now he was leaning on the glass too, gazing down as if into an aquarium, "do you think you're going to live here the rest of your life?"

"The rest of my life?"

"You're so young," he said. "You look so young. You don't look a day older than when you and Wayne moved here."

"Oh, come off it, Leonard. I'm thirty-eight, and if that isn't bad enough, I'm going to be a grandma."

"No!" he said. "I knew Janie got married, but she can't have a baby. She's just a little kid."

"She's starting right in, poor fool, just like I did."

"But she was only in third grade or something when she used to play with Barb."

"Tell me about it," Susan said. "Jimmy was six."

"God," he said, "has it been that long? Well, I'll tell you one thing, and it's the God's truth—you sure don't look like anybody's grandmother."

"Well, thank you." She straightened up. "Why don't you just paint your living room blue? You like blue? Paint it blue."

"It's the bedroom I want blue."

"Okay, the bedroom."

"But I'm not sure. Susan, help me. You're a woman."

So I am, Susan thought. The sun beating down on her head must be getting to her. She could feel it burning on her arms and shoulders. "I think my ice cream's melting."

"Bring it on over to my house, I'll make you a frappe. Use my new blender, well, it's not new. I got it at a yard sale."

"All these yard sales," Susan murmured.

"I spent all last weekend going to yard sales. I didn't know what else to do with myself."

"There must be something."

"I'd like to start dating, but I can't."

"Why not?"

"Eileen would kill me."

Not likely, Susan thought. A nice, mature woman with her mind on civic action?

"She doesn't want the divorce, you know."

"Oh, that's what they all say," Susan said, sharply, and then was sorry, because he might not be lying. She couldn't meet his eyes—amber-brown, like Rusty's. They used to be bedroom eyes, foxy. "Leonard," she said, "can I ask you a question? Why are you wearing a sweater on a day like this?"

His bushy eyebrows shot up. "I guess I forgot to take it off. I've been up since four. It was cool then."

"Well, you should take it off." It was an old man's sweater—loose at the neck, grimy sleeves, and it had pilled all over the chest area, also the stomach.

"I will, when I get home." He turned around so his buttocks were against the car. He looked as though he meant to stay there forever. "I went out at five and picked blueberries."

"I didn't get much," Susan said, "in the way of blueberries this year." She pulled her tank top away from the flesh of her midriff and blew down into her bosom. "I've got to get home. I'm roasting."

"Come home with me, and I'll give you some blueberries."

"I can't. I've got to get these groceries in the refrigerator."

"Well, take them home, and then come on over."

"I can't. I've got about a ton of laundry."

"Let the laundry go. Do it tomorrow. You'd be doing me one helluva favor if you'd just come tell me what to do."

He wasn't going to move, she could see that. Going to stay right there until she said she'd come home with him. She got out her keys, clomped around to the driver-side. Dumb to go to the market in clogs.

He was standing too close again, right behind her. She couldn't open the car door.

"Leonard . . . ," she began. It wasn't up to her—no, it wasn't—but someone should tell him, someone should tell him. "I'll pop over," she said, "for a minute, but first I've got to get these groceries home."

He was into his blue Bug before she had her seat belt fastened. Stunning how fast that man could move when he wanted.

Jimmy wasn't up yet, and it was after ten o'clock. Nobody to help with the groceries. She carried them all in, clomping around, but the noise didn't wake him. Break a leg in these shoes some day. Too old to wear them. Too old to be carrying in groceries for a sixteen-year-old kid.

And why had she'd agreed to go over to Leonard's? She'd been going to ride her bike down to the lake, swim her mile, lie in the sun. By the time she got home from his place, the beach would be too crowded. So maybe she could get a quick swim before dinner. Find out if that kid of hers was going to be home. The lake was open till eight; all she'd miss was some sun. Ruin her hair, but that was okay. No date tonight, weeks and weeks since she'd had one. Stay home and read; she had three new romance novels. Stay home and read, stay home and worry. And a fat lot of good it did, all that worrying. Hadn't kept Janie out of trouble, wouldn't keep Jimmy. He'd be out with those friends of his; they were too old for him. Out drinking beer and what else—cruising? Nice of Wayne to leave her with teenagers' problems. Wherever he was, he wasn't worrying. He didn't even know about Janie's wedding, didn't know about the baby. Wayne, a grandpa—if that wouldn't shake him.

All right—she folded the last of the paper bags—all right, lady, no more grumbling.

She wasn't going to go into his bedroom, she told herself, pulling up behind Leonard's VW. Pine needles littered the top already—matched the rust spots. She could remember when the car was new. Needles lit silently on her windshield; they covered the ground right up to the house. It must be the drought that made the trees shed like that. Getting out of the car, she almost slipped.

Cool air, cooler than in the car. The cottage looked bleak; she couldn't see the lake. It should have been pretty—the pines, the white clapboards, but there wasn't so much as a single flower, just blueberry bushes, and she saw no berries. He must have picked them all this morning.

The front door was open. She called, "Leonard?"

"In here." He came toward her from the gloom. "Come on in. I was looking at my bedroom."

"I can't stay." But she stepped inside.

Hardly any light came in; the place was freezing. A bare room; there weren't even curtains. Nothing but a chair, one of those recliners, grungy brown naugahyde. The kind you saw at yard sales.

"Sit here, Susan."

"No, I won't sit down."

"I don't blame you. It's not very homey."

She shivered. "It's not that. How long have you been here, anyway?"

"About a million years. No, about six weeks."

"But you're not going to stay here, are you?"

He hitched his pants. "It's a question of cheap rent."

"But you can't stay here for the winter." No wonder he wore that sweater. Probably lived in it. The fact was, it looked slept in.

"I was thinking I could maybe get a couple of space heaters."

"But it's so tiny. This is the smallest living room I ever saw."

He sighed. "You should see the bedroom."

"I don't even have to," she said. "Forget blue."

"Antique white?"

"Couldn't hurt." She could see into the kitchen—not a table, not a chair. "How come you don't have any furniture?"

"I have my chair," he said. "I've got Barb's old bed. Well, I don't have her bed, but I've got her mattress. I thought I'd build a platform. You know, I'm handy."

"No, I didn't know," she said.

"Or I thought I'd get a double-size futon or a queen."

"I'd hate to see a queen-size anything in here. Oh, Leonard, it's depressing." He shouldn't be living in a place like this.

"It'll be better when I'm settled. Come look at my kitchen."

Should've changed to sneakers, she thought, clomping across the floor. Should've worn my winter coat.

"I get the sun in the afternoon, and it looks more cheerful. You have the view of the lake from here—see? The corner window."

He was standing too close again; he smelled dank, like old lake water in your bathing suit.

"Can I get you some orange juice or something? How about a drink?"

"A drink?" The clock over the refrigerator said ten-forty.

"Hell," he said, "it's Saturday. I could make you a Bloody Mary."

"You said you'd make me a frappe."

"Then a frappe it is." He got out the blender. "Go sit in my chair, get a feel for the room."

"I've already got a feel for the room." She watched him take the ice cream from the freezer. A few frozen dinners were all that was in there.

"I want to get a love seat or a couch. Tell me where to put it."

"You haven't got a whole lot of choice."

"I know, but where's the best place?"

"There isn't any." Now, that wasn't nice. "What I mean is . . ." But he'd turned on the blender, so she wandered into the living room, tired, all of a sudden. She'd like to sit down but not in that recliner.

The naugahyde was cold against her bare arms and legs. She stretched, and her clogs fell off onto the floor. Why was she doing this? She'd never meant to stay. She'd wanted to get Jimmy to cut the lawn. Should've left a note, not that he would read it. But no, it was too hot to cut the lawn, at least it had been.

Leonard turned off the blender. He was whistling. "You want your blueberries now or later?"

"I thought I was going to take some home."

"You can do that too."

"Now is fine. You know," she said, "you really ought to wash your windows."

"I thought I'd just leave them filthy. Saves on curtains." She would've laughed, but it all seemed too pitiful. He was loading things onto a tray. "Look," he said, "I got all this at a yard sale."

He had put the blueberries into two yellow plastic containers. Whipped butter must have come in them, or margarine. Someone ought to tell him those weren't bowls.

"What do you think of the glasses?"

"Well, they're good and big."

"I thought they were pretty."

Turquoise leaves and vines trailed up the sides. "The only trouble is," she said, "they make the frappe look green."

"It *is* green." He looked pleased. "Secret ingredient."

"Such as what?"

He set the tray on her lap. "See if you can guess. Go ahead, taste it." He picked up his glass.

The frappe tasted cold; it was cold and minty. "I don't want to guess. What's in here?"

"You like it?" He sat down on the arm of the chair.

"What is it?" All he did was perch there, but she couldn't look at him.

"Crème de menthe."

She set her glass down. "I don't think I can manage all of this."

"Just have what you like."

"I don't think I want any of it."

He leaned down close. "I know what you want." She couldn't believe he had actually said that.

"I don't think you do."

"Here, give me the tray."

"Yes, take it," she said, "please."

He set his glass on it and lifted the tray. "I suppose this ought to go back in the refrigerator."

"Right."

But he didn't get up; he set the tray on the floor. Then, before she could move, he was back, leaning over her.

"I have to go home."

"You don't want to go home."

"Don't tell me what I want to do."

But it would be hard to get up unless she really pushed him, and she didn't want to do that. She was just embarrassed for him.

"What you really need in here, you know, is some kind of table."

"I need a lot more than that, Susan."

"Yes, but you could start with a table."

Her teeth were chattering, and not from the cold. She felt his hair graze her forehead, one of those long strands. "You could probably find one at a yard sale." She put her hands up against his chest. "Somebody's probably buying just what you need right this minute."

"Susan, Susan," he said, "you're so young."

She could feel the beating of his heart through the sweater. His mouth came closer, his lips already pursed. Maybe if she didn't look . . . She closed her eyes; his hand cupped her chin.

His kiss was gentle, but his mouth was cold. Cold, so cold, as cold as she was. He drew back and smiled. She had to get out of here. How? She pulled a little grimy ball of wool off his sweater.

Then, all on their own, her fingers were pilling him. "Oh, God," she said. "Look what I'm doing."

He paid no attention. "Did you know you were sitting in a magic chair?"

"Look," she said. "I'm sorry, but this is all wrong."

"Right here." He took her hand. "It's got a magic button." He was guiding her hand to the end of the chair-arm.

"Listen to me, Leonard . . ."

But he wasn't listening. He pressed on her forefinger; the chair shot out, and there she was, sprawled on her back, looking up at him. "I'm lonely," he was saying. "Aren't you lonely sometimes too?"

"Let me up." He had a knee on either side of her. "Look, I don't want this. It's a mistake."

"I can make you happy. You won't be sorry."

"You're putting me in an awful position."

"It'll be better when I get the futon."

"What?" she said.

"It wouldn't always be like this."

"That's what I'm telling you—it isn't going to be." Her arms were getting tired from pushing against him.

"I'll get a real bed."

"No!" she said.

"Please, Susan, just this once."

"Leonard, cut it out!"

"Just once—what would it matter?"

"Damn it, Leonard!" She gave a great shove, and he toppled off, caught himself, managed to stand up. The blueberries were rolling all over the floor; the tray was filling with pale green liquid.

"You came here," he shouted. "What did you come for?"

She was down on her knees, looking for the clogs. They must be caught somewhere under the chair.

"You wanted to come."

No, I didn't, she thought.

"What do you think you are—a schoolgirl?"

Just give up on the clogs, just get out of here, leave them. She leaped up, ran for the door, slipping on blueberries. Then she was outside on the warm pine needles.

She thought he was following her across the yard, but that was his anger coming after her. It caught up with her just as she reached the car.

"Think about it, Susan—you're not getting any younger."

Cowbird

Ellen had already fastened her seat belt and checked that her tray was locked flush in the seat-back ahead of her, but automatically she went through the motions—like a good little girl, she thought; she was forty-seven. No one else was paying any attention to the flight attendant, who double-pointed to the emergency exits so fleetingly that Ellen could barely follow her gesture, though it was something she always liked to know—which exit she was supposed to go to. It wasn't even a safety concern; she just wanted, as always, to do the right thing.

The right thing—she was doing it now: flying out to L.A. to take care of her mother. The library had given her a six-week leave; Margot wasn't expected to last longer than that.

The flight attendant was holding up the oxygen mask. "If you are traveling with a child or someone infirm, put your own mask on first and *then* tend to the other person."

To take care of yourself first—Ellen almost laughed. Learning on a plane what she'd never learned at home. And her mother had modeled it so well, too, not that Margot would've thought of it like that. She never would have thought of it at all. There was no need. She had Dad.

And then she had Cat. And Cat knew all about it.

"Cat will pick you up at the airport," Margot had instructed, and Ellen didn't say, "Over my dead body." Instead, she muttered, "I'll take a cab." But Margot said, "You know Cat will be glad to."

And there, in a nutshell, was why Ellen hated Cat—maybe not hated, maybe just resented. Or maybe both hated and resented.

She hadn't seen Cat for at least twenty years, and already she felt indebted.

Cat had shown up at the front door on a cool but sunny Saturday morning. Mama was in the backyard, weeding, so it was up to Ellen to let Cat in. Through the little window in the door, she saw a tawny-haired woman with a narrow chin and strangely pale eyes. They were bluish green or greenish blue, and their gaze was intent, like the stare of a cat: unblinking, as when a cat stalked a bird.

She couldn't help it: a shudder rippled through her—a frisson, she would say, when she had learned the word. Fear or dislike made her fingers clumsy, though she managed to get the little window unlatched.

"Yes?" she said, as if she didn't know who this was, as if it hadn't been "Cat, Cat, Cat" ever since the beginning of the semester. The new fifth grade teacher—that was Cat, and her classroom was right across the hall from Ellen's mother's.

"Hi, I've come to help Margot weed." The thin lips stretched into a big, wide smile, showing blunt, white teeth—not like a cat's teeth at all.

"Just bring Cat around to the back," Mama had told her. It was rotten luck that she was the one who had to do it, but Tim was down the street, mowing the Millers' lawn, and Dad was off doing the grocery shopping, as usual. Nobody else's father went to the market every Saturday, but no one else she knew had a mother who worked, either. Dad said, "Your mother already has enough on her plate. She shouldn't have to spend Saturday morning at the market." It was his way of making it up to her for all the dinners she cooked when she was just as tired as he was, if not more so, since she was on her feet all day teaching a class of third graders, while he, principal of the town's other junior high, spent most of his time at his desk. In any case, people were entitled to do at least some of the things they wanted, or so he said, and what Mama wanted that day was to weed the geraniums. Other Saturdays, she might work in her potter's studio out in the garage, or go back to bed after breakfast and read a novel.

"I'd like to get started," she had said, leaving Ellen to deal with Cat.

Ellen unlocked the door, intending to step outside, but Cat was stepping in, just as if she'd been invited. She stood a few feet into the living room, looking around—at the framed Impressionist prints that hung on the wall behind the sofa, at the antique rocker with the tapestry upholstery, the lamp table that turned out to be walnut, not oak, under four layers of white and yellow paint.

"Pure Margot. She sure gets away with eclectic!" Cat fixed her pale eyes on Ellen and laughed. "Where is she?"

"Out in back," Ellen could say, at last.

"Maybe I could see the house later." To Ellen's relief, Cat stepped outside again. "Lead on, Macduff."

So Ellen went on ahead, as if she really were leading, as if Cat couldn't have found the backyard on her own.

But she didn't like walking in front of Cat. She hadn't thought about this when she put on shorts instead of pedal-pushers; it hadn't occurred to her that Cat would see her legs, which were long and scrawny, with thighs that didn't meet.

"Hey, could you slow down?"

Ellen stopped. Cat was limping. Was one leg shorter than the other—something wrong with her hip?

"I had polio," Cat said, as if she'd read Ellen's mind.

Ellen didn't know what to say. She said, "Oh."

"When I was ten."

"Oh."

"You're what, now—thirteen?"

Ellen nodded, though she was still twelve. She already knew how old Cat was—thirty. Thirty years old and still living with her mother! Ellen knew because she'd said, "How old is she, anyway?" Her own mother said, "You don't know the whole story." Cat was a courageous, valiant woman. Not only that, but a gifted teacher, "one of those marvels who really love teaching." She got her students to do the most interesting art-work—vibrant paintings, gorgeous color schemes. She was better at inspiring the children than Margot was, and Margot was the school's art teacher.

But all this was the gospel according to Margot.

"Your mother tends to disparage herself," Dad had told Ellen. "She thinks less well of herself than she deserves. You should take all that with a grain of salt, and don't you start doing it yourself! Understand?"

Ellen said she did. But she didn't. She always believed what her mother said. Only recently had she begun to see it as a kind of lie and as something else—she wasn't sure what.

Mama was kneeling at the edge of the geranium bed. She had the faded red kerchief over her hair that Tim used to wear tied around his face when he was being the Lone Ranger. Even when she was wearing old gardening clothes, she was beautiful.

"Cat!" she cried, getting to her feet.

Her smile was warm and somehow certain, a smile that was just for Cat, not for Ellen.

"Damn it, I tried to like her," Ellen used to say, when, against her better judgment she found herself ranting about Cat—to her college roommate, to Alex, her husband; she knew her grudge against Cat had gone on way too long, had followed her into adulthood like a curse. "I couldn't even get myself to feel sorry for her."

It should have been easy. It wasn't just that Cat was crippled from polio. It was that she came from such a tragic background. She was the next-to-youngest of six too close-together children, the only child who'd been given away—to her mother's sister when she was three. She had to learn to call her aunt "Mother" instead of "Auntie," and she had to call her mother "Auntie Phyllis." She didn't understand why her real mother had given her away. Or, later, how her mother could have done that and then had another baby, another daughter—one that she kept.

Cat's new mother didn't want a daughter; she wanted a slave— someone to do the laundry and wash the floors, cook dinner, clean up. Cat *toiled* in a way no child should have to do. No wonder she considered Ellen spoiled—not that she ever said so, but Ellen already knew she didn't help out the way she should. There would be periods of a few weeks when a new regimen would be introduced: the children were going to wash and dry the dishes. But the squabbling, the squabbling! Their mother would rather do it herself than have to listen, and somehow Ellen knew this too. So Tim was released because Ellen was, and Ellen was excused so she would have more time for her homework. She was a plodding student, a grind, learning slowly but determinedly, sometimes unable to finish tests. The time just went, and all of a sudden it was gone, and you had to turn in your paper, and she wasn't done. But all the answers up to that point were good, so she got her A but felt slow and obtuse. She wished she could have been quick-witted and brilliant, or at least have had some kind of talent. She was so unlike her mother. Even her hair was a dull brown—and limp, whereas Mama's made you think of velvet or chocolate. Yet Dad was her real father, she was absolutely sure of that. Therefore, she couldn't be adopted.

Cat really was adopted, and neither of her mothers loved her; but she was able to become Mama's great friend. How did she do it? Simply by being there, every Saturday morning, helping in ways Ellen never would have thought of. It was Cat who weeded the maidenhair fern and tied up the Cécile Brunner rose that climbed the garage. Ellen was supposed to be mopping the kitchen linoleum and hand-washing the tile floors of the two bathrooms—another of those intermittent regimens that were going to teach responsibility and enable her to feel she was contributing. She did the work slowly, feeling obstinate, as if these Cinderella-jobs would never be finished. From the bathroom window, she could look down at her mother and Cat in the back yard. They always seemed to be having such a good time.

"Why does she have to come over every single Saturday?" she finally asked, knowing the question might annoy her mother, though it wouldn't anger her.

Her mother thought about it. "It's the high point of her week."

"It's the high point of *your* week," Ellen managed not to retort. But it was the low point of the week for her, no question. When she saw Cat and Margot laughing and talking, she had all she could do not to wish Cat were dead—killed in a plane crash, run over by a milk truck. But she could wish with all her heart that Cat had never been born, just as Cat's mother must have done.

And if her own mother had felt that way, if Mama had given her away? Ellen had never thought of this before, and it filled her with a sorrow she had never felt either, a sort of stunned sadness as if she were lost, like Hansel and Gretel, left in the forest. But empathy just made her hate Cat even more. *Empathy*. She even hated the word, though she had learned it only recently.

"I hated everything," she told her first therapist, a man her parents took her to when she was fifteen, overcoming their repugnance for psychological interpretation, saying they were worried about how unhappy she seemed. "When I was thirteen, I even hated my friends. And I still do," she added, delighted to see his eyes widen, "except they aren't my friends anymore."

Sitting with them on the lawn at lunchtime, listening to them brag about their boyfriends, whispering and giggling while she chewed her sandwich, she only thought how obnoxious they were, how boring. Not friends, just girls she'd known since grammar school. What could she brag about? Nothing. Their boasting seemed all bravado, a farce—like what Mama did, only in reverse. The realization came to her one day out of nowhere. When people complimented Mama on her pottery, never once did she just say, "Thank you." Instead she had to point out the flaws: the glaze was too thick here, the color not right. Someone told her, "You're too critical," and Ellen remembered what Dad had said. But now she saw what Mama was doing: getting someone else to do her bragging. And she was ashamed of her—it was so obvious. Risky, too: it required an accomplice. If no one contradicted her, then what? Still, if it worked, it inflated the ego. Ego—Freud's word: Ellen was reading about it. Her parents were beginning to seem to her ignorant. Even her father. She had nothing to say to him. "Ellen, the Silent" they called her at school.

"Isn't there someone you'd like to have over?" her mother sometimes asked, as if she were still a little kid. Tim had friends who often came to play. They climbed the avocado tree in the back yard, the eucalyptus tree across the street; it stood at the edge of the vacant lot where you could hide in the tall, swishing grass. When she was younger, she used to play with them—Ellen against the tribe of small boys. But at thirteen she was too old for that—or they were. It would've been fun to have someone she could go with to the movies. Once in a while the whole family went, and there were times when she had actually gone with her mother when it was some movie Dad didn't want to see. He tended to like Ma and Pa Kettle films and Westerns; her mother liked what he called "weepers."

But Margot had started going to the movies with Cat. Cat would come over just before noon instead of in the morning, and off they'd go to the matinee. Other times, they worked in the studio, pounding clay; Cat was learning to use the potter's wheel. She was a natural at that, too, Margot said. Ellen had never felt like a natural at anything. At least she was no longer washing the bathroom floors while her mother did something interesting with Cat. There was a woman who came once a week now and did all that; she even ironed the sheets in the mangle, and Dad had bought and installed a dishwasher. So all Ellen had to do was iron her own blouses and her skirts, which were very long; it was the New Look.

Then, at school, she learned to sew—something, at last, that she could do well. Her basting was a line of perfect half-inch hyphens exactly one-half inch from the seam's edge. If she didn't stitch something right the first time, she could rip it out and do it over. "Why do you care?" a girl in the class asked her, watching Ellen re-do the top-stitching on her apron's bodice. Ellen knew but also knew enough not to say, "Because I know I can get it perfect." The class had treadle sewing machines, and no one could sew as slowly as Ellen. Stitch by stitch, the needle went down, caught the loop from the bobbin, pulled the thread up. Her feet rode the treadle, she had the rhythm; it was the only activity where she felt coordinated. Cooking was a different story. That teacher was a terror; everyone was scared of her. Once she had yelled, "What are you doing with that cinnamon?" Ellen had been about to measure a half-teaspoon, not realizing that Miss Gruby had pre-measured the spices. They made applesauce, French toast, scrambled eggs, and cocoa, and that was all Ellen knew how to cook when she got married. Perhaps, she thought, she had inherited her mother's lack of domesticity. The thought pleased her; her mother's meals never had: the carrot salad with raisins, the chipped beef on toast, the canned fruit cocktail, the gritty canned pears. The meals Dad sometimes cooked were even worse, because he invented things— horrible combinations: canned-salmon casserole—again with raisins, a watery beef soup with string beans in it. Ellen disliked raisins, she loathed string beans, and just to glimpse the coins of yellow grease floating on the soup's surface could make her gag. Both parents, strangely, could cook delectable fried chicken, but neither of them must have wanted to since they hardly ever did.

"Why do you think that was?" her second shrink asked. Ellen said it was because frying made the stove a greasy mess.

"You're so literal," he said, disappointed or disapproving; sometimes it was hard to tell the difference. It occurred to Ellen that she had learned to enjoy disapproval; she rather enjoyed not playing the game. Maybe her role in life was to be a disappointment. Thwarting—what you did to people you couldn't please. She knew she was a disappointment to her mother. She knew her mother liked Tim better.

And why not? He was a darling little boy, precociously kind, not a sad sack like Ellen. Until he was three or four he had blond ringlets; then his hair began to darken until it was like their mother's. She waited for him to lose his sunny disposition too, but he grew up to be kind and easy-going. Good-looking, like Dad. A lot smarter than she was.

By sixteen she no longer hoped to turn into a swan.

Tim was sorry, but he couldn't meet her plane. He had to go to his daughter's dance recital.

"Don't worry about it," she'd told him on the phone. Of course he must go, even if it meant that Cat was going to pick her up. Anna was only four; she was going to be a daffodil. "It's okay, doting dad."

"'Doting dad?'" Ellen heard him echo.

What a shame, she used to think, that he was blessed with no irony, but then neither of them had any wit to speak of. It touched her that he'd turned out to be such a delighted parent, though where had the genes for that come from?

She herself had sworn she wouldn't have children. Then there she was, pregnant, her senior semester in college, waddling around in maternity clothes. She still remembered the first day she wore the black maternity skirt to class, with a striped black and turquoise smock covering the skirt's cut-out stomach. When she passed her former French professor in the hall, he said, "Bonjour, Madame," instead of "Mademoiselle," a greeting that made her feel stripped of privacy. Would she and Alex have gotten married if she hadn't been pregnant? She took it for granted not, though when she (stupidly, determinedly) asked Alex, he would say, "Probably, eventually," an answer that only led to closer questioning. He quickly learned to say, "Of course we would've." Good Alex—not that she believed him. But Good Alex couldn't lie forever. Bad Alex finally said, "Jesus, how many times have you asked me that, will you shut up about it if I say no?" and all she had then was the satisfaction of having driven him to tell the truth, she with her mulish insistence on knowing it. She loved her children but did not dote on them. They were grown up now, in their mid-twenties. They had turned out better than she'd allowed herself to hope, neither Elizabeth nor Stewart married as yet and nobody blissful but nobody anguished, both of them competent in their jobs. Reasonably happy—what more could one ask? Temperamentally, they were Alex's children, for which she thanked heaven, atheist though she was. They treated her with a kindly, laid-back affection that she could not imagine feeling toward Margot. It was such a relief that they were fond of her. She had been so afraid she'd be a damaging mother, a mother whose children rightly hated her. At least they had always known she would rather be doing something with them than scraping paint off a table by herself in the back yard. Maybe, she sometimes thought, if Margot had been a serious artist, her remoteness might have been more forgivable.

"My mom was a dilettante," she told another of her therapists, using the Italian, not the French pronunciation, which caused him to frown. "She wasn't exactly an artiste manqué, she was more like an artistic *person*. I don't know—if she'd ever had any real ambition, maybe that would've been worse. But we kids simply weren't her priority, and we knew it."

"A narcissist."

"No," Ellen said, "she just liked to be by herself, she liked to be alone. Even when Dad was still alive. He understood. She's an introvert, for Christ's sake, and so am I, but I don't like to go places alone."

And her mother did. She might even prefer it.

"She never remarried?"

"God, no!" Ellen laughed.

"How would you have felt if she had?"

"Are you kidding?"

It was a heart attack that killed her father at fifty-four. He had just come back from having lunch in the school cafeteria—a hot dog, he told his secretary.

Poor Angela. She had burst into tears and so had Ellen but not Margot, who, with a set face, leaned forward in her chair and handed Angela a folded rust-colored handkerchief across the coffee table. She had a drawer full of these small, cotton squares—yellow and maroon, aqua, chartreuse. She always had one in her purse, in her pocket, but Ellen had never seen her use one. Now she understood: they were for other people's tears. She had never seen her mother cry.

～

After Dad's death, Grandma came over a little more often—Margot's mother; Dad's parents were dead. Grandma was a feisty little woman in her seventies who lived alone by choice and still swam in the ocean. She went square dancing on Wednesdays and Saturdays, and was determined that Margot was going to come with her, at least on Saturdays.

"Don't start," Margot warned, but Grandma didn't know when to stop. She said forty-nine was too young to be a widow.

"Look," Margot said, after some weeks of this, "I've had my man, I've had my marriage. It was a good marriage, and I don't want another."

"Why not, if it was so good?"

"None of your dratted business!"

Margot looked so fierce that Ellen relaxed in relief, but Grandma laid her hand on her heart, as if about to die of shock.

In an instant, Margot was squeezing her mother's narrow shoulders, "I'm sorry, I'm sorry, you know I didn't mean it. But you and Tim and Ellen are enough for me. And Cat. You're my family."

"Oh, Cat."

"Yes, Cat."

"I see," Grandma said, still wounded.

So Cat had become part of the family, and Ellen knew exactly when that had happened.

It was the Saturday Dad left the car in the driveway and came limping into the kitchen without any groceries. He told Ellen, "Go get your mother." But Margot had just left. "Her car's still here."

"She went to the movies."

"Christ, that woman!" He caught himself, "Beg your pardon," and sank down at the kitchen table. Somebody had stepped on his foot at the market and it hurt, he said, like the very devil.

He asked Ellen to bring him a large pan—the old dishpan would do—with some warm water in it and some Epsom salts.

"Salts?" Ellen said, not sure she understood.

"Just bring me that red box by the Ajax."

The two smallest toes on his left foot weren't bleeding, but they were already the color of blood blisters. He said he was going to go lie down, as soon as he was done with the soaking. "Christ!" he said, again, wincing, and Ellen was afraid she'd gotten the water too hot, but he said, "No, no, it's just that it stings." Then he said, "Will you bring in the groceries, please?"

She had thought maybe he hadn't been able to buy any groceries; she didn't know when his foot had gotten stepped on. Somehow she'd had the idea that it was before he did the shopping, and now the thought of him limping around the store, with his foot hurting, made her feel like crying. As for what made him think he had to *ask* for her help, as if she wouldn't have gone out to the car, at least eventually, and looked to see if there were groceries, that was what she got for gloating over "that woman," whichever one he meant; it wasn't just Cat that she hated by now. She was scared. Her mother should have been here.

Mama didn't come home till nearly three. They'd seen some movie with Gary Cooper in it. "What a beautiful man," she sighed. As for Cat, she had gone straight home. She was late, and her mother would give her hell, as if Cat were still a five-year-old.

"A grown woman—under that sadistic old harpy's thumb. Did your father get saltines?" She was opening the cupboard that would have held crackers if Ellen hadn't put them in a different place—for no particular reason, just a mild assertion of autonomy: the cupboard next to it. "Guess not."

"He hurt his foot."

"What do you mean?"

"Somebody stepped on it."

"In the market?"

"It looked all red. It looked like it hurt."

Her mother didn't seem to feel at all guilty, just concerned. "The man's a saint." She went off to see what needed to be done.

The toes got infected—they didn't heal. The vice-principal had to take over. He was a short, aggressive man who wanted to know when her father was coming back—or *if*. Why was his foot not healing, what was the problem? No one was supposed to know that Dad had diabetes; it might make people think he couldn't do his job, but this man got so angry when she said, "I don't know," that Ellen was afraid she would somehow let it slip.

"He's going to have a sympathectomy," she blurted, one day.

"What's that—a sympathectomy?"

"I don't know." It was an operation that was supposed to improve the circulation of blood to the limbs, but she wasn't sure she had the name right.

"For a girl as big as you, you don't know much, do you?"

"No," she all but whispered.

For weeks after her father had the operation, he was hospitalized. His foot was propped on a stack of pillows. Penicillin dripped onto the infected toes. Every evening Mama drove into Los Angeles, to see him. Once a week or so Ellen and Tim went with her. But most of the time it was Cat who accompanied her.

Dad said he wanted to talk to Ellen, just Ellen. She came and stood next to his bed, trying not to see the raw, infected toes.

He reached out and took her hand. "It takes a lot out of your mother to come in here every night. It's a long ride, a lot of driving."

"Cat does most of the driving," Ellen wanted to say. It was what her mother had told her. At least Cat didn't come along when she and Tim did. The drive took almost an hour, each way.

"I try to tell her not to come so often, but she won't listen." His voice cracked. He waited a moment. "I know you're helping her as much as you can." But Ellen knew she wasn't helping at all; she didn't know what to do, and it made her sullen. There was no one to tell her what she was supposed to be doing. Dad gave her hand a squeeze. "Don't let her get too tired." Tears started running down his cheeks before he could swipe at them. Ellen said nothing, just stared at the floor. She had never imagined her father could cry. "Give me a tissue." He was embarrassed too. "Listen—about Cat . . . she's being a good friend to your mother. I know you don't like her, but try to be nice to her."

"I'm always nice to her," Ellen cried, stung.

"You're not in competition," Dad said. "You understand me? Your mother loves you as much as she loves me. You don't have to worry about Cat."

But Ellen knew that wasn't true. If she and her mother and Cat were in a lifeboat and there was only room for two, her mother would choose Cat and tell Ellen she had to jump overboard and drown. She might want to take Ellen too, but she would take Cat, because Cat was an adult and could be of more use.

"Now, be cheerful," Dad was saying. "Go tell her I want to see her."

Later, when it was time to go, Ellen and Tim went out of the room first. Something made her turn around when she was out in the corridor. Her mother was collapsed into her father's arms, and they were clinging together as if, in the whole world, they had only each other.

If he were still alive he'd be eighty-four, Ellen thought, as the plane flew over the Rockies. There was snow on the peaks, though this was May. It looked fresh and cold down there, uninhabitable. Pristine forever, somehow like her mother. Her mother had been so beautiful, still was, her pure, white hair in its way as lovely as when it had been the deep, rich brown. Small wonder Dad had been so in love with her, and Margot had surely loved him, in her own way. Privately. They had not been a demonstrative family. But what would the two of them have done together? It was hard to imagine them retired. Retired couples had to do things— travel? It was what her mother did now; her interest in making pottery had left her, though she had taken up needlepoint several years ago. She went on group tours, usually by herself. She had discovered, to her surprise, that she loved cruises. Dad would've hated them. He would have told her to go have fun, and off she would have gone—alone or with a friend, probably Cat. He would have stayed home and read—detective stories, history, working his way through the Durants' many volumes: the Greeks, the Romans—*Caesar and Christ*. Ellen could imagine him watching baseball on television; when he died, they didn't own a set. Maybe he would have taken up gardening. Once he had said something about growing carnations, and for a while there had been in the dark garage a box full of damp earth and coffee grounds in which worms were supposed to be proliferating. She could remember Mama saying that she would try them in the geraniums. Alex's attempt to grow mushrooms in the cellar had been a failure too.

A few months after Dad died, so did Cat's mother. The week before the funeral, Cat came to stay for a while. Ellen could never get out of Tim how long she stayed; he didn't seem to have paid attention. It didn't shock him that Cat slept with Margot in Dad's bed. The bed was two single beds pushed together to make one that was king-size, but still: Cat in Dad's bed—it was wrong. She had only just arrived when Ellen came home for the weekend. Ellen would have stayed in the dorm if she'd known.

She overheard the two of them talking in Margot's bedroom. If she sprawled on the bathroom floor beside the open furnace vent in the wall, she could hear Cat, who must have been closer to the vent, but not all of what her mother said.

"I can't stay in that house . . ."

"You're going to stay right here."

And then the words that froze Ellen's blood: "I'd like to stay here forever."

"Well, you can't," Ellen said, in her mind, thereby missing what her mother replied.

"She can't stay in the same house as her uncle," Margot explained, "uncle, step-dad, whatever he is. He's been chasing Cat around for years. Cat tried to tell her mother, but she wouldn't listen."

A rescue mission—was that what Cat was? If so, why had Ellen never seen it before? All those good deeds that Cat had done—the gardening, the marketing, the chauffeuring—they were stored up somewhere, just waiting. Some day Cat was going to want to cash them in. Margot didn't seem to realize. She thought Cat's generosity was pure altruism. Or maybe she considered that she herself was such good company that she was reward enough.

"What if she comes to live with you?" Ellen taunted Tim. "How are you going to like living with Creepy Cat?"

But Tim merely shrugged. He was a senior in high school and hardly ever home; he had a job, delivering liquor. He also had a scholarship to Stanford for the following year.

"It seems to me," Ellen's grandmother said, "that if anyone's going to come live with you, it should be me."

Nobody moved in. In the fall, Tim moved out, and then their mother was alone in a three-bedroom house. Neither Ellen nor Tim came home from school very often, just for the long vacations. Not Thanksgiving. Ellen went to a friend's—she had friends now and a boyfriend, the one just before Alex. As for Cat, Ellen didn't think much about her, and when she did, it was more as a theoretical question.

"I think Cat was in love with my mother," she used to say—to a therapist, to a friend, and later to Alex, though usually when she'd had a glass or two of wine with dinner; she had a very weak head and was easily tipsy. "I don't think Cat probably ever made a pass at her, but I think maybe she threw herself on my mother's mercy. And Mom probably said, 'I'm sorry, I can't help you.' She would've been kind but surprised and firm, and Cat would've known there was nothing doing. Not to gloat, but she probably wondered what about all that devotion, all those years she'd given my mother. Hell, she was leading my mother's life, doing what my mother wanted. But the day-to-day companionship—could that have been enough? I mean, they were friends, but they were *only* friends . . ."

"You never sound too sure of that," Alex had been known to say.

"Well, you know, Cat wanted a mother, but Mom wasn't enough older to be Cat's mother, unless she'd had Cat when she was, like, nineteen."

Alex had heard all this before. He finally said, "Don't you think it's about time you and your multitude of shrinks figure out why you're so obsessed with this poor woman?"

"Why shouldn't I be obsessed? She tried to take my place, she tried to push me out. It was *my* nest. Fucking cowbird!"

He laughed—not a mean laugh but a trifle exasperated; he was a nice man, a good man. Ellen was lucky to have him, though she was getting sick and tired of having to remind herself so often. "You just said your mom wasn't old enough."

"She took my place as Mama's *friend*."

"Ellen, you never were her friend, you're her *daughter*."

Oh, how that ultra-rational tone annoyed her, especially when he was uttering some ultra-stupidity. "I never said the place she took was a place I ever had."

"Or even should have had."

That did strike home. "All right, I'll quit talking about it."

"Good girl," he said. "Better yet, stop thinking."

And she did stop—for months, even years at a time. But then something would rekindle those feelings—when she thought Alex might be having an affair (and it turned out he was, and they got divorced, and he remarried), or when two of her friends went to a movie she wanted to see, without asking if she wanted to come with them. She was right back there, watching her mother and Cat gardening in the back yard when she was supposed to be cleaning the bathroom. Apparently, you were never too old to feel left out, abandoned, cut to the quick when someone else was preferred— those childish things, all those childish things, those feelings she had somehow brought on herself but never had a right to. She'd assumed they all fell away when you grew up, leaving you strong and knowledgeable and entitled. She should be ashamed of being the way she was; she knew it.

There were times when, if she could have been someone else, she would have traded in an instant.

The years passed. Cat and Margot were still good friends, though there were rifts, fallings out. Ellen didn't try to keep track of them. Most of them she suspected she didn't even know about. She was only really aware of the first one. The summer after graduation, when she and Alex came to stay with Margot for two months, Cat never even once came over. Nor did Ellen hear anything about her. She didn't think about it. She was very busy, getting things ready for the baby. They had bought a house with the down-payment Alex's parents had given them, and she was trying to paint at least the room that was going to be the nursery. She managed to do that and paint the other bedroom too, but her water broke after only one wall in the kitchen. Her mother-in-law painted the other three while Ellen was in the hospital having Stewart.

It was just to be polite that Ellen finally asked about Cat, one Saturday when she brought Stewart for a visit to his grandmother. Margot seemed inattentive, even stressed, at any rate too busy to pay attention to Stewart. She was on sabbatical, at UCLA, working toward her Master's, having gotten tired of teaching third grade and decided to become an art supervisor. It would mean traveling around to various schools instead of spending all her time in one classroom (across the hall from Cat, Ellen intuited. It was December and still no sign of Cat).

"And so how is Cat these days?" she asked, her voice extra-polite, the kind of voice Margot used to use when she inquired about the Master's in Library Science that Ellen would have been pursuing if she hadn't had a baby in September.

"I'm sure she's fine," Margot said.

"Haven't you seen her?"

"I'm just so busy."

Busy writing papers. No time to baby-sit. Busy making pots for her ceramics class. Pots, plates. She had to make a tea set, and it turned out to be a lot harder than she would have thought. The cups wanted to warp; they did not want to be all the same size. They were all imperfect, though she'd been throwing pots for years. But Ellen couldn't muster much in the way of sympathy. Here was her mother, taking classes at her alma mater, and here was she, stuck at home with a three-month-old baby, her own Master's having fallen prey to pregnancy. She knew she ought to be glad for her mother, but the fact was, she had a bad case of envy.

Her mother got an A in her ceramics class but did not feel she deserved it. It was, she said, a humbling experience, which made Ellen, for the first time, try to gauge Margot's arrogance. To her, the vases and casseroles looked fabulous. There were some small, flared bowls glazed teal green. Lovely little things. How Ellen coveted them, though of course she never said so. But Cat apparently wanted them too. Cat was apparently back in the picture. And, next thing Ellen knew, the little vases were gone.

"Oh, Cat liked them, so I gave them to her for Christmas."

Ellen was a grown up person by then, a mother, so she couldn't have felt that wrench that was so much like jealousy, though more like a spasm than a stab. It left her feeling woebegone, just the same. Feeling woebegone, Alex said, in his young pomposity, was a condition reserved only for children—for children, Ellen thought, and wives who hated their little houses and, sometimes, their husbands.

Ellen's grandmother didn't think a still-young woman should spend the rest of her life making pots.

"I'm not," Margot said. "I'm going back to teaching. I don't really want to write a thesis."

Then, in the spring, there might have been another falling out, because once again Cat was nowhere in evidence.

"Well, of course I see her at school," Margot said, "but she's got lots of other friends. Which is good. For a while she was living with another teacher, but I guess it didn't work out as well as they hoped. She's bought a house."

"What's it like?" Ellen asked.

"I've never seen it."

"Why not?"

"She never invited me over."

"Isn't that a little odd?"

Margot looked regretful. "She's been hurt by too many people."

"Were you one of them?" Motherhood was making Ellen bold. And she was pregnant again, though Stewart was only seven months old.

"I suppose so," Margot said. "I never meant to."

But then everything would be all right again, and every once in a while, Ellen would run into Cat at Margot's. Cat seemed utterly taken with Ellen's children—a side of Cat Ellen had never imagined.

"I'll baby-sit for you any night but a school night."

The way Cat rested her cheek against Elizabeth's blond curls, the way she smiled and held her, convinced Ellen that she really meant it, but she never took Cat up on her offer. She didn't want Cat in her life. It didn't matter to her anymore that Cat was still in her mother's. She stayed at home with her kids—a fifties mom, the kind of mom her mother hadn't been.

It isn't going to be the way it used to be, Ellen thought, as the plane prepared to land. She looked down at the thousands of houses they were flying over on their approach to LAX, houses on square lots with square turquoise swimming pools. She watched them growing larger and larger, as if a zoom lens were at work, bringing them closer. The square lots were probably fifty by a hundred, not really square. She had lived in one of those houses, feeling stifled and not knowing why, thinking it was the babies, the marriage, when it was land, the absence of open land. Now, when she drove to work, she passed fields full of Canada geese. There were trees—maples, ash, pines, even the occasional elm that hadn't died. If only the plane would never land.

It touched down, hard, with a bump, and Ellen held onto the arm rests and braced herself.

She had said she would wait at the arrivals curb, where Cat could just swoop by and pick her up, but Cat wanted to meet her at the gate. Maybe they both would be unrecognizable. Maybe they should each be carrying a sign. Without the sign, they would miss each other, and Ellen could take a cab after all. "She's got the same hair," Margot had told her—the same tawny gold as before, not strawberry blond but paler, a color that had always come out of a bottle.

So, yes, there was that tawny head in the midst of the throng of people waiting to greet the passengers. It was Cat, all right, and her hair might look the same, but her face looked older— she was sixty-four or -five by now, the skin not so taut across the cheekbones, but a good, firm neck, no wattle. Same pale eyes, same thin lips, none of those furrows above the upper lip that she herself was getting. Actually, Cat had held up very well. Was plastic surgery a possibility? When she saw Ellen, she waved, but Ellen had seen her first and had therefore caught the registering of startled recognition, because of course Ellen was older too, and she did not dye her hair, which was still dark but beginning to go gray, and she didn't wear make-up, though every time she saw Tim, he told her she ought to. But Alex hadn't liked make-up, and she had hated the way it felt, so she had worn none since college, not even lipstick. She knew Tim was going to tell her she looked tired and washed out. She would say it was the appropriate way to look.

Don't let her hug me or kiss me, she prayed, as Cat approached, arms outstretched. They hugged, Ellen using only one arm, because she didn't want to put her carry-on down. But no kiss.

"I thought maybe I should have a sign . . ." Cat began.

"That's just what I was thinking, but you look just the same."

"So do you."

Lie Number One. Might as well go whole hog: "It's so nice of you to do this, I would've taken a cab . . ."

"I'm just glad you didn't come on a school day."

"You're still teaching?"

"Of course. It's my life. How many bags have you got?"

"Just one—it's a duffel."

"Smart of you."

They headed for the escalator, Ellen making sure she didn't stride along too fast. She hadn't forgotten Cat's limp, and besides, her carry-on was heavier than it should be. She had brought too many books, as if the town didn't have a quite decent library, the library of her childhood.

Cat stepped onto the escalator ahead of her and Ellen found herself looking down at Cat's head, into the darker hair at the scalp: gray roots of the golden hair growing out.

"Is she in pain?" Ellen asked, when she and Cat were in the car, heading north. "Is she conscious?"

"She mostly sleeps. She's getting shots of Dilaudid—morphine—for the pain."

Her mother had not wanted to die in a hospital. She did not want to die in a hospital bed. Tim had arranged for two health aides to cover days and nights, and the Hospice nurses checked in twice a week. But two days ago Margot had given up trying to eat. She was still drinking Ensure, but reluctantly.

"It's as if she's decided to hurry things along."

"I'll make her some custard," Ellen said.

"Well, don't be too disappointed if she doesn't want to eat it. Everything makes her nauseous, and the nurse said not to feed her unless she asks." Cat put her left blinker on and changed lanes. "And don't expect her to be able to talk much, either. She's not really 'here,' except once in a while—you know?"

"But I was talking to her on the phone just day before yesterday."

"Things keep changing," Cat said. "She's withdrawing."

But then, unexpectedly, she would come back. Just that morning, when the minister of her church came to visit, she had roused herself out of what seemed to Cat a possible coma and smiled, even talked a little. She made a joke: "So this is what it's like to croak."

"How did the minister react to that?" Ellen asked, but she was thinking: Church? Her mother had started going to church? She had never gone to church, had always claimed to be an agnostic.

"I don't know. The teakettle started whistling."

Ellen studied Cat's profile, the kind of profile that ought to be on a coin—the still-firm jaw-line, the small, yet authoritative nose.

"You're looking wonderful," she blurted.

Cat actually blushed. "Thanks. I try."

She speeded up, leaving no more than a car's length behind the large silver van ahead of them, but Ellen felt no tightening of the jaw or the abdominals. Usually, when someone else was driving, she felt so nervous she had to hang onto the hand grip above the door. When she was still married, she had only to reach for the hand grip to drive Alex crazy. "Take a pill," he'd bark. She'd say, "I already did," and he'd say, "So, take another." Sometimes he said, "Why don't you just close your eyes?" But it was worth it to annoy him if she could allay some of that anxiety. Why then, with Cat, did she feel so oddly calm?

Something about Cat must have changed.

"Cat!" Ellen burst out, in an access of something—gratitude? It felt like gratitude and warmth and relief. But instantaneously a doomed feeling was also forming, which told her she might regret anything she uttered. "I'm sorry . . ." For what? She sat up straighter, still unsure what she was trying to express. "I know I was a horrible teenager."

"Not to worry," Cat said.

The conviction was growing: she should keep her mouth shut. She blundered on anyway. "No, I want to tell you . . . I just couldn't be nice, I was just so jealous."

"I know."

"I wanted to do all the things with Mama that you did."

Cat whooped, as if she couldn't help it. Then she said, "Don't worry about it. I understood. But thanks." She laughed again, as if genuinely amused, and Ellen didn't know what she felt, besides confused and embarrassed.

She told herself she hadn't meant one word of her apology. Sacrificing the pathetic, neurotic teenager she'd been! She had caved in before anything had even been asked of her. As she always did. Her life was nothing but appeasement.

"Oh, shut up," she admonished her brain, but as usual her brain kept on going.

Her mother lay asleep, in her own bed, her face beautifully serene but her hand placed on her right midriff as if to quell the pain. She was dying of liver cancer, discovered two months ago. It had metastasized, no doubt, from some other site, and no treatment was possible. In any case, she told Ellen and Tim when, in a conference call, she announced the diagnosis, she didn't want any treatment. She was seventy-nine, she had lived her life. It reminded Ellen of when she said, "I've had my marriage."

Sitting beside her, Ellen searched her mother's face. She was searching for Mama, but here was only Margot, the person this woman was for everyone else. Mama must have disappeared long ago, a long time before the lovely hair turned white.

Cat came to the doorway. "I'll come back tomorrow."

Ellen roused herself and thanked her, surprised to note that she wished Cat weren't going. She heard the back door close and felt let down—tired, as if she had already been here for weeks. It was unclear to her what her function was to be. Perhaps she had come here only to wait.

She picked up the hand that was resting on the bedcovers and held it between her own hands to warm it.

"I think I thought I was going to take over from the nurses," she told Tim, that evening. "You know—do errands, read to her, maybe fix little tidbits too delicious to refuse . . ."

"I thought you were simply going to *be* here."

He looked older; he looked like their father—the same dark eyebrows, the same deep lines around the mouth. He had their grandmother's intensely blue eyes, eyes Ellen had always wished were hers. In a family of blue eyes, hers alone were hazel.

She hoped she was going to see him often; she had seen so little of him over the years, living a continent apart, each with families; he'd been married twice, had a child from each marriage.

"I'm an idiot," she said.

"You always were. But we loved you anyway."

"Really? You think Mama loved me?"

He winced. "What a question!"

"No, I mean it. I used to take it for granted, but at the same time I always wondered. Because maybe she couldn't—you know, just couldn't. Because I was me. *Dad* loved me."

"They both loved you. They both loved *us*."

"So you never wondered—you just knew?"

"Jesus, Ellen!"

"All right, all right . . . how was the recital?"

"My little Pavlova." His smile was fond. "Anna was dressed all in yellow and green."

"Sounds very fetching."

"They didn't actually do much dancing. They were supposed to be rising out of the ground from seeds."

"Bulbs," Ellen said.

"Okay, bulbs."

"Did she miss her grandmother not being there?"

"No, she doesn't realize."

"Were they close at all?"

He frowned. "I don't know about close. She lets Anna play with her shoes."

"Her shoes?"

"Well, you know, Anna likes to try on other people's shoes."

"You think she's going to grow up to be a psychologist?"

Tim just looked at her.

"Never mind," Ellen said. "You can't blame me for trying. Tell me, what do you think of Cat these days?"

"She's been dropping in every day. In fact, all sorts of people have been here—teacher-friends, people she met at UCLA. She was in some kind of sewing circle . . ."

"Needlepoint," Ellen said. "She always brought her needlepoint with her when she came to visit. Where are those needlepoints? They should be framed."

"I thought she was making pillows," Tim said.

"They may have started out to be pillow covers, but they turned into art. She didn't work from a pattern, the design is all hers. Remember the one she called 'View From the Turnpike'?"

He shook his head. "Sorry."

"The dark maroon one, the color trees get in the spring, when they're budding, before they leaf out—well, you wouldn't know, you've never been east. Why is that, Tim—why have you never come to visit?"

"Too busy, I guess. But some day . . ."

"I'd like to have that needlepoint, if you don't mind," Ellen said. "It means a lot to me. I saw her begin it, and I saw her working on it when she visited."

"Well, consider it yours."

"It's still hers," Ellen said. But it always would be.

Maybe, she thought later, it was enough if just one person loved you.

The nurses kept offering her cups of tea, and Ellen accepted them, though she didn't much like tea. It was kind of them. The day nurse even gave her a hug. It was that obvious, Ellen guessed, that she was depressed.

It had happened to her almost immediately. Stupid of her, but she hadn't anticipated feeling so superfluous, ineffectual—unable to do anything for her mother and not only that: ignored, shut out, more lonely than she knew how to cope with. She was in an alien land, among alien people, even though—or else because—it was the house she'd grown up in. Her mother slept most of the time, as Cat had said. She didn't respond when Ellen tried to talk to her. The doctor, who stopped by once a week, said not to give up; she could hear even if she couldn't speak. Ellen should talk to her as much as she liked. But not expect Margot to talk back.

She did, though—once. Ellen was sitting at her bedside, saying how sorry she was to have been such a depressed, unpleasant teenager. Later, she thought: Don't I ever learn? because her mother, without opening her eyes, said, "Unpleasant? You were *dismal*." And then she said something worse: "You were so awful about Cat. I used to wonder how I ever got such an awful daughter!" Ellen was so shocked it didn't even occur to her to feel hurt. All she could think was: What good am I doing here? Maybe Margot had stopped eating in order to flee her dismal daughter, even if that meant she had to die sooner. Maybe the best thing she, Ellen, could do for her mother would be to get the hell out of there.

Cat stopped by, most days, after school. Ellen would fix her a cup of tea. Cups of tea were all she felt like offering—something she herself didn't want. It was all she would do for Cat, the real daughter; she brought the tea to Cat in the bedroom. Sometimes Cat held Margot's hand or stroked her forehead. Once, Ellen heard her saying, "We had some good times, didn't we?" But another time, just as if Cat didn't know Margot could hear and understand, she said to Ellen, as Ellen handed her the tea, "Oh, I gave her that little bottle on the dresser. You suppose I could have it back when . . . you know . . . *after?*" Ellen, appalled, could only nod. After that, as if the idea had taken root, Cat began to ask for other things—things she had given Margot over the years, or so she said: an amethyst ring she'd gotten her in Puerto Vallarta, a red scarf that had been a Christmas present, a lovely plate that Ellen had always thought Margot made. So many things.

"She keeps asking, and she's right in the room, and Mama can *hear*," Ellen told Tim. "I never know when she's going to do it, or I'd hustle her out. I've told her Mama can hear, but she pays no attention. What's the matter with the woman?"

"I have no idea."

He was trying to figure out where to move. He and Lisa wanted to buy a house in a good school district. Anna would be in kindergarten next year. Cat would know where the good schools were. "I'll have to ask her, next time I see her."

But they didn't run into each other. Cat came straight from teaching; Tim came after dinner. His visits were a help, a relief. They broke in on the stony absence of meaning that was anger, she supposed, though she didn't feel angry. She was as helpless against it as if she'd been still a child, as if the trajectory of her whole life had circled back to this regression. Was this what had lain in wait for her when she was a teenager? She hadn't known then what she was dreading.

The day nurse told her to take a walk, get out of the house, go to a movie, go shopping. She gave her errands to do: buy an avocado and some chips and she would make some of her famous guacamole. But Ellen didn't want any guacamole. When she got in the market, she felt lost and disoriented. She would push the carriage up and down the aisles. Where was prune juice? The same thing happened in the pharmacy.

One night, while the nurse was changing a diaper, out of the blue Margot said, "I didn't know you pooped your pants when you croaked." The nurse laughed and said, "Well, now you know, honey." But Ellen couldn't laugh. Then, all of a sudden, she did. Her mother didn't; she receded back into sleep. Another day, when Ellen was sitting next to the bed, watching her mother breathe, Margot suddenly said, quite loudly, "Cat has hard hands."

It was the last thing she said, and the next night she died. Tim wasn't there. Ellen was asleep. The night nurse came and woke her up. So Margot had died alone, as she had lived. Alone, as she had preferred.

An astonishing number of people came to the memorial service. For a loner, Tim said, she had an awful lot of friends.

"You know, I never worried about her. She always seemed totally self-sufficient. But then, here are all these people, and I haven't a clue who most of them are."

"Being a loner doesn't mean you're friendless," Ellen tried to tell him. "It just means you enjoy being alone."

"I don't enjoy being alone," he said.

"For me," Ellen said, "it all depends."

The stoniness had turned into a relief that mimicked jubilation—the end, no doubt, of the anxiety, the waiting. But Ellen would catch herself smiling, quite as if she were glad her mother was dead. She knew, because people smiled at her in the grocery store, people who would have looked away quickly the week before. She had three weeks left of her leave of absence. She could stay on and help Tim clear out the house, for they would put it on the market, the sooner, the better. She had no illusions that going through their mother's things would be easy. Tim seemed glad she'd be staying.

"Maybe Cat," he said, "would like the plants."

"You don't like house plants?"

"You've seen our place. We're trying to move—soon, I hope. Damn, I never asked her."

"About the schools, you mean?"

"Right."

Cat wanted the plants. She said she would come get them on Saturday, about nine, if that wasn't too early—in fact, she could stay and help sort through things. It flashed through Ellen's mind that Cat thought she was going to worm her way in just as she had done with Margot.

Then she was ashamed of herself and said, "It's awfully nice of you to offer . . ."

But Cat's help was the last thing she wanted. She wanted to work with Tim, or go at her own pace.

She thought too long. Cat said, "See you Saturday."

"What the heck," Tim said, when he heard the agenda. "Let her help."

"I don't want to be beholden."

"Look, she's a giver, it makes her feel good to help people. You're giving to *her* when you let her."

"Oh, bullshit," Ellen said. "That's not the whole story." But he was a man; he didn't want the whole story. The whole story was that Ellen didn't want Cat around, period, and why couldn't Tim understand that one, simple fact?

"Ask her about the school districts while you're working. I'll come over about noon to see how you're doing."

Cat was carrying a square white box when Ellen answered her knock at the back door, and for one insane instant she thought Cat was bringing her an orchid.

"I thought you might like to have these."

Mystified, Ellen took the box into the kitchen and set it on the counter. Whatever was in it, she didn't want it, she didn't want anything Cat could give her. Nothing on earth would ever make her like Cat.

And she didn't have to like her. Margot was dead.

The cover was stuck. Ellen slid her thumbnail along one edge, reluctantly easing it off. Spears of gold tissue paper pointed up, uncrushed, a nest for two small teal-green vases.

For a moment it was hard to breathe. Then she said in a low, rough voice, "You can't give me these! She gave them to *you*."

"I always thought you should've had them."

Where, Ellen wondered, would she have gotten such a notion? If Margot had wanted Ellen to have the vases, she would have given them to her, and she hadn't. If she had, Ellen could never have parted with them. But now she didn't even want them. No, no, of course, she did. She wanted them from Margot but not from Cat. For Cat to be giving her the vases was patronizing, an insult—like saying, "You're even needier and greedier than I am." But no one could be as needy or as greedy as Cat.

Ellen closed her eyes. She mustn't look at the vases. Or touch them. Or pluck them from their nest. Her hands were not to be trusted. If they acted on their own—but what kind of monster could even imagine it? Think instead of the mess to be swept up—not worth it just to horrify Cat. And how sorry, how desperately sorry she'd feel to have destroyed something Margot made, something so beautiful.

She'd like to go out to the studio and smash everything in it. She hadn't been out there yet. Cat said Margot had quit using it.

She waited until her hands stopped trembling, then lifted the vases out, one at a time, setting them down carefully on the counter. They were as perfect as she remembered but smaller.

"Why?" she asked.

"I just figured you would want them."

But took them anyway, Ellen thought.

"I don't think it even occurred to Margot you might like them."

Right, Ellen thought. As far as her mother was concerned, she hadn't really existed. There was only Cat, Cat, Cat.

But now it was leaking out of her, the fury that had protected her. And tears were about to leak out of her eyes. A thin wail was already beginning to vibrate somewhere high in her nose.

"Hey," Cat said, hugging her. "Hey, hey . . ."

She stroked Ellen's hair and patted her on the back, and against her will Ellen felt the grudge deserting her.

Then she could speak and even grab a paper towel off the roll attached to the underside of the cupboard. She mopped her face, blew her nose.

"Cat, are you sure?"

"I want you to have them."

Only doubt and suspicion remained to protect her; they were kicking in reliably but all too weakly.

"It's totally dear of you," she told Cat at last. "Sorry I got all hysterical."

"Not a problem." Cat glanced at her watch. "I've got three hours. Where do you want to start?"

They would start with the clothes, Ellen said, because the clothes would be easier than all the rest; there was so much stuff, the stuff of decades. Margot had lived here for almost fifty years. She had filled up all the closets and cupboards, all the shelves; she had stored things under her bed. Friday, Ellen had gone through her mother's bureau, and three of the four drawers were already empty. A couple of satiny bras and underpants had surprised her. They'd gone into the plastic bag for the Good Will. As for the jewelry, she had left it all in the top drawer; maybe Tim's wife would want it. Not that there was much—some earrings, bangle bracelets, the amethyst ring that Cat had mentioned.

The ring was quite hideous, anyway it was gaudy: a huge deep-purple amethyst set in coarse gold prongs. Why Cat would have given such a ring to the elegant Margot, Ellen couldn't begin to imagine. Margot had been glamorous without the adornment of jewelry, glamorous even with a kerchief tied around her head. It was time, Ellen thought, to give herself a little credit. It had been tough to be the dull, unglamorous daughter of such a woman. She had survived a mother who hadn't much liked her. Survived. Not just outlived her.

She had set the ugly ring in its black velvet box on top of the bureau and then, for some reason, put it back in the drawer. The needlepoints were what Ellen wanted to find on her own. She should have looked for them yesterday.

The clothes were done in short order. Without taking a break, they started on the kitchen. Yard sale items—spatulas, wooden spoons. Pots and pans in the lower cupboards.

"My God," Ellen said, "here's the pot my father made his awful soup in." She set the blue enamel pot on the stove.

Cat hefted it. "Light. I could use it."

"Take it, by all means."

"Where's the lid?"

Go ahead, Ellen thought. Kneel on the floor with your head in the cupboard. What burrowing creature did Cat remind her of?

"I don't think it had one," she finally said.

In twenty minutes or so the lower cupboards were clear. The upper cupboards were going to be harder.

Dishes, so many dishes—bowls, plates, many of them made by Margot: a dinner set for four—soup bowls, salad plates, the works.

"You're going to save these, of course?" Cat stood in front of the cupboard, her hand on the edge of the door.

"I think Tim wants them."

"If he doesn't, could I have them?"

For an instant Ellen didn't know what to say. She wanted the dishes herself if Tim didn't. "If he doesn't, then I thought I would ship them East," she said, and saw Cat make a disappointed moue. Damn it, she thought, she was *my* mother. But she felt ungenerous, stingy. Cat had given her the vases, and all she had given Cat was an old soup pot. But it wasn't all hers to give or otherwise dispose of.

Without asking, Cat was already stacking the other dishes in the cartons—pottery not made by Margot but still very handsome: a breakfast set with a dull gray-green glaze; square black salad plates. Margot always had nice things.

"I think I ought to ask Tim about those, too," Ellen cautioned. She could feel the onset of a tension headache. With any luck Cat would get one too and decide to go home. As for the drinking glasses—yard sale, definitely.

"Oh, all right," said Cat. She set the carton on the counter next to the stove.

Ellen checked her watch. It was now nearly eleven. They had been working for nearly two hours. Surely they could stop for a while, and then Tim would come.

"What about the hutch," Cat said, "in the dining room?"

"Don't you think we've done enough?"

"I hate to stop when we're on such a roll."

"Not even for some coffee—tea, maybe?"

"Not for me. I'll start on the hutch."

Oh, no you don't, Ellen thought. Cat wasn't exactly helping. She was looking through Margot's things for herself. Cat wanted. Cat had always wanted. It was what Ellen had always known, always felt.

But, what the hell—the hutch had only two drawers. Without answering, she followed Cat into the dining room.

"I'll have to wait for Tim on this, too," she warned, but Cat was already opening the drawer on the right. Mama's sterling was stored there in gray non-tarnish cases, the spoons rolled up and tied, the forks, the knives. One small spoon lay unprotected, an outcast, and Cat picked it up, held the spoon against her cheek. She was smiling, as if to say, "I dare you to refuse me this." Embarrassed as much for Cat as for herself, Ellen nodded okay; her whole face was burning. For Cat must have removed the spoon from one of the cases some time before Ellen arrived; it was untarnished.

She had to step back; Cat was opening the other drawer. "She probably had a lot better idea than I did what was where," Ellen told Tim later. During the three weeks while Margot lay dying, Ellen had never had it in her to explore. She'd been half-dead herself, it seemed to her now, as if she had been dying in synch with her mother. It hadn't felt right to her to look for anything until her mother was dead, not even for the needlepoints. But here they were, spread flat in the drawer, "The View from the Turnpike" on top.

"These are so wonderful," Cat said. "Maybe better than her pottery." She pulled out the other drawer again and laid "View" on top of the silver. Three canvases in all, each totally different.

One for each of us, Ellen thought. But that too was for Tim to help decide.

"She was a great lady," Cat said, putting the needlepoints back in the drawer and closing it. "Now let's tackle under the bed, then I'm done for today."

Or any other day, Ellen thought to herself. She hoped her mother at least had aspirin in her medicine cabinet.

Under the bed were open boxes of articles clipped from magazines and newspapers: notices of art shows, book reviews, all with a layer of dust. Ellen sneezed.

"I guess she hadn't looked at any of this for a while."

She had boxes of articles under her own bed. It was the archivist in her, she liked to think. She was going to go home and clear out her house.

"I run a pretty tight ship, myself," Cat said. She dumped the box of articles into a trash bag. "I try not to keep any magazine more than a month. If I haven't read it by then, it's gone."

"It must be wonderful," Ellen murmured, "to be so organized. Oh—shouldn't we have put those in the Recycle?"

Cat made a face. "Don't be so *good*."

"Good?" Ellen said.

"You were always so good."

"How do you mean—'good'?"

Cat just sighed. Then she said, "We always had to be so careful." The pale eyes looked less amused than hostile: an angry cat about to scratch.

Ellen said nothing, could think of nothing. She stared at Cat until Cat finally looked away. And then, just as if she hadn't said anything unsettling, Cat said "So, shall we attack the bureau?"

Ellen was in such turmoil that she didn't have the wit to say "I've already done it." Whatever she had done didn't count anyway.

But Cat would find out. She watched Cat jerk the top drawer open as if she owned the bureau.

"Here it is."

Cat reached in for the black velvet box. She popped open the lid and showed the ring to Ellen, holding the box up to the sunlight, so the amethyst sparkled. "She never wore it much. She thought the stone was too big, and the ring was too loose—on me too, unfortunately." Cat extracted the ring from its box and forced it over the enlarged arthritic joint of her ring finger. "She had arthritis too, so she only wore it once in a while to please me, because look . . ."

The heavy stone made the ring swing around so the amethyst would only have been visible from the palm. All Ellen could see from the top of Cat's hand was a band of gold like a wedding ring.

"Liar!"

The word burst out of her mouth, and once she had said it, she could not stop.

Her Dust, Her Sun

"Don't you think it's about time you gave me my keys back?" Sally said, on the phone, and Martin was so irked by her insistence on this finalizing ritual that he didn't answer immediately, which meant he didn't answer at all. "Or were you planning on keeping them for your collection?"

No answer there, either. What happened to women—did their intelligence desert them—that they became so ordinary in their eagerness to hurt? Six months ago, she'd known how to make him bleed. Now her clumsy attempts, so wide of the mark, gave him a kind of disappointment; she was becoming, retroactively, an unworthy opponent, calling all their months together into question. And perhaps that was her intention, though he'd never known her to be so subtle. In her bitterness—was it bitterness?—she was becoming a woman who would have bored him.

"I'll mail them to you," he said, not questioning why she had to have them back, the symbolism too obvious. "How about if I just throw them away?" was on his tongue, but that was her level.

"I found a record of yours—I assume you want it, it's that one I couldn't stand: "The Medieval Sound." There's a book too, and I'll be damned if I'll mail it."

"What book?"

"Henry James—collected stories. It isn't even your book. It's got Loretta's name in it."

169

Not going to defend himself. Just get off the phone. He said, "Okay, okay, what is it you want me to do—come and get this stuff?"

"Well, it wouldn't just kill you, would it?"

The last thing to disappear: their power to annoy, their last hold: this ability to make your life unpleasant. The obstinacy, the lack of grace, the sheer determination to be an irritant.

"Oh, hell," he said, "just throw it out, give it to the Good Will. I don't care."

"Fine," she said, sounding unexpectedly cheerful. "And you mail me the keys."

Score one for her. He said, sarcastically (score two), "When was it you wanted me to come?"

"When I'm not here."

"Well, when is that?"

"I'll be gone all day Sunday."

His cue to wonder where? "You win," he said, tired of the game.

"You pitiful ass," she said, and hung up.

He'd already unlocked the front door and started up the stairs to Sally's condo when the old feeling struck: here he was, in her script, pitiful ass that he was, turning in the keys to her heart and so on. He could hear Petulia meowing behind the door. The key stuck in the lock, as it always did. Then the door was open, and he was using his foot to keep the cat from getting out, a routine he'd all but perfected during his five-month stay here. The stench of the litter box assaulted him; he'd forgotten how pungent the smell was. Dust balls forming in the hallway, as usual. Here lives, they proclaimed, a woman who does not use the mop as often as she might. With what dismay they'd smitten him on his first visit. "I don't care what you think of me," they said to him now. But why was he looking for messages, or was that in her script too?

There, on the table at the end of the hall, were the things she'd left for him: the record in its white and black jacket, the book, and, completing the tier in decreasing size, something she hadn't mentioned—a pair of navy socks, rolled into a ball. Not his, as she must have known. Why did she want him to come when she wasn't here? No note, nothing about where to leave the keys. He picked up his belongings and put the keys beside the socks. The sun was beaming into the kitchen.

On impulse he stepped into the room. Remarkably clean, for Sally—no dishes in the sink, the counters bare. He'd always thought it a cheerful room.

He was dead-tired; he sat down at the table. The trips to Maine were doing him in. He seemed to have spent the last two months driving—nearly five hundred miles every weekend. Had it been worth it? The answer was no. He could have gone up during the week, as soon as summer school was over, but weekends were his slot. Someone else had the weekdays. Who? Eve's kids, other friends. Other men. Eve made no secret of it.

Who cared? He wasn't jealous, just tired of the inconvenience. If he'd cared, he might be jealous. Impossible to imagine "caring," as they all put it, about a woman again.

Petulia was sharking around his ankles, shedding her long orange fur on his pant legs. He stood up, and she grabbed him around the shin. "Ouch!" he cried. Her claws needed clipping. "Let go," he said, bending down to unhook her. He got a glass from the cupboard, checked the freezer. No ice cubes—when were there ever? Nothing but a glaze of ice in the tray. "Hey!" he yelped, as she grabbed him again. No food in her dish. None in the refrigerator. "You're out of luck. Sorry." No dry food either. "What's she been feeding you—scrambled eggs?" The cat kept meowing. He replenished her water. What was the matter with Sally? He didn't hate cats, just didn't much like them. "If you had any food, I'd feed you, damn it. I'm not *all* bad," he told Petulia. Not all bad, though Eve seemed to think so. Sally certainly did. Forget Gretchen and Loretta.

On the other hand, he thought, running the water until it was cold on his fingers, why should he have his nose rubbed in shit? The young guy, the cellist, who stayed so late a week ago—why couldn't they rehearse some other day? "Oh, we do," Eve said. (Stupid of him to ask.) She was a bit too forthright. Her ad had spelled it out. "I've tried monogamy." ("You were reading the Personals," Sally cried, "when you were living with me?" But what had she expected?) Eve and her string players—they got together, all right. Lying out on the deck, watching for shooting stars, easy to see in that dark Maine sky. Sun-bathing, bare-assed, none of them on the look-out for late lobstermen, someone sailing. It was all right, he supposed; it was okay. So Eve didn't get that tan just on Saturdays with him (a little too tan she'd gotten, a peculiar maple color). Basically, he was just tired of it: come up Friday night, but not too early. Don't get there too late; don't arrive hungry. If you want something to drink, bring it with you. Then the glass of wine by the fire, the star-gazing. Bed. (Better not be too tired.) Morning: the five-mile hike or the bike ride, Eve living all summer long in that gray jogging suit. No eggs in the house; she didn't believe in eggs. What did she believe in? Berries, yogurt. The jar of peanut butter he'd brought had disappeared, big jar, too, probably eaten by some violinist. Such a fool he'd felt, sneaking out to his car for a hunk of pepperoni, handful of onion thins. In that place, food, not sex, was clandestine. What he wouldn't give for a woman who would cook for him again!

"Yeah," he said, out loud, and laughed, re-hearing what Eve had told him yesterday morning: "You're the most narcissistic creature I've ever encountered." Her voice was full of unaccustomed wonder. And all he'd been able to retort was, "Even worse than you?" Trying to turn it into a joke. Why did he let her persuade him to go sailing? He was no sailor—he knew it, she knew it. Trying to be a good sport—a futile enterprise for him, as she put it. The best he could do was go along with what she wanted. Yes, it was marvelous to watch her slim, lithe body, leaning dangerously, it seemed to him, out over the water, her long, dark hair blowing in the chilly wind. But then the boom came around and cuffed him into the drink, the water cold enough to freeze your balls. Did it on purpose. Laughed. Not funny. He should've gone home then, but his clothes were soaking wet. "Good!" she said. "You'll get to see the sunset." As if he hadn't seen enough sunsets by now. In the morning, Eve kept telling him, watch for the heron.

So he'd seen it at last, this morning—almost missed it: gray, not blue, larger than he expected, standing motionless in the shallow water. He never saw the long bill descending, the quick dart that must have punctured the water's surface. He looked away at the crucial moment, took a sip of his coffee, blinked. No matter how he watched, all he saw of movement was the bill pointing up, the long throat swallowing something—a periwinkle? The shore was all minute snail shells, not sand. A small fish, maybe. An hour, at least, of that stillness. What was there to wait for? Something that never happened. Waiting, waiting, until he was as frozen as the heron. And then it turned away, its decision arrived at, and stalked on those disjointed-looking legs up over the slabs of rock and on to the next cove; and that was all.

Leaving him prey to some strange feeling: he was the only one to have seen this, the only witness. He'd never thought of waking Eve. But then, it was nothing new to her. His thought was: now that he'd finally seen it, he could leave, not come back. And all the way here, as he drove, he'd thought: Give me the city, preserve me from nature.

He set his glass in the sink and picked up his record and the book. Petulia went into a frenzy of renewed hope. It was her meow he couldn't stand; she was part Siamese, though it didn't show: orange ball of fluff, a small cat. The week he'd moved in, she'd been in heat, and, good God, what an unearthly yowling that was! He couldn't tolerate it—who could?—and Sally had finally had her spayed. She hadn't wanted to do it—over-identification with the pet by its owner? But she'd promised to get rid of Petulia if he moved in; on their cruise, she would have promised him anything. Rome, Naples—she was so happy; in Tunis they woke up to music and camels, watched them from their stateroom's balcony. She hadn't had much luxury in her life, and neither had he. She loved it all—the mints on the bed-pillows, the white terry-cloth animals fashioned from hand towels, clever elephants, dragons, puppies. She cried over the abandoned dogs running through Pompeii, had to buy them a pork sandwich in the café. Could be she had tried to find a new home for Petulia; she said she'd tried—but not too hard, he could bet. "How can you want me to give up a kitty you know I love so much?" She was lying on the bed, with the cat on her chest, the apricot fur looking like a continuation of her own hair. "I don't suppose it's occurred to you we could have her put to sleep," he said, not meaning it. She'd stared at him in horror, finally said, "It's not like you're allergic to cats, or anything." Hostile laughter when he said he was allergic, all right. The nights he'd lain awake, listening to the crunch of dry cat food, the scrabbling in the litter-box, light from the bathroom piercing his eyelids like daylight. Cats—they were supposed to be able to see in the dark. You didn't really try very hard, he told Sally, in his head. Had he ever known a woman less accommodating, any woman, that is, who made a pretense of being, which Eve didn't?

The Medieval Sound: he would've been sorry to lose this record—there was so much on LPs that wasn't yet on CDs. The jacket too, with its pictures of kortholts and crumhorns. "The racket of regals and racketts," Sally had termed it, her own roots in Streisand, Carly Simon. "What was the attraction?" Eve wanted to know, early on, but who could remember? Not great sex, that was for sure. Loretta—that was great sex. But Sally? "It sounds like such a mismatch." Probably was. But she was a woman who sang around the house—sang pretty badly, at least not well. Yet, it was worth something—the pure cheerfulness. "And then," he'd said, "there was the cooking." "I never in my life," Eve said, "heard anything so disgusting." "Oh, yes, cooking," he said, teasing her, as Sally had teased him. How long till he realized she sang also to devil him, imitating somebody, maybe Streisand? She'd blow on a grass blade to mimic a crumhorn. A fun-loving woman; she made him wince. Was he supposed to have antics of his own? "You poor soul," Sally said, "how did you get to be so serious?"

He set the book and record down again and headed for the bathroom, Petulia running after him. Strange, but he felt more at home than when he'd lived here. Was this why Sally wanted him to come when she was gone?

The litter box looked clean, though it stank to high heaven, and—no surprise—the light was on. She left it on all day, as if Petulia couldn't see in the daylight either. Turning lights off after her—a losing battle. "Look, I've been leaving lights on for the last eight years. I like it bright, okay? It's cheerful." When he was through in the bathroom, he flicked the switch off.

The bedroom door was closed, but he opened it, expecting to see an unmade bed, the Sunday *Globe* scattered upon it, the phone buried in there somewhere. But the bed was made, and nothing was on it. She must be expecting a guest tonight. He could hardly resist the temptation to go in and lie down; he was, in fact, desperate for a nap. Incredibly, the black stain was still on the wall behind the wooden headboard, remains of the spider he'd had to smash. How could Sally not have cleaned it off? Answer: she probably never even noticed it. Not for her to lie around, staring at walls. Loretta—she could stare at nothing for days, tears welling out of her big, sad eyes. And Sally—her eyes also filling. But she'd known, she must have known, there'd be an Eve, just as Loretta knew there'd have to be a Sally. She'd been around, Sally had; she knew what she was getting into. So he wasn't perfect. "Yeah, well, you're a lot more imperfect than I thought."

Bad enough if the spider had been something delicate, a Daddy Longlegs or at least something small, not that thick-bodied creature, legs dense as fringe. If Sally hadn't been astride him, he might not have seen it. It would've lowered itself down onto the back of his head. What sound could he have made that she mistook for passion? All he could remember was crying, "Oh, Jesus!" To spin down suddenly from the ceiling, stop three feet from his face—for what purpose? Doing something quick and nasty with its legs. Getting ready to drop a plumb line, itself the bob. Sally bending down to him; he tumbled her off, sat up, grabbed a magazine from the floor, and smacked the spider against the wall. "You asshole," she said. "I was about to come." Not one of their better fucks, but there was always something.

New, maybe old, spider webs in the ceiling's corners. He'd kept them swept, after that. Lame duck month, late contribution. He hadn't done his share, she said. A month of arguing. What was his share? It was her home, full of her stuff. Full of her, no room for him. One room, if you could call it a room, hardly space for a smallish bureau. Stuck out there over the porch, all those windows. Cold when he moved in, hot when he moved out. What was he, anyway—a boarder? Easier to live among strangers, the cleaning divided up, assigned. This week you vacuumed; next week: KP. But where he lived now had already served its purpose.

They should've moved somewhere else, some condominium with the right number of rooms and copper plumbing, bought new furniture, thrown out the kitchen table, handsome once— now scarred with water rings, heat rings. Sally and her children. The cigarette burn at the edge—that was her husband. The whole tribe, careless; they didn't take care of things. This was where he'd had to write his bills, correct papers, his own room unusable—that terrarium. But why hadn't he known better? Why hadn't Sally? Answer: the cruise, that happy week. But anybody could be happy in Italy.

It wasn't just being happy; it was being free, through with Loretta; it was over, that business. No more hearing how she'd given up a good life for him, left a good man, left her husband. If it was such a super life, what was she doing screwing around? He'd never meant to break up her marriage, or his own. "Then why did you tell her?" he could hear Loretta asking (and he could see her too, lying there on his bed, staring up at the ceiling). "So I'd have to stop seeing you," he'd said. (Was it his doom to remember women, weeping?) "Oh, bullshit," she'd cried, tears running down past her ears, into his pillow. Might as well not have answered; she always thought she knew better, always thought she knew why he did this, did that. "You're just doing the same thing with Sally that you did with me." As if it were her right to tell him. "You think you're in love with Sally. You're just tired of me." He didn't contradict her. At least, he said, Sally didn't analyze him. "Don't worry. She will." And so she had. But he hadn't the wit to see it coming, in Italy.

"Guess who's picking us up at the airport."

"I thought we were taking a cab," she said.

"I arranged it with Stevie and Phil before we left."

"Why?"

"I want them to meet you."

"But not at the *airport*!"

"They love to go to the airport."

"To pick up their father and some strange woman?"

He'd told her that she wasn't a strange woman; they were going to be impressed.

"You mean impressed," she said, "that I'm not Loretta?"

But he'd had no doubts. Well, maybe a few. "There'll be two of us," he'd told Phil; he hadn't said "a woman." Someone he wanted them to meet, he said, not "someone I'm going to live with."

So, there they were, at the gate, such good kids, waiting. Good-looking kids, too, both of them, Phil looking more like him, now that he'd got contacts, the same dark eyes; he looked older than twenty. Even Stevie, his hair still blond, was less like Gretchen. They'd shaken Sally's hand, politely.

He was the one who was suddenly nervous. "I thought we could stop somewhere and grab a bite."

"That's okay, Dad. We're going to eat later."

If he hadn't been so pigheaded, it might've begun to filter through to him that the boys were impatient; the plane had been late. But he hadn't come down from his week's high.

"Maybe some ice cream. How about a sundae?"

"We don't have time, Dad. Mom needs the car."

How could he have managed not to think? That was Gretchen's car they'd be driving.

And he could remember looking at Sally. Her skirt was wrinkled, her blouse starting to come out from the waistband in back. This was no young chick; this was a forty-one-year-old woman. Strained, uncertain smile. And the way she was standing—her chest all caved in. Loretta wouldn't have trailed along, last on the escalator. She wouldn't have wandered around the luggage conveyor, looking for her suitcase. She would've stood there and made sensible conversation. Where was Sally's suitcase? It wasn't his they had to wait and wait for. Then Customs. Nothing to declare, but she had to fill out some form. Random selection. His sons' time she was wasting.

He could see himself starting for the exit, the boys in tow, the three of them waiting for her; she'd waved them on. And he'd gone, knowing that her suitcase was heavy, heavier than his own. Too heavy. He'd gone anyway, crossed the street. She was still waiting for traffic. She was fifty feet behind. He could've yelled, "You need some help?" He could've given his own suitcase to Phil. But all he could think was, why did she have to be here? He'd walked around the car, checked the tires, while Phil was opening the trunk. "I should've taken a cab," she used to say. "Why didn't I have the guts to?" But it would've had to be to his apartment; she'd left some stuff there, and she didn't have a key.

"Now we can go," he'd said, when she finally reached the car; and he'd grabbed her suitcase and flung it in on top of his own, slammed the trunk.

Were his sons ashamed of him? She said they should be, but that was later, after they were home. Walking around in his kitchen, ranting.

"Acting like I was some stray that just happened to glom onto you, somebody you'd maybe met on the plane!"

"That was *you*," he cried. "*You* acted like that."

"Why did you run off on me in the parking lot? Why did you have to sit up there in front and exclude me? All that: 'How's the car been running, did your mother get it tuned up?' Why did you say, 'Now I have to take her home'?"

She wasn't supposed to have heard that. He'd thought she was already out of earshot. But the car door was still open; she'd leapt out, as soon as they pulled up in front of his apartment.

"You wanted me to hear it."

"I didn't even know I was going to say it."

And he hadn't known; it had just come out of him.

"It was so stupid," she cried. "Don't you think they knew you were lying?"

He knew it was stupid. Did she have to rub it in? So he was a coward, but she didn't even look like a respectable woman. Standing there on the sidewalk, her clothes all rumpled like some floozy, smiling and waving, "Nice to meet you both." Playing the game, once she knew what it was. "We may as well go right on." Impersonating somebody he'd imported, the accent vaguely British. Then: "You can just put that in your car," to him, who was carrying both suitcases to the door of his apartment, not looking around to see if the boys had turned the corner yet; let them see. "If you think I'm going to stay here tonight, you're crazy."

She had come in, though. What was she going to do—spend the night on the sidewalk? "I want to go home," she kept saying, but he'd known not to take her home. Not in that state. She wouldn't sit down. "I can't stay *here*." Walking around, until he threw himself down and grabbed her around the knees to make her stop. He must have looked like a supplicant.

"Oh, get up," she said. "What're you doing? Get up, for God's sake!"

Leaning against her thighs, his eyes closed, he'd found the right words. "Are you ever going to forgive me?"

"No," she said, "no." Then: "Ass that I am—probably. But I *told* you it wouldn't work."

"I know, I know."

In the morning: the silent ride home. Not a good night for either of them, she on the sofa. He'd listened to the clock ticking. Not a sound from her. No crying, not a snuffle, the sleep of the just.

A stupid argument: who was going to carry in her suitcase? "If I could carry it at the airport, I can sure as hell carry it now." No, he wanted to carry it. "Oh," she said, "pitiful," her favorite adjective. He'd lugged the suitcase up the stairs, put it on her bed. Sunlight streamed in through the windows; dust motes flurried up from the bedspread. She was already on the phone, calling the friend who'd kept Petulia. "You want some tea?" she asked, but he was leaving; she seemed relieved.

All downhill from there. Wounds don't make you closer. Yet, he'd moved in, lived here. Not a trace of him. Nothing of him in this place, never had been. More of him in his wife's house—still: the coffee table he'd made, his mother's silver. Let Gretchen keep it. The kids could have it, their wives. Paintings, books.—let her keep it, all of it—the house, the car, his sons, his boys. She'd earned it, keeping his house, mothering his children, putting up with everything. His wife.

"You still call her your wife."

As if she didn't. "It's your wife," she'd mouth, her hand over the phone.

"I have to go over to my wife's this weekend."

"Your 'wife's'?"

"I was married to her for twenty-three years!" he could remember expostulating.

"That whole time, didn't you ever call her 'Gretchen'?"

"I have to go over to Gretchen's Sunday."

Sally, sardonic: "You have to go where?" And then: "'Have to'? You *want* to, why can't you be up front?"

It didn't matter what he was, he couldn't win. Sullenly: "I want to see my kids."

"Why can't they come over here?"

"They don't feel comfortable."

"It's you who doesn't feel comfortable."

"All right, all right. It's me."

But she wouldn't leave it. "It's not as though I was Loretta."

But she might as well have been. They might all have been—Sally, Eve. And sometimes he wished, yes, he wished she were Loretta, Loretta who wanted him no matter what he did.

Eve: a curiosity. Even in sleep, she looked invincible, her bony face not soft and slack like Sally's, Loretta's. She was a novelty. When, apart from her, did he even think of her, except times like now? As for him, he was the man who came up on weekends.

"Whatever you do," she'd told him, months ago, "just don't fall in love with me." He hadn't. But someone must have. Who was she talking about last night?

"He was so desperate. I mean, who asked him to burden me with his love? There he was, on his knees, with his head in my stomach."

"What did you do?" She wasn't talking about him; yet, in some way she was.

"Oh, I just told him to get up, and I took him sailing."

This morning—the way she came out of the bedroom, yawning, stretching her arms up, already dressed in her jogging suit. From the low couch, she looked so tall—long legs, long arms; she could touch the ceiling. Something almost threatening about the way she stalked toward him. He'd put one hand on the coffee table that was between them. Then one smooth roll, and she was in a shoulder stand on the rug, silhouetted against the gray water— still, upright, like the heron.

"Which would you rather," she'd said, from this crazy position, "go for a bike ride or take a hike?"

Neither, he said. He had to get going, had to be somewhere in the early afternoon. Had to get the hell out of there, was what it was.

The Memola pad he'd installed was still attached to the kitchen cupboard. A little organization: his one contribution, not that it seemed to have done much good. Three words on the pad in Sally's large scrawl: "Cat food, Brillo." The marking pen came off its velcro with a faint rip.

"This is no way to live," he wrote, below "Brillo." "How could you let Petulia run out of food?" He rubbed this out with a paper towel and wrote, "House looks good, but keep an eye on those dust balls," rubbed this out also and was about to replace the marker, then wrote, "Those aren't my socks."

Petulia ran ahead of him to the front door, streaking past his legs so fast she almost tripped him. He shooed her out of the way with his foot, and backed through the doorway—another successful exit. All in all, he had gotten rather good at it.

Only, as he drove to the turnpike, his jubilation left him. What am I doing? he wondered, and it struck him that he was thinking this more often than he used to. Or was it just what he always asked himself, when he was through with one thing and had, as yet, nothing?

The Accompanists

"If you loved me, you'd love to hear me snore," Martin said. He was standing at their hotel-room window, gazing down at the wet London streets.

Her bed creaked, and he glanced around, but her eyes were still closed. At least she was dressed—skirt, blouse, all but her boots.

"It's not like it was just you," she said. "There was somebody else right behind my head. Then some woman started coughing . . ."

"I never heard a thing."

"You never do."

Half-true, at most: he either slept or he didn't. She was the one who'd slept on the plane—through the rattle of ice, people ordering drinks, the pop and hiss of the cans of mix. They'd sat by the galley, the bar cart in front of them, and she'd slept through it all, her head on his shoulder. Maybe they could sleep alternate nights.

"Come on, Denny, let's get going." She groaned but sat up, blondish hair falling forward. "What did you do with the key?"

"On the bureau."

He went over and checked. Not easy to lose; it had a long, metal rod attached to it.

"Your skirt's kind of linty."

She yawned. "I don't care."

"Well, you ought to."

She gave him her dead-eyed look.

"Sorry." He wasn't old enough to be her father. On the other hand, she wasn't old enough to be his peer. Surely he could at least try to remove the lint.

"Catch!" He tossed her boots over to the bed and headed for the bathroom, to dampen a towel.

He'd had no idea, this morning, that she was in here, had just assumed, on seeing her empty bed, that she'd gone down to breakfast without him, typical Denise behavior. "No!" she'd yelled, when he switched on the light. Naked Venus, rising from the tub, stepping out of pillows and yellow blankets. No Botticelli, this disgruntled female. Startled, then amused, then turned on, he'd reached for her. "Not now," she'd cried, "for Christ's sake, not *now*!"

Her skirt was wool—maroon, like her boots. The lint was yellow, like the blankets "Blanket lint," he diagnosed. He sat down on his bed and beckoned. As he swiped at the skirt, he could hear her yawning.

"Turn." She didn't always cover her mouth. "Again?"

"I think you're making it worse."

He gave up and slung the towel across the room in the general direction of the bathroom. "You want your jacket?" She nodded. "Please." He got it for her from the wardrobe, held it while she slipped it on. Even then, he thought, she might have headed back to bed had he not propelled her firmly toward the door.

He followed her down the dimly lit corridor. Her step was jaunty, even on no sleep. He liked walking behind her; her hips swung, her skirt. At the elevator, he handed her the room-key.

She dangled it in front of her face, letting the rod swing like a pendulum. Her eyes went vacant. "Sleep, sleep."

"Put that in your purse."

"Yes, Pa."

A few families still sat in the dining room. Plenty of tables over by the window. A man and a woman lingered at one of them, where a yew hedge pressed up against the glass.

"Would you like to sit over there?" Martin asked; the hedge was full of lively sparrows.

"This way," the hostess said, and they followed the prim black dress to a table near the kitchen.

An Asian waiter was with them in an instant. "Blue card or white card?" he asked, in perfect, stilted English.

"Blue," Martin said, and showed his card. To Denise he said, "Never mind. You don't have to find it." Just once, he wished, she would keep track of things. Already she had left her umbrella somewhere—the Underground? the British Museum? the Indian restaurant where they'd had dinner?

"Please," the waiter said.

"Yes," Denise said, smiling up at him. "Otherwise, how would you know I was even staying here?" The waiter didn't smile; he said nothing. "You could've invited me in right off the street," she said, to Martin; and there at last was her card, inside her passport. He watched, to make sure she put the passport back in the zipper-pocket.

"Continental breakfast," the waiter said, asked about juice, and was gone.

She took a roll from the basket and tried to tear it. "So now they're having breakfast together."

"Even though they can't seem to sleep together."

Crumbs exploded across the table. "I'm talking about that couple by the window."

But they weren't a couple—that was what struck him. The man looked sixtyish—pudgy, balding. The woman? Smooth blond hair, slant cut. Blonder than Denise, a bit older. But young—early thirties? She was leaning forward, stubbing out her cigarette.

"They were on our plane," Denise said.

"They were?" If he'd seen that blonde, he would have remembered.

"He's wearing a wedding ring. She isn't. They didn't sit together on the plane." He was surprised she'd noticed so much—and must have looked it. "Damn it, Martin, you have this myth: nothing crosses my mind except music."

He could feel the flush spread up his neck. Yes, he was patronizing; he couldn't seem to help it. The fourteen-year age difference could have been twice that. His sons were over half her age. How could she know what he knew? was the feeling. And she didn't, either—didn't even read a newspaper. Once he'd told her George Eliot and George Sand were brothers. She'd given him her dead-eyed stare. Then she'd said, "Oh, I thought they were sisters."

He found her often delightful but, all too often, wearing, and he must've been out of his mind to take up with yet another musician. At least his last girlfriend had played the piano, an instrument he enjoyed; he played a little himself.

The waiter set down their tomato juice. "So, what do you think?" Denise asked.

"About what?"

"Did they meet in the elevator?"

"Haven't a clue."

She grinned. "I think they're having themselves a tryst."

"A tryst!"

"He's an adulterer," she said, in a stage-whisper. "He's got that look."

"I was an adulterer, and I never looked like that."

"You didn't have five kids in college, that's why."

"He doesn't have five kids, or he couldn't afford London." Couldn't afford that blonde, he meant.

"He's here on business. His company sent him."

"From where?" Playing the game, but where was this leading?

"Pennsylvania. That's where his wife is."

A rack of toast came, and their coffee. She poured him a cup from the squat nickel pot. Good strong hands. Not small, not lovely. Nails cut shorter than his own. Just hands. You'd think a harpsichordist would have elegant hands.

The other metal pot held warm milk—he'd forgotten. The marmalade—that, he did remember. The same marmalade in every Bed and Breakfast; there had been no hotels for him and Gretchen, even though it was their honeymoon.

He watched the blunt fingertips try to peel the lid.

"Here, give me that."

She dropped it on his palm. "She's not a happy woman."

"Who?" For one cloudy instant, he'd almost thought she meant Gretchen.

"Her—over there."

"What makes you think so?"

"She looks unhappy."

"Oh, you and your looks."

"She's got this apartment, she doesn't cook, she eats sandwiches or else frozen things from the freezer . . ."

"That's where most people keep frozen things."

"Yes, okay. Anyway, she's tired of coming home to an empty apartment."

That stung him. He said, rather grimly, "Maybe she likes her empty apartment, the way you keep telling me you do."

"I haven't got an empty apartment."

True. It was full of keyboard instruments—harpsichord, clavichord, virginal, organ. Where was she going to put the new harpsichord she'd ordered—an Italian, somewhat smaller, only one manual. Already you could hardly get to the sofa, which was where she slept when he stayed over.

Her fingers were at work on another container of marmalade; he had placed the opened one on his own plate.

She hadn't noticed. "They're leaving. Wow, would you check that walk!"

Nice ass, and didn't she know it! The man touched the small of the woman's back, a proprietary gesture, somewhat annoying.

"You do have a leer."

"You told me to look." The couple moved out of sight beyond the glass partition. "Some day you'll be glad if I can work up a leer."

"Same day," she said, "as I love your snoring."

When they came out of the dining room, the bald fellow was looking at maps at the porter's desk. He had his overcoat on. No sign of the woman.

They converged on the elevator, the three of them, the man wheeling suddenly, as though going back for something. As they stepped in, he took the side near the buttons. Martin reached to push number 7. Already glowing. Just don't say it, he willed Denise, but as if the closing of the door released her, she said:

"You were on our plane, I think."

"I came in yesterday." The voice was southern. "You folks get on in Boston?"

Denise was nodding.

"Washington."

"Are you here for long?" she asked.

"One more night. Then it's on to Munich."

"Munich."

As if she didn't know where it was, as if she hadn't done a concert there with her group.

The man smiled. "Germany." Poor dope.

The elevator stopped. Denise stepped out, and the three of them turned left down the corridor. Martin waited for her to say, "Oh, you're right next to us," but she didn't. She was rummaging in her purse for the key. The man gave them a little nod and let himself into his room.

"The snorer," she said, unlocking their door. Behind her, he said, "Sshh!" "How could he possibly hear?" she scoffed.

"Maybe he's got ears like yours."

It seemed to him she closed the door more firmly than she needed to, but everything she did annoyed him today, even when, on tiptoe, she kissed his cheek, and backed off, smiling, "Impossible."

The chambermaid had been there, and the satiny bedspreads, smoothed over the pillows, seemed to cancel the night spent apart, promise another chance. He gave up too easily, Gretchen said, on everything: on her, on the marriage, even—it was true—on the woman who had parted them.

He got Denise's coat from the wardrobe and laid it on her bed. Goose down—plump as a comforter. But she flopped down, her boots on one purple sleeve.

"Hey," he said, "aren't we going?"

"In a minute."

"For God's sake, Denny." He knew her minutes.

It would be noon before they got to the National Gallery, and he wanted some time there, not to be rushed. She had it in mind to eat lunch in a pub, and that was fine, but the pubs closed at three. Something for each of them, they had agreed. Today, after lunch: Westminster Abbey. Hampton Court for tomorrow. Then Greenwich. After that it was York. Yesterday: the British Museum. Her day; she had to check on some composers—Vicente Rodriguez, Joseph Ximenez, a whole raft of people he'd never heard of. It shouldn't take more than an hour or two to find out what the holdings were. And then, if there turned out to be something promising, she could come back some other time—without him. It sounded as though she'd just thought of all this. But she had her letter of recommendation, the letter she needed for her reader's pass. She had thought it all out, just neglected to mention it. She would meet him at noon, she said.

It was left to him to take their luggage, go on to their hotel; it took all morning. The room would not be ready till one, and he was too tired to explore on his own. Cups of coffee in the lounge. Just staying awake was a challenge. Finally he'd left the luggage with the porter and walked over to the British Museum, wandered around among the Egyptians, gone to meet her in the book shop at noon. But she hadn't come.

Back to the hotel to check in, then back to the museum. By two she must have finished, because at three he found her asleep in the room. And that was their first day—a wasted day, as far as he was concerned.

"*One* minute," he said.

She murmured, "Yes," and yawned.

He sat down in the chair by the window, his coat slung across his knees. "Man Waiting For a Plane That Isn't Coming"—that would be the title, he thought. It peeved him—he couldn't help it—it peeved him to see her lying there. The two beds pained him. At the Cape last summer she'd slept in the kitchen. On the floor, in her sleeping bag. Not that they didn't start out in the same bed, and he never knew when she left him, but in the night he knew; his body knew. He would put out his hand. Gone. At home, when she left, he insisted she wake him. "I'm going." Two, three in the morning. The sounds of her departure were what stayed with him: the dead slam of her car door, not quite catching, the cold, cautious grinding of the motor.

His snoring. It wasn't his snoring. Not *just* his snoring, she said. The way he slept. He ran in his sleep like a dog dreaming—some new tic? Restless feet. With her it was hands.

How long before she'd be playing—on the night table, in a restaurant? Spidery creep among the crumbs. Music he couldn't hear. "It's rude," he said. She just laughed. At the beach, she had played something on his back. A rondeau, she said. Couperin, no, Rameau. Just teasing, but he wanted her to stop. "Enough," he said. She went on, finishing. "Now scratch it. You owe me." But she stroked his back instead, as though to smooth away the music she'd played. As if she could wipe away what his back had learned—not just the mothlike flutter of the trills, the mordants. No—how she'd gone on and on. "Haven't you ever been able to sleep with anyone?" He had asked her that, then feared the answer. But persisted: "Hasn't anyone ever woken up and found you in the same bed with him?" She'd grimaced, looking down at her hands, said, "Give me time." Time. They'd been together eight months and she couldn't even stay in the same room, it looked like.

He heard a door pulled shut. The business man leaving. She mustn't sleep now.

"Denise!" he cried.

They'd be lucky if they managed to take the same bus.

The sidewalk was bricked and uneven, like Boston's. He guided her around the thawing puddles, where the ice had been smashed by bolder feet. Not raining yet, but they'd need his umbrella. The air was raw, cold on his ears.

"You know," she said, as they stood in the bus shelter; her skin was pale from the cold, "I'd really like to go to the Portrait Gallery."

"We won't have time."

"I mean instead. They've got that portrait by Branwell Brontë—the one of Charlotte and Anne and Emily? And then there's another one of just Emily, but I don't know if that's there or not."

"You'd rather see Branwell Brontë than Vermeer and Rembrandt?"

"Yes—I would, actually."

"I think we could safely skip Westminster Abbey."

"That isn't what I meant—I go see Branwell, you go see Rembrandt. I mean, they're right next door to each other."

He'd thought they had come here to be together. "Hey," he said, "if that's what you want."

Their bus came. They climbed up to the top, where in front there were just some school boys. She sat by the window, looking out, rubbing circles in the film of condensation. Did she truly not think of herself as defecting? Was the assumption that he wouldn't mind? His arm pressed against her pillowy coat sleeve. Beneath the down, her arm didn't give.

In Trafalgar Square: more ice, the pigeons skidding around in the fountains. Yesterday, snow covered all of Wales, the fields white and gray, then brown and rime-rimmed. "Swindon," the pilot had said. They'd be near there, Martin said, if they went to the Cotswolds. And how did he know—she might go to the Cotswolds. He might decide to go there himself.

The mist drifting down chilled the bridge of his nose, as he gazed up at the statue of Nelson. He pointed to the National Gallery. "I'll meet you up there. Two on the dot."

He'd have to skip the Italians. He wanted to find the Van Eycks, Van der Weydens. Four rooms of Rembrandt—that was pushing it. He was tempted to go straight to Vermeer.

He made himself stand in front of each painting: The Woman Taken in Adultery, The Deposition. He could see into Room 28, where the two Vermeers were hung.

In 1967 what had he seen? This addition hadn't existed then. The Leonardo cartoon, the famous Vermeer, the other Vermeer—not quite as famous. Musicians—young women, both playing virginals. He remembered not paintings but his new wife, with her knot of pale hair, her slender grace, remembered trying to slip his arm around her waist as they went together from painting to painting. "Please—not here," she'd said. (Not here, not now. He could feel his attention slide.) The gift of enjoyment, she had said. Somewhere, it must have been Windsor Castle, they had come unsuspecting upon a Vermeer, had gone through a doorway or rounded a corner and there it was, just hanging there. Gretchen had let out a little breath. She had taught him what he was looking at. "You study aesthetics in the abstract," she said. All theory. Except he had learned.

He had to sit down. It was cooler sitting down. But a pack of tall Germans came thronging in; Hendrickje Stoffels bathed behind them. Where, he wondered, was the nearest drinking fountain?

Too far away, wherever it was. The heat, yesterday's stress, the plane trip—he felt slightly sick. See the Vermeers and get out in the air. He got up and went to Room 28.

The artist had used the same virginal in both pictures. No, not quite true: different inner lid landscapes. But the same stand, the same marbled blue case. Here was the young woman in her pearly dress, standing at her instrument in the chilly light. He didn't remember the slight greenishness of her face, but the feel of the room was delightfully familiar. Small—he'd forgotten how small the paintings were, had forgotten that they were under glass. The woman's slight, tucked smile drew him forward. He must actually have taken a step, for the thick velvet cord pressed against him, keeping him out, as was intended.

For whom was her smile—a violinist? Recorder player? Perhaps a singer? He'd never quite realized that someone must be standing there in that space between painting and viewer—a presence unseen but almost palpable. So obvious, yet he had never seen it. She might just have said, "Shall we try it again?" She was waiting for the soloist's nod.

In the other painting, too, the music had stopped, but this young lady was numb with chagrin, her confidence shaken, she might even be frightened, her spirits as blue as her taffeta dress. She must have made too many mistakes, counted wrong, played naturals instead of sharps, and the cellist—no, gambist—had walked off in disgust, so abruptly that he'd left his instrument behind. Then, temper under control, he'd come back—to coach her; tell her what she'd done wrong.

How, Martin wondered, could he have failed to see that these women were both accompanists?

But now he was beginning to remember what Gretchen had told him about the symbolism—what the abandoned viol in the second painting meant, and the pictures hanging on the walls—Cupid, in the one and in the other, "The Procuress." And he saw that he had made it all up, all of it, seeing with eyes that weren't his. No epiphany, after all, just empathy of a sort. He'd had a regression, become Denise. It left him feeling somewhat shamefaced. Too bad. He had felt, for a few moments, ebullient, as if he had found a new road to Truth.

It was only one-thirty, but he'd had enough.

He didn't expect her to be early. He was quite content to lean on the balustrade, letting the drizzle slant in on his face. Quite content. He gazed down at the square, at the hundreds of pigeons flapping and wheeling, the gray sky, dozens of black umbrellas. He was looking for a purple coat.

And there she was: Denise of Assisi. On both outstretched arms pigeons roosted. A flock of them pecked by her feet. She dropped her arms; the pigeons flew up; she was brushing off her sleeves.

Running down the steps, he lost sight of her. At the corner he had to wait for the light. The green walk-signal flashed, and he was across, flying down more steps into the square. The pigeons scattered, the people steered clear. When she turned around, he almost ran into her.

"What's the matter?" she cried, her eyes wide. "Am I late?"

He was laughing through gasping. "It's raining."

"You came charging down here to tell me that?"

He opened the umbrella; she took his arm, and they walked down a side street where he'd glimpsed a pub.

"Guess who I saw in the Portrait Gallery."

"Not the adulterer again . . ."

"They're quite the lovebirds."

"Did you see any paintings or just them?"

"I saw Branwell—oh, wait till I show you!"

Postcards, he thought, sitting across from her in the pub, but it was a sheaf of toilet paper she handed him.

"Isn't it great?"

What was great? "NOW WASH YOUR HANDS" was printed on each thin, slick section.

"Oh," she said, "what did you do that for?" Without thinking, he had crumpled the paper in his fist. "Now I'll have to get some more."

"Why—to write people on?"

"No, I just want it. But Mozart would've."

He nearly said, "Thank God you're not Mozart." He asked her what she wanted to eat.

"Pork pie and cider and trifle, if they have some."

He went up to the bar and ordered.

And there, on the other side of the room, leaning toward each other across the table, there sat the adulterer and his blonde; her hair looked platinum against the dark paneling. She was laughing up at him, that old guy. How did he rate—that fellow?

He took the food back to the table. They were here, he told Denise—the adulterer and his woman. Their four lives were entwined, their fates entangled. Tomorrow they'd be at Hampton Court; on Friday they'd be on the train to York.

"No, he's going to Munich. Remember?"

"They're going from here to Westminster Abbey."

"We'll give them the slip." Her cheeks were flushed. "We'll go to the V. & A." She was laughing. "I'd rather go there anyway. They've got the first Elizabeth's virginal."

Now was his chance to tell her—about the virginals in the paintings, about the young women, the unseen soloists. But it was too late; he had somehow missed the moment. Or, more likely, he thought, there had never been one.

The Glass Harmonica

He watched her saunter toward the ocean, across sand still gray from the weekend of rain. The white straps of her bathing suit crossed in an X, bisecting the ribbon of paler skin; she had worn her two-piece suit other weekends. Her skin was golden. She was walking away from him.

The first wave broke low, heavy with sand. Brownish foam shot up around her knees. She flinched, as if the water had stung, and began to wade out through the small, sandy waves. When she was up to her midriff, she stopped—gauging, he thought, the rhythm of the darker surf: long lines of foam, breaking far out and, beyond them, the long, rising mounds of green. She shaded her eyes; the sun had come out. He saw her decide and plunge, swim fast through the backwash of foam. Dive. Surface. Dive again. Once more; then she was swimming up and over the swells, out to where the water was calm.

She turned and swam parallel to the shore. Her head became a caramel-colored dot. He didn't care if she swam or drowned, whether she got cramps in those slim, strong legs, those arms that could hold her whole body above him, while sand from her hair rained lightly down. He might take the car and drive back to the cottage, change the bed, sweep up the sand. She could walk home; it was only a mile. If she didn't drown, she would find him gone. The greenhead flies were already biting him, going for all his tender places—the undersides of his knees, his thighs. She did not have any tender places. He slapped at the flies, killed a few, but more and more of them zeroed in on him. There must be something in his blood that drew them. Leave, he told himself. Go ahead. He would get in the car; he would drive away. In the end, of course he stayed.

So that he saw her come out of the water. She had been swimming for nearly an hour. She was stumbling; once she fell backwards; he didn't go to help her. Her heaviness, as she plodded up the slight incline, was so unlike her buoyancy in water that he simply watched: she was a stranger. He would have gone to help a stranger. She stopped, when she was a few feet away, and gave herself a shake, like a dog; he felt the cold spatter on his legs. In the sunlight her hair was bronze. Her eyes and her nose were red. Was that how she would look if she cried? Goose bumps had risen on her golden skin. She lurched forward, dropping face-down on her towel. He watched the flies dart under her arms. Memorial Day—a memorable day. It was lodged in his mind like a grudge.

"I want to tell her in person," he said, but Carol was trying to pull up the bed-sheet. In the dusk her hair looked almost black; it hung, straight and thick, past her shoulder blades. He waited until she had settled back beside him. "Now do you think you could pay attention?"

She gave the sheet another twitch, and everything changed, like a snowscape. He watched the gently rising slope that was emerging between her pelvic bones. Who got pregnant these days by accident? "Well, I didn't do it on purpose," she'd wailed, "and I didn't do it all by myself, either." How, why—it didn't matter. The odd thing was: he was pleased. Pleased! He'd be forty-three when this child was born. A new family—it committed him.

"I have to get up," she said. "John's probably starving."

As if John would even think of food while that radio program was on. "I've only had it for two years," a man's voice was saying, "and this is the third muffler, I swear to God."

You could hear it over the window fan. Try to make love, try to have a conversation. And if he could hear the radio, John could hear them. "Well," Carol kept saying, "what if he does?" They had different ideas about privacy, clearly, different ideas about a lot of things. He could see how the differences were going to emerge—first the salient ones, like her toes making peaks, then the minor molehills, the knee-size mounds. And some would push themselves up very slowly until they became Matterhorns.

"I just want you to understand," he said.

"I understand better than you think."

"Are you driving through a lot of water?" the radio asked.

"I just don't want her to hear it from someone else."

She had brought her hair around from behind and now she was plaiting it under her chin—one long braid: a circus beard.

"You just want to see her again."

He flipped the sheet off them both and sat up. "What if I do? What if I do? It has nothing to do with us." He leaned over and gave her shoulders a little shake. "I don't like unfinished business, that's all." Her dark eyes filled. "Come on, be brave."

"I thought it was finished."

"You know it is, in that sense. Sweetheart, you're everything Denise isn't."

"But why do you have to take her to the Cape?"

"She can help me move the desk."

"You're not leveling," Carol said. "You want to take her to the cottage one more time."

How he hated it when she said, "You're not leveling." Right up there with calling vegetables "veggies." And yet, these were such minor annoyances. He knew he could love her; he already did.

Or would he love anybody who said she loved him—anybody, that is, with such beautiful eyes?

He stood up. "Did I ever tell you . . ?" But that was too maudlin. He settled for, "Damn it, I love you."

"If I say my wife has beautiful eyes," he might say, the first day of class, "what kind of utterance am I making—a statement, a proposition? Am I saying there's a property called 'beauty'? Am I saying it inheres in her eyes? Am I saying the same kind of thing as 'Her eyes are brown'? Or am I merely saying, 'My wife's eyes please me'? Do some, or most, of us have to agree that they're beautiful? Where does that leave my subjective perception?" And so on, and so on. He used to hold up the piece of melted aluminum, useful remains of one of his saucepans, and ask, "Is this an art object?" Someone would usually mutter, "What is it?" and then he would talk about function, origin. He could count on some wise-ass to say, "If that's art, it isn't any good," but most would sit there and say nothing. Week after next: that sea of neutral faces.

"What're you thinking about?" Carol said.

"Your eyes."

"No, really."

"Really." Were they really going to marry?

She was resting her elbows on the kitchen table. Her skin was particularly luminous this morning. Happiness or pregnancy? She should have been painted by Ingres: her nearly black hair, the teal blue of her bathrobe.

"And I'm thinking this is the last day I've got to do the tune-up. I've got faculty meetings all next week." Every single day except Friday, and then the long weekend, Labor Day weekend. He pushed his chair back. Through the window he could see John on his skateboard, splashing past the Valiant through the drying rain puddles. Around the car he went, his T-shirt fluttering, and disappeared, all but his small dark head. The tockety-tock of the wheels got louder.

"Does he absolutely have to do that now?"

"I don't suppose." She drew her bathrobe together. These small crimes he was always committing; he was going to have to be so careful.

"What if I asked him to help me?"

"You know he'd love it."

How to restore that glow—he knew how. If only she wouldn't be so grateful.

He got his toolbox out of the Valiant's trunk. At home he could have worked alone. How was he going to learn to love John? The poor kid was always around. If they went anywhere, so did John.

He was going with them next Saturday to the Hatch Shell. The Boston Ballet. John liked ballet?

He gave all six plugs a loosening twist with the wrench. His own fault—he'd gotten himself into this. "John," he called as the boy whizzed by, "you think you could change some spark plugs?"

John ran the skateboard up onto the grass. In the wonderful silence, he came running back. A face like his mother's—as open, as pleased.

"Sure."

He gave himself a little hoist; his feet didn't quite touch the ground. A grunt, a slam on the wrench with his palm. Not bad. The small hand reached around.

"Here's one."

The skull in back was round, like Carol's; the hair neatly followed the curve of the ears. A nice little boy, a beautiful kid. Perhaps this time he'd have a daughter? His own sons were in college already.

The car wouldn't start. Martin said, "Oh, shit."

"It's probably your distributor cap," John said. "I bet it's wet." Yes, and he was probably right. "I'll take it off for you." So let him try. "Go ask Mom for a rag." A bit much, that, Martin thought, but, hey, it made him laugh.

She was standing at the sink, stringing celery.

"Your son needs a rag."

"Is he driving you nuts?"

"No, he's being a help."

Her hair hung forward in two long braids. There was something straight and sturdy about the part and innocent about the neck. He came up behind her and put his arms around her, careful to keep his grimy hands off her smock.

Her head was way below his chin; he could look down and see the red embroidery she'd done across the front—poppies or something. Very nice, but the smock looked like a maternity top.

"So," he said, "are we having veggies for lunch?"

"This is for the tuna sandwiches, silly."

She got him a rag from the sack in the broom closet. He gave her a kiss and went back out.

John said, "I couldn't get it off." He was nearly crying. "I couldn't get the spring clips off."

Martin said, "Well, let's see." He laid his hand on the back of John's head. "It's pretty hard. It's hard for me too." They were both so good—the mother, the son—far better than he deserved.

Each time he phoned, he had gotten the harpsichord—a Three-Part Invention, if memory served—then: "Sorry, I can't come to the phone. Please leave a message after the beep." A new tape, thank God. The one she had in the spring said, sepulchrally: "You've reached the voice of Denise. Leave a message if you want the rest of me." It had opened with a few bars of flashy Scarlatti. Foolish to give her name, he kept telling her, foolish to word the tape like that.

August: he must have called twice a week. To be gone for so long wasn't like her. Still, she was often away. He used to know where she was—Amsterdam, Cologne. He hung up each time before the beep. He was going to have to leave a message this time, something short, like: "Call me."

But she cut in, saying, "Hello, hello?"

Before he thought, he said, "Where the hell have you been?"

"Vancouver, out at the music festival." And then, sounding surprised, she said, "Martin?" Only three months, and she couldn't recognize his voice? He asked how she was. Fine, she said. She had a new car, a station wagon. Distantly, she asked after him.

His voice came out thin. "I've sold the cottage. I'm going down Friday to get that desk." He could hear how strained he sounded. "I thought you might like to come."

"What desk?"

"The one in the bedroom." As if there were more than one. When she didn't answer, he said, "Denny?"

"You couldn't go on Saturday?"

"No."

A long silence. Then: "Why . . ."

"I'm going to the ballet." Not that it was any of her business now.

"No. I mean why do you want me to go?"

"We need to talk."

"About what?"

"I need to see you."

More silence. Then, unenthusiastically: "I guess I can."

Like those friends of John's, who, when Carol said, "How about some lunch?" had to think about it before they said, "Okay" as if it were a favor. He supposed she could look on this as a favor—as he ought to.

"Great," he said. "Can you be here by eight?" Tell her eight, she might make it by nine.

He dreamt he was making love. He and some woman were in a car, then a bed. People kept walking through the room. They were all at a party; he was back in the bed. The woman said, "and you should check your compression." In his dream he knew he was dreaming, and when he woke up, he heard himself laughing. Six-fifteen. The radio came on. A trio—sounded like Brahms.

Denise used to say, "Does it have to be on?" Did he have to have a radio in every room? Silence—that was what she liked. She would go around turning the radios off. And only in the car would she listen, though neither of their cars had a good radio. He'd given her a Blaupunkt for her birthday, hoping she'd be pleased. Embarrassed instead. She was just so ungracious. "No, I can't take it. Really, truly, you shouldn't have." But he'd given her only the radio, not the speakers, afraid to try to give her too much. "But I don't have birthdays" was what she'd said next. She could quit, he said, at thirty-five. At last she had thanked him, adding, "But I think I'll wait till I get a new car." March then. In June, when he came to get the books he had lent her, he saw the radio—still on her dining table, still in its box, forgotten gift, the stacks of music grown tall around it, flyers for her chamber group piled on top of it. Cancelled was what he felt.

The kitchen radio was blaring away. He turned it down, put the coffee water on. Out in the trees the birds were waiting. Sunflower seeds for the redwood feeder, thistle seed for the plastic cylinder. He was barely back indoors, and there were the goldfinches. "Thistles," his kids used to call the finches. They didn't have finches in Fresno, probably, which was where their mother had moved.

Call Carol, he thought, as he stood at the sink. Steam from his coffee drifted toward the window. A titmouse was pocking a sunflower seed. Perfect aim: wham, wham, wham. Holding onto the branch and the seed. Beside it, the full-grown baby begged, fluttering flat to the branch. "You're some con artist," Martin said. The adult gave one hop, popped the seed in. A whoosh of wings: the birds were gone. The tiger cat from next door had leapt to the railing, was creeping along toward the swinging cylinder.

"Get out of here," Martin said. "Thhh." He leaned close to the screen and said it again. The cat crouched, gave one blink. Who would scare the cat off when he moved? Who, for that matter, would feed the birds?

Call Carol, he thought again, in the shower. "Call me," she'd said, "before you leave?" Five-minute shower, cut it to three. Denise used to walk right in. "Mind if I pee?" Her face would appear around the curtain. "My, my. Sex-xy!" Whatever house he and Carol ended up buying was sure as hell going to have more than one bathroom. He'd done his part, he'd sold the cottage—the last thing that was his.

He would call just as soon as he was dressed. Both pairs of shorts were in the laundry. So, he'd wear jeans. He had time to do laundry. Shirts, socks—he started sorting. T-shirts, a pair of Carol's white cotton briefs. Healthier, she said, than nylon—you shouldn't wear nylon to run in. Should a pregnant woman even be running? It was ten of seven—he'd missed her.

When Denise used to bring her laundry, they'd watch the news, Animal Kingdom, Wild World of Animals, whatever it was, somehow wind up making love. She would make those crazy noises. "Pretend you're humping a hippopotamus." Wispy bras draped over the backs of his kitchen chairs, tiny stretch-bikinis drying on the doorknobs. Domestic bliss—all false. No one was ever going to be as important to her as her music.

The phone in the bedroom began to ring. He knew it was going to be Denise, cancelling.

"Did I get you at a bad time?" Carol said.

"I was just waiting for you to get home."

"I didn't run."

"How come?"

"Oh, I don't know. I just wanted to . . . talk."

"Okay."

He sat down on the bed and worked his right foot through the pant leg. She'd be sitting on the edge of her bed too, legs stuck out straight, ankles crossed. She'd be wearing her kelly green running shorts. No, she'd just said she hadn't gone. Where was his patience? He couldn't focus. He stuck his other foot through.

"What's the matter?" he asked.

"Oh . . ." She gave a little groan. "I know I shouldn't say this, but . . . I trust you."

"You'd damn well better." He tucked the receiver under his chin, stood up, got the jeans yanked up, zipped. Why didn't she know not to say such things? But of course she did; she must feel very shaky.

"It's just that I really do love you."

"I'm glad." He couldn't say it: "I love you too." Not on demand, not in this mood. He closed his eyes, trying to see her the way she looked when he knew he loved her, when her cheeks were flushed and her hair was loose. He thought he heard a car pull up.

"Marty?"

The Venetian blind was closed. He said, "Yes?" rather loudly.

"You don't want to talk right now, do you?"

"I'm distracted. I'd better call you back."

By stretching, he managed to reach the blind. A sleek silver station wagon was parked in his driveway, and Denise was already getting out. She was wearing a long blue shirt—one of his. She'd swiped it that time—for rags, he'd thought. The way it hung halfway down her thighs, you'd think it was all she had on.

He said, "Let me call you when I get home."

"I probably won't be here."

"No?"

She was getting something out of the rear of the car. When she reached in, the shirt rode up, and he felt an adolescent twinge of disappointment, because of course she was wearing shorts. She hoisted a familiar duffel bag to her shoulder and started across the lawn.

I'm going to take John to 'Return of the Jedi.'"

"Again?" Martin said.

Carol laughed. "I told him this was the very last time."

Her hair was longer—down to her shoulders. Curlier, the way it always was in the summer. Lighter, a brighter blond.

"We might take Brian."

He dropped the slats. "Well," he said, "have fun." And then, because he wasn't giving her what she wanted, and she was so good and he was so rotten, he said, in a burst of remorse, "I do love you" and couldn't tell—was he lying? All he knew was, he felt pissed at Denise for some reason. He couldn't even count on her to be late.

So, no, he wasn't very welcoming. "Why," he said, "are you wearing that shirt?"

She slung the duffel bag down from her shoulder. "Everything I own is in here."

"You've never heard of laundromats?"

She stared up at him, her eyes cool and blue. "Why're you being so awful?"

He was being awful—that was a fact. He stepped back from the doorway. "Would you like to come in?"

"Five minutes ago, I would've said yes."

"Oh, come on."

She left the laundry on the doorstep. "Looks just the same."

"Not for long. I'm buying a house."

"Oh?" she said, turning around.

But this was not the way he wanted to tell her. Start over. "I don't suppose you want any coffee."

"I don't suppose you've got any orange juice."

She went ahead of him into the kitchen and opened the refrigerator while he was still thinking. Her rubber thongs left grass clumps on his carpet; there were blades of grass between her toes.

She sniffed the carton of orange juice. "Is this okay to drink?"

He nodded. "Your car—it's a Volvo?"

"Yep."

And him with his miserable Valiant. Lucky if it got them to the Cape and back. In his brain an idea was forming.

"I screwed up," she was saying; she leaned against the counter, her foot against the cupboard behind her. "I measured wrong. The Dowd's too long. I can't get it in unless it's upside-down . . ." She took a swig of juice from the carton.

What was she saying? What did she mean?

". . . plus I have to leave the tailgate open."

"I want to go look at your car," he said.

"I'm going to trade it in on a van." She came out with him.

Oh, but it was an elegant car. Gray interior, bucket seats— leather? Politely he asked, "When did you get it?"

"Just before I went to Vancouver."

Over eight thousand miles on the odometer. She hadn't driven out by herself, he could bet.

"I had to take the little Italian."

"Who's that?" he said. "What little Italian?"

"Jesus, I just told you the Dowd wouldn't fit. I would've had to put the passenger seat forward, and then I couldn't have taken Marge."

Marge. Who was Marge? The gamba player, she of the ample rear. You could carry a harpsichord; the back seat must fold forward. He could get both the desk and the book case in here.

"Tell you what," he said. "I'll make you a deal."

"You don't have to tell me. I already know. I can do my laundry if we take my car."

"When we get back," he said. "Not now."

～

But they had never had any luck on trips. He shifted down—third, second; the southbound traffic had come to a halt again. A lung-corroding exhaust spewed from the blue station wagon stopped ahead of them. VW 412—kids loved them. The brother of that friend of John's had one.

Cars were stopped for as far as he could see, while the northbound traffic sped along. If only he weren't in the middle lane, he'd be tempted to turn around on the median—get a ticket; it would be worth it. Twenty minutes of start and stop, and they hadn't even gotten past Dedham. Rush-hour traffic—he just hadn't thought. He shifted into neutral, put the brake on. The sun was fierce, glinting off the silvery hood, off the chrome of the cars ahead. His sunglasses were in the Valiant, naturally.

"Could you please close your window?" She was waving her rubber thong in the air, trying to disperse the smoke. Her sunglasses made her look like Darth Vader, like somebody who ought to be riding with bikers.

He pushed the button that closed the window.

"Thank you." She reached into the paper sack on her lap. Carrots. Carol would have brought a picnic lunch; they were taking a picnic to the Esplanade. Taking a picnic, taking John. That was what he'd be doing tomorrow.

"What's with these carrots? Some new addiction?"

"It helps you cut down on your smoking. You didn't even notice I'd quit, you rat."

"Why, lovey!" he said, and could feel himself flush. But she didn't seem to notice.

"You want one?"

"No, thanks." Great unpeeled things—unwashed too, by the looks of them. She was picking off some kind of threadlike roots.

The kids in the VW had turned their engine off. Bare feet stuck out of every window. He started to lower his again; the blare of rock came in.

"Please!" she said, indistinctly. Her munching was going to drive him crazy.

"How about if we turn on the radio?"

They both reached, and her hand brushed his; she drew back. So they mustn't touch? Guitar music, sounding strangely muted, filtered in over the tick of the engine. The fidelity ought to be a lot better, if this was the radio he'd given her. Blaupunkt, it said, very small, on the dial. He couldn't see any name on the speakers.

"I've really been enjoying the radio," she said, rather stiffly, as if she felt as constrained as he did.

"What kind of speakers are these?"

"I forget."

"So where did you get them?"

"Why?"

"Well, did you listen to them before you bought them?"

She turned to look at him. "How could I?"

"You have the guy switch back and forth . . ." Why was he explaining, why was he bothering? If she didn't mind how the radio sounded . . . Give her a decent radio, she had to get cheap speakers. Or did some other good friend give her the speakers?

"They were in a box," Denise said, and coughed. A speck of carrot landed on his jeans. "My God," she said, and began to laugh. A year ago, she would have wiped the carrot off, smoothed it off, caressed his prick through his pants, maybe even unzipped him. "How disgusting," she said. Three months. He flicked the carrot to the floor. The cars were starting up. They crept forward twenty feet and stopped.

". . . on the clavichord," the announcer said, an unfamiliar voice. Denise said, "Lurtsema must be on vacation."

As they'd all like to be, Martin thought. Next year damned if he would teach summer school. Next year? He'd probably be working two jobs, teaching and working nights as a programmer.

They were devoting the hour to baroque keyboard music, the announcer said. Martin almost said, "Oh, no, you don't." He pushed a button on the right, got country-western. "Where's CRB?"

"Oh, come on. I want to see what they're playing." She changed the station back.

"Carl Philipp Emanuel Bach," the announcer was saying. And there was his old enemy, his personal enemy: the harpsichord, her instrument, sounding as it always did—like the copulation of skeletons, somebody said.

"What's that quotation—how does it go? You know—the one about skeletons?"

"Shhh! I want to hear who's playing."

She would be able to tell just from listening. She was leaning close to the radio, as if that were where the sound came from.

"I think it's Kipnis," she said, after a moment. She sat back. "So what was it you wanted to know?"

He couldn't remember. The cars were inching forward again. Maybe all this traffic was going to the Cape—not rush-hour traffic. Labor Day traffic. Why hadn't he thought of this?

"Igor Kipnis," the announcer said. Denise said:

"Ha!"

Martin said, "Oh, him." Was that the harpsichordist whose concert he'd dozed through? No, someone else, someone she'd studied with. Slept through a concert—he couldn't help it. The instrument was so faint and boring. Snored, she said. She should be glad he hadn't coughed. If only she had played an instrument he liked—the piano, say, or perhaps the cello, something with a little warmth, anyway an instrument which, if you had to tune it yourself, only had four strings, not a hundred and eighty-three of them. Harpsichords were art objects, he could remember telling her, holding forth as they stood outside in the heat, on the steps of Jordan Hall, where he'd first encountered her—in May, over a year ago now. She was wearing a blue sleeveless dress. She was waving her arm, calling, "Ticket, ticket." He had gazed up into her smooth, pale armpit, and he had bought her extra ticket. Harpsichords, he said, were not musical instruments. Yes, he admired the way they looked, but that was to be taken in by appearances. "The fact remains," she said, "you slept."

"Jean-Philippe Rameau," the announcer said. Surely she wasn't going to make him listen to any more. He reached for the button.

"Wait a minute. I'm going to play this in October."

She could hear it any time she wanted. She probably had a tape. He hadn't brought her along so she could shush him. Why had he brought her—for company? But alone was what he always felt with her.

"You may play with a group," he'd shouted, at the beach, "but you're never going to be anything but a fucking soloist." No one close enough to hear him. What did she want him for? Nothing but sex—and only when *she* wanted it, which was actually quite a lot. "Control-freak—you want to call all the shots." "Oh?" she said, and he yelled at her again: "You make me feel used and degraded. I don't even think you're human." Again she said, "Oh?" Then she turned and sauntered away, and he thought he had never felt so abandoned by anyone.

He could see flares in the road ahead. He said, "There must've been an accident."

No response. She was sitting absolutely still. Tuned out, didn't hear him. She had done so literally: tuned him out—one hundred and eighty-three strings. Never knew when he got up from the sofa, never even looked around. He was at the door when she said, "There! Sorry it took so long." Wimp that he was, he came back and sat down, and she never knew, still didn't know, how close he had come to leaving. Just started to play. Rameau then, too. It was for this thin, chilly sound that she had forgotten him.

"I'm going to get married," he said. She said nothing. He looked at her profile. Not a quiver. "I'm going to be a father again."

The three lanes were being funneled into two. The state police were waving the cars to get over; firemen were hosing down the highway, and there, pointing down the grassy slope, was a red pick-up truck with its side dented in. But no ambulance, no second car. Perhaps it had been towed away.

Mozart, the announcer said: the A minor sonata, the Rondo, played this time on the fortepiano.

"Why don't you get one of those," Martin said, "seeing as how you've already got a virginal and a clavichord and a Volvo."

"I've got one on order," she said, "but I won't be getting it for a year or so." She rolled her window down and dropped what was left of the carrot out. "It doesn't look like anybody was hurt."

No blood, no bodies, nobody hurt. How would she know if anybody was hurt? They were picking up speed—second, third. The feet sticking out of the VW had retracted. He shifted into fourth. "Look . . ." he said. It had been a bad idea; they shouldn't be going to the Cape together. "Listen . . ." he said, but she had put her feet up against the glove compartment, and now she crossed her right foot over and with her big toe changed the station. For things like that he had loved her.

"Denny . . ." he said.

"There's a hedgehog."

"Groundhog."

A Norwood exit was coming up. He could get off, turn around. Take her home. Write her a letter.

The radio was silent, and so was Denise. He needed to get that desk. If he didn't go today, he'd be going with Carol and John, on the weekend, when the traffic was just as bad. No—it was better to go today. Why couldn't two such clever people make it?

Unearthly sound, ethereal whine. It was that ad for the glass harmonica. Invented by Benjamin Franklin, the announcer said, and now they were being made by a firm in Waltham. Their cost was comparable to the modern harpsichord's.

"That's next," he almost said, though he knew nothing about it, not even what it looked like or how you played it. He imagined vials, tubes, glasses of crystal, filled, it might be, with some kind of liquid—spirits of something, a tincture, ether.

"Listen, Denny," he said, "I have to talk to you. I've got something I have to tell you."

But she was receding from him, actually receding, lowering the back of her seat. All that was left of her was her feet, her legs, the fringe of her shorts.

"Okay," he heard, from somewhere behind him, "tell me who you're marrying."

Landmarks

All summer long and for part of the spring and fall too, Meg would leave the kitchen door open for Sylvia, though sometimes, when she was trying to fix breakfast or dinner and didn't want to be tripping over a full-grown Canada goose, she closed the door and made Sylvia stay outside no matter how Sylvia carried on; she had a piercing and indignant honk. Or if Matt was stomping around upstairs, getting up late, as usual, because it was the weekend or summer and he had not yet managed to find himself a job, which of course he should have done in the spring like all the other kids, Meg shooed Sylvia out, saying, "Go mingle with your own kind."

But Sylvia must have been imprinted as a gosling with a bony red-haired woman, because she paid zero attention to Sylvester, who was supposed to be her mate, and it was Meg whom she followed around, not twelve-year-old Marilyn, never mind how many lettuce leaves Marilyn tried to entice her with, though when Marilyn held out clumps of grass, Sylvia would amble over, mistrustfully pausing on each webbed, dark-as-charcoal foot, and snatch the grass clump, dirt and all. She would walk off, shaking the grass clump the way Meg had once seen her shake a half-grown mallard duck that had been swimming in the wrong wading pool: grabbed it by the neck; that duck never was the same again but lurched around forever after with its head at an odd angle and a limp. "Maybe," Meg said, "if you squatted down and held out just a few blades . . ." But Sylvia ignored that offering altogether, turning her white under-tail on

Marilyn to nip blades of grass so short Meg couldn't even see them from the doorway; the kitchen garden was mostly dirt, hardly any lawn left or anything else, just a border of yellow chrysanthemums along the stone wall and a few daffodils in spring. Marilyn must have brought the clumps of grass from out in front where Jonathan was digging up half the lawn for a vegetable patch. "Did I ever tell you," Meg heard her say, years later, to the boy she was going with then—Ron, Don, whatever his name was—"about being rejected by a goose?" And Meg could see poor Marilyn, in her plump phase—it was just before she started her adolescent growth spurt; she was eventually to be taller than Meg, nearly as tall as Jonathan—squatting there in her too-tight blue shorts, her dark hair falling in a tangle around her plump, sullen face. The little guilty thrill—Meg remembered that too: Sylvia was *her* goose, preferred her. Or did that feeling come later? "My mother," Meg also heard Marilyn say, "was a little peculiar. I mean, she let this goose, for Christ's sake, have the run of the house. It used to bug the hell out of my father."

But not always, not in the beginning, Meg thought. There were those years—two, maybe three—when Jonathan was working at home. Up at five, by five-thirty at the typewriter: technical stuff she didn't understand. By one or one-thirty he'd be in the garden: weeding his bok choy, tying up his snow peas, edging the flower beds where his violets grew. She could remember his bringing her a violet, white with tiny purple speckles; it was like the blue spatter-ware she collected. His purple violets and his white ones had hybridized. Had she ever seen anything like that? No. The next spring he was weeding carefully around the violet's seedlings, hoping they would breed true, and they did. So that by now she had quite a colony of them out there, more each year, though she had quit digging them out of the lawn, stopped trying to put them back where they belonged.

Digging in the earth. She could see him as clearly as she could see Marilyn: bare tanned back, arms getting stronger, sunlight giving a sheen to his short black hair. Could see him, all sweaty, building the first duck house, out there with Matt: Hold this, hand me that. And Matt—pale, freckled face getting sunburned; he wanted to be indoors building rockets. He would have been maybe thirteen and a half.

But they needed the duck house and one for the geese. Raccoons had discovered the ducks; a family of them came at sundown. She knew when they came—all the ducks would be quacking; perhaps she should not have clipped their wings. So far, she had gotten out there in time. They were not raising ducks, Jonathan said, for raccoons.

They were raising them for the eggs, the best eggs in the world: big golden yolks, clear whites. Four Pekin ducks meant four eggs a day. But it seemed a kind of crime to keep taking the eggs, keep the ducks laying until their bills were pale amber, their feet whitish yellow. Four virginal matrons—they should have a drake. "Just asking for trouble," Jonathan said. But that wasn't where the trouble lay.

It was seeing all those ducks in the young man's yard, all those different kinds: the white call ducks and the mallard look-alikes, miniature; she bought a pair of each. Domestic mallards: a pair of those too. Sylvester: offspring of geese the young man had raised. Then Sylvia: he got her from somewhere else. So that somehow one trip to buy a Pekin drake turned into an ongoing thing, like shopping. Eleven ducks instead of four. Eleven ducks plus two geese.

In the spring the ducks interbred, canny about where they hid their nests. Then there were black ducks mottled white and white ducks spotted black—twenty-eight ducks but still only two geese. More houses were needed, at least two, but Jonathan was out of his building phase; she didn't realize that until he threw the hammer across the yard. Then she said the first thing that came to mind: "Aren't you ashamed! You could've hit a duck in the head." And he yelled, "I wish I had."

But in the beginning: a common enterprise. What did Marilyn know of their leisurely days? They might spend a rainy afternoon in bed. Or a sunny one, and he'd say, "Aren't we naughty," setting the alarm so they would be up and acting normal by three o'clock, when the school bus brought the kids home. Sometimes, though, Jonathan couldn't wake up, and once Marilyn asked, "Is Dad sick?" When he came downstairs, he was in such a stupor he said he must have sunstroke; it had rained all afternoon. That was sunstroke from this morning, Meg was quick to explain, but Marilyn said, "It was cloudy at school." Matt was who finally said, "Marilyn, drop it." By then Jonathan had gone outdoors. He stayed out there, digging up chrysanthemums, until supper was ready. A very private man.

But Marilyn remembered how angry he had looked—having to move all those plants out to the front, so Sylvia wouldn't eat the blooms. Which she never did, just tweaked them off one by one as if they were targets and she perfecting her aim; she could catch a gnat in mid-air. And only once, when Meg was late clipping her wings, did she fly into the front yard and tear up the lettuce Jonathan had so carefully tended. She was not "always" doing that; she had all the lettuce she could want. Meg got it from the supermarket—slatted, lidded crates full of discarded leaves. No, Sylvia was just trying her wings. Or perhaps she wanted the grass. Jonathan's lawn was the best on the street, a perfect lawn without one weed.

"Goose shit everywhere," he cried, that time. He'd be damned if he'd hose it into the flower beds. Nothing would serve but that Meg must come pick it up: dark green turds, solid with grass, not watery like the stuff Sylvia squirted in the house. She did that when she got over-excited; it was something about television, male voices. She would set out for the living room as if she were drawn, her dry feet plicking across the dining room floorboards. Jonathan himself peeled back the rug so Sylvia could stand there and watch. She honked at the newscaster; Jonathan would laugh. Her neck was straight as a stalk. "A remarkable goose," he said, and it was only later on that he used to watch the news upstairs. He did that because he kept his sherry in the bedroom, puritanical about not having liquor around. They had tried Sylvia on nature programs, but she couldn't care less, would turn around and leave; she had a stately, jerky walk. "Out," Meg would say. "Go make Sylvester shut up." The panicked honking would die down. But Sylvia did not so much as greet him. Did she even know she was a goose?

She knew, when the wild geese flew over, calling back and forth in the spring and in the fall. They landed sometimes in the field behind the duck yard. In the spring it was pairs; they mated for life.

Sylvia and Sylvester had never mated at all, so far as Meg knew; and she had watched. She ran the hose at full force into the yellow wading pool, hoping the rushing water might remind him of what he surely must know. But all he did was run around the yard, running lopsided because his right wing was pinioned. He ran through the pool, dislodging the hose. "He's retarded," Matt said. Maybe he was. Sylvia fled to the kitchen garden. Three years old, and she had never laid an egg.

"Are you sure she's a she?" Jonathan asked.

All Meg had was the young man's word. He had sexed both geese when they were young, examining the cloaca; you turned the goose upside down. But she was not going to try that with a goose that was grown. It was all she could do to hold Sylvia on her lap while trimming those long flight feathers. The three toenails on each foot were like claws; they could rip through aprons and polyester pants; they could rip skin. And Sylvia would be pinching Meg's forearm with her bill, leaving bruises. "Damn it, Sylvia, it's for your own good," Meg would tell her, tell herself, as Sylvia flew-ran out of the kitchen, stampeding the ducks clustered by the doorway. White down floated in the air; watery greenness streaked the linoleum and Meg's arms. Marilyn had a real knack for wandering in about then. She didn't need to say anything, but she did: "Gross." Once—Meg could not have been more surprised—she went over and got the roll of paper towels. Without commenting, she started to wipe up, and Meg, touched, thought: How adult. Another time, she asked—sincerely, Meg was sure, "Wouldn't it be better if she flew away?"

Migratory instinct must have been what made Sylvia start out on foot. Sylvester, though he would not come into the house, would follow her through an open gate, down three stone steps, and along the driveway to the road. The neighbor from across the street came herding them back; Meg saw them go by the kitchen window, and that was the first she knew. The geese had been walking smack down the middle of the street. Didn't Meg hear all the traffic come to a stop? The driver of the school bus had put his red flag out, put on his flashing red lights, made all the cars sit there and wait. That Matt. What call did he have to be so defiant when, after school, she lectured him about the gate, really hit into him the way she hadn't for a long, long time. Consequences, she said. Responsibilities. "Everybody on the bus knew those were your geese," he cried, and for a moment she almost thought he might burst into tears, though he was nearly sixteen. She didn't know who was more surly these days—he or Marilyn.

Probably it was Jonathan. The free-lance work wasn't coming his way. Weeks of interviews brought nothing; in the winter he found a job. "Gone captive" was the way he put it; he worked long hours. It was up to Meg to haul in the bales of nesting straw and the hundred pound bags of duck pellets and cracked corn; she divided them into bags of fifty pounds. Matt showed no inclination to help, and she had her pride, would not ask him. He should have been able to think of it himself. In the spring she sold the Pekin eggs to the organic farm up the street and then Easter ducks in batches of six, but the sales did not begin to pay for the feed. If only the geese would reproduce.

They did not. She would sit in the doorway of their house, feeling the warmth of the rotting straw rising behind her, getting heavy-eyed from so many ducks dozing at her feet, their bills tucked under their wings. It would take a plane flying overhead to wake her up, not that she heard it, but something alerted the ducks; they started out of their sleep just as if the plane had been a hawk, and every head tilted, one eye looking skyward. Only the geese were not disturbed, but nothing disturbed them—not the mating madness of the randy drakes, not the squawking of the broody ducks. "What is the matter with you?" she asked them, because something must be. The goslings would have brought twenty-five dollars apiece.

The young man asked her to tend his incubator for him; he was going to school now, working nights. He brought the incubator and twelve heavy goose eggs, Emden and Toulouse. It felt wrong to be taking his ten dollars just for turning the eggs in the morning and the evening, making sure the temperature stayed right, smoothing water over the thick, hard shells. On the lid of the incubator he had etched a cross and below that: BLESS THIS HATCH. She did not realize those scratches and lines were letters until the twenty-eight days were nearly up.

The goslings had a hoarse, wheeping cry. They had big naked-looking eyes and long necks. "There," Meg said, when Sylvia came in to see them, "if you'd done things right, you could've had some of these." But Sylvia snaked her head into the carton, hissing. In just a few minutes every gosling would have been in worse condition than the crippled duck, so Meg took the carton into the living room and set it on the hearth.

"Is this necessary?" Jonathan asked; he was lying on the couch. "Did it ever occur to you to keep that goose outside, where she belongs?"

But that was not the Jonathan she knew, speaking. That was Jonathan after three glasses of sherry, and anyway it was the children who did most of the complaining. They said the goslings stank, but what could you expect? They walked through their mash; they tipped over their water. She had to keep finding new and bigger cartons. When everybody was gone, she let them run loose in the kitchen for a little while. They did not follow her; they were not imprinted unless it was with each other. The young man was late fetching them; he gave her an extra five dollars. She took the money in to Jonathan, her small contribution, but he looked at her with something so close to contempt you would have thought she had earned it by unsavory means.

He did not have time for the vegetables anymore, and Meg did not have his green thumb. What flourished was the duck straw she used for mulch; it seeded itself and came up wild oats. By the end of the summer, the Pekins had stopped laying; only the mallards and the call ducks went on and on, laying small green eggs with an off-taste like onions, a strong flavor. "They taste," Marilyn said, "like worms." And she also said—but this was later, "When I was sixteen, my idea of luxury was a chicken egg for breakfast." Such nonsense, Meg could not help thinking. At sixteen Marilyn was no longer eating breakfast; if you were going to be tall, then you had better be thin. As for Matt, eggs of any kind gave him an eczema. Jonathan hardly ever ate at home by then.

He left, the summer before Marilyn went off to college. He had done his duty as he saw it, or so he said: supported a wife and two children "and God knows how many ducks." He did not mention the geese. He would continue to help Meg until she could support herself. It was time, he said, she stood on her own two feet. Matt, home from college, had no comment; he had always been a silent child. But Marilyn said, "How can you be so surprised?" She had seen it coming for years, ever since Meg put the goslings in the living room.

But Meg really had not had an inkling. Those rainy afternoons did not seem so long ago, six or seven years; she had thought they would return.

The drug store hired her as counter help; the available shift was one to eight. By the time she got home, it was already dark. She had to feed the ducks by flashlight.

Raccoons came again. Meg no longer kept track, but she could tell that every night there were fewer ducks. She asked the neighbor across the street if her son would like a job; but sometimes he played late at a friend's, sometimes he just forgot. And the geese were too much for him, Meg guessed. They were gentle, not fierce like other geese but willful; if you chased them, they wouldn't go in.

And so one night she found Sylvia standing by herself. "Where is he?" Meg asked, playing the flashlight around. The ducks came to their wire doors and quacked, but all Sylvia could do was honk. It had been raining; the duck yard was mud. The tufts of gray feathers by the fence were wet.

She could see how it must have been—the geese asleep together in their house. The door was open, the raccoon crept in. The rain must have drowned out any rustling. One quick bite through the neck, and that was lt. She bad not thought a raccoon would attack so large a creature as a goose.

But he was not so large; he looked quite small, lying there just the other side of the fence. One leg was chewed off, the wilted foot still attached. The thigh meat was gone and part of the breast.

She picked him up by his remaining leg and hurled what was left of him into the field, his body whishing through the air as if in flight. Then a landing so soft it wasn't a thud, just an object falling into tall sodden grass.

"You have to go in," she told Sylvia, raising her arms, but Sylvia wouldn't go near her house. She shied and ran around the yard; perhaps she smelled the blood. "Well, come on, then," Meg said, leading the way, and: "Come on, you fool goose," when Sylvia wouldn't come, and, "Fool, fool," bitterly to herself, when the flashlight hurtled through the dark and went out. It needed no great aim to hit a stone wall.

She stood at the sink, washing off the dirt. The cold ache in her fingers seemed right. If only she hadn't thrown out Jonathan's sherry—she had never liked it; it would be like medicine. Go back out into the muck and the dark? She closed her eyes: Not that much of a fool. Sylvia would have to come of her own accord. Meg stood in the doorway and called.

There was no answering honk. In the heavy air her voice seemed to die. Lettuce, she thought, and then, the TV, and she went in and turned it on. Her own muddy shoeprints led back to the kitchen; she strewed the bits of lettuce among them. All she could do. She sat down to wait; she used to sit there to clip the wings.

The dim gray breast was what she saw first, then the dark line where Sylvia's neck began, the twiglike legs walking into the light, and at last the dark goose shape.

"Now, get in here," she tried to say but could not. Sylvia hopped in as she always did, both feet landing at the same time.

She headed for the lettuce as if nothing were wrong. "Now, you see," Meg said, closing the door, "you're going to have to find a new home."

But that was not Sylvia's job; it was Meg's. She called the young man whose goslings she had hatched all those years ago, not that many. He had married, his mother said, and moved to upstate New York. She knew no one who wanted ducks and geese; she certainly did not want them herself. But try the Audubon sanctuary, she said; and in the morning Meg did.

"How many?" the Audubon woman said. Her incredulous laugh floated over the phone.

"Fifteen," Meg repeated. She had just counted. "And one Canada goose, a female." She could hear people talking. Someone said, "If we did that for everyone . . ."

"All right," the woman said, at last. They would take the ducks for their domestic pond. There was a separate pond for wild geese. Meg almost said, "But she isn't wild."

None of the lettuce crates were big enough for a goose. She loaded the ducks into the car, one crate on the front seat, one on the floor. The other two had to go in back with Sylvia. Meg carried her out, wrapped in a beach towel. When, years later, she heard, "My mother was a little peculiar," she thought: Yes, and if you only knew. But Sylvia rode very well back there, first standing on the seat, then huddled down. She was panting, the way geese did when they were scared.

A young woman in jeans unloaded the ducks. She glanced at Sylvia and said, "We'd better drive down."

Chain-link fencing enclosed the pond. Geese were in the water and standing on the shore. In the winter, the young woman explained, a lot of these flew south but some stayed. Others flew in from the north. She hopped out of the car. "We'll let her wings grow." And then, because Meg was just standing there, she said, "Here, I'll get her." She handed Meg the key to the gate's padlock, and when Meg turned around, she had Sylvia at arm's length, dangling from a pinch-grip on the upper wings. "You can open the gate." She tossed Sylvia inside, shut the gate herself, snapped the padlock. "We keep the pond open all winter."

But no shelter, Meg thought; there was no shelter, and Sylvia had never been in snow except by choice.

Sylvia stood alone by the fence. The geese came slowly from the water and converged.

"They're a little xenophobic at first," the young woman warned.

The geese closed in with lowered heads. Some of them had broken wings. Meg couldn't watch; she thought: You watch. A bedraggled goose had Sylvia by the breast, gray feathers in its bill when she broke free.

"But pretty soon they'll leave her alone. You can come visit."

"Yes," Meg said.

She went once, then not again. She was looking for a goose with shorter wings. So many geese, and they all looked alike, except for the ones with the injured wings. Sylvia could be one of them. It was December; her wings would have grown.

Not enough for her to fly south; Meg thought, when snow lay deep on the ground. But spring came at last and, with it, the wild geese, flying in pairs over the house.

When Meg heard them honking overhead, she would go to the kitchen doorway and watch, half-expecting a pair to land, though the wading pools were gone now, the duck houses torn down. She thought that there must be some permanent landmark—the stone wall, features of the land—something that a goose would recognize as home as readily from the air as from the ground.

In the Dark

The first time I saw Roger, he was standing in the doorway, just standing there, gripping an extra-large suitcase. I keep thinking he was wearing dark glasses, but he couldn't have been; he arrived at dusk. He did wear glasses—but clear and horn-rimmed. He had on a three-piece business suit. The suit was the same sandy brown as his hair, about the color of a dead Boston fern. The rest of us were in sweat pants or jeans. "Wear comfortable clothes," our instructions had said. We were starting a weekend for the divorced and separated—fifteen of us, now that Roger was here.

"So that's everybody," Chuck said, from the sign-in table. "Run upstairs and find a room. You can fill out your name tag when you come back down." He had told all of us the same thing, but when he spoke to Roger he sounded impatient. Maybe that was just because Roger was late.

Without saying anything, Roger turned and sprinted up the stairs, his suitcase banging against the risers.

We sat there, waiting for him, nobody talking. Chuck was fingering his scraggly red beard. The wall clock ticked—five minutes, ten. Then Helen, my roommate for the weekend, said suddenly, "You think he's unpacking?" and everybody laughed. Another woman said, "He's probably changing his clothes." But when, at last, Roger came charging downstairs again, he was still in that same tan suit.

"We're just using first names," Chuck told him, shortly. He clapped his hands. "Let's move down to the mats."

We scrambled down to the floor, relieved to be doing something—anything—after all the waiting.

Helen assumed the lotus position. People in the lotus position make me want to say, "Show off!" but Helen was a very fit-looking lady in her fifties, and I guess if she wanted to show off, she was entitled. The rest of us settled for sitting cross-legged—all but Roger, who couldn't seem to do it. Maybe his pant legs were too tight, or maybe his knees weren't flexible enough. He kept looking around, from one person to the next, and I don't think it helped that his gaze fixed on Helen.

"Why don't you take off your shoes?" Chuck suggested.

Roger looked flustered but said, "Good idea!" We all watched him take off his shoes. Then he took one leg in each hand and managed to get the ankles crossed. I wanted to say, "Oh, Jesus, just sit any way you can," but you could see that he wanted to do it right. His glasses started to slide down his nose. With his forefinger he pushed them up. When he leaned forward, they slid again. "On this weekend," Chuck was saying, "we're going to be talking about something called separation anxiety." All I could think about was the anxiety Roger was causing me. He was sitting with his arms clamped around his shins; his glasses were at the end of his long, thin nose, and a lock of hair had fallen over his eyes.

Chuck told us to form groups of three and tell each other who we were. Roger, after he'd had such trouble getting more or less comfortable, didn't look like he intended to move.

"Shall we do a good deed?" I said, to Helen, because no one was sitting down with him.

"If we must," she said, none too happily. We went over to Roger. "How about we're your group?"

He said he'd be honored. As if mesmerized, he watched Helen weaving her feet up over her thighs.

"I don't see how you can do that."

She laughed. "I teach yoga. Shall I keep going—age before beauty?" She took a deep breath. "I'm recently divorced, I live in Newton, both my kids are in college . . ."

"I used to live in Newton," Roger said. He began to talk about the excellent school system.

"Is this what we're supposed to be doing?" Helen asked.

"Rosemary," he said, "where do you live?"

"Wayland."

"Do you ever shop at Sudbury Farms?"

"Once in a blue moon," I said. "Why?"

"I might've seen you in the market. I live in Sudbury—anyway, I did. By any chance, do you know the Grays?"

"Let's stick to the subject," Helen said. "Roger, are you separated or divorced?"

His forehead squinched into a pained-looking frown. "I'm in between."

"What's between separation and divorce?"

"My wife's getting a divorce."

"So you're separated," I said, but he said, "*I'm* not separated." Helen's eyes gave an "I give up" roll. "How long have you been divorced?" I asked her.

"Six months—six months, last week." She stopped, as if hating to go on. "It's been . . . hard. I didn't know I was going to miss marriage like this. I don't mean I miss Eric—God, no—but I'd really like to be married again."

"Boy, would I ever not!" I cried. "Never!"

Roger said, "Don't ever say 'never,' Rosemary," and Helen said, "You're still so young, you don't know."

"Oh, yes I do!" I was twenty-five, old enough to have come to a couple of conclusions and decisions. For example, I'd given my best friend, Maureen, permission to call my parents in Michigan if she ever saw me getting serious about anybody again. I meant it as a sort of joke, but she said, "The kind of men you're attracted to, it'll save time if I call your folks right now!" We had something of a falling out over that remark but made up, after a while, as usual.

"You're both very fine women," Roger said, reprovingly. I asked if he had any children. He said, "One."

"Boy or girl?"

"A girl."

"How old?"

"Eleven—no, ten. Shelly's still ten."

Helen said, "I suppose she lives with her mother."

"She'll be eleven, just before Christmas—we were still living in Worcester, we had Christmas in Worcester, we didn't move to Newton till January of '74, but then Brenda didn't like the house, so I built the house in Sudbury, but if you subtract '73 from '84, it looks like she's eleven."

We were all silent for a moment. Then I asked, "Where does Shelley live now?"

"Sudbury."

"And where do you live?"

"Connecticut—Hartford. Do you know Hartford?"

"Not really."

"You'd take the Mass Pike to Route 86 . . ."

"I do know where it is," I said.

"I don't like cities," he said. "I like towns." He began to talk about cities versus towns. A few minutes later Chuck called us back to the group.

"That couldn't have been what we were supposed to be doing," Helen muttered. She lowered herself to the mat like a dancer. "Trying to talk to that man's like pulling teeth—and every damn one of them a molar."

"Roger," Chuck was saying, after no more than an hour, "I'm sorry but I can't let this go on. I keep saying I want to hear about you, and you tell me about some engineer at work. You've told us about three different neighbors. Now, are these neighbors you? Is this engineer you?"

"No," Roger said, as if baffled.

"All right, then I don't want to hear about them. I don't want to hear any more unless it's about yourself."

Roger stared at the floor just in front of him. He said nothing else for the rest of the evening.

I was afraid he was going to become a sort of scapegoat and said as much to Helen, after lights-out. We were both trying to get comfortable in our cots. The accommodations in this place, at one time an abbey, were what I would call Spartan at best. The walls didn't extend to the ceiling, and instead of a door, there was a coarse, heavy curtain. So we couldn't talk; we had to whisper. The one high window had a grille of bars—for what purpose I couldn't imagine.

"He brings it on himself," Helen hissed. "I've no sympathy whatsoever, I just find him annoying,"

"I feel kind of sorry for him," I admitted.

"Oh, my dear, you're not a rescuer!"

"No, no, definitely not."

"Thank heaven," she said, and wished me good night. But I kept thinking about Roger until I finally fell asleep.

At breakfast, there he was again, sitting across from us at the refectory table. He was wearing a long-sleeved powder-blue shirt and jeans that were brand-new—dark and stiff. (I'd noticed, though, as he walked into the room, that they fit him quite well; he was narrow-hipped and slim.) But half listening to him talk ("Who'd like some sausage? There's a lot of bacon left"), made me think of Bobby, my ex, who also used to wake up talking non-stop, to the point where it felt like I was getting a brain transplant. "I can't pay attention to you yet," I tried to tell him, but he never got it through his head. The only way I knew to actually make him shut up was to act as if I wanted sex. He'd be out of that bed in two seconds flat, and I never knew a man who took such long showers. The thing was, sometimes I wasn't acting, so, yep, we had our irreconcilable differences.

"Rosemary," Roger said, "you aren't eating."

"That's all right, I don't eat in the morning."

"But that's bad for the system."

"Not *my* system."

"Oh," he said, "you sound like Shelley. She never wants to eat in the morning either. I keep telling her you can't go off to school on an empty stomach. I tell her, just eat one egg for Daddy." There was a fond look on his face. "How about an egg?"

"No, thank you."

"Toast?"

A triangle of toast appeared in front of me. I shook my head.

"Try it."

"Leave the girl alone!" Helen barked.

Roger almost dropped the toast in my coffee. That's what his wife always said, I thought—Brenda, he'd said her name was.

"It's okay, Roger. I eat a big lunch."

He placed the toast on his own plate, glumly.

"What we're going to do now," Chuck announced, when we'd all finished breakfast, "is going to take the next two hours."

The Blind Walk. You were supposed to choose partners— someone you felt secure with. One of you walked around wearing a blindfold; the other was the silent guardian—no talking, only touch allowed. After an hour, you traded roles.

Cowardice made me head toward Helen. I hadn't had much to do with anyone else, so far, and the truth was, I felt pretty alien; I'd never been to anything like this weekend before.

"Have you got a partner?" Roger blocked my path.

"No talking!" Chuck handed me a square of navy flannel, which, not thinking, I tried to tie onto Roger over his glasses.

"I'd better take these off."

"Roger, I don't want to have to tell you again."

"It wasn't your fault," I whispered.

The blindfoldees began groping along the walls and the furniture. Not Roger. He took off as if he could see. First the dining room, where the caterers were still wiping down the tables. He paused in the doorway for a moment. Then back down the hall, to the stairs. Up he went, without a stumble. A left turn; he stopped at each doorway, counting. I followed him into his room.

He sat down on the cot that was next to the entrance. I sat on the one just across the room, glad that this was a silent hour. I'd spent a fairly sleepless night. For the monks the cots were probably the equivalent of a hair shirt, and no doubt Helen was a really good person, but, sweet Jesus, how she snored!

Roger was taking his wallet out of his pants pocket; thumbing it open to the snapshots: a little blond girl, standing beside her bicycle; another one of her, younger, at the beach. He wanted me to take the wallet, so I did. There was a picture of him, smiling, looking happy, with a scared-looking two-year-old astride his shoulders. No current pictures of Shelley, no pictures of Brenda.

Below the blindfold, his mouth looked sad. He was leaning against the wall like a casualty or a prisoner; sunlight coming in through the high, barred window made stripes of shadow across his face. I got up and put the wallet in his hand and then, on impulse, touched his cheek.

It made him smile. He had a mouth that I liked—lips not too full but not thin like Bobby's. A kissable mouth. I think mouths tell a lot, and I was determined to avoid any man with a mouth like Bobby's. What are you supposed to do with a husband who won't kiss you, who doesn't want to, who has, in fact, an aversion? "What's the matter with me?" I shrieked at Maureen. "Have I got the world's worst case of halitosis or what?" I couldn't understand it; he hadn't been like that before we got married. "It's not you, it's him," she used to insist, because I was getting a real case of self-disgust. But I didn't believe her; it had to be me. Something about me turned him off. When I asked him if he was gay, he said no, he just didn't like saliva. It seemed to me we could work around that. But finally he said, "It's like you've turned into my sister." Not that he had one—a sister, I mean.

I sure as hell didn't want to have to rehash all this with a bunch of strangers; it was bad enough trying to tell it to the marriage counselor we went to. And it seemed to me that I'd thought about it enough. But according to Maureen, I was too cured. I was supposed to be grieving, not numb. I was supposed to feel abandoned even though I was the one who'd left. What total crap,

I told her, but she said, "Please—do it for me. You've got to work through your feelings, all you're doing is repressing them. Plus you've got to get it through your head—damaged men aren't safe. *Hear* me?"

So, here I was, sitting on a cot in bored silence, wishing I were home asleep. "Self-discovery and personal growth"—that was what the flyer had promised. Jargon, I said. To Maureen, normal speech, but she was secretary to a pair of shrinks.

At last we heard the gong. Roger stood up and held out his hand. It was a nice, dry hand, very warm.

My turn: I spent the whole hour sitting on the sofa in the Group Room, half-aware of people shuffling past. Sometimes, somebody tried to sit down, but Roger must have warded them off; he was sitting at the other end, guarding me, and, oddly, that did make me feel safe. I slipped into that reverie state you get in just before you fall asleep, and what I was thinking about was my wedding, in the Arnold Arboretum. It was May, the lilacs were in bloom. Bobby was handsome in his white Nehru jacket, and I was wearing a dress of my grandmother's—also white, from around 1900: long sleeves, fitted bodice, full skirt with bands of lace called insertion. I wore my hair in one big braid then—the same chestnut brown, my mom said, as my grandmother's. Maybe it was bad luck to wear that dress. My grandparents broke up when my mother was ten.

"Rosemary sat," Chuck said, when we talked about the Blind Walk. "Rosemary sat, and Roger ran."

But, I thought, Roger didn't run after he showed me the pictures. Chuck wasn't right about everything. For all I knew, he was wrong about everything. I didn't trust him. He seemed to like it when people cried.

So, for him the afternoon must've been a success, because everybody who said anything ended up bawling. I saw Roger dab at his eyes; it was when someone was talking about her son. Kids—at least I didn't have to worry about kids. Actually, I didn't have much to worry about at all. I enjoyed my job. I had good friends. I should have had better sense than to listen to Maureen.

At dinner we were all so quiet that Chuck said we needed a break. Helen went upstairs for a catnap. I decided to wander around by myself. I would've gone outside, except Chuck had said not to. He was probably afraid we'd all jump ship, and it's true: the thought did cross my mind. But instead I went exploring, from room to room—this was a huge building, sometimes used for retreats; stone outside, stark white walls inside, with dark, varnished woodwork like you used to see in schools. I tried to imagine it inhabited by the monks. In one room there were midget tables and chairs, like the ones in the day-care center where I worked.

By the time I got back to the Group Room, it was empty, but somebody had built a welcoming fire, and the sofa was over in front of the fireplace—just waiting for me was the way it felt. What luxury, after the rigid cot, to stretch out on my back and relax. So what if I didn't belong in this group? Tomorrow, by late afternoon, I'd be home, giving Maureen a piece of my mind. I'd certainly had enough of hers. She said I should take a lesson from Bobby—as if Bobby ever had anything to teach me. Bobby, I knew from mutual friends, was out there, dating up a storm.

I could fall asleep on such thoughts and often did. No chance of falling asleep on them now. Whoever pushed in from the veranda sent the door banging against the wall. Nobody rushed around like that except Roger. I sat up. He dropped half his armload of logs.

"I'm sorry, I'm sorry! I disturbed you." He picked up the logs, as if someone were timing him. "I was just going to build up the fire."

I lay down again and watched him. He placed a new log and then another—so carefully that not a spark was released.

"There," he said, when he was through, as if now we could have a real conversation. He stood with his back to the fire. "Are you enjoying the weekend?" I said not exactly. "But it's interesting, isn't it? I'm glad I came. I've met some very fine people." He hesitated, not looking at me. "I think *you're* a very fine person."

"Thank you," I said. Why disillusion him?

"Only, you shouldn't have said what you did about not remarrying."

"Why not—if it's true?"

"It was ugly—it sounded bitter."

"I'm not bitter. I'm just glad it's over."

"I'm not," he said. "I liked being married."

"I liked being married at first."

"But you weren't married for very long, were you?"

"It seemed like a long time," I said. "Two years."

"Fourteen," he said, "counting the separation."

"You count the separation?"

"I'm not divorced—yet." He brushed his hair back from his forehead. "Why should I be divorced? Shelley needs a father. I'm a good father. I don't understand Brenda."

I didn't doubt it a bit.

"I think I was a good husband. I mean, I tried." He half-turned, to hold his hands to the fire. "I did the laundry, I did the marketing. The minute I came home from work, I'd set the table. Brenda used to say, 'I wish you'd go read the paper,' but I was glad to help, I liked to do it. She never worked. She went back to school for her Master's, and then she threw my clothes on the lawn. Was that fair?"

"It doesn't sound very fair," I agreed.

"And now, when I come up to cut the lawn, she gets in her car and drives away."

"You come up from Hartford to cut the lawn?"

"It's when I come for Shelley. The lawn's just starting to grow."

"But it isn't your problem now," I said, "is it?"

"I don't see why not. I planted the lawn."

I didn't know what to say. Finally I asked how often he saw Shelley.

"Every other Saturday. This was my Saturday, but I'm here instead, so I said I'd come up next weekend. But Brenda said, no,

if I wanted to do something else on my Saturday, that was just too
bad, and I'd have to wait. But I'm going to stop off tomorrow on
my way home and say hello."

It sounded like a bad idea to me, but I could see there was no
point in saying so.

"You remind me of Shelley," he said, after a moment.

"You mean because I don't eat in the morning?"

"No, it's because you're little and quiet."

I puzzled over this. I am five feet, six. "But I'm not really little,
and I'm not usually this quiet."

"That doesn't matter," he said. At least I didn't remind him of
his wife. "I don't understand why your husband would leave you."

"Who said he did?"

"Then who left?"

"Well, I did."

"By mutual agreement?"

"Sort of."

He looked confused but said, "I see." Then he straightened
up and threw back his shoulders. "He must have treated you very
badly."

"Not on purpose." Poor Bobby—he didn't understand his
Rosemary-phobia any better than I did. "But I *like* you so much,"
he'd keep repeating. And I liked him too. And therapists liked the
both of us, but nothing did the least bit of good.

Roger cleared his throat. "Wayland's a nice town," he said.

"I'd like to get around to everyone tonight," Chuck began.
"I'd like to hear from the people who haven't spoken." There was
a silence so tense you could hear people breathing, and I jumped
when an ember crackled. "Helen, what're you getting for yourself
this weekend?"

Getting for yourself—how unappealing. Helen sighed. "I
guess I've got to do it." She began to talk—about her husband, her
marriage. Eventually she cried. I thought if I never cried again it
would be too soon.

"Paul," Chuck was saying.

I began to think of having an attack of some kind that would give me an excuse to leave. Or maybe I could just go up to my room and lie down. But meanwhile here was Paul, who missed his little boy.

"She took him to Oregon," he said, and stopped.

"It hurts, doesn't it?" Chuck said. Paul nodded, unable to speak. "You hurt. Can you say, 'I hurt'?"

I wished I had the nerve to tell Chuck he was a bully, but he had gotten the result he was after: Paul, a two hundred pound, all-muscle policeman, was weeping. "I hurt," he said, at last.

Chuck let Paul cry for a few more minutes; then he said, "Roger, what's the pain about?"

Roger had his face in both hands by now, but when he took his hands down, his cheeks were dry.

"What are you feeling?" Chuck asked. "How did you feel when Paul was crying?"

"Sad."

"And what else?"

"Sorry for Paul—very sorry."

"And how do you feel now, right this minute?"

"Fine. I'm okay—I feel fine."

"You don't look to me like you feel fine."

Roger nodded. "I had the flu or something last week."

"What I'm seeing isn't the flu."

"It might've been a cold."

"Look," Chuck said, sounding almost angry, "we'd like you to share with us, but you don't have to. You don't have to share with us if you don't want to." Leave Roger alone, I thought. "If you don't want to share," Chuck said, "I'd like you to say so."

Roger took a deep breath that turned into a sob. "I want to. I don't know how." Tears streamed down his cheeks. "Why don't I know? What is it about me?"

I was wiping my nose on the back of my hand. The tears were dripping off my chin. Someone slid me the box of tissues. I grabbed a wad and sent the box back. Roger was talking on and on—about his child, about the lawn; and the whole time, I sat there, snucking and sobbing. It wasn't his fault, he couldn't help it, but wouldn't you have to leave a man like that?

"What's going on with you, Rosemary?" Chuck finally asked. I blew my nose and shook my head. "Why were you crying?"

"Because Roger was."

"Other people cried, and you didn't cry."

"Roger's just very human," I said.

Chuck pointed his beard at me. "We're all human." I would've liked to ask if he was sure. "Does Roger remind you of someone?" he persisted.

"No," I said, "except maybe my ex-husband."

"Did you love your husband?"

"Yes," I said, because I didn't see any reason not to lie.

We broke up around midnight. We'd all pitched in a dollar, and someone had gone out after dinner to buy wine. The men dragged the sofa over against the wall, and we brought the mats up close to the fire.

"This is like Girl Scout camp," Helen said. "We should have a sing-along."

My cue to escape. I went out to the veranda and leaned over the railing.

A few minutes later, someone came up to me and put his arms around me from behind. I knew it was Roger; we didn't talk. The night air was chilly, and we were both shivering. Inside, the others were singing. I heard Chuck say it was a quarter to one. "You can stay up as long as you like. You can sleep through breakfast. But I want everybody ready to work by nine." People began to say good night. Pretty soon it was quiet.

"Let's go in," Roger said.

The fire had died down; the room was almost dark, just a little glow from the embers.

"Let's put the sofa back," he said, so we did. He sat down beside me and put his arm around my shoulders. "You're a good person." I didn't argue. He kissed me. "You loved your husband." He kissed me again and then again, and it felt as if he were making it up to me for Bobby. We sank down on the cushions, and I quit worrying about whether we had arrived there solely through misapprehensions.

I did wonder, though, before we went up to our cots, how we were going to look at each other in the morning. I said so, but Roger whispered, "It's already morning." And he put his forefinger gently against my lips and said, "Don't think ugly thoughts. It was beautiful, Rosemary."

At breakfast, I gathered he'd changed his opinion, because he didn't even wish me good morning. So, that's that, I thought, let down but not surprised. In my limited experience, it was how men reacted.

But at the last minute, as we were walking to our cars, he caught up with me in the parking lot.

"What's your last name? What's your phone number?"

I told him, because I didn't want to make an issue out of something that was very likely never going to be one.

I was truly surprised when he phoned, the next night.

"I've been thinking about you." He sounded a little embarrassed. I said I'd been thinking about him too. Actually, I'd been thinking about the scene on the sofa, replaying it like a favorite movie.

By Wednesday it began to lose its reality. For Roger too. He called up and talked about the weather in Connecticut.

"Are you feeling uncomfortable about what we did?" I said, rashly.

"Oh, no," he said. "It was beautiful." But I could see that he'd just as soon forget it. "My timer just went off. Why don't I call you Friday?"

On Friday we talked about the follow-up meeting that was scheduled for the coming Sunday. Was he planning to go? "Yes," he said abruptly, "and I'd like to take you out to dinner afterwards.

Maybe we could go out to lunch too, or breakfast. I was thinking of driving up tomorrow afternoon."

"Would you like to stay here?" I asked.

"Oh, no, dear." I think this was the first time he called me "dear." "I wouldn't want to impose. Why don't I just pick you up for the meeting?"

"Fine," I said, hoping I didn't sound disappointed.

We went to an Italian place for dinner. The follow-up meeting hadn't been very interesting. Only about half the people showed up.

"I wonder why Helen didn't come," I mused. Maybe, I thought, she was avoiding me. She never asked where I'd been, when I didn't come upstairs with her.

"I tried to see Shelley this morning," Roger said.

"How was that?"

We talked about Shelley all though dinner.

At eight-thirty I said I was tired. He didn't seem to hear me. At nine I said I had to go home, and we left.

"I was going to go back tonight," he said, as he walked me to my door, "but I think I'll stay over and start back early. I should get a room. Do you have a phone?"

I just looked at him. Then I unlocked the door and said, "It's in here on my desk." I got the phone book out of the drawer. He seemed puzzled—perhaps by its use? I sat down on the couch and waited. His back was to me, but I heard a sigh.

"Roger," I said—I'd try one more time, "you're welcome to stay here tonight if you want to."

"Oh, no, dear," he said, just as he'd done before. "Thanks, anyway." But he placed the phone book on the desk and came and sat at the other end of the couch.

He began to talk about the economy. After a while, I said I wasn't interested in the economy, I was interested in him. He looked startled. I asked him about his parents, his childhood. Dutifully he told me about his childhood, about the various jobs he'd had. "I worked my way through college. I've had to work all my life, not like you women."

"I work," I murmured.

He stood up. "I should go." The clock over the mantel said ten. He stood in front of the fireplace, talking. I hadn't lit a fire, but several times he held his hands out to the grate, as if warming them.

He started in on politics. Did I think Reagan was going to win the election?

"Probably," I said.

The hour grew later and later. Eleven-fifteen. At last I lost patience. "Roger, tell me something. Did we or did we not make love in the Group Room after everybody'd gone to bed"

He blushed. "You don't remember?"

"I remember, but you don't act like you do."

"I remember," he assured me. "It was beautiful."

I didn't know what to do. I put my feet up and covered myself with the afghan. He sat down in the chair by the fireplace. I didn't know how I could have been so stupid—I didn't have a thing to drink in the house.

He said nothing. I said nothing. I began to wish I hadn't given up smoking. I didn't have the nerve to try to seduce him. I couldn't understand why he didn't leave.

At last I heard another sigh. "Well," he said, "I think it's probably too late to find a room, so I guess I'll take you up on your offer—if it's still all right."

"Of course it's all right," I said. "You have two choices—this couch or the bed with me."

He only had to think a minute. "The bed. It probably gets cold in here later on."

I showed him where my bedroom was and went into the bathroom and put on my nightgown and my bathrobe. When I came out, Roger was in my bed, with the covers drawn up to his chin. His glasses were next to the lamp on the nightstand, and he looked as blind as an infant mouse.

I got into bed.

"Are you going to sleep in your bathrobe?"

I said no and took off my bathrobe.

"Are you going to leave the light on?" he asked, in the same worried voice.

"No," I said, and turned off the lamp.

One Good Man

"Janet?" the caller says. "This is Joe Kincaid."

Kincaid, Kincaid. Statistics? Calculus? It's Joe *Shore* she's got the conference with—in only half an hour. Kincaid: nobody she's got this year. Maybe one of last year's students.

"Give me a clue," she says. Why do people do this? How can they expect her to keep track? Twenty years of students.

"This *is* Janet?"

It's eight-thirty already, and she hasn't had breakfast. She lets her impatience show. "Yes!"

"I'm going to put pennies up your ass," Joe Kincaid says.

She freezes, the phone still at her ear. Then, before she can stop herself, she says, "Why so cheap?" and hangs up, the way she should've done right off.

Lord, Lord, what came over her? She's had crank calls before; she knows better. Crank calls—what she gets for listing herself as "Janet," instead of letting herself be reduced to an initial. It isn't as though Bernice didn't warn her.

There's no time to call Bernice, who's probably left for the library. She phones anyway.

"Now, why do you think you said that?" Bernice says, not "I told you so," bless her. She sounds sympathetic, a little amused, as if she had all the time in the world.

"Come over for dinner," Janet says. "We'll analyze my motivations."

"Are you upset? You're upset."

"Not really."

"I'll come about six."

"No, come straight here."

But she *is* upset, must be, can't find her black boots, and she just wore them yesterday. Does she have to wear boots? Yes, because it snowed last night. She can see a dusting on the construction project across the street; it hasn't melted off the girders. She never thought she'd see the day when she was glad Joe Shore is always late. She finds her boots—under her desk in the living room.

She's not upset, she thinks, hurrying to the subway. She's nibbling on a piece of bread—the heel. She's got to go to the market, get bread, buy onions; she'll fix Bernice chicken breasts. Riceroni. On the way home, she'll pop in the market. The market she has to go to is out of her way. If they had to tear something down, why did it have to be the A & P?

Joe Shore is leaning against the wall outside her office. His All-American College Boy face looks sullen.

"You're perfectly right to be angry with me," she says, "but I got an unexpected phone call."

And all of a sudden she's studying his face—for signs of guilt? Marks of depravity? The only significant change in his features is: he yawns. Nevertheless, she finds herself listening to his voice as he stumbles through his questions. He is hopelessly confused about standard deviations, and here she is speculating about what other deviations may be confusing him. Anybody could be named Joe. It's probably not even the caller's name. He could've made it up, picked it out of the phone book.

"It's that he gave a name," she tells Bernice, over sherry. They are sitting at either end of the sofa, facing the two large windows. In the dusky light the curtainless panes don't look so grimy; the spider plants hanging there don't look so sick. Through the leggy fronds she can see the dark skeleton of the steel beams across the street and, through the grid, the last of the rosy sky. First destruction, then construction: five-story parking; it's going to cut off her view. "I thought he was a student. I trusted him."

"Like when that guy pretended to drop his change," Bernice says, "and I was helping him pick it up, and the woman snatched my purse."

"Like that," Janet says. City living. "What's an obscene phone caller doing making phone calls at eight-thirty in the morning?"

"He's probably out of work," Bernice says. Then she says, "You'd better change your phone number."

"I can't." Not when finally, at last, after years of hassling, she's got the phone company to print her right name, right address. It would be a lot easier, the representative seemed to think, if people in Boston didn't move and change their names so often. She's gone back to her maiden name. That was three years ago. She's moved twice. That's often?

"Well," Bernice says, "maybe he won't call again." She tucks her feet under her rust-plaid skirt, rests her arm across the back of the sofa. Her bangle bracelets clink together. The ice cubes in her sherry: a fainter echo. "Ice in the sherry?" Steven used to say, a complaint. "Why not just put the bottle in the refrigerator?" The refrigerator barely holds milk and orange juice. He had eyes. Why should she explain? She is always explaining. "I like ice in my sherry." Another explanation. "But why do you keep putting it in mine?" She used to get—not crank calls but calls from Steven.

"He's going to call again," she says.

"Next time, you hang up. No question."

They stare at the phone on the desk across the room. Black touch-tone. It knows when it's going to ring.

"He could give another name," Janet says. "I can't just hang up on people."

He knows where she lives. She's given encouragement. How does she know he's not watching her apartment? He could be watching now. This is nonsense.

"I think it's time you got curtains," Bernice says. She runs her fingers through her hair, and her bracelets slide down her arm. This year she's blond. Last year she was a redhead. "Let's go to Jordan's Saturday morning."

Janet's eyes fill. Over-reacting. But what a good friend Bernice is, a better friend than she is. She reaches for the pack of cigarettes she bought at the market. When she picks up the matches, she tips over her sherry.

"I'm an absolute flake," she says, but Bernice is on her way to the kitchen. The reddish brown liquid spreads across the glass-topped table, pools at the chrome edge; the ice cubes skitter. "Never mind," Janet cries. "Really—don't bother. I have to get the carpet cleaned anyway." The coarse brown pile has already absorbed the dribble.

Bernice scrubs at it with a wet sponge and the dishtowel. Down on her hands and knees, for God's sake. Trying to squeeze in, between the sofa and the coffee table.

"That's the best I can do." She sits back on her haunches and, reaching inside her blouse, runs a thumb under each bra strap.

"I like your blouse," Janet says, instead of "Thank you." Dull gold silk; it must be new.

"I've had it for a month," Bernice says. She fixes Janet with the particular look that spells determination. "This may not be the best time to bring it up, but I think we should write that ad."

"No," Janet wants to say but doesn't, though she wishes Bernice would stop pushing. Enough already, she keeps saying—enough grieving over that shit, Steven.

Bernice rocks back on her heels and stands up, not leaning on the sofa. Dance aerobics have done wonders. She hasn't lost any weight, though, Janet thinks, then wonders how she can be so uncharitable. She's not exactly depressed, but it's as if she's looking through a graying mesh.

"See, if you run the ad yourself," Bernice persists, "you're in a better position."

She's standing in the doorway of the kitchen; the kitchen isn't big enough for two. Janet squeezes lemon juice over the chicken breasts. She unhooks the garlic press from the pegboard. No, no garlic. Bernice is meeting a new man tomorrow night, a man who ran an ad in the *Boston Phoenix*—in the "Person to Person" section at least, not in the "Personals," which is for kinkies. It's perfectly safe, Bernice insists. Of course you meet them in a public place. You don't give them your last name. All they have is your phone number. Janet shudders. She hangs the garlic press back up. Her over-protective routine—what she did with her children. Bernice doesn't give a hoot whether she smells like garlic.

"You're safer," Bernice continues. "*You* get to do the screening. You've got *their* phone number. And it separates the singles from the married. If they send you a box number, they're married."

"I just can't stand the idea," Janet says. You don't go advertising unless you're desperate. You don't go answering other people's ads either. Naturally, she can't say this, shouldn't even be thinking it— not in this day and age, when everyone does it.

"It's nothing to be ashamed of, damn it."

Up-front at last! is Bernice's attitude. Gone, thank God, all that disgusting coyness. True, the last man Bernice fell for said she'd better learn to act less eager. But he was a creep and a jerk, and who needed him? Her time has arrived: she is a healthy, hot-blooded woman.

As for her own blood, Janet thinks, ripping the top off the box of Riceroni, it moves, if it moves at all, through tiny, constricted capillaries. The last arterial pulsing was with Steven. She says:

"What if nobody answers?"

"My God," Bernice says. "What am I going to do with you?" She comes around to the counter and pours herself more sherry. No ice cubes. "How did you get to be so negative? As if I didn't know—I could just kill Steven."

The fire's too high, the butter is browning. If she, Janet, could feel like killing Steven, no doubt she wouldn't be so negative. How wrong it is that who she wants to kill is Mary Anne—for being only thirty-eight, for appealing to Steven. And she used to like Mary Anne, a topnotch secretary.

"He couldn't help it," she tells Bernice. "He's a creep and a jerk."

"I think it's time to stop making excuses for men," Bernice says. She reaches over Janet's shoulder and switches on the hood fan. It would be nice, Janet thinks, to have a big-enough kitchen. You don't have to be cooking for two to have one. Bernice knocked out a wall, put in granite counters; she's got cupboard space she doesn't even need. You can do that in a condo—remodel. Why is she still living in this depressing apartment?

"And I think," Bernice says, back at the doorway, "it's time you quit carrying the torch for Steven." She raises her glass: the Statue of Liberty.

"I'm not carrying any torch." When ice fills her veins, why talk of torches? She is supposed to be browning, not scorching, the Riceroni. She takes the frying pan off the burner.

"Not much you aren't," Bernice says.

"Well, I can't avoid him."

He drops in her office. He wants to stay friends. "I'm concerned about you, Janet. You're looking peakèd." It's winter, she says. You're supposed to look peakèd. "I want you to be happy," he says, and lays a hand on her shoulder. Ice? He has managed not to say "happy, like me," but she knows how hard it must be for him, what a struggle. Mary Anne likes beards. He has grown one—scruffy, patchy, multi-colored. It makes him look older, she'd like to tell him, but you have to pay too highly for those meaner impulses.

Avoid him? She wouldn't give him the satisfaction. Who she avoids is Mary Anne.

"We're going to write that ad," Bernice says, "after dinner. Which plates do you want me to put on the table?"

"The red ones." Red plates are cheerful. Janet pours the water into the Riceroni. Steven used to watch the news while she cooked. She gets out lettuce and a carrot to grate into it. Thinking of Bernice, she leaves out the scallions.

"Are we having wine?" Bernice asks.

"Of course." The big bottle of moselle—that's the real reason there's no room for the sherry.

"I'll just rinse out our glasses."

"Don't be silly. Use clean ones." If she had a bigger kitchen, she could have a dishwasher.

Bernice edges behind Janet and gets the glasses from the cupboard. "The other advantage when you run the ad yourself," she says, as if they were still on the subject, "is: you don't have to try to figure out who this guy is, when he calls you and says, 'This is Joe Schmoe, you answered my ad,' and you answered ten, but they all think you just answered theirs, naturally." She puts the glasses down and hugs Janet. "You *are* upset. I'm sorry."

For Janet has flinched at hearing "Joe." How ridiculous. She lifts the lid off the Riceroni.

"You're letting all the steam out."

"I don't really have my wits about me, do I?"

"No kidding," Bernice says. "You haven't turned on the chicken."

"And you want to cook with me? You think I'm going to be even halfway competent with a couple of strange men hanging around, waiting for their dinner?"

"They won't be strange," Bernice says, "by the time we have them to dinner."

Because they'll meet them first, she says, as she tears up lettuce. They'll meet them for coffee or a drink. They'll screen out the wimps and the crazies. By the time they get to the dinner stage, they'll have winnowed out the chaff. Credulous, Janet thinks. Bernice is so credulous. She thinks they're going to meet someone interesting. She thinks they're going to have fun, mini-parties— her moussaka, Janet's chicken. Stuffed vine leaves, flan, chocolate mousse. People to cook for. They both love to cook. Who can cook anymore? Janet wonders. She can't even fix a simple dinner.

But it's turned out well, even though the market didn't have shallots, even though she left out the garlic.

"The chicken is super," Bernice says, "even without the garlic."

When Janet used to leave the garlic out, cooking for Steven, he'd frown and put his hands together, making steeples. "I don't know, Jan—it's not up to your usual standard. It lacks—*je ne sais quoi*—but something." And that's the difference, she thinks, between men and women.

"About the ad," she says, trying to sound energetic, upbeat, "where would we run it?"

Bernice sighs. "If we lived in New York, we could try the *New York Review*. But there aren't any men in Boston who read it."

"That's nonsense," Janet says. "Steven reads it."

"So he's the only one. Don't you remember—when I ran that ad and all I got was answers from places like Zaire? For Christ's sake, I wasn't looking for pen pals."

Janet helps herself to more salad. She doesn't want to be negative, but if she ran an ad and only out-of-town people responded, she'd think nobody local liked her ad, not nobody read it.

"As for the *Singles' Almanac*," Bernice goes on, "it's like the *Want Advertiser*. You know, 'Fifty years young' or 'considered good-looking.' Then there's 'My friends say I have a good sense of humor.' No, we're going to have to run it in the *Phoenix*."

Before she thinks, Janet says, "How can you expect anyone normal to answer ads in the *Phoenix*?"

"I answer ads in the *Phoenix*," Bernice says, "and you know it. There are perfectly decent ads in the 'Person to Person.'"

"I know," Janet says. "I wasn't casting aspersions." She pours them both more wine from the bottle on the table.

"The man I'm meeting tomorrow sounds quite interesting."

"Well, I'm glad," Janet says. "What sounded interesting?"

She doesn't like her own tone of voice: snippy. Bernice puts her fork down. You'd think those bracelets would disturb people at the library.

"I don't think I really care whether he's interesting or not," Bernice says. "I just want an adventure. At least I'm trying. I'm not sitting around moping."

"I'm not moping."

"You are."

"I am," Janet says. She watches Bernice dish out some more Riceroni. Pretty hands. Her own hands are getting age spots.

Bernice wears rings, flashy rings. She's wearing an enormous pearl, not fake, "a huge, incredulous pearl," as Janet once read in an interview of some model or starlet. She clipped the interview; she was going send it to *The New Yorker*, along with "Race horses can rnu, but they can't do much else" and a hospital's ad for an "intravenus nurse." What happened to those clippings? She had a whole collection. They disappeared, her last move, like her wedding ring. Photographs too. Of the kids, friends, of the house in Arlington.

"If you want the truth," Bernice says, "I have a hunch he's married."

"Why? Where do you get that?"

"Well, he was a little secretive. He kept saying he had to have a woman who was understanding. He kept saying, 'Is there anything that would make you reject a man?'"

Janet can think of all sorts of things that would provoke rejection. Married is certainly one of them.

"Then why are you meeting him?"

"Oh, hell," Bernice says, "let some other poor fool do his laundry and cook his breakfast."

"We're going to write that ad," Janet says, and she gets up with more energy than she's felt all day, goes across to her desk and gets a pad of paper and a pencil. "So how do we word this? 'Two women in their forties . . .'"

"Two attractive women," Bernice says, through a mouthful of Riceroni.

"Why do we have to say 'attractive'?"

"What do you want to say—'gorgeous'?"

Maybe Bernice is what men mean when they ask for "Rubenesque," but who is gorgeous? Attractive? That is just so neutral. "How about 'interesting-looking'?" she suggests.

Bernice stares. "Are you serious?"

"But 'attractive'—that's so boastful."

"All right. 'Two women, early forties . . .'"

"Don't you think we should at least be truthful?"

"My God," Bernice says. "You're impossible. Okay, here it is: 'Two women, pushing fifty, one short and fat, one short and skinny' . . ."

"You don't have to go to extremes," Janet says, "do you? Don't we need something to attract their attention?"

"Squat and skinny," Bernice says. "That'd attract their attention." Janet laughs. "That's better. You realize you haven't laughed all evening?" She sips her wine. "Maybe we should write something cryptic, be a little mysterious. Here we go: 'Two adventurous women, attractive forties, want a couple of good men for spring rebellion . . .' "She gives Janet a roguish look. "There must be one good man left somewhere in Boston. You think we could share him?"

"*Share* him?"

"Say we find one good one," Bernice continues. "I mean really good. We'd probably like the same one anyhow. Think of the problems. But if we set out to share him, we wouldn't be jealous, would we?"

Jealous, Janet thinks. How to ruin a friendship. She is jealous of Mary Anne; she'd hate to be jealous of Bernice, her best friend these days—for the last three years. The friends you make in Advanced Degree Singles: other single women.

"I mean," Bernice is saying, "you could have him half the week, and I'd take him the other half. Who wants him full-time anyway?"

"You do," Janet almost says, but that would be snide. She says, "Think, think—who's going to do his laundry?"

"You are," Bernice says. Janet starts to giggle.

"He might like my chicken better than your moussaka."

"I don't think that's the problem."

"Then what is?"

"Finding him!"

The ad they finally come up with reads: "Two adventurous women, forties, professionals. One blonde, one brunette, both attractive. Like movies, dancing, theater—the usual. Come sample our cuisine. You'll stay for the meal. Looking for one or two good men in Boston/Cambridge."

"I don't want to put that ad in," Janet tells Bernice on the phone, the next morning. Too late. Bernice stopped on her way home to Cambridge. She slipped the ad into one of those mail boxes she knows is a real one, not a dummy. And that's what you get, Janet thinks, for succumbing to drunken impulses. It's a stupid ad, one of those things you write but don't mail. Besides, she isn't interested in dancing.

In the middle of explaining regression lines, she remembers she didn't wish Bernice good luck for this evening. She'll call her, make sure she got home safely. As she comes out of the classroom, Steven says, "Hi," and she blushes. If he knew what she's done! He says, "You're looking good—not so peakèd."

"He was into whips," Bernice says, when Janet calls her. It's morning. She fell asleep watching TV in the living room.

"God," Janet says. "He came right out and told you?"

"Of course not." Does Bernice sound just a bit testy? "He kept talking around the subject until I got the picture." Janet can't help wondering: did Bernice misinterpret? After all, at first she'd thought this man was married.

"Well," she says, "at least he wasn't married."

"The hell he wasn't."

"I'm sorry. Jesus!"

"What about you?" Bernice says. "Did you hear any more from your crank caller?"

Joe Kincaid. She'd forgotten about Joe Kincaid. Why did Bernice have to remind her? As if she didn't know! Sharing a man, indeed—how idiotic!

There are anywhere from six to fifteen single women to every single man in Boston, she reads in the newspaper that night. It's not the *Globe*; they were out of *Globe*s, she stayed so late, working.

Not going to haul all those tests home. Joe Shore's still confused.
How discouraging. Perhaps if she used data in her examples that
meant something to him? The number of women per available
men might mean something. She gets out her graph paper. Surely
there must be some age group where they're numerically equal. In
her classes there are still more men than women, but that's because
it's math. Oh, everything's discouraging.

Love and work. What did Freud know? About work, not love.
He didn't even know that much about sex, at least for women.
Work. She should sell out, be a consultant, quit teaching. If she
didn't have tenure, she could move to Alaska, where the men
outnumber the women, or used to. She should move, in any case,
buy a condominium. What is she waiting for? Why buy curtains?

The windows are too big for ready-made curtains, she discovers
on Saturday. She's going to have to order custom drapes. Bernice
says:

"So order them."

"I don't want to," Janet says, though she does order them.
In the old days, she'd have made the curtains herself. Now she's
too busy. No, even if she had the time, she wouldn't make them.
What's lacking is interest. She's not interested in nesting. Not by
herself, not alone. Bernice is way ahead of her. She was right to
buy a condo. From the street, you'd never suspect how nice it is
inside those ratty-looking three-deckers. It isn't just Bernice, either;
all the single women Janet knows have bought condos. They've all
got off-white walls and snazzy kitchens, Navajo rugs on the floor,
and plants in baskets. Nesting, as if they'd settled, meant to stay.
Decisions!

"I should go to school for a while," Janet says, when they're
through with the curtains. She's ordered off-white, of course;
anything else would be overpowering. "I don't want to go to
school. I don't want to go home." That apartment is not home. The
last home she had was Arlington. Everything's found a home in
Bernice's condominium: the framed art work done by her friends
and her children. She's got a stereo system. What is this—envy?

Comfortable, plushy couches, interesting curtains. Rusts and golds, like autumn.

But Bernice says, "I don't want to go home either."

They take the Red Line over to Cambridge and have lunch in a Soup and Salad. They go see the uncut version of "The Leopard." A debauched afternoon. It cheers them. They end up having a drink at Bernice's.

"I just happen to have an eggplant," Bernice says, "and some potatoes."

When Janet goes out to buy wine, she finds herself thinking, Yes, but owning a condo would be like having tenure.

Presidents' Day. Janet has Monday off. She stays home and works. All day long she talks to no one. She tries to reach her daughter in L.A., but Amelia doesn't answer. Janet remembers: Amelia's in Hawaii. She was going this week with her new boyfriend. Bernice isn't home either. Janet gets her answering machine. She calls another friend, also single. "Can't talk now," the friend says. Meaning: "Bill's here." Bill or whoever. It's a beautiful sunny day; they're having a thaw. Janet sits at her desk and stares out the window. The bare girders across the street rise out of mud; sun shimmers on the oil-slicked puddles. In the afternoon light, there's no disguising how really filthy the windows are.

When she runs into Steven in the hall on Tuesday, she's startled by how healthy he looks. He's got a sunburn. He's been to St. Thomas, he says, and she remembers she didn't see him Friday. A little vacation, four days, can do wonders, he chuckles. Mary Anne has not got a sunburn; she isn't even tan, Janet realizes. Mary Anne is brushing her short auburn hair over the sink in the ladies' room. She looks as though she might have been crying; she looks peakèd.

"Steven," Mary Anne says, brushing, brushing, "is an asshole."

It's got to be prurient curiosity that makes Janet ask what happened.

"He met somebody twenty-six."

In the fluorescent light, Janet's hair has a reddish cast that looks unnatural. Home-dyed is what it looks. Time to go professional.

"His daughter's twenty-seven," she says.

"That's what I mean," says Mary Anne.

Janet decides to give a dinner party. She will invite Mary Anne but not Steven.

On Saturday the *Phoenix* comes out, and Janet buys it. Their ad is supposed to be in this issue, but she can't find it. She reads every single ad in "Person to Person." Not there. She's relieved as well as disappointed. She calls Bernice.

"The fuckers ran it under 'Personals'," Bernice says.

"Oh, no!"

"Oh, yes. Look on the right-hand page above the ad for phone sex."

"Which ad for phone sex?"

"The biggest one," Bernice says. "It's right beside 'Foxy lady wanted for spanking.'"

"Oh, no," Janet says again. Yes, she sees it. In there with the escort services and the massage ads. How could they?

"Listen," Bernice says. "On Monday—could you call them?"

"Why me?"

"I can't call them from the library."

"Why don't we just forget it?"

"No!" says Bernice. "It makes me angry."

It doesn't make Janet angry. It's more like she feels wounded. Misunderstood. But it's just a mistake, nothing to be ashamed of.

It's not a mistake, the woman at the *Phoenix* says. She has checked with the department manager. No, she says coldly, it was a considered decision. The ads placed in "Person to Person" aim at romance, dating.

"But that's what this is," Janet says.

"It says you're professionals."

"We're a college teacher and a librarian, for God's sake," Janet says.

"That's not how it reads. Then you say, 'Come sample our cuisine.'"

"That was an invitation to dinner." Explaining, explaining.

"It's ambiguous," the woman says. "And you ask for one or two good men."

"Well, there probably *is* only one." The woman doesn't laugh. Probably some young thing, one of those women who don't realize yet what they're going to be up against. If they want to reword the ad, she tells Janet, it can be run under "Person to Person."

"Do you want to run a different ad?"

"Hell, no," Janet says, and now she *is* mad: disgusted with the whole venture, angry at Bernice.

"I think we should write another ad," Bernice says, when Janet tells her. She seems to find the mix-up amusing. She's going to tell her kids about it and her ex-husband.

"Well, I'm not," Janet says. She's not in communication with her ex-husband.

She gives the dinner party. She invites Mary Anne and some other people from school but not Bernice. She cooks lamb vindaloo, makes her own paratha. She does the yogurt with the pureed mint and onion. She walks over to the Haymarket to get the lamb and the mint.

A month goes by. She has Bernice over to celebrate getting curtains. And also to help hang them. She serves pork chops with apple sauce, nothing fancy. She asks Bernice if she wants the spider plants. "Throw them out," Bernice says. Janet takes them down to the dumpster. You can't see through the five-story parking anymore. Thugs and muggers could hide in the dark honeycomb. Voyeurs could stand across there and look in her windows. It's just as well she got curtains, but she's going to have to remember to draw them.

Bernice says she's lost eight pounds. She can wear her old jeans again. Motivation is all. She's been seeing someone she met at the library. He's one of those men who have "Take care of me" written all over them, but he speaks nine languages; this summer he's going to Italy. Janet has gone to three concerts and two movies by herself, and all she has seen at the concerts and movies is couples.

"Did you ever call the *Phoenix* to see if we got any mail?" Bernice asks, as she's about to leave.

"Of course not," Janet snaps.

"Well, why don't you?"

"No!"

Bernice makes a face. "All right, I will."

And she does. They have a ton of mail, she tells Janet, and the *Phoenix* wishes they'd come get it; it's taking up three tubs. "They're going to throw it all out on Friday. Why don't you pick it up?"

"Why should I pick it up?" Janet says. "Why don't you?"

"I don't really need it. I've got my hands full."

Kill, kill, Janet thinks. She does some reflecting. Steven's tan has begun to fade. He's been hanging around her office, saying things like, "I miss your chicken." He has shaved off his beard and looks much younger.

On Friday morning, she sticks a trash bag into her purse before she leaves for school—one of the sturdy kind, dark green; she's not going to take any risks with those No Name bags that keep tearing. At noon she takes the subway over to the *Phoenix*'s office.

"Thank God," the young woman behind the counter says. She flips her braids over her shoulders. "It must've been some ad!" She piles stack after stack of envelopes on the counter. "There must be hundreds of responses."

Janet says, "Thank you," and sweeps the envelopes into the trash bag. She hasn't got time to go home. She rides the subway back to school, hanging onto the pole near the door. The trash bag nestles between her feet, deflating gradually; it seems to be getting heavier on her toes. Why is this woman taking her trash for a ride on the subway? Nobody looks even curious. People in the city do stranger things.

She stuffs it into the cubbyhole under her desk. Is it actually leaning against her ankles, or is this her imagination? Every once in a while, she can hear the plastic crinkling. The contents are making themselves at home, settling.

Steven looks in and says, "How about going for a drink at the Copley Plaza? They've got a jazz pianist I want to hear. You always liked jazz piano."

Janet says, "Mary Anne is who likes jazz piano." How about coming anyway, Steven says, and for an instant she's tempted. It's so nice to be invited, so nice to be wanted. But then he says, "It'll do you good."

"I've got people coming over," Janet says. "I can't."

She lugs the trash bag to the subway. She has a depraved thought: she could have left it on the train. Even now, she could throw it in some other apartment building's dumpster. How irresponsible! Who knows what's in here?

She does. The likes of Joe Kincaid.

How is she going to dispose of all these letters? she wonders, dropping the trash bag onto the sofa. Is she going to have to buy a paper shredder? She turns on the TV, slips her coat off. When she comes back from hanging it up in the bedroom, the trash bag has already hunkered down. It's collapsing upon itself, sagging inward; the neck droops to the side and slightly forward: a despondent guest she can't get rid of.

She turns the TV up so she can hear the news, while she chops up onions and bell peppers for a Western.

Time to buy that condominium. From the kitchen, the trash bag looks as if it's watching television.

The Vole Truth

Oh, be not like the meadow vole,
Fickle in heart, absent of soul,
His only goal to screw as many
Females as he can.
But emulate the prairie vole,
Who, huddled with his pair-bond mate,
Is hers for life, as vasopressin,
Like cocaine, rewards his brain.

Oxytocin makes her his,
He will help her with the kids.
Their life, though short, is full of bliss,
As yours could be. Remember this
And think: perhaps it's not too late,
Your genes need not dictate your fate.

Les, who supplied the title, said, "Send it to the *Poetry and Medicine* section in *JAMA*," but Jess didn't think the *Journal of the American Medical Association* would accept a poem with the verb "screw" in it, and she was pretty sure there'd be other reasons. In any case, she had written it not for *JAMA* but for Les, who was a meadow vole, if she ever saw one, in dire need, she told him, of a good dose of vasopressin.

Trouble was, he looked the same to her as when she'd fallen in love with him, thinking (as she also told him) that he was the human equivalent of a prairie vole. As she could see, at first he didn't much like being compared to a rodent but bore with her heroically, because he wanted her to take him back. Jess, against her better judgment, found this flattering. "When he shows you what he is, believe him," she had read once in the *Boston Globe's* advice column. Excellent advice, but who could follow it? If Les wasn't who she'd thought he was, then who was he? It seemed to her that the telltale discrepancies should show up physically. But they didn't, no matter how many times she replayed the first time she laid eyes on him, looking for warning signs or else reassurance.

There he was, standing behind a lectern, waiting for the roomful of Census job-applicants to take their seats. He was tall— 6'3" or so—straight, confident, in his mid-sixties, she figured. Just to look at him you'd know he had to be part Irish, that his hair, wavy and gray, must once have been black.

Grinning out at them, he waited for the room to quiet down. He wore silver-rimmed glasses, was slightly buck-toothed. He riffled through some papers on the lectern—the test, Jess assumed, that they were here to take. Solemn, his face looked somewhat gaunt— irresistibly ascetic, she thought. Although everyone was waiting in silence by now, still he said nothing.

Then, at last, he spoke:

"Dearly beloved, we are gathered here together . . ."

A few people snickered, Jess not among them. Nobody groaned. He shuffled his papers.

"Oops—wrong stuff."

More people laughed. Jess clicked her tongue. So corny! But she admired the risk he had taken. It didn't enter her head that, in less than six months, he'd be telling her, "Jess, you are my woman."

Or that he'd be calling her "sweetheart" and "darlin'."

Or that he'd be moving into her living room.

In the morning she dabs Tigress on the inside of her wrists and behind her ears—the Fabergé cologne that the Vermont

Country Store has revived, brought back to life, like an out-of-print book. She wishes they had brought back Aphrodisia too, always her favorite; her mother was the one who liked Tigress, saying it smelled like lead pencils. It never smelled like lead pencils to Jess, always seemed too strong, but now she needs all the strength she can get, because it is happening again.

A woman named Delilah is after her man.

Not that Jess has thought of Les in so proprietary a way. They have lived together, now, for almost ten years but never considered marriage. Les has already been married twice, and he made both his daughters promise to come kneecap him if they ever heard him mention marriage again. Jess was only married once, but that was enough, and she told her son to just shoot her and have done with it, never mind taking her out joint by joint. They are both in their seventies, Jess older—seventy-six two months ago; Les is seventy-four, going-on seventy-five, and they are both too old for this sort of thing, or so Jess keeps telling herself, but Les is still a terrible flirt, mostly with nurses and waitresses. Sometimes Jess thinks if she hears him say "A psychiatrist?" to one more waitress when the waitress asks, "Can I get you anything else?" she will have to act out in some way, but that way has not yet become clear to her. Jess and Les—they go together at least in rhyme, though they haven't much more in common except that both of them like to eat out; Jess no longer cooks, though she used to enjoy it. Now it hurts her back and knees too much—she can't stand up long enough even to fix scrambled eggs for breakfast. She does so anyway but relies heavily on instant oatmeal. Dinner is beyond her.

Delilah is only seventy-one, and she has no back or knee problems, is a strapping woman, thick-waisted, broad of beam, whom Jess can imagine walking along beside a covered wagon or behind a plow. Les has described her as "slight," which makes Jess wonder whether anything in his brain ever agrees with what is in her own; they may have been talking at cross-purposes the entire time they have been together. More and more often she thinks this is true. They have a nomenclature problem; it isn't just adjectives. When Les says "hall," what he means is the flag-stoned entry porch, which one of the visiting nurses calls "the mud room." What Jess visualizes is the hallway upstairs onto which the bedrooms and the only bathroom in the house open. It took her several years to interrupt the instantaneous association, to block that picture in her mind of the upstairs hall when Les said something like, "I put the shovel and the bamboo rake in the hall." She was a long time learning not to ask, "Why did you do that?" in a perplexity that was all too genuine. She still gets the misguided visualizations—can't help it, it's automatic—but she knows they're probably wrong and doesn't act on them. "You have caused me to censor my brain," she tells Les, for this translation difficulty has spilled over into her conversations with other people too. She's developed a basic doubt that anyone she talks to is saying what she thinks they mean. They are all speaking private, impenetrable languages. This causes her to answer hesitantly, and sometimes, in despair, she doesn't answer at all, which makes people think she is deaf. But she is not deaf, just a little hard of hearing, not enough to warrant a hearing aid.

Delilah, on the other hand, understands Les perfectly. She is the sharpest bridge partner he's ever had—they're on the same page, the same wavelength. They play bridge together four afternoons a week, in various towns, with various groups. Before they started playing together, Les was dissatisfied with all of his partners, who were nothing, in his estimation, but beginners. It takes a lifetime to become even somewhat proficient at bridge, he warns Jess frequently, so there's no point in her taking it up now; she would never be good enough. Jess pats his shoulder and says not to worry; she has never had any desire to learn bridge or any other card game. She would as soon try to do sudoku, which Les also enjoys, though he has no scruples against cheating. She'll stick with crossword puzzles, thank you, in the hope that the process will help preserve word retrieval. As far as she can see, it doesn't. The words are down in there somewhere, like fish that hide along the bottom of the pond—golden carp, weaving silently in and out among the roots of lily pads, flashing to the surface only when you have quit looking for them.

Les is better at crossword puzzles than Jess is. He started doing them when he was a teenager, so, despite the fact that the only books he reads are about bridge (though one year, to impress the son-in-law who is an internist, he took a subscription to JAMA), he has a good vocabulary and knows all those puzzle words like "adit" and "etui." Also he knows more about sports and characters in old TV cop shows. Which is just as well, since he is of the generation whose men needed to be better at everything than their wives and lovers, as well as smarter. Although there is no reason why he should even mention the subject, he likes to pontificate about why a husband and wife should never be bridge partners. Ten percent of divorces, worldwide, are caused by bridge misunderstandings, he says, sounding certain of his figures, because he has made them up. His current bridge partner is very good, yes, but if he were married to her, he would be partners with someone else, because, good as she is, she's not as good as he is, though it's true she's getting better every week. She's working hard to improve her skills and to that end brings him the bridge column from the *Boston Globe*, which she copies at the Senior Center in whichever town it is she lives in. They both do the bridge problem, then discuss it on the telephone, and sometimes Les doesn't come right home after bridge but stays on afterwards, so they can discuss the solutions when it is quieter. Jess has gone so far as to ask whether what they're doing is a courtship via bridge problems, but Les has not deigned to answer that question.

At seven in the morning, two months ago, when Jess picked up the phone to check her bank account (something she does every Monday), to her surprise, Les was already on the line with someone—a woman. "Sorry," Jess said, and hung up. She assumed he was talking to one of his daughters, but when she came down to fix breakfast, he started to bluster.

"It's not what you think!"

"Which is what?" Jess asked.

"I was talking to my bridge partner."

"So?"

"She just had a wart removed."

"At seven in the morning?"

"What difference does it make what time it was?"

"You know that's not what I meant."

"She was worried," Les said. "It was on her face. She was afraid it was going to leave a scar."

"Did it?"

Instantaneously, Jess had been visualizing a wart on a chin, a woman's chin, and one on a woman's nose. Since she had no idea what the bridge partner looked like, the chin and nose actually belonged to one of Les's former bridge partners, a woman named Dottie.

"She doesn't know yet. She's still got a band-aid."

So here was Les, all concerned about another woman's wart, and yet it hadn't worried him one bit that Jess had stayed in bed the day before, after being sick all Saturday night, throwing up into a waste basket. Les, who sleeps on the living room sofa, because he chooses to, hadn't been aware she was taken ill. When he finally yelled up the stairs to see why she hadn't come down to fix breakfast, Jess asked him to put some saltines into a baggie and toss them up to the landing for her. She was feeling hollow and thought they might settle her stomach. It used to work eons ago, when she was pregnant. He did that and then got involved in watching golf and the Patriots and never thought of her again until it was time for dinner. Then he was annoyed, because she hadn't actually explained that she didn't feel like going out to dinner, and now he would have to forage for himself, something he wasn't good at, though Jess often thought he would have been an excellent provider if he had been a Neanderthal, sallying forth to kill an antelope or stealing food from another family.

"You could get Chinese take-out," she suggested, over the phone. He was on his cell, hanging out the kitchen door.

"Fuck that!" he said. She could hear him through the floor as well as over the phone.

"You could have them deliver it."

"I'll go get a steak and cheese."

It seemed to Jess that he was unduly put-out; after all, she was the one who was sick. He didn't offer to get her anything, so she didn't ask him.

Because Les didn't volunteer Delilah's name, Jess took to referring to her as The Warthog. She had only just begun to realize that The Warthog and Les played bridge together so many times a week, and it was beginning to percolate that maybe bridge was not all these two were playing. Two afternoons a week, she herself volunteered at the local branch of the library, where she sat behind the counter and checked books in and out. So she was really not paying much attention to what Les might be up to. When, a few months before, he'd asked whether she would mind if he had a female bridge partner, Jess had said no, of course not. Now she recalled that he'd had a little inward smile when he asked, the left corner of his mouth twitching up as if an imp controlled him.

On her best days, indeed she would never begrudge Les a fulfilling friendship. On the other hand, on all days she would begrudge him another affair; he has had at least one since they started living together. All too obviously, it seems to Jess, he cares a lot about The Warthog. If she is playing bridge in the evening, he calls her to make sure she got home safely. They talk on and on—about how her partner screwed up, Les reports. Jess wouldn't know; she goes upstairs. All she knows about The Warthog is that she lives in senior housing, and the only reason she knows this is that Les has been dropping these little bits of information. Les has always been very secretive—in the high school pictures of him Jess has seen, he looks downright sneaky—but now that Jess has found out about The Warthog's existence, he seems to welcome any opportunity to talk about her. He has that desire to have her name on his tongue, even though he's not yet using her name.

Eventually he does use it. "Damn it, her name is either De-lee-la or De-lie-la."

"How can you not know?" Jess asks.

"People pronounce it different ways."

Somebody, he says, asked her at bridge, and she merely smiled and said, "Either way."

"Just like Jeanne Crain," Jess says, but Les looks at her blankly. He does have the grace. after a moment, to say:

"Jeanne Crain?"

"The actress?" Jess prompts. "Ice rink?" Then she says, "Oh, never mind."

Jess grew up in Santa Monica, California. She was used to seeing actors and actresses every so often, and she actually saw Jeanne Crain twice—once in a sedan that was pulling up in front of the Catholic church in Santa Monica and once at the Sonja Henie ice rink in Westwood. Jess was only fourteen, and she was thrilled. Jeanne Crain was just as pretty as she was on the screen, and her partner, someone said, was her husband. This was so much more exciting than glimpsing José Iturbi speeding past them in a convertible on San Vicente Boulevard or hearing about how a friend's brother had seen Leslie Caron at the restaurant where he was a dishwasher.

Naturally, Jeanne Crain soon attracted a crowd and had to quit skating and start signing autographs. Somehow, from somewhere, Jess procured a piece of paper, and somehow she got a turn—even more amazing, for she was small and people often jostled her aside. Best of all, Jess, to her own surprise, got up the nerve to ask a question: "How do you pronounce your name—Jean or Jeannie?"

And Jeanne Crain, smiling her enchanting smile, said, "Either way."

From this association, Jess gets the idea that The Warthog must be charming.

She herself is not charming; she has always been aware of that. Sometimes she can make people laugh, though hardly ever Les. And she can have interesting conversations with friends and even strangers but, again, not with Les. They somehow have nothing to talk about anymore, though when they were first working together, doing the census, they did laugh a lot, mostly at Les's jokes. Each week, Jess reported to Les; he was her crew leader, her boss. She used to think this was why he still thought of himself in that light, but gradually she realized there was another reason: Les has to be head of household, king of the pride; everyone else is an underling. She can see how this might come about if your household consisted of yourself and three women. Early on, she believed he was a man who really liked women, but she's come to realize that he sees them as not quite human. What they think or feel simply doesn't interest him; she mostly manages not to take this personally, because even his phone conversations with his daughters are of the "How're you, I'm fine" variety. But ten years of this have dimmed her ego, made her feel irrelevant, boring. "You're a total behaviorist," she's been known to tell him. His response is always, "What's wrong with that?" People's motivations have never intrigued him. "What do I care why they did it?" he'll ask. All that matters is what they did. If he hurts someone's feelings, he says, "They'll get over it."

"Where's your curiosity?" she asks him, from time to time.

After the seven o'clock phone call, Jess started thinking back, and the way she figures it, Les has probably been involved with The Warthog for the last six months. For at least that long he has been getting angry with her, Jess, every day once, maybe twice a day, unless they happen to have had sex, which they still do, every week or so, usually on weekends, when Les has no bridge games. All Jess has to go by is remembering that this happened before, during the third year they lived together, when, as it turned out, he was having an affair with his then-bridge partner, Dottie. Having an affair apparently makes Les irritable. If Jess can't quite hear what he has just said, he erupts with, "Jesus Christ!" even though it would be difficult for anybody to understand him when he isn't wearing his teeth and has his hand over his mouth. The various hums of the humidifier, the oxygen concentrator, and the air purifier don't help either, and this is in addition to the TV, which is on 24/7. Add to the cacophony the whirring of the stove fan, the swishing and clicks and roars of the dishwasher, the beeping of the microwave— but why go on? Jess might as well be as deaf as Les accuses her of being. She says she will get her hearing tested, but he says there's no point; she won't like a hearing aid; there will be too much ambient noise, and she won't use it. She begins to see that he wants her to behave in ways that annoy him; he is looking for pretexts. More and more he finds them.

"What did you do with the sugar packets I brought home from the hospital?" he will demand.

"What sugar packets?"

Chances are they're still in the pink plastic wash basin along with yet another bottle of body wash, another spray deodorant, more talcum powder that they will never use. Les always wants to bring these things home, saying the hospital will just throw it all away, but Jess is the one who throws it away, which makes her feel wasteful and guilty. As for why Les gets especially furious with her when he is involved with another woman, Jess can only think he must be wishing he were living with someone who could understand him. She can see how that might be, though she has lived with Les for all these years without his, in any sense, understanding her, and it has never made her furious, just somewhat forlorn.

He and Delilah have a purely platonic relationship, Les finally volunteers. This, Jess finds herself unable to disbelieve, though common sense tells her she ought to be skeptical. She believes, because she cannot do otherwise. If she didn't believe Les, she would have to kick him out, for she will not put up with another relationship like the one he had with Dottie. Or so she tells herself. The relationship with Dottie was not platonic, though Les to this day insists that it was. But Jess had found empty Viagra packets in his car's glove compartment—samples, with all the pills pushed out. There was persistence here, there was endeavor. Nonsense, Les said; they weren't even his. Somebody at bridge had handed them to him to throw away. "You can't expect me to believe that," Jess had cried, scandalized to realize he thought her that much of an idiot. "I don't care whether you believe me or not," Les retorted. He went on to say he was too old for sex anyway, too old and too sick;

he had COPD, a disease he had brought on himself by smoking since age ten. Back then, he was not yet on oxygen, tethered to a fifty-foot plastic tube.

Jess did not learn to distrust him. She loved Les; she couldn't help herself. With love came trust; it was not rational. Because she loved him, she wanted him to be happy. If he wasn't happy with her, he should go somewhere else. Dottie was not a viable candidate; her grandchildren slept over too often. "You could get your own place," Jess suggested, but he said, "I can't live alone. Besides, I like living here." The living room—that was what he liked; it was very large and opened into a galley kitchen. Yes, it was a nuisance to have to go upstairs to use the bathroom, but he had always liked sleeping in the living room, even when he was married. He could leave the TV on all night. From the time he moved in, they have lived more or less separately, Les downstairs, Jess upstairs, Les lying on the couch, watching sports, Jess, lying on the bed, watching movies and cooking shows, reading novels or sometimes writing poems she doesn't usually show Les. Still, they used to have a low-key companionship, like sleepy, sedentary cats who swat at each other from time to time. They don't really know one another, Jess thinks, but sometimes you just have to admit that and give up. They're roommates, housemates—more than that: lovers, but less, so much less, than she wants them to be. She wants him to be interested in her, not The Warthog. What makes that woman's warts and welfare so involving? He is—what is the word?—enamored; he has that focus. When Jess first met him, he had it for her, but it dissipated after he moved in. Why does this happen? After Dottie, Jess had the sense to tell Les to leave, but then he started coming around again, laying little presents on the bench in the entry porch—a serving of bacon from his breakfast in a restaurant, some crab cakes from another place they used to eat. And this was when he gave her the title for her poem. She thought if he came back, he would be faithful. He even said he'd be a good prairie vole. "If you want someone else," she said, "be honest, move out." He said, "I'm not going to want anyone else. I want *you*, darlin'."

But now here is De-lee-la or De-lie-la, and he's not moving out; he's too sick. He says Delilah thinks he should move into senior housing. There's going to be a vacancy on the second floor in her building. Someone's dying. Les should get on the waiting list.

"Is that what you want?"

"I don't know," he says, and Jess can see it's true. He seems lost. "I'd probably spend just as much time here as I do now."

What presumption! Jess thinks. She says, "What would you do about oxygen—have a machine in both places?"

November: Les catches a cold from Delilah, which he gives to Jess. Her cold lasts for three weeks. His turns into double pneumonia. Now is when Jess begins to realize how thick he is with Delilah, who visits him in the hospital every morning, according to his younger daughter, Laura. Laura, concerned about her father, has taken some vacation time and come up from Florida. She's staying in Jess's guest room, because her sister, also here from out of state, is sleeping on their mother's couch. Jess is very fond of both girls. Whatever his faults, Les must have done something right to have raised such nice children, he and his first wife, whom Jess also likes. She has made Jess feel welcome at Easter and Christmas gatherings, and she gave Jess her recipe for party mix.

Laura makes mushroom omelets for breakfast, then, about ten-thirty, goes to the hospital.

"What is it they're putting on his feet?" Jess asks idly, one morning. "It makes them smell like eucalyptus trees."

"Oh, that's some stuff Delilah makes," says Laura, not thinking. "Ointment," she says, looking guilty, blushing.

"*She* puts it on his feet?"

"It's got menthol in it."

"Every day?" Jess asks, not to be diverted.

"Well, every day I've been there."

Such devotion! Jess thinks. Les has terrible feet: callused, cracked, with fungal toenails growing every which way. Delilah must even love his feet.

"She only stays a couple of hours," Laura goes on. "She has to leave at eleven to go play bridge."

"Will I be running into The Warthog if I come to visit you in the morning?" Jess asks Les, that afternoon.

"If you met her," he says, not answering the question, "you'd probably be friends. And quit calling her that."

Jess takes the jar of ointment out of the night table drawer. "Is this doing some good?"

"The nurses seem to think so."

Jess unscrews the cap and sniffs. "Reminds me of my childhood." Then she says, "Does she also wash your feet with her hair?"

"Can't," Les says. "Hair's too short." He tells Jess not to start being catty. He says again that Jess would like Delilah if she knew her.

Delilah, it turns out, came to visit Les the last time he was in the hospital, too, and the time before that. Laura had run into her but hadn't mentioned it. The daughters stay out of their father's personal life. Both are friendly, easy-going women, living competent, fulfilling lives. There is none of the mild unhappiness that Jess has battled all her life, from childhood on. Because this melancholia is her natural state, she has always understood that she would be no one's first choice. She's convinced Les would be happier with The Warthog, whom he's described as "bubbly." Jess has never in her life been bubbly, in fact sees herself as a semi-depressed introvert who probably shouldn't be living with anybody at all unless it's on some isolated Norwegian fjord. Lately, checkers in the market have begun calling her "Miss" instead of "Ma'am," and she knows, or thinks she knows, what that means: she is losing her sexuality, maybe even her gender; soon, people may be calling her "sir." Before getting to know the daughters, Jess had never encountered people she considered "well-adjusted."

So here was this great friendship, about which Les, for months, had said nothing, and it had been going on for a lot longer than she'd realized.

"I asked you if you minded me playing with a female partner," Les says, when Jess asks again just how intimate this friendship is. "You said you didn't."

"And I didn't," Jess says. "Was that a mistake?" She wants the truth.

"Of course not."

She thinks it probably was. Again she remembers the little tug at the corner of his mouth, the involuntary half-smile almost like a wince. It was his putting-one-over-on-you smile. What would he have done if she'd said yes? And why did he even ask her?

"Have you had sex with her?"

"Hundreds of times."

"You should probably go live in her building," Jess says.

The day she finally meets The Warthog, is the day she finally gives in and starts referring to her as De-lee-la. Their meeting takes place in the hospital, where else? In Les's room. Jess has expected to run into her some day, just the way she came to expect she would run into Dottie, after she had encountered her in both the market and the Mall. The affair was more or less over by then, might actually have been over, but you never knew with Les. Jess ran into Dottie three or four times, and the final time, either the third or fourth, Dottie told Jess that she'd had to break up with Les because he liked too much kinky sex. "What do you consider kinky?" Jess asked, but Dottie said, "I don't want to talk about it." Genuinely curious, or else in the grip of one of her masochistic spirals, Jess asked Les what kinky things he had done with Dottie. "I never did anything with Dottie," Les said, from which Jess deduced that he had probably done a lot of kinky things with Dottie, whatever kinky meant. Because he often said the exact opposite of the truth, when the time came for Jess to ask about Delilah, she thought "hundreds of times" could possibly mean none at all. But it could also be an instance of truth by hyperbole. On the other hand, she was so used to being wrong, she never trusted her own conclusions. After running into Dottie all those times, she had come to expect to keep on running into her, so that when a total stranger rapped on her car window one afternoon when Jess was sitting in the market's parking lot, she made the instant assumption that the rapper was Dottie. When it wasn't Dottie, she for a split second assumed it was another of Les's women, wanting to talk about who knew what, maybe kinky sex. But the woman only wanted to tell her that her headlights were still on, so Jess turned her headlights off and went into the market. She had been sitting in the car, listening to *Eine Kleine Nachtmusik*, because, though she had never liked that vapid composition, she didn't want to go into the market. They might not have a handicap cart available, and riding one around the store was the only way she could manage; she was not up to pushing a carriage for such a distance as marketing required. Besides, she felt an obligation, like it or not, to hear the piece to its end. As a child she had been told the story about the young Mozart, so upset by someone's breaking off a performance in mid-measure that he sickened, his fever rising and rising until someone had the wit to go finish the piece.

When Jess finally runs into Delilah, Les has already been in the hospital for several days. He has been ending up there more and more often, lately, because when Les can't catch his breath, he suffers acute anxiety, which exacerbates his breathing difficulties. There are times when his nebulizer treatments don't relieve the problem, and he can't keep increasing his dose of Xanax, though this is in fact what he does. The only thing Jess knows to do in these circumstances is call 911. Within minutes, the ambulance and the fire engine and the police arrive, the fire engine all but blocking the narrow street they live on. There ensues an argument with the ambulance driver about which hospital to take Les to, the one that's three miles away or the one seven miles distant, where his pulmonologist has privileges, an argument Les has won all but once. The ambulance driver announces that it is not his responsibility if Les dies en route, and he always has to make a phone call to his superior to let him or her know what they are doing. The driver and EMTs talk in loud, authoritative voices that reverberate in Jess's large living room. The room is crowded with men in dark uniforms who stand with their hands on their hips and seem excessively vertical, maybe because they are arguing with Les, trying to talk him down. But Les finds unexpected breathing volume and shouts at them until they put him in a chair and carry him off down the front stairs. Then everyone is gone, and Jess is by herself in the peace and quiet. She wants to stay there, in the peace and quiet. She gets into her car and drives to the more distant hospital, arriving before the ambulance, which follows a less efficient route. The time when the driver wouldn't take Les to the hospital he wanted, Jess went there out of force of habit, expecting him to arrive any minute. When he didn't come, the triage receptionist phoned the other hospital, but he hadn't yet been entered into the computer, and for a few seconds Jess entertained the idea that he had been kidnapped. She went through all the phases of imagining how she would feel if he had been kidnapped. Sometimes she does this, thinking how she would feel if he died. She knows thinking about these things won't ward off their occurrence but does it anyway, even though it makes her ashamed, since sometimes, thinking of the peace and quiet, she knows she would be glad.

At the wrong hospital, Jess finally met Delilah. At last! Jess hadn't realized how the meeting had been hanging over her. It was the third day of Les's hospitalization, and so far—lucky Les—he had no roommate. Jess thanked the volunteer who had brought her up in a wheelchair. Slowly she wheeled herself past the empty bed, unable to see Les, even his feet, because the privacy curtain was drawn all the way around him. She was just beginning to wonder if that was in fact Les behind the curtain, when the silhouette of a tall, wide-shouldered woman appeared.

"Wait, please. Les is on the commode."

Her speech held a trace of a foreign accent, which Jess, without any grounds at all, decided was Iranian. Although the woman was wearing tight jeans and a brown-plaid shirt that matched her hair, Jess assumed she was a nurse. She still didn't question that assumption when the woman said, "Can you reach the toilet paper, hon?" Lots of nurses called the patients "sweetie" and "luv"; when Jess was in the ICU a few years back with heart problems, there was a nurse who called her "darling." Nobody but Les had ever called Jess "darling," though her mother called her "dear" and her ex-husband, "toots."

"How about a wash cloth?" the woman asked, and Les must have nodded, because she sashayed toward Jess—a peculiar swaying walk, the kind of walk you might try to perfect when you were fourteen but would then grow out of unless you were Marilyn Monroe. This woman was not Marilyn Monroe. This woman was downright homely. She had a big masculine-looking nose and a pugnacious chin, a chin that was just made for a wart. It was the chin that told Jess who this had to be. "Excuse, please," The Warthog said and, leaning over Jess, pushed the wheelchair backwards, until Jess was out in the corridor. Then she clomped into the bathroom in what looked like hiking boots and turned on the water in the sink full force.

Jess remained sitting in the wheelchair. Once, when she was a child, her kitten had slipped into the bathwater. It had been teetering along the rim of the tub while Jess took her bath. Jess expected it to try to jump right out, but the kitten had just sat there, up to its neck in warm water, looking stunned, as if it had landed on another planet.

Jess could have gotten out of the wheelchair. Instead, she wheeled herself back into the room. The Warthog was already behind the curtain. She was murmuring something to Les that Jess couldn't hear.

And Jess stopped, not wanting to proceed. She shouldn't be here, didn't want to be. It was noon; she had expected to feed Les his lunch; sometimes it was the only way to get him to eat. But here was The Warthog, staying late for some reason, and the room wasn't big enough for both of them.

How could Les have fallen for this woman? Dottie had been no beauty either, but, based on what he'd said about The Warthog, Jess had been envisioning a woman of grace—tall, fine-boned and elegant, the kind of woman who could make her, Jess, feel like a big galumph, though she was barely five feet two and weighed a hundred and eight. For Les to see this cow, this water buffalo as *slight* must mean he was thoroughly enchanted, as in *A Midsummer Night's Dream*. And what recourse was there against enchantment?

The Warthog was coming at her again, this time carrying the gray plastic bucket from the commode.

"His stools are still a little hard," she said, "but the MiraLax should fix him right up."

She lifted the bucket and Jess ducked, wheeling herself past the Warthog and over to the bed. With her cane, she swept the curtain aside. Les was sitting up, his smile uneasy.

"How are you?" she said. "*You* tell me."

"Well," he said, and cleared his throat, "I guess you've met De-lee-la."

A week later, Jess is still in shock. Delilah has enormous, unquestioned confidence. She must assume she has superior entitlements, because right in front of Jess she hugs and kisses Les—on the forehead or the cheek, perhaps not on the lips. And she combs his hair and washes his face, as if Les were her doll and Jess didn't exist. What has Les told her—that he's merely a boarder? That is what, as it turned out, he had told Dottie.

Maybe, Jess thinks, she should brazen it out—tousle Les's hair, kiss him, embrace him. But she doesn't do that even in front of the daughters, only when she's alone with Les.

And now not at all. She's no longer welcome.

"I really don't want your cold," Les says.

Jess says, "That's Delilah's cold."

But it's a cold that belongs to Jess now. It's here to stay. It seems to go away for a week; then there it is again. Six months, six colds. In the hospital, she wears a mask—for hours, for she usually stays till other visitors come, or if no one shows up, till eight or nine o'clock, though she doesn't like driving home in the dark. Les doesn't want to be left alone. In the nursing home she can sit farther away from his bed; he usually has a private room. But then he says, "Where's your mask?" It makes him anxious if she doesn't wear one. "I haven't got a cold," she reassures him. He says, "You're probably coming down with one." He hasn't allowed her to get near him for months, and she can't help feeling this is Delilah's doing.

Ten days in the hospital, ten days in the nursing home, home for a day or two, then back to the hospital. He likes it best in the hospital. The nurses pay attention to him, joke with him, tease him. Delilah visits him every morning, even on the weekends, whether he's in the hospital or the nursing home.

"Have you considered moving in with her?" Jess asks, on a day when he seems to be feeling a lot better. Surely she is thinking only of his happiness.

"How could I live with her?" Les yells. "Her apartment's only big enough for one person."

"You could pool your resources and rent a bigger apartment."

"She hasn't got any resources. She's on food stamps."

Jess scowls at him like the science teacher she used to be, but he just shrugs. "I'm not going to support her."

"You are a truly rotten man," she tells him. Does he really stay with her just because of her house? "I don't understand how so many people can love you."

"What's not to love?"

"Oh, don't get me started."

At least he is nothing like her father. Her father was a stern, straight arrow, a man of intimidating integrity. But this man delights in being evasive, prides himself on his deceptions. Not that he isn't often generous, even kind. He has done, in fact, quite a few caring things, such as buying Jess a crock-pot because she said she wanted one, and taking her to Hawaii and on a cruise to Alaska. But she's never sure of his motives, suspects, against her will, that these good deeds are atonements. "Stop being so negative," Les used to tell her, but distrust spreads; it's corrosive. She trusts him with money but not with women. She thinks he's had more affairs than she realizes. When she told him he was a meadow vole, he was tickled, after his initial annoyance. Unlike Jess, he likes the way he is. All he says he wants is the power to please her—in all ways, not just sexually. She hates herself for doubting him, but she can't help it; they're no longer snuggling, and she needs that dose of oxytocin, unavailable to her now that she's Typhoid Mary.

"Here comes trouble," waitresses used to warn, when she and Les trooped into restaurants where he was known.

He still wore a wedding ring. "That's going to come off." The marriage had been on the rocks for years, he said. His wife, his second, was about to throw him out. "Why?" Jess should have asked but didn't. She didn't make a decision to believe him. Trust just happened. "Any day now," he had added. They were both recently retired, Les from the pharmacy, she from teaching. "So," she said, "what are you looking for—a lily pad?"

She should have noted that he didn't answer.

If she could have foreseen how things would be in ten years—how sick he would be, for he wouldn't stop smoking, how unfaithful he would be, what would she have done? Gone right ahead, she supposes. But does she really deserve Delilah?

She feels even smaller than she actually is, around this woman—dwarfed, shrunken almost to nothing. When Delilah is in the same room, Les shrinks too; he becomes a little old man confined to his bed. They're a little old couple, like people in a fairy tale, the ones who are going to be given a magic pitcher if they offer water to the thirsty wayfarer. The pitcher will never run out of water. The wayfarer is a god in disguise. Delilah is huge, Delilah is Olympian. Maybe she has come down to earth to test them.

Jess tries to stay out of her way. When she visits Les in the hospital or the nursing home, she phones in advance to see whether Delilah's still there, for Delilah has taken to staying later and later. She now also answers the phone, because Les is so short of breath. If he does answer, his voice is faint and quavery and he says, "Here, talk to Delilah."

"Les is on his nebulizer," Delilah reports, or "on the commode," or "He's eating his lunch." "He'll talk to you later," she says firmly, as if she is Les's office manager. Why has she taken over Les like this? What has made her do it?

Dottie said he was the most oversexed man she'd ever known, but it turned out she'd only known two, the other one her husband. Maybe, Jess thinks, Les and Delilah are secretly married. One of these days, she will wheel herself into his room and be greeted by "Meet the new Mrs. Greentree!" It would shock her but somehow not surprise her, for he is becoming a different man. He has turned all his phone calls over to Delilah by now, even the ones to his daughters. And she is communicating directly with both of them, sending extensive e-mail reports, daily. Jess would never have thought of this; she dislikes dealing with e-mail. It is borne in on her that she hasn't kept the daughters well-informed. It's a good thing, she decides, what Delilah is doing. She asks for the reports to be copied to her, too.

Clearly, Delilah has won.

"I know you less and less," she tells Les, one afternoon, in the hospital, but he must hear it as "Les and Les," because he says, "What're you talking about?"

"Do you love Delilah?" she finally asks.

"I love *you*." He frowns. "I *think* I love you."

"Ten years and you still don't know?"

"But Delilah's re-invented me." He gives her a flash of his old raffish grin. "She made a new man of me."

"What does that mean—a 'new man'?" It strikes her that she doesn't want to know.

He shrugs and spreads his hands. "If I ever recover, I'm going to *live*."

Does that mean go off with Delilah? If she can bring him back to life, can Jess object? She wishes he could get well and go live in Florida, play in old people's bridge tournaments, or whatever. He doesn't like Florida except in winter. So, somewhere else then, but out of her life. No, Florida. It's far enough away. He and Delilah can rent a condo. A segment of ocean can be seen from the bathroom; there will be a dinky, leaky pool that seagulls will crap in. The inhabitants of the other units in the building will be French

Canadian so that Les, who won't set foot out of the United States of America, will feel like he's living in a foreign country. No, no, she really wants him to be happy, though Delilah's happiness does not concern her. But she won't try to deprive him of someone who's good for him. She loves him, she wants the best for him. There will be ocean views from the living room; the pool will not leak; seagulls will fly clear of it.

She manages to feel like this some of the time. Some of the time is better than nothing. Other times, she hopes Delilah will have a heart attack, a stroke, a brain tumor. A heart attack would be most appropriate.

Sometimes, unpredictably Les rallies. He talks with energy and at great length, telling his visitors complicated stories about his teenage and army pranks. And he eats his dinner himself, doesn't have to be fed, and flirts with the nurses, who go away laughing. But the next day, he'll be looking gaunt and sad-eyed, and will refuse to eat more than a string bean or two. Then Jess will often eat his dinner, because he's not going to eat it and it's getting late and she's hungry. She feels compelled to admit this to the aide who takes away the tray and to the nurse who checks his vitals.

"Why do you insist on telling them?" Les asks, but she wants them to know that his appetite isn't as good as it looks. "Delilah eats my lunch sometimes, and they don't give a hoot." Once, in fact, arriving a little earlier than usual, Jess surprised Delilah sitting in the visitors' chair, wolfing down meatloaf and mashed potatoes while Les napped. It seemed to Jess that there was something feral about this, but maybe Delilah just hadn't eaten breakfast.

"I can't stand by and watch good food go to waste," she explained, to Jess's surprise, for Jess had long-since got over expecting Delilah to explain anything she did, though she would like her to explain where her overwhelming entitlement came from. Les is no use whatsoever. He knows hardly anything about her that he will admit to.

"Where did you say she grew up?"

"Somewhere in the Midwest."

"In the United *States*?"

"Where else?"

"Then where did she get that accent?"

"I don't know what accent you're talking about."

It seems to Jess that Les would know more about Delilah if he loved her, but that, she is fully aware, may be wishful thinking. (A) He knows more about Delilah than he's telling and (B) He doesn't know all that much about anybody.

"What a peculiar upbringing you must've had," she used to muse, though unsure whether upbringing explained much of anything. But whence came this desire to conceal the truth—any truth, as if it were a priceless secret? A long time ago, in between marriages, he'd owned a Jaguar XJS, he said. It was white, a beautiful car, a car he hardly ever drove. What he drove to work was his mother's old Chevy; he kept the Jaguar in the garage. People would have judged him differently if they'd known about the Jaguar; he liked setting them up to be wrong. No wonder she and Les are forever at odds, when she wants to be loved for who she is.

"Doesn't it occur to you," she asked him once, "that you're setting *yourself* up to be mis-loved?"

"'Mis-loved'—is that a real word?"

"Loved as someone you're actually not?"

"I don't care why I'm loved," he said, and she could see that this was true. It only matters to him to be loved; he goes around in disguise, like that thirsty god. But he won't be lied to, won't stand for that, though he lies and lies to everyone else. Sometimes he probably tells the truth. A random reward, to throw everyone off.

"She'd be too much for me," he says to Jess, one afternoon. "She's like a force of nature." He seems to be continuing a conversation that he had with someone else, perhaps one of his daughters. "I couldn't live in her building, she'd take me over." Since he's not well enough to live anywhere but medical facilities, Jess takes his comments as denials of his condition. Then for several days in a row, he tells Jess that he doesn't love Delilah, and he mentions several times that they've never had sex.

"Does Delilah realize this?"

"That we've never had sex?"

"That you don't love her. I think you love her."

"I hardly know her."

That's probably true.

It's too late for him to get to know Jess, but about a month before his death, he starts telling her he loves her—several times a day, for almost a week. Jess thinks but doesn't say, "Are you confusing me with Delilah?" Why is he saying this, what does he want? Maybe just to leave her with a pleasant memory?

She tells him, "I love you too," because it is true, and he says, "I know you do." But once she says, "I don't feel lovable. What I feel is tired and disgruntled."

"Even so, you're lovable, sweetheart." It is the dearest thing he has ever said to her, and she knows she will remember it and weep.

"I'm sick of this life," he says.

What he wants is to come home to die.

The hospital bed gets set up in the center of the living room, parallel to the couch, between the fireplace and the coffee table. The commode has already been here for months, for those few days when he's been home. Jess can carry the bucket upstairs to the bathroom, as long as she goes step by step, with great care. As for the urinal, she empties it into the kitchen sink and then, ridiculously, runs the garbage disposer. It would be easier if Les were in the guest room upstairs, across from the bathroom, but then meals would be an insoluble problem. When Jess brings Les his breakfast or dinner, she can only carry one plate at a time. She needs a cart. They don't have a cart. She's been needing a cart for the last four years.

There is one further request.

"I want Delilah to come visit me every morning, same as she's been doing."

"Delilah here—in my house?" Jess cries.

"She's been here before," Les says, unwisely. "In any case it's only Monday through Friday." Delilah will refrain from coming weekends.

Jess can stay upstairs during these visits, or come down and hang out in the kitchen. Or she can sit on the couch and be part of the conversation.

A front-row seat to watch Delilah caressing him or helping when, lying on his back, Les tries to position his penis in the urinal?

"No thanks."

If Les cared about her at all, he wouldn't ask this of her. But it may be his last request. Whether he loves her is not the issue, or even whether he loves Delilah.

Maybe she can just pretend Delilah isn't there, maybe all she has to do is stay upstairs. But, no. Delilah empties the commode bucket here, just as she did, that first time Jess met her. At least she knocks when she comes upstairs. If she wants to empty the bucket, Jess decides, let her. It was no lie when she said she was tired. She finds herself reluctantly grateful. "Thank you for all your help," she says, because indeed Delilah is doing a lot. When the Hospice bath nurse changes the bed, Delilah carries the sheets and towels down to the laundry in the cellar. And before she leaves at noon, she brings it all back up to the living room and folds it, placing it neatly on an armchair. "Feel free to make yourself some tea," Jess says. "Or, if you want, there's instant coffee." One day, she goes so far as to offer soup.

"Oh, no thanks," Delilah says. "I brought some rye bread and some pickled herring."

Jess no longer detects any trace of an accent. Maybe, she thinks, there never was one.

And maybe Delilah *is* just a dear, dear friend, with nothing romantic going on, nothing sexual. Certainly that has to be the case now that Les is so sick. Illness was, after all, what he was pleading, back when he and Jess were still talking about such things. But when the bath nurse comes in the afternoon instead of the morning and Jess sees Les lying naked on his narrow bed, thinner than he ever was but still a fine figure of a man, she finds such a relationship hard to believe. A few times, Les came home really late from his Friday afternoon bridge game. He said he'd felt so tired he had to lie down at the senior center, and he'd fallen asleep. He'd seemed to emanate sexuality the first time this happened, and Jess couldn't help her suspicions.

"Oh, Les," Jess hears herself say. "Oh, Les!"

It is horrible to be jealous at seventy-six. She thinks of Delilah helping the morning bath nurse, and she understands what "racked with jealousy" means. Is there no place she can go—perhaps to visit her son on the west coast? There are plenty of people around by now. Both daughters have come home again, but both are staying together in a motel.

When Jess comes downstairs, after Delilah has left, she often finds a kitchen full of people: the bath nurse, writing up his notes, the Hospice nurse talking to a daughter or two, and sometimes, Les's first wife, who is a Eucharistic minister and can give Les communion.

For Les, who has never gone to church during the entire time Jess has known him, has remembered that he is a Catholic. Someone has given him a rosary, which he calls "my beads."

"Where are my beads, I can't find my beads," he will say, in a panic, and someone will have to feel around his ribs or get down on her hands and knees, to peer under the bed. He clutches the beads in one hand and wears an oximeter clamped onto the third finger of the other; so he can see his oxygen level at the push of a button. Laura gave him the oximeter for his birthday; it is yellow and black, like a cartoon bee. "My two talismans," he calls them. He asks to see a priest.

The priest comes on a Sunday afternoon when nobody but Jess happens to be around; the family's all off watching a softball game that one of the granddaughters is playing in. Jess goes to sit on the front porch while the priest hears Les's confession. When he is finished with Les, he comes out and asks Jess if she would like to receive communion too. Jess is surprised to find that she's tempted but says, "No, thank you. I'm not a religious person." She has gone suddenly from being full of jealousy and resentment to an apathy of both mind and body. She feeds Les scrambled eggs and instant oatmeal but often doesn't eat, herself.

The Hospice nurse, whom Les already dislikes, takes him off everything but Xanax and morphine. Gone—everything that was supposed to make him better, gone—everything that was to keep him alive. No more fish oil, no more baby aspirin.

"Your primary care authorized it," Jess explains, but Les can tell what she isn't saying. Her own heart sank when the nurse made the cuts.

"She's trying to turn me into a fucking addict."

"The morphine's supposed to relax the airways."

Jess suspects the morphine is killing him more quickly than he would die on his own. No, the nurse says. His lungs are shot. His body is shutting down.

"You can take all that stuff if you want," Jess finally tells him. "The nurse just thought it might be easier."

"For whom?"

"You, mainly." She feels so dishonest, citing rational reasons that aren't the real ones. "You want to keep on taking your usual meds?"

Les looks at her hopelessly. "No," he says.

A few minutes later he says, "I'm scared," and Jess can't comfort him with talk of heaven.

"I would be too," she falters, knowing, as she says it, that she is failing him.

After that, he seems to set his mind to dying. He doesn't want to see the friends who come to visit him. He's furious with Jess for letting people in, caring more about hurting them than tiring him.

"But they've come quite a distance," Jess protests.

"Let them come look at me in my casket."

When everybody has gone home and there are just Jess and the night nurse, Jess will stand by the bedside and watch Les sleep. His mouth is open; he's not wearing his dentures, his cheeks are sunken. He already looks dead. But his breathing seems peaceful now, more peaceful than when he was in the nursing home. Probably, she thinks, it's because of the morphine.

The nurse increases the dose again, and now Les sleeps most of the time. He is too weak to get up for the commode and has to wear diapers—strangely cumbersome things. He lies there, unhelpful, inert, and Jess can't lift him. She leaves him to his nurses, for they have a day nurse too by now; it feels to Jess as if she's giving up on him. Les said he wanted to die, but he doesn't; his body keeps on going and going. Yet each day he's also farther away; they are going in different directions. She can't reach him. When could she ever? Les is less. Mumbling to himself. Once he laughs.

"Happy Father's Day," Laura says, the Sunday before he dies, and Les, as if he were wishing her Merry Christmas, echoes, "Happy Father's Day."

There is no further reason for Jess to stay upstairs. She walks into her own living room without knocking, used to seeing Delilah sitting on the couch or standing beside the bed. Once she surprises her sitting on the edge of the mattress, leaning over Les, murmuring, "Go peacefully, my darling."

"Is she his sister?" the day nurse asks Jess, after Delilah has left.

"Not hardly."

"She seems to love him very much."

"Lots of people do," Jess tells her, wondering, as she has done so many times, why that is. What is it that is so lovable about Les? What makes waitresses and half the nurses say he's a sweetheart? A certain warmth? A boyishness? "He's such a great guy," Delilah said, which made Jess want to slap her. But she's right. Something about Les makes you want to hug him. Why couldn't he have cared enough about himself to save his lungs, quit smoking?

Jess has another image of him in her head, dating from their week in Hawaii. Though on oxygen, he still looks healthy. He's standing on the lawn outside their rented condo, near the low hedge that divides the lawn from the beach. He's wearing khaki shorts, the kind with lots of pockets; his chest is bare and tan. But in the grass lies a turquoise plastic tube that follows him around like an unruly snake, coiling and flopping when he moves; the end that isn't in the canula attaches him to the oxygen-concentrator in the condo. Smoke from his cigarette wafts away in the breeze along with the oxygen that can't be seen. Jess waits for his nose to go up in flames; some day his hair will singe. When he started spending so much time in the hospital, he couldn't smoke, but it was too late by then.

Les fears the flames of hell, despite his beads and his confession, despite the fact that he hasn't had a chance to commit any further sins. Sex outside of marriage is a sin, the priest told him, and this seemed to upset Les unduly. "So, now I'm a sin?" Jess expostulates, caught between incredulity and outrage. "What about Delilah?" Les doesn't answer that except to say he wants to talk to another priest.

What does he think, Jess wonders—that she, like God, has forgiven him? She hasn't. She is no Christian. She thinks it's wrong for sins to be forgiven. What you did, you did; you're forever responsible. Forgiveness by the damaged party makes no difference. Not that she believes in retribution, but why should you go free while your victim lies bleeding?

"Did he tell you he loved you?" she wants to ask Delilah, who is sitting on the couch with the day nurse beside her. Delilah—big, strong Delilah—is crying; the nurse has her arm around her. According to the night nurse, Les was going to die today, and he just did so, a few minutes ago, while Jess was upstairs in the bathroom. Except for Delilah, the room is silent, no longer filled with harsh, rattling breathing.

"I kissed him on the forehead and told him I loved him," Delilah says, in between sobs. Jess almost wishes she could feel sorry for her, but she has her father's heart, stern and unrelenting.

The day nurse says, "We were just sitting in the kitchen, chatting, and I realized I wasn't hearing any sound from the living room."

"At least," Delilah weeps, "the last words he heard were 'I love you.'"

If he heard anything, Jess thinks.

Just a few days ago, when Les was still eating oatmeal and ice cream and scrambled eggs and could still talk, he said to Jess, of Delilah, "I don't know what I'd do without her." Why couldn't Jess have asked him then: Do you love her? He might, finally, have told her.

"He lied to me," Delilah says. "He told me there was no other woman in his life."

He was a man, Jess thinks, who over-valued the truth and had to keep it all to himself.